P9-DTV-389

"GO BACK TO BED," HE SAID.

Her eyes were huge with shock.

He rounded on her again suddenly. "You are right, Rebecca," he said through his teeth. "You know nothing of what battle is like. Don't mouth platitudes at me. And I thought it was agreed that he not be mentioned between us. You promised that he would not. It is not to happen again, do you understand me? Julian is dead. Let him go."

She turned away, but he grabbed her wrist and spun her back to face him. He hauled her against him and lowered his mouth to hers. It was not a tender kiss. Ghosts were clawing at him and he fought to banish them, to impose the reality of the present on the dreams and horrors of the past. She was his wife. They had been married less than three days before. This was their honeymoon.

She was clinging to him when he lifted his head again, her body arched in to his. She should have slapped his face—hard. Instead, she was playing the part of a dutiful wife as he suspected she always would. His anger intensified. He hated her at that moment. He stooped down, scooped her up into his arms, strode across to the bed, and tossed her down onto it . . .

It had not taken long for rationality to return to her

BUY TWO TOPAZ BOOKS AND GET ONE FREE ROMANCE NOVEL!

With just two purchases of Topaz books, you'll be able to receive one romance novel free from the list below. Just send us two proofs of purchase* along with the coupon below, and the romance of your choice will be on its way to you! (subject to availability/**offer good only in the United States, its territories and Canada**)

Check title you wish to receive:

☐ *WILD WINDS CALLING*
June Lund Shiplett
0-451-12953-9/$4.99($5.99 in Can.)

☐ *A HEART POSSESSED*
Katherine Sutcliffe
0-451-15310-3/$4.50($5.99 in Can.)

☐ *THE DIABOLICAL BARON*
Mary Jo Putney
0-451-15042-2/$3.99($4.99 in Can.)

☐ *THE WOULD-BE WIDOW*
Mary Jo Putney
0-451-15581-5/$3.99($4.99 in Can.)

☐ *TO LOVE A ROGUE*
Valerie Sherwood
0-451-40177-8/$4.95($5.95 in Can.)

☐ *THE TURQUOISE TRAIL*
Susannah Leigh
0-451-40252-9/$4.99($5.99 in Can.)

☐ *SO BRIGHT A FLAME*
Robin Leanne Wiete
0-451-40281-2/$4.99($5.99 in Can.)

☐ *REBEL DREAMS*
Patricia Rice
0-451-40272-3/$4.99($5.99 in Can.)

☐ *THE RECKLESS WAGER*
April Kihlstrom
0-451-17090-3/$3.99($4.99 in Can.)

☐ *LADY OF FIRE*
Anita Mills
0-451-40044-5/$4.99($5.99 in Can.)

☐ *THE CONTENTIOUS COUNTESS*
Irene Saunders
0-451-17276-0/$3.99($4.99 in Can.)

*Send in coupons, proof of purchase (register receipt & photocopy of UPC code from books) plus $1.50 postage and handling to:

TOPAZ GIVEAWAY
Penguin USA, 375 Hudson Street, New York, NY 10014

NAME_____
ADDRESS_____ APT. #_____
CITY_____ STATE_____ ZIP_____

TANGLED

by

Mary Balogh

A TOPAZ BOOK

TOPAZ
Published by the Penguin Group
Penguin Books USA Inc., 375 Hudson Street,
New York, New York 10014, U.S.A.
Penguin Books Ltd, 27 Wrights Lane,
London W8 5TZ, England
Penguin Books Australia Ltd, Ringwood,
Victoria, Australia
Penguin Books Canada Ltd, 20 Alcorn Avenue
Toronto, Ontario, Canada M4V 3B2
Penguin Books (N.Z.) Ltd, 182-190 Wairau Road,
Auckland 10, New Zealand

Penguin Books Ltd, Registered Offices:
Harmondsworth, Middlesex, England

First published by Topaz,
an imprint of Dutton Signet,
a division of Penguin Books USA Inc.

First Printing, March, 1994
10 9 8 7 6 5 4 3 2 1

Copyright © Mary Balogh, 1994
All right reserved
Topaz Man photo © Charles William Bush

 REGISTERED TRADEMARK—MARCA REGISTRADA

Printed in the United States of America

Without limiting the rights under copyright reserved above, no part of this
publication may be reproduced, stored in or introduced into a retrieval system,
or transmitted, in any form, or by any means (electronic, mechanical, photo-
copying, recording, or otherwise), without the prior written permission of both
the copyright owner and the above publisher of this book.

BOOKS ARE AVAILABLE AT QUANTITY DISCOUNTS WHEN USED TO PROMOTE PROD-
UCTS OR SERVICES. FOR INFORMATION PLEASE WRITE TO PREMIUM MARKETING
DIVISION, PENGUIN BOOKS USA INC., 375 HUDSON STREET, NEW YORK, NEW YORK
10014.

If you purchased this book without a cover you should be aware that this book
is stolen property. It was reported as ''unsold and destroyed'' to the publisher
and neither the author nor the publisher has received any payment for this
''stripped book.''

For Jacqueline
My elder daughter
with love

O, what a tangled web we weave,
When first we practice to deceive!

—SIR WALTER SCOTT

1

England, February, 1854

She was not going to go to the quayside. She had told Julian that already. Plenty of women were going to stay with their men until the bitter end, of course. She watched them now from the window of her hotel room, standing there straight-backed and calm-faced, so that anyone observing her would have thought that she felt no emotion at all, that the scene beyond the window had nothing whatsoever to do with her.

The Guardsmen of the Grenadiers' Third Battalion were marching smartly along the streets of Southampton, making a spectacular show with their swallow-tailed red coatees and tall black bearskin caps. The curious and the patriotic lined the streets, cheering them, calling out encouragement, waving handkerchiefs. And women were there—wives, sweethearts, mistresses—moving along the pavements beside the marching troops, most of them gazing at one particular man with longing, unhappy eyes. Soon they would be saying good-bye to their men.

Perhaps forever.

It was February, 1854. Perhaps many of the men marching so smartly along the street would never see the end of the year.

They were to sail only as far as Malta—as a precautionary measure, the government claimed. It was very unlikely that there would be war. The Tsar of Russia would be foolish not to back down when he was threatened with the might of both England and France. But the Tsar continued to make his presence felt in the Black Sea and the Mediterranean. He continued to try to take advantage of the crumbling Turkish Empire.

The British had not been involved in any major war since the Battle of Waterloo almost forty years before.

But British overland trading routes to India and the East were being threatened, and the British were clamoring for a fight. The government, however, claimed that there would be no war. They were sending troops to Malta merely as a precautionary measure.

Rebecca, Lady Cardwell, kept telling herself that as she gazed downward onto the street and waited for Julian to come back to their room to say good-bye. She would not go to the quayside. Perhaps there her control would desert her—in public. It was not to be contemplated. She almost had not even come down from London. The thought of going as far as Southampton with him but no farther had been excruciating agony. But the thought of not going as far as she could had been worse. She had come.

Those poor women in the streets below, she thought, watching them, many of them with children. Only a few of the wives had been allowed to go with the enlisted men, their names drawn by lottery. The rest had to stay, most of them to be cared for by the parishes in which they lived. They were to live on charity while their men were preparing to offer their lives in service of their country.

Many officers' wives were going, of course. They did not have to participate in the lottery. Rebecca would have gone, too, but Julian would not allow it. She had miscarried only the month before—for the second time in their two-year marriage—and he was afraid that she had not recovered her health sufficiently to undergo a long voyage and live in an unfamiliar climate.

She had pleaded with him—how was she to live without him? But to no avail. He had deliberately taken her question literally and told her that he had made arrangements for her to return home to Craybourne during his absence. Doubtless he would be back in England almost before they realized he was gone.

But Craybourne was not home. Not really. It was the home of the Earl of Hartington, whom both she and Julian called Father. But in reality he was neither Julian's father nor her father-in-law. He was Julian's godfather, who had taken Julian in as a five-year-old orphan and brought him up with his own son. Rebecca did not really want to go to Craybourne, but she had no choice. Julian had said she was to go there—until he returned.

Rebecca set her forehead against the glass of the window. Until he returned. What if the Tsar continued to be stubborn? What if the British and the French held firm? What if there was war after all? What if—? But she straightened up again and turned with a falsely calm and cheerful smile as the door opened abruptly behind her.

"Look whom I've brought home with me, Becka," Captain Sir Julian Cardwell said, his voice cheerful, his good-looking face animated, his eyes sparkling with the excitement of the occasion. "He was skulking along the street and unwilling to come up with me. I had to convince him that you would be mortally offended if he did not take his leave of you before going off to war."

Major Lord Tavistock closed the door behind them. David. The Earl of Hartington's son. Looking apologetic and, as always, ten times more handsome than any other man she knew, including Julian. He was taller than Julian, with a greater breadth of shoulder and chest, with narrower waist and hips, and longer legs. He was darker than Julian, with those blue eyes making Julian's gray ones look quite ordinary. But then he had neither Julian's sunny good nature nor his charm. Nor her love.

She disliked David. She had no wish to have him there in her hotel room. He was an intruder. She had only a short time left with Julian—perhaps only an hour or less. She was greedy for every minute of that time alone with him. But it was not David's fault he was there, she had to admit. Julian had brought him, insensitive perhaps to her need to have him alone for the final hour. Or perhaps he found their parting as difficult to contemplate as she and was trying somehow to take some of the emotion from it.

"David," she said.

"You'll wish me to the devil, Rebecca," he said, coming toward her, his right hand outstretched. "I'll say good-bye, then, and leave you alone with Julian."

Good-bye. Perhaps she would never see him again. Perhaps there would be war after all. Perhaps he would be killed. She disliked him, but Julian had always thought of him as a brother. And she had once played with him and looked up to him as something of a hero—a long time ago. She had even sighed over his growing good looks for a while as a girl until her moral upbringing and her own firmly held principles had made her realize that he was not at all the sort of young man who was worthy of her devotion. More recent events had confirmed her in that opinion. But she did not want him dead.

She must feel some trace of fondness for him after all, beneath the dislike and the disapproval.

"David," she said, looking earnestly up into his eyes, "look after yourself. Keep yourself safe." Her hands were clasped before her. She would not take his outstretched one. But suddenly—she did not know how it had come about—she was in his arms, her own tight about his neck, his about her waist—hugging him as if she would never let him go. Her eyes were tightly closed. "Keep yourself safe."

"And you, Rebecca," he said. His arms tightened as if to squeeze all the breath out of her. "I'll take care of Julian for you."

And then he was striding back across the room and opening the door. He spoke without looking back. "I'll see you downstairs, Julian. Five minutes. No longer."

She had never done anything so unseemly in her life, Rebecca thought, running her hands over the full, flounced skirt of her green dress. And then his final words echoed in her mind. *Five minutes. No longer.*

She clasped her hands again and forced a smile to her lips. She would not disgrace herself. "Julian," she said, looking into his face, memorizing it just as if she expected to forget it the moment he sailed away, "take care of yourself. Don't forget to write." As if she were his mother. As if he were going away to school. He was going to war. Perhaps there really would be war. Perhaps . . . In spite of herself she felt her smile wobbling and her hands clenching each other painfully.

"Becka," he said softly, opening his arms to her. His normally sunny, charming smile had deserted him, "Becka."

She hurried into his arms and set her forehead against his shoulder, against the hard shield of his scarlet coatee. She set her arms about his waist and was aware that she could not feel him, but only the uniform he wore. It was as if he had already been taken from her.

He laughed and rubbed his cheek against the top of her head. "I knew you would be like this," he said. "Like a marble statue. I wish I had insisted on sending you home from London so that we would not have had to go through this."

"It would have been the same there," she said. "There would have been the moment of parting. It was unavoidable. Oh, Julian." She fought tears.

"Becka," he said, holding her close, "it is just to Malta. Just an expensive and pointless exercise. We will be home by summer, mark my words. The government does not want war."

Three minutes must have passed already. Two left. She breathed in slowly and lifted her head.

"Becka," he said, framing her face with his hands, gazing into her hazel eyes. "Becka, my darling."

"Julian." There were world and universes of things to be said, yet all she could do was whisper his name.

"I have to be going," he said, smiling. "Smile for me."

She tried, felt the impossibility, and shook her head quickly.

"Well, then," he said, lowering his head until his lips touched hers, "kiss me, Becka."

She kissed him with desperate tenderness. It might be for the last time. The very last time. She tried to will time to a standstill.

"My darling." He had drawn his face back a few inches. "I shall miss you every hour of every day until I am home with you again. You know that, don't you?"

She nodded. "I love you."

He patted her shoulders briskly and moved back from her to check the sword at his side and reach for his cap. He was smiling again. "You'll take the train back to Craybourne tomorrow morning," he said. "You'll be there before dark and Father will have the carriage at the station to meet you. You will be quite safe. Miss Houghten will be with you."

"Yes, I'll be quite safe, Julian," she said. "You must

not worry about me. Go now. It would not do to be late.''

"And have to swim after the ship?'' he said, grinning. "No, by Jove it wouldn't. My men would not have been so well entertained in a decade.'' He was opening the door and stepping through it.

There was a moment when panic grabbed at her, when instinct would have had her across the distance between them, grabbing at him for one last kiss, one last goodbye. A moment when she wanted to plead with him to take her with him after all. But she was not a creature of instinct. She was a disciplined, rational being—or so she told herself.

"I'll wave to you from the window,'' she said.

"Yes, do that, Becka,'' he said. "Remember that it is only as far as Malta. There is more danger on the streets of England than there will be there.''

"Yes,'' she said.

The door closed.

He was gone.

She stood where she was for a few moments, drawing steadying breaths, resisting the temptation to tear open the door and go hurtling down the stairs after him. She crossed the room to the window on trembling legs instead and looked down.

Most of the red-coated soldiers had disappeared. David stood on the pavement below, facing away from the hotel. She felt a surging of resentment against him. It was his fault that Julian was going away, perhaps to war, perhaps to his death. If David had not bought a commission in the Guards and come home several times looking dashing in his uniform and bringing stories that had sounded unutterably romantic and exciting to a country-bred young man, Julian would not have thought of buying one for himself just before their marriage. Julian had always looked up to David, had always tried to keep up with him and emulate him. Though Rebecca could not imagine why it was so. David had always been wild and thoughtless. Sometimes cruel.

Her lips tightened. Yes, cruel. Flora Ellis had been their playmate and friend all through their growing years. She had been of thoroughly respectable lineage even though she was only the daughter of the vicar of Cray-bourne, whereas Julian was a baronet and David was a viscount and son and heir of an earl.

And yet now Flora was living alone and disgraced with her infant son while David was sailing away with his battalion, unconcerned about their fate. He had refused to marry Flora even though she had been abandoned by her family and ostracized by everyone else for a long time.

For that, Rebecca thought, she would never forgive David.

And then Julian came out of the hotel and joined him, and the two men turned to hurry along the street in the direction of the quay. For a few sickening moments Rebecca thought that he would not look back. But he did, removing his cap and waving it jauntily in the air, grinning up at her. A boy on his way to some exciting adventure, eager to be gone.

Julian. Her husband. Her love. The man she had adored from childhood on. She raised a hand, palm out, though she did not wave it. She did not smile. She stood thus until long after he had disappeared from view. Until there was a knock at the door and it opened behind her.

"Rebecca?" a woman's voice asked softly. "Do you need company? I'll go away again if you don't."

Rebecca closed her hand upon itself and lowered it. "Don't go away, Louisa," she said. "Let's do something. Let's see what Southampton has to offer by way of shops and other sights, shall we? We have only the rest of today here to see all that is to be seen."

She turned to smile resolutely at the companion Julian had insisted on employing for her after her first miscarriage well over a year ago. She no longer resented his decision. She and Louisa Houghten were friends.

David waited on the street until Julian came out of the hotel and joined him. He was glad he had no wife. He would not relish making the decision of whether to take her or whether to leave her behind. He did not approve of taking women to war—and contrary to what Lord Aberdeen, the Prime Minister said, he was convinced that there would be war. On the other hand, he did not think he would be able to say good-bye to a wife in England, knowing full well that there was a strong chance he would never see her again.

He did not think he would be able to do it. It had been bad enough saying good-bye to Rebecca a few minutes ago. He closed his eyes briefly. Rebecca. Had he pulled her into his arms, or had she come there herself? It did not matter. Throughout their growing years they had been friends and playmates, almost brother and sister for a while. And Julian had been there in the room with them just now. It had been a natural gesture, to hug each other like that.

But God, he would not be able to leave her if she were his wife.

Perhaps he would never see her again.

"Whew!" Julian said, coming up suddenly beside him. "Fresh air. Let's go, Dave."

"That bad?" David looked at him sympathetically.

"Worse," Julian said. "Women get intense about these things. At least Becka does. But she doesn't ever have the hysterics or anything like that, I must admit. She can always be counted upon to behave like the true lady she is."

They were striding along the street in the direction of the sea. As soon as the tide was favorable, they would be sailing.

"She will not be at the window?" David asked. He would not look back himself.

"By Jove." Julian turned back, swept off his cap, and waved it in the air, grinning cheerfully. "Poor Becka. She still has not recovered her spirits. She wanted that child badly. She feels a failure as a woman and a wife without children, and other nonsense like that."

David remembered the whiteness of her face and the blankness of her eyes when he had called on her a few days after her miscarriage.

"She is better off staying home," Julian said. "Becka wasn't made for the rough life. It's hard leaving her, though. I do love her, Dave, though I know you some- times doubt it."

David felt his jaw harden. He did not want to pick up the bait—not at the moment.

"I do," Julian said. "No other woman has ever meant anything to me except Becka. I married her because I love her. There was no other reason."

"You don't have to defend yourself to me," David said. "I am not your keeper, Julian. Not any longer. And it will mean nothing to you if I say I am disappointed in you. It never did."

"Well, there you are wrong," Julian said, his good humor deserting him for once. "Your good opinion always mattered to me, Dave. More than Father's. I have always admired your self-control and your strength of character."

"Strength!" David laughed harshly. "A fine way I had of showing it. Allowing you to manipulate me all through boyhood."

Julian winced. "That was not a kind word to choose, Dave," he said. "You're still angry because of that woman you saw me with in London a week or so ago. She meant less than nothing to me. She was just a whore. I wouldn't even recognize her now if you were to set her before me. It was just that Becka has been ill since losing this child, and even before she lost it I was having to go easy because of her losing the last one."

David made a sound of impatience and contempt.

"I love her," Julian said mulishly.

"Your marriage is your own concern," David said. "If you choose to risk hurting Rebecca, I can't stop you. But don't expect me ever to lie or cover up for you again. I think I did it one too many times. Perhaps it would have been better for Rebecca to have known the truth before she married you."

"About Flora?" Julian said. "By Jove, that was a mess, Dave. I'll always be grateful, but you don't need to keep bringing it up."

"You promised me then," David said.

"Yes, I know." Julian flashed a smile at him. "Promises like that just aren't easy to keep. For you, perhaps. You don't seem to need women the way I do. But I mean to reform. From this moment on there is only Becka. God, that was agonizing back at the hotel room, Dave. There is never going to be anyone else. Are you satisfied? I do love her, you know."

David did not answer for a while. He was thankful to see that they were approaching their destination. The quayside was thronged with red-coated Guardsmen and clinging, sobbing women. "Yes, Julian," he said at last. "I know that."

It was true too. It was small consolation, but it was true.

2

Malta and the Crimea, 1854

Life on Malta was tedious. There had been a surge of energy and eager anticipation when the men left England, an expectation that at last they would see action. But action was slow in coming. Although Britain and France declared war on Russia at the end of March, another two months were to pass before the British forces were moved closer to the scene of possible hostilities.

They had to make their own action. But because there was not much to be made, boredom was widespread. Only a few of the men managed to ward it off. Captain Cardwell was one of them. He began an affair with Cynthia Scherer, wife of Captain Sir George Scherer of the First Coldstream Guards.

It was not a particularly secret affair. Nothing much was in army life. Perhaps the only officer of either the Third Grenadiers or the First Coldstream who did not know about it after the first week or so was Captain Scherer himself. The couple were at least discreet enough to carry on their affair while he was busy about his duties.

No one thought of telling him. Even apart from the fact that it would not have been the honorable thing to do, there was the fact that everyone liked Julian Cardwell. His sunny nature and warm charm were appealing even to his men. No one censured his behavior openly and probably very few privately. Julian was the sort of man who needed women, and everyone knew that his wife's delicate health had forced him to leave her behind in England.

Major Lord Tavistock stayed tight-lipped about the affair for three whole weeks, although he shared a billet with Julian. It was none of his concern, he told himself.

Besides, he knew from long experience what Julian's reaction would be if he did give in to the temptation to
remonstrate with him. There would be the charming boyish smile and the assurance that Cynthia Scherer meant
nothing to him. There would be the renewed assurance
that he loved Rebecca and was going to be faithful to her
from that moment on. And the damnable thing was that
Julian would mean every word of what he said—as he
always did. No, he would stay out of it, David decided.

And yet all his resolutions were thrown to the wind
when he arrived back at his billet from a meeting earlier
than expected one afternoon to find that he had walked
in only scant moments after what would undoubtedly have
been an extremely embarrassing scene. He came to an
abrupt halt in the doorway and stared pointedly at Julian
on the bed.

Julian smiled his engaging smile. "Would you be so
good as to wait outside for a few minutes, old chap?"
he asked.

By the time David, his back to the door of the room,
heard the woman leave, he was white with fury. He had
been telling himself for longer than five minutes to go
away and find something else to do for a while, to forget
about it, not to get involved. But he knew he was going
to do just that, just as he always did.

"This is not to happen again," he said curtly when he
was back inside the room, the door firmly closed behind
him. He convinced himself that his outrage was purely
over the use that had been made of his room. His anger
was justified.

Julian was reclining on his untidy bed, only half
dressed, his hands clasped behind his head. He grinned.
"Are those orders from a superior officer?" he asked.
"Sorry, old chap, that scene was not in the best of good
taste, was it? I was not expecting you."

"She is a married woman," David said. Though that
was not the real cause of his fury at all just as the fact
that they had used his room for their bedding was not.

"I suppose that is better than carrying on with someone's virgin daughter," Julian said. "Come on, Dave,
you have to admit the truth of that."

"It would not be the first time," David said, unbuckling his sword belt and setting it and his sword on the table.

"A low blow," Julian said, grimacing. "I have always regretted that mistake. You know that, Dave. It happened in a moment of thoughtless passion. I wish you wouldn't keep reminding me."

"Your life has been made up of moments of thoughtless passion," David said coldly. "I thought perhaps you would grow up, Julian. I thought perhaps marriage to Rebecca would mature you. You seemed fond enough of her. But you have been married for more than two years and you are twenty-four years old and there is no sign yet of any change for the better."

He sounded like a moralizing, killjoy judge, David thought, and resented the fact that Julian always seemed to bring out that side of him—and cursed himself for not having walked away from the sight of Julian and Lady Scherer in bed together.

Julian swung his legs over the side of the bed and reached for his shirt. "Your trouble, Dave," he said, stung, "is that you never learned that life is to be enjoyed. I honestly don't know how you can handle celibacy—you *are* celibate, I assume? I certainly wouldn't recommend any of the whores hereabouts unless you want an alternative to dying from cholera or dysentery or battle wounds."

"People can be hurt while you are selfishly enjoying life," David said. "Scherer, for example. Rebecca. Flora Ellis."

"Cynthia is bored," Julian said. "I am bored. We are not in love, Dave. This is no grand passion. Becka will not be hurt because she will never know about it. And it makes no iota of difference to my feelings for her. I miss her, if you want to know the truth. I wish she were here instead of Cynthia. God, how I wish it. But she isn't so I have to make the best of what there is."

David sat down on his own bed to pull off his boots. He would not call his servant. There was too much of a strained atmosphere in the room to be shared with an outsider.

"The silent treatment," Julian said. "It always comes to this and you have always been expert at it." He smiled winningly. "Look, Dave, I know you think I treat Becka rottenly, and you are right, damn you. She is everything a man could ask for and more, isn't she? And she loves me. It never ceases to amaze me that she loves me. But she is not always available. Either she is ill or—or she is a thousand miles away. What am I expected to do?"

There was no point in arguing further with Julian. It would not even be an argument. Julian would capitulate almost immediately and be contrite and charming and full of good resolutions. He really had not changed. And the trouble was that David loved him now as he had always loved him—from the moment of Julian's arrival at Craybourne at the age of five. The seven-year-old David had welcomed this new brother into his lonely life with open arms and a yearning heart. He had felt instantly protective of the smaller, younger Julian, with his rumpled fair curls and big gray eyes and mischievous grin. Even as a young child Julian had had a natural charm.

In those days David had been afraid of his father, whose hand could feel remarkably heavy after some wrongdoing. Oh, he had loved his father too and felt that love returned in full measure. But he had been afraid that love might not temper severity in Julian's case. Julian was not his father's son and Julian was incurably mischievous. David had been afraid that Julian might be punished more severely than he and even perhaps turned off and sent to live elsewhere. The very thought had filled David with anxiety. And so almost from the start he had developed the habit of shielding Julian from detection and punishment whenever the child had got into serious mischief—as he did occasionally. Many was the spanking David had endured for an offense he had not committed.

Protecting Julian had become a habit. The spankings had progressed to more severe thrashings as they grew older, and David had been aware of his developing reputation—among the servants and neighbors—for wildness and even slyness since no one ever saw him commit all his various offenses.

Finally, when he was seventeen years old, he had realized that it was a pointless and undesirable habit. He knew very well by then that his father, though stern, gave unconditional love to both boys. And David had begun

to consider it a weakness in himself to be so used by his
foster brother—though to give Julian his due, he was always charmingly grateful for David's interventions and
always brimming over with resolutions to reform his
ways. His essential weakness had seemed charming, even
lovable, in a young boy.

But the habit had been more deeply ingrained in David
than he had realized. There had come the time several
years later when Julian had come to him frantic and
white-faced. He was within three months of marriage to
Rebecca and he claimed to love her dearly. But there had
been a moment of thoughtless passion—he did not know
what could have possessed him. He really did not. And
he did not know what to do.

Flora Ellis was pregnant.

It would be dreadful for Rebecca to discover the truth.
The humiliation, the scandal for her would be more than
Julian could bear. And it was her he loved. He knew it
now and would know it forever after.

And so David had done it once more—and had regretted it ever since. He had agreed for the last time to take
the blame. For Rebecca's sake. And because he had believed against all the evidence of his experience that
marriage would change Julian.

He had done it because he loved Rebecca himself—
always had and always would.

And so once more he had allowed himself to become
the scapegoat. And he had lived ever since with the guilt
of having interfered in something he should not have
touched. Julian—and Rebecca—should have been left to
work out the problem somehow together. Julian should
have been forced to take responsibility for his action for
once in his life.

And yet, David thought now with a feeling of some
self-contempt, he still loved the foster brother who had
come into his lonely life like a little bundle of sunshine.
Despite disillusionment and bitterness, he could not hate
Julian.

"Just be careful," he said after a lengthy silence,
bringing the argument to a rather lame end. "You would
not want to humiliate Scherer quite this publicly, Julian.

And you would not want to hurt Rebecca. She deserves better.''

Julian combed his fingers through his fair hair. "You were always my conscience, Dave," he said. "I suppose you realize how wretched you have made me feel? As always it's your silence that does it more than the words. I'll be done with the bloody woman. There. Are you satisfied? I'll be as celibate as a monk. It's good for the soul or something like that, isn't it?" He grinned.

"Something like that." David threw his coat from him and felt the deceptive coolness of the air against his shirt sleeves. "Lord, I hate this heat. Why can't someone invent a uniform to be worn in hot climates?" He stretched out on his bed and closed his eyes. "Wake me when something exciting happens, will you, Julian?"

"You might find yourself in an everlasting slumber if I do that," Julian said. "How about getting up for dinner in two hours' time?"

"That sounds exciting enough," David said, yawning hugely.

It was only after the British forces had been moved from Malta to Gallipoli in May that David became aware that the affair had resumed. Though probably it had never stopped, he thought. Probably Julian and Cynthia Scherer had merely become more discreet.

David said nothing all through the summer—even after June took them to Varna in Bulgaria and the unhealthy heat and the chronic outbreaks of cholera and fever and dysentery started to kill off the men by the thousands long before they saw any military action. The affair continued unabated. Perhaps soon they would be finally at war, David thought grimly, and the boredom would be at an end for Julian. Perhaps soon celibacy—and marital fidelity—would be a necessity rather than a choice.

Indeed it seemed that he would be proved correct. In September the British and the French landed in the Crimea and the enemy was finally engaged, first in the storming of the Alma Heights on the 20th and then, after a few minor clashes, in the Battles of Balaclava on October 25th and Little Inkerman the following day. The Guards established their camp up on the Chersonese Plateau, between Balaclava to the south and Sebastopol to the north. Even the officers had only tents in which to live. It seemed impossible that any clandestine affair could be conducted under such circumstances.

But Julian, of course, had always thrived on challenge and danger. He spent the night following the Battle of Little Inkerman in Captain Scherer's tent while the captain himself was on picket duty. David lay awake most of the night, cursing himself for so wasting his energies and for worrying about a man who was not even his brother. Sometimes, he thought, love could be very akin to hatred.

Julian returned to the tent he shared with David a safe time before dawn, and David cursed himself again for his feeling of relief. He said nothing though he did not even pretend to be asleep.

Julian sighed and wriggled into a nominally comfortable position on the ground. "Life begins to get interesting," he said. "The attack to our rear the day before yesterday, to our front yesterday. I wonder where the next one will come from. Or will we take the initiative, Dave, and attack Sebastopol at last? That is what we came here to do, after all." He yawned.

"Pretty soon we'll see all the action we can handle," David said.

"The sooner the better," Julian said. "I didn't join the military just to lie on my back staring up at canvas all day and all night except when there is picket duty to relieve the tedium."

"Go to sleep," David said.

"I've already gone," Julian said, yawning again.

He had returned safely. But obviously something had gone terribly wrong. Late in the afternoon of the same day, David entered the open space ringed about by officers' tents, a general gathering place for all off-duty Guards' officers. He found that he had walked into a crisis.

A dozen or so officers were standing about the edges of the space, rather like spectators at a prize fight. Julian stood in the empty center, his booted feet set apart, his hands clenched into fists at his sides, looking rather pale and tense. Captain Scherer, both his arms held by fellow

officers, was having a glove pulled free of one clutched
fist. He was glaring at Julian, his normally florid complexion almost purple, murder in his eyes.

"No, don't George," one of the two officers was
saying. "Once you have thrown it down, you will find
yourself in a hell of a mess. Think again."

Captain Scherer pushed off his two friends with a snarl
of rage though he had no glove left to dash in Julian's
face. His hand went to his side and with a scraping of
metal his sword was free of its scabbard. Julian's hand
went to the hilt of his own sword.

"Cut it out! Both of you." Major Lord Tavistock's
voice whipped about the space like a lash. One quick
glance about had shown him that he was the senior officer
present. "Put it away, Scherer, if you don't want to be
facing a court-martial. Drop your hand back to your side,
Cardwell. We don't need to be starting to carve each
other up when the Russians are poised and ready to do it
for us."

Neither of the two central figures in the drama moved
for a few moments. They continued to stand with eyes
locked on each other's.

"Major Tavistock is right, George," one of his friends
said, relief in his voice. "General Bentinck would not
look at all kindly on two officers of his brigade dueling,
especially while on active service. Not to mention the
Duke of Cambridge. Or Raglan himself for that matter."

"Leave it, George," the other friend said. "At least
for now. The matter can be dealt with later, after the war
is over."

"I'll give you both ten seconds." David's voice was
cold and hard. There was no thought now to any personal
feelings. He was an officer, imposing his will on others
as a matter of military discipline.

Captain Scherer returned his sword slowly to its scabbard after perhaps five seconds. Julian's hand fell away
from the hilt of his sword.

"Look out for yourself, Cardwell," Captain Scherer
hissed through his teeth. His eyes had not flickered from
Julian's. "You have not heard the end of this matter. You
may feel assured of the fact that your useless life has
been reprieved for only a short time."

"I'll be happy to give you satisfaction any time, any place," Julian said, his voice quiet and steady. "Court-martial or no court-martial, Scherer."

When Captain Scherer finally turned away, Julian strode toward his tent without another word. David felt the tension drain from his body even as he felt inner fury mount. It would serve Julian right if Scherer had run him through—he had a reputation for being handy with his sword. It would be no less than Julian deserved.

David and Julian avoided all reference to the incident during the few days that remained before they went into action themselves. Cynthia Scherer disappeared from the camp. She had been sent back to Balaclava, David heard. He hoped fervently that from there she would be sent to England.

The Russians launched a massive surprise attack at dawn on Sunday, November 5th—in a dense fog. Thousands of Russian soldiers marched in huge columns up onto the heights from Sebastopol to the northwest of the British camp and from across the River Tchernaya to the northeast. Battle raged all day, the numerically weaker British pushing back wave after wave of attack, both sides enduring terrible slaughter.

General John Pennefather's Second Division fought alone for several hours, reinforcements not coming up until the situation looked desperate. In particular it seemed that the Russians were about to turn the British right flank when they took possession of the Sandbag Battery overlooking the steep slopes of the Kitspur on the east side of the battlefield, driving back the defending soldiers of the Forty-first and Forty-ninth.

Rescue came just in time in the form of the Guards, the Grenadiers in the center, the Coldstream to their right, the Scots Fusiliers to their left. They drove the Russians back down the slope and then held the position in line, their discipline keeping them from making a wild pursuit of the fleeing enemy. But the men of the Fourth Division, also newly arrived, felt no such restraint and went hurtling down the slope in hot pursuit of the enemy to the bottom of the Kitspur. In the heat and excitement of a battle that seemed to be won, The Coldstream Guards followed them and then many of the Grenadier Guards, despite the fact that several of their officers, Major Lord Tavistock among them, bellowed at them to hold the line.

David plunged downward after his men through the heavy oak brushwood on the hill, sword in hand, holster loosened on his pistol, cursing volubly. The Russian masses were still fleeing and showing no immediate sign of standing and reforming. But even so it was dangerous to pursue and leave the Sandbag Battery above them defended by only a small remnant of the Guards. There were other Russian columns still up on the heights and constantly resuming their push forward. He must round up his men, and anyone else's men he happened to run into for that matter, and herd them back up the hill—at sword point if necessary. Heads would roll for this.

Matters were not improved by the fact that the remains of the morning fog combined with the smoke from the guns made all about him almost invisible. And yet in the course of ten minutes or so he had dozens of men toiling back up the hill, and he constantly ran into other men, singly, in pairs, and in small groups, and sent them on their way with blistering curses and menacing sword.

His was not the only waving sword. Suddenly through the smoke and the fog he came across two men, one prone on the ground, the other with a booted foot on his chest and his sword poised to run him through.

"Don't kill him! Take him prisoner." David had snapped out the order even as his brain was interpreting the scene before his eyes. Both men were British. Captain Scherer was the one down. Julian was about to kill him.

"For the love of God, stop!" David bellowed as Julian turned his head sharply in his direction. "Have you gone mad?"

"Stay out of this, Dave." Julian's voice was harsh and nearly unrecognizable. His eyes were wild with the savage blood lust of battle. "This is none of your concern." And his sword flashed downward.

David heard a shot. Above the constant roar and the deafening thunder of guns from across the battle field, he heard a single shot and watched Julian look back at him, surprise in his eyes, before crumpling at the knees and pitching forward across the body of Captain Scherer.

David looked down blankly at the pistol in his hand.

Shrouded in smoke and fog, the moment seemed unreal. This time and this place seemed to bear no relationship to the deadly battle that was raging above and all around. And no relationship to anything else for that matter. The battle and all else were forgotten.

"The devil!" The shaking voice belonged to Captain Scherer. "He was demented, Major. I would be dead if it were not for you. I owe my life to you." He was pushing at the body that had fallen across his own.

David watched a steady hand return his pistol to its holster and felt someone's leaden legs carry him across the distance to the two entangled bodies. He turned Julian's over gently and glanced at the small deadly blood-outlined hole just above his heart. He touched three fingers to Julian's neck. There was no pulse.

"He's dead," he said to no one in particular.

Captain Scherer was struggling to his feet, clutching his bloodied sword arm. "You had no choice, sir," he said, his voice aggrieved, "other than to watch him kill a brother officer in cold blood. You had no choice."

"Julian." David's lips formed the name, but it was doubtful that anyone would have heard even without the din of the guns.

"He died in battle," Captain Scherer said harshly. "A hero's death, sir. Shot by a fleeing Russian. They are calling, sir."

Three Russian battalions were advancing along the heights above them, cutting them off from the remaining Grenadiers at the Battery with the Duke of Cambridge and the Colors. Voices were yelling at all those left on the slopes of the Kitspur to get back up.

They might never have made it if the French had not come to their rescue as they fought their way through the Russian columns to the Colors and then continued to fight forward with the remaining Guards to take the colors and themselves to the safety of higher ground. But the French came in the nick of time and drove the columns back into St. Clemens' Ravine.

Even so many men did not make it through. Captain

Scherer did by some miracle, despite a useless right arm. Major Lord Tavistock, fighting by sheer instinct, his sword flashing in all directions, his mind numb, fell wounded and would probably have been finished off by a Russian bayonet had not a sergeant and a private dragged him with them to safety. He lost consciousness as he was being carried back to the hospital tents, a musket ball through the muscle of his left arm and one embedded between the calf and bone of his left leg.

He almost died. It was amazing that he did not. Many thousands of the wounded who wanted desperately to live did not do so. He did not even want to live and yet did.

He cursed the surgeon who would have amputated both his arm and his leg, and threatened him with death or worse if he did so. Both balls were removed at the hospital at Balaclava. And then the fever set in, the fever that killed far more men than either the wounds or the shock of amputation ever did. The fever made him quite unaware that he was moved yet again and set on board ship and transferred to the barrack hospital at Scutari. Perhaps he would have died there—almost certainly he would have done so—if there had not been a group of lady nurses newly arrived from England who insisted on organization and cleanliness and air and space.

Even so it was amazing that he lived. One of the nurses—their leader—warned him that he might not.

"Your wounds are healing nicely, Major," Miss Nightingale said to him quite matter-of-factly some weeks after his arrival, "and the fever has receded. But you are dying. You know that, don't you?"

For all the care she showed her patients, she was not a woman to mince words. Major Lord Tavistock only just stopped himself from telling her to go to hell. She was a lady after all.

"Only you can heal yourself the rest of the way," she said. "Your real wounds are ones I have no skill with, nor the surgeons either. You cannot forget all the killing?" Her voice was suddenly gentle, understanding.

"I killed my brother," he told her with closed eyes.

She did not answer him for a long time, and he did not open his eyes to see if she had moved away.

"I do not know how literally you mean that, Major," she said. "Do you have a wife? Or a mother and father? Or any family? Anyone to grieve for you when you are dead? Is it not self-indulgent to die when you might live?"

When he finally opened his eyes, she was gone.

He had killed Julian. Julian, whom despite everything he had loved. He might have yelled again and deflected that downward flashing blade. Or he might have shot an arm or a leg. Instead he had aimed for the heart.

He had killed her husband, the man she loved more than anyone in the world. He could never go home and face her. He tried not to picture her being told the news when it was brought to her. He tried hard but could see nothing else behind his eyes for hours at a time, whether he was awake or asleep. The thought of finally having to come face-to-face with her, knowing himself to be her husband's murderer, made him long for death and become envious of those about him who died with such apparent ease.

He tried not to picture his father being given the news of Julian's death. And then he pictured his father learning of his own death too. He was his father's only son, his only child. His father had opposed him buying a commission with the Guards when his position as a landowner in his own right and as heir to an earldom should have kept him at home. But he had had to get away. He had had to get away from *her*. An ironic fact, as it had turned out, when his joining the military had brought Julian into it too a mere few months before his marriage.

Could he deliberately die and cause his father all that suffering? Could he?

He finally decided to live—almost as if he had total control over his own fate—when he overheard one of the surgeons and Miss Nightingale discussing the desirability of shipping him off back home. Home was the very last place on earth he wanted to be. If he must live in order to avoid going there, then he would live.

He was back with his regiment in the Crimea soon after Christmas and was able to suffer with his men and fellow officers all the indescribable horrors of the winter there without adequate clothing or housing or food. He almost welcomed the suffering. During the coming year he distinguished himself in action time and again, acquiring for himself a reputation for daring and stern devotion to duty. He also acquired one of the new and coveted Victoria Crosses, a medal awarded for extraordinary valor.

Captain Sir George Scherer had been sent home, an invalid, after the Battle of Inkerman. Captain Sir Julian Cardwell, buried with so many other officers and men on the Inkerman Heights, was remembered as a hero and as something of a lovable rogue.

David found his grave. He went there only once—with dragging footsteps—soon after returning from Scutari. It was a mass grave. Someone had bungled and buried officers and enlisted men all together. It was customary to bury officers in individual, carefully marked graves. But Julian had been piled under with everyone else—with all the others of all regiments and ranks who were known not to have returned alive up the Kitspur.

All had been confusion and inefficiency after the battle as well as during it, it seemed. David grieved that he had not been there to identify the body, to give Julian a decent burial befitting his rank. He stood looking down, stony-faced, at the large, snow-covered grave.

Julian was there. Julian, his brother. The man he had killed.

He never went back.

Major Lord Tavistock carried his secret and bore his guilt alone.

3

Craybourne, England, July, 1856

The Peace of Paris was signed in the spring of 1856, ending what came to be known to history as the Crimean War, one of the hardest and most devastating wars in which the British had ever participated. The survivors of the army that had left Britain more than two years before, including the maimed and the wounded, began to return home.

Rebecca Cardwell still wore black. The veil and the heavy crape had been set aside with reluctance after the first year, but she continued to wear mourning just as she continued to mourn. She had loved him. He had been light and gaiety in her life for so long that she could not remember a time when he had not been. Julian had been her life. She still did not know how to live without him.

Now the pain had become sharper again. And the guilt. She stood in the window of her private sitting room at Craybourne, the Earl of Hartington's country home, staring along the driveway to where it turned into the trees half a mile away. She had stood thus each afternoon for the past four days, waiting for the carriage to return from the station, and supposed she would do so each day until he finally came as he had informed his father he would this week.

David.

She had wished David were dead. David instead of Julian. She had cried bitterly about the unfairness of it, about the fact that it was Julian who had died and David who had survived. She had read somewhere that the good die young, that the evil live on. It was a thoroughly silly idea, but even so—why had it had to be Julian who had died? He had been so full of life and love and laughter.

It had not taken long for rationality to return to her

mind. And guilt. How could she wish for another man to be dead only so that her husband might live? As if one change in reality could effect the other. She did not wish it. She did not wish David dead. She only wished Julian alive. She wished they had both survived.

It was just that she had known as soon as the grim-looking soldier had arrived at Craybourne and asked to speak with the earl privately. She had known that one of them was dead. She had not hoped it was David—never that—as she had waited, sick at heart and sick to the stomach, pacing the tiled hall outside the library, refusing Louisa's company. But she had hoped and hoped that it was not Julian. She had drawn a shaky hope from the fact that the soldier had not asked to speak with her. But hope—if there had been hope—had fled when the library door opened and the earl, looking grave and drawn, had asked her to step inside.

She had known then that it was Julian, not David. The earl had not needed to tell her. But she wished with the last pitiful shred of hope that after all he was calling her in to break the news of the death of his son. She had wished that after all it was David.

But it had been Julian. Dead in the Crimea in a battle they called Inkerman. Dead several weeks before word reached her.

No, when she thought about it rationally, she did not wish that David was dead. But she did hate him. If it were not for him, Julian would never have been in the Crimea. He would still be alive. Instead of which he was dead and buried in a place where she could not even lay flowers on his grave. She leaned forward to rest her forehead against the cool glass of the window. But she straightened up again at a knock on the door. It opened before she could answer.

"Rebecca?" The Countess of Hartington peered around the door, smiled, and stepped inside the room. "I thought you must be up here. You really should have come walking with us. It is a beautiful day."

"I know you and Father value your time alone together," Rebecca said.

The countess clucked her tongue. "William and I have been married for almost a year," she said. "We are no

longer on honeymoon. Why will you persist in feeling
that you do not quite belong here with us, Rebecca?''
She seated herself on a chaise longue and motioned Rebecca to take a seat too.

Rebecca had always felt that she did not quite belong
even though she had never for one moment been made
to feel unwelcome. She had come to Craybourne because
Julian had told her that was where she must go. And she
had stayed there after his death because there was nowhere else to go. She had been unable to go to Julian's
estate because he had never lived there—and after his
death it had passed to a cousin of his. She had been
unable to go back home because her own father had died
shortly after her wedding and her mother had gone to
live with a younger sister in the north of England. Rebecca's brother, Lord Meercham, had leased the house
in which they had grown up—eight miles from Craybourne—and taken his family to live in London, though
more often than not they were traveling about the country, moving from one house party to another. The settlement Julian had left her would have made it difficult for
her to set up alone anywhere.

''I have never said so. Father is kind to me,'' she said,
sitting in an armchair beside the fireplace. ''Extremely
kind.''

''But you feel all the awkwardness of living in a house
which you ran for well over a year,'' the countess said,
smiling ruefully, ''but where you now feel you have no
function. And you feel the awkwardness of the reversal
of our roles, though I have never pressed the point, Rebecca, and never would. And I did ask you if you minded.
I am not sure I could have brought myself to marry William if you had been dreadfully opposed to the idea.''

Rebecca looked down at the hands in her lap. ''I was
happy for you, Louisa,'' she said. ''And for Father. He
had been alone for so many years. He must have been
lonely, I think. And I would not have dreamed of trying
to prevent what the two of you had mutually agreed upon.
It is just that when I married I dreamed of a home and
family of my own and now—oh, now there is nothing.
But I would rather not talk about it. Self-pitying people
are tedious to be with. I am well blessed.''

She did not quite speak the truth about Louisa's marriage to the earl. She had not been happy at the time. She had been deeply shocked when she had realized very gradually what was happening between her companion and the Earl of Hartington. Louisa was a quiet, rather plain woman, six years Rebecca's senior, a gentleman's daughter fallen on hard times. And yet suddenly she had been scheming to become a countess and mistress of Craybourne—or so it had seemed at first.

And yet she should not have judged as she had done, Rebecca realized now. She should not have assumed that the whole business was sordid, that Louisa was a scheming adventuress. The marriage appeared to be progressing well. There seemed to be real affection between Louisa and the earl. And it was true that Louisa had never tried to be anything but a warm friend to Rebecca.

There had been some awkwardness, of course, at the changing of roles. Rebecca had been mistress of the house until the wedding. Now she was a homeless widow living with relatives—and not even quite that. Though she had never been made to feel an outsider. She had to admit that. It was all in her imagination.

And of course her loneliness had been accentuated by the loss of her companion and of her position in the house all at the same time—and less than a year after her loss of Julian.

"You should put off your mourning soon," the countess said gently. "It has been well over a year, Rebecca. You must start going about again. There are many wonderful gentlemen left in the world, many of them eligible. And you are so lovely. I have always envied your beauty."

"Perhaps soon," Rebecca said. "For putting off the mourning anyway. I could never marry again."

The countess's smile faded suddenly. "Oh, dear," she said, "I am feeling so nervous, Rebecca. Aren't you?"

Rebecca raised her eyebrows.

"But of course you are not," the countess said, laughing. "Why should you? You have done nothing to incur his wrath. I have. Do you think he will resent me? Do you think he will believe I am trying to supplant him in William's affections? Do you think he will believe I was merely a fortune hunter?"

"David?" Rebecca said.

"I am his stepmother," the countess said, grimacing. "And only two years older than he. And he will know that I was your employee and that most reprehensible of all creatures, an impoverished gentlewoman. Do you think he will come today, Rebecca? He said in his letter that he would be leaving London within the week."

"Perhaps today," Rebecca said, "or tomorrow. One never quite knows with David." Perhaps he needed a week or so of wild living in London, the war over, his commission sold.

"Thank God he lived through the war," the countess said. "I don't know if William would have been able to take the shock had he been killed."

"Yes," Rebecca said. "Thank God."

But the countess bit her lip in dismay. "Oh, Rebecca," she said, "I am so sorry. How tactless of me." She held a hand over her mouth and was silent for a while. "Will his coming home be welcome to you or not? Will it help to see him and talk to him about your husband? Or will it hurt to remember that they left for the war together?"

But Rebecca was not given the chance to answer. Both ladies jumped to their feet suddenly and exchanged glances.

"Horses?" the countess said. "Is it Vinney back from the station? The train must have come in."

They went to stand side by side at the window, watching to see if the carriage would veer off in the direction of the stables as it had done for the previous four afternoons or if it would proceed up to the house. It passed the turning to the stables.

"I must go down to William," the countess said breathlessly when the carriage slowed on the terrace below them and they could see trunks strapped to the back of it. "I would prefer to be with him rather than have to make a grand entrance later. I have never felt so nervous in my life. Come with me, Rebecca?"

"Yes," Rebecca said. She did not want to make a grand entrance either.

They hurried down the stairway to join the Earl of

Hartington, who was just emerging from the library into
the hall.

Major Lord Tavistock had been wounded again in 1855,
a nasty bayonet gash that had opened up his neck and
shoulder. It was a wound incurred in saving the life of a
young private soldier, whom many men of his rank would
have considered expendable. It was the act that had won
him the Victoria Cross. He had lost copious amounts of
blood, but he had survived. The scar was still livid. Both
his leg and his arm ached on occasion and sometimes
when he was tired or when he was not paying sufficient
attention he limped. But if he compared his condition
with that of many other men who came home with him
after the peace had been signed, then he had to admit
that he had nothing to complain about. At least he still
had all four limbs and both eyes.

And of course so many thousands did not come home
at all. For a long time he had wanted to be one of them,
had even tried to be one of them. But he had survived.

He longed to be back in England. He had decided long
before that if he survived the war, he would sell out and
spend the rest of his life in the country on his own estate,
looking to the well-being of those dependent upon him.
It had been an indulgence to join the army and leave his
responsibilities to a steward.

He wanted to put it all behind him. He wanted to forget. He wanted to be healed. Not of his wounds—they
had healed as much as they ever would, he supposed. Of
other wounds that were not physical. His soul needed
healing. Perhaps if he could just start a new life and
make something worthwhile of it, he would be able to
forget. He would be healed.

Perhaps.

He had to go to Craybourne first. He knew that. He
must see his father. But he dreaded going there and spent
four days longer in London than he needed to conduct
the little business he had there. Craybourne would be
different. His father had a new wife. He could not imagine his father with a woman. His own mother had died
in childbed when he was only two years old.

His father's wife was only thirty years old—and she

was the woman Julian had employed to be Rebecca's companion. David could not remember what she looked like though he must have met her once or twice. He dreaded meeting her now. He feared that she must be frivolous and mercenary. He feared that his father would be unhappy, would be realizing now after almost a year that he had made a mistake.

Or perhaps he feared for himself. Perhaps he feared no longer belonging. No longer having his father to himself—as if he were still a small boy and needed that security.

Or perhaps what he feared most, what delayed his homecoming for four days, was something else altogether. Rebecca was still living at Craybourne, as she had since Julian had sent her there when he sailed for Malta. She had nowhere else to go, of course, but even if she had, his father would have persuaded her to stay. He had always treated Julian like a son. He would think of her as a daughter-in-law.

In the course of almost two years David had somehow managed to persuade himself that he had had no choice in what had happened during those dreadful seconds on the Kitspur during the Battle of Inkerman. The choice had been between Julian's life and Scherer's, and he could not in all conscience have watched a murder being committed in cold blood. He had, after all, been an officer in Her Majesty's service, dealing with two fellow officers. It had been immaterial that one of them was Julian. If it had been anyone but Julian he would have done the same thing without a qualm of conscience. He had assuaged his guilt with the obvious truth of that thought, even if he had not banished it. The thought had enabled him to go on living—somehow.

But he would rather do anything else in life than go to Craybourne and have to face Julian's wife. His widow. Rebecca.

The drive from the station seemed shorter than he remembered, perhaps because he did not want to reach the house. Despite the four days and the steeling of his mind, he was not ready. Before he could quite gather himself together after the train ride from London, they were through the gates and among the trees. And before he

had adjusted his mind to that fact, they had rounded the
bend in the driveway and left the trees behind and there
at the top of half a mile of rambling lawns, was the house
itself. Home.

David shifted uneasily in his seat.

A few minutes later he climbed the horseshoe steps to
the main doors, which were being thrown back even as
he set his foot on the bottom step, and wondered if his
father would be there in the hall to greet him or if he
would have to steel himself for an entrance into the drawing room. But all nervousness and all thought fled as he
stepped into the doorway and his father came hurrying
toward him. The next moment they were locked in a
close, bruising embrace.

"My son," he heard the earl say. His father had never
been a demonstrative man, though David had never
doubted his love. But he clung now wordlessly, without
shame. "My son," he said again.

"Papa." They released their hold on each other finally
and David looked at his father, an older replica of himself, their eyes on a level. The handsome, rather narrow,
rather severe face had acquired dignity with age. The
dark hair was silvered at the temples, perhaps a little
more than it had been two and a half years before. "It's
good to be home." The words seemed inadequate to the
emotion of the moment.

A woman had moved up behind his father's shoulder.
David dared not look. He could feel his heart beating in
his chest and could hear it hammering against his ears.
His father turned and set an arm about her waist.

"This is my son, my dear," he said. "David, this is
Louisa, my wife. I believe you have met before."

She was small and inclined to plumpness, though she
was by no means fat, fashionably dressed in a blue, tight-
bodied dress, its wide skirt made fuller by three deep
flounces. She had light brown hair and gray eyes. Her
face was amiable and rather plain. David could not remember her. But she was a surprise. It was difficult to
see her as his father's wife, as his companion, his lover,
despite the fact that his arm was still about her waist.

"David?" Her voice sounded anxious and he realized
that she must be as nervous about meeting him as he was

about meeting her. He realized too that she must have greeted him by his title at former meetings. But she was his stepmother now.

He inclined his head to her. "Ma'am?" he said. "It is a pleasure to meet you—again."

She smiled suddenly and he could see that she was not entirely without beauty. "You are so like William," she said and flushed. "So like your father. I had forgotten your looks, though we did meet on one occasion, I believe. Was your journey tedious? Trains are so noisy and dirty, I find, though wondrously fast. You must be ready for tea."

He felt himself relaxing. Until something—a small flutter of movement perhaps—drew his eyes in the direction of the stairs and the shadows to one side of them. She was almost invisible. She was wearing black—Oh God, she was still wearing black. His stomach turned over. He had forgotten that she was taller than average. And he had forgotten the way she had of holding herself so regally erect. He had not forgotten her hair. Even in the darkness of the shadows he could see that its pure gold had lost none of its luster. It was parted at the center and looped down smoothly over her ears. Her face looked as if it had been sculpted of alabaster. Had she always been so delicately pale?

"Rebecca?" he said. Somehow it seemed as if there were no one else present except the two of them. He took a few steps toward her.

"David." Her lips formed his name though he felt the sound more than heard it.

And he knew with a painful rush that he had been fooling himself for well over a year, that nothing was over, that nothing could be forgotten, that there could be no healing—ever. For he was the one who had clothed her in black and put that alabaster look on her face. He was the reason she was standing there forever alone and in shadow instead of in the light and the sunshine with Julian.

He had killed her husband. He had shot Julian through the heart.

"Rebecca," he said, reaching out his hands to her

without knowing that he did so, "I am so sorry." She would never know how sorry.

She set her hands in his, two slender blocks of ice, and he squeezed them tightly until he could feel the hardness of her wedding ring.

"I'm glad you are safe," she said. "I'm glad you came home, David."

He stood staring at her, wanting to take her into his arms and hug her as he had hugged her at Southampton the very last time he saw her, wondering if she needed to be hugged at that moment.

By her husband's murderer.

His father's hand clasped his shoulder. "Let's all go up for tea," he said. "We can talk there."

David released Rebecca's hands and offered his arm. She took it and they walked up the stairs ahead of his father and his father's wife, all of them strangely silent.

They had talked and talked through tea, the three of them, and again over dinner. There seemed no end to the questions his father and Louisa had to ask David, and he showed no reluctance about answering them. All of Louisa's nervousness seemed to have evaporated. She looked entirely happy by the time they all adjourned to the drawing room and the earl asked her, as he often did, to play the pianoforte and sing. Louisa had a sweet voice.

She was playing and singing now, the earl behind her, one hand resting lightly on her shoulder, David standing at her other side.

Rebecca sat in the window seat, where she usually sat in the evenings, though both the earl and Louisa frequently urged her to join them at the pianoforte or beside the fire if it was a chilly evening.

He had changed. He had aged. He was thinner—at least his face was. His figure still looked powerful beneath the dark evening suit he wore. He looked more like his father than ever, tall and dark and severe. Except that there was a new softness about the earl's eyes, put there no doubt by his contentment with his new marriage and perhaps by the safe return of his son from war. Whereas David's blue eyes were hard and bleak all at the same time.

They were eyes that had looked on suffering and horror

and death and could not forget. Or so it seemed to Rebecca.

But he had lived through it. Julian had not. There was little physical evidence of David's ordeal except for the shockingly livid scar on his neck, which showed above the collar of his shirt and which he had told the earl extended all the way down his neck and along his shoulder. Courtesy of the Russian tsar, he had said lightly.

Rebecca had shuddered deeply. Julian had received his death courtesy of the Russian tsar.

She found herself resenting David more than she wanted to and feeling guilty at her reaction. He was safe and loved and being made much of by his father and by Louisa. It was all over for him. It was his past. He had the rest of a lifetime to look forward to.

Julian was in a grave in the Crimea.

It was unfair. And her bitterness was unfair, she knew. Such were the realities of war. She was not by any means the only widow the war had created. At least she had not had children to be orphaned, though she might have had two if circumstances had been different. So many poor widows of the war had children.

"Rebecca?" She had been so deep in thought that she had not noticed him crossing the drawing room toward her. He was standing in front of her now, dark and elegant, looking down at her from those hard, opaque blue eyes. "You no longer sing?"

She used to sing, during her childhood and during her girlhood, both at home and at Craybourne during the frequent visits she had made there with her parents—the earl and her father had been close friends. She used to love to sing at Craybourne as she grew older because the two boys had liked to watch her and listen to her. David used to turn the pages of her music until Julian had ousted him. Then David would sit at a distance watching her while Julian sat beside her smiling his appreciation and flirting with her to the extent her very proper upbringing would allow.

"Your father wants to listen to Louisa," she said. "He is fond of her, David."

"Yes," he said. "I have seen that. Will you join us at the pianoforte?"

She shook her head quickly. The conversation at tea and at the dinner table had encompassed every topic concerning the past two years, it seemed, with one glaring omission.

"Were you there?" she whispered. "Did you see it happen?"

Although there was a lengthy silence, she could see by his eyes that he understood what she was asking.

"Yes." His voice was no more than a whisper too.

"They said he was a hero," she said, leaning forward and looking earnestly at him. "That was all. They seemed to know no more. I suppose all men who die in battle are called heroes, aren't they? At least to their surviving loved ones. Thousands of heroes for each battle."

She watched him swallow.

"Tell me what happened," she said. "Tell me how he died."

He shook his head. "Perhaps it is better not spoken of, Rebecca," he said.

"Why?" She gripped the edge of the window seat on either side of her until her knuckles turned white. "Because he did not die a hero's death? Because it was too horrible to describe? Because I will be upset? He was my husband, David. He was my love. You know that more than anyone. I must know. Please, I must know. I think perhaps it is because I do not know that I cannot let him go. I cannot believe that he is dead, that I will never see him again. I still cannot believe it after almost two years."

His hands were clasped behind him. His eyes bored into hers.

"There were not many of us," he said, "but we had repulsed an attack by a large column of Russians. We had driven them down a steep slope and were pursuing them, putting them to rout. Julian led the charge in his usual madcap, utterly courageous way. He was shot through the heart."

Yes, that would be Julian. If she just had him in front of her now, she would shake the life out of him. A bullet. Through the heart. He would not have felt a thing. He would not have known.

Julian!

"Are you all right?" David's voice was soft.

"You could not have stopped him?" she asked. "You could not have shielded him?" She knew that her questions were foolish, childish. She resented the fact that he had let Julian go on ahead. He had been Julian's superior officer. He should have been leading the charge. He should have stopped that particular bullet.

"We were all charging, Rebecca," he said. "I was wounded myself during the retreat that followed. Those were the wounds that landed me in the hospital at Scutari."

She spread her hands palms-up in her lap and looked down at them intently. "So you were not there when they buried him," she said. "You did not see how he looked. Whether his face was at peace or showed suffering."

"It was at peace," he said. "I turned him over before going back up the hill. I had to make sure that he was dead."

She closed her eyes.

"He was my brother," he said softly.

She was sorry for her unreasonable resentment. Yes, wild as David had been, he had always been fond of Julian, she believed. And Julian had loved him and emulated him and always craved his approval. Julian had joined the Guards because David was one of them. For the first time she realized that David must have been distraught at Julian's death. And he had witnessed it.

"I am glad you were there," she said, looking up at him again. "I hope he knew you were there. He would have known, wouldn't he? You were in the same regiment. Yes, he would have known."

He frowned and said nothing.

"Thank you for telling me," she said. "Thank you, David."

It was foolish for the pain to be so raw again after so long. It was self-indulgent, perhaps, to let pain go on and on. To grieve interminably. Perhaps Louisa was right. Perhaps it was time to put off her mourning.

But the pain was raw and new again.

She got to her feet and drew away from his outstretched hand. "Please excuse me," she said, hurrying past him. And then she noticed the earl and Louisa, standing beside the pianoforte, looking at her.

"Rebecca," the countess said, "let me . . ."

But she smiled at them and hurried on by. "Please excuse me," she said.

Perhaps these tears were necessary, she thought, blinded by them as she hurried up the stairs and into her room. Perhaps these were not a foolish indulgence. Perhaps these were the healing tears at last.

At last it was real. David had seen him die. David had touched his body and turned him over and confirmed that he was dead. He really was buried in the Crimea. He really was.

Julian was dead. He was never coming back to her.

He was dead.

4

"I should have refused to answer," David said. "I should not have stirred it all up for her again."

"She was fond of the boy," the earl said. "And he left at a bad time, when her health was delicate. She has never recovered from his death."

"I should not have told her anything," David said.

Louisa came across the room toward him and set a hand on his arm. "I know her well," she said. "We have always been close. I believe it was because she did not know, David, that she has found it so impossible to accept. Upset as she is tonight, I believe it will help her to know the full story."

"Foolish boy," the earl said. "He led the charge, David? He took unnecessary risks? How typical of Julian."

"It was that sort of battle," David said. "It was not one that could be fought by the book. It was one that was won by individual effort and foolhardiness. We were so damnably outnumbered—pardon me, ma'am."

"Louisa," the countess said, smiling. "It is an embarrassment to be your stepmother and only two years older than you."

"Louisa." He nodded. "This must have been a tedious evening for you with nothing but talk of war and armies. And now this upset. My apologies."

"It was inevitable," she said. "You have been gone for well over two years, David, and there have been only a few letters. Your father has been frantic about you."

"Frantic, my dear?" the earl said.

"Yes." She turned to look at him. "You have scarcely mentioned him, William, or your anxieties about him. But do you believe I have not known that you have thought of little else since I first came here? Do you think I do not know you?''

The earl raised his eyebrows and looked at David. David could not recall seeing his father grin before. He had rarely even seen him smile.

''And now I am going to leave the two of you together,'' the countess said, ''so that you may talk freely to each other without fear of either boring or horrifying me. I shall look in on Rebecca on my way up. Good night, David. Good night, William.'' She raised her face to her husband, and he kissed her briefly on the lips.

It looked strange to David, seeing his father kissing a woman.

They talked until the early hours of the morning—about the war, about Julian, about the earl's decision the previous year to marry again, about David's decision to sell out of the army, about his plans to move to Stedwell, the estate he had never yet either lived on or managed for himself. He was going to give the housekeeper and steward there one month's warning before going there.

It was a satisfactory homecoming, he thought as he finally said good night to his father and closed the door of his room behind him. It was wonderful to be with his father again, and he had felt a cautious and unexpected approval of his father's wife. It looked as if it might be a happy marriage. And he had a good future to look forward to, an interesting one. A challenge.

He wondered suddenly as he unbuttoned his shirt if Rebecca was sleeping, if she was still crying. He wondered if she had any suspicion at all that he had lied to her. He wondered if his father had any suspicion. He wondered, his hands stilling on the buttons, how each of them would react if they knew the truth. If they knew that the bullet that had stopped Julian's heart had come from his own pistol.

He felt a familiar coldness and dizziness buzzing in his head. They must never know, and that was all about it. Apart from himself, there was only one man who knew the truth and George Scherer, wherever he was, was unlikely to tell it. And so David felt again, but more intensely than he had yet felt it, all the heavy burden of his secret. A secret that he could share with no one.

I killed my brother, he had told Miss Nightingale. That was the closest he had come to telling the truth. But he had been unable to say any more though he had sensed that she would have listened. But as she herself had said, she had skill only in healing the body. She could have given no absolution to his soul.

No one could give that. Not even God. God might have the power to forgive sin, but He could not erase guilt. And this particular sin had been committed not against God, but against Rebecca.

He had not expected to find her still in mourning.

He had not expected that.

Flora Ellis lived with her son in a small cottage on the Craybourne estate, half a mile from the village. She was accepted there now, time being a healer of most ills, though she felt no wish to move back there. It suited her to live a little apart but also to be close to other people. She did not mind going into the village now that there was no chance of meeting her father there. Her father had been vicar at the church there at the time of her disgrace. He had recently been moved to another parish at his own request. He had not spoken to his daughter since the day she had announced her pregnancy.

She had steadfastly refused to disclose the name of the father, though it was generally believed that he was David Neville, Viscount Tavistock. His father, the Earl of Hartington, had after all given Flora the cottage of a deceased former housekeeper to live in, and had apparently supported her since her own father had disowned her, and her son too since his birth almost four years before.

Flora even had a few friends, among them Rebecca Cardwell. Rebecca called on her frequently at the cottage, though Flora never called at the house. They often went walking together, Richard with them. Rebecca enjoyed the friendship of someone who was quiet and kept to herself. And she enjoyed watching Richard grow even though there was some pain in knowing that she might have been watching her own children grow if only she had been able to bear them. She tried not to brood on the matter. Although she had always been quiet, she was not naturally of a gloomy turn of mind.

Rebecca called on Flora the morning after David's return home. She had had to get out, away from the house, into the air. She had a headache, caused by all the crying she had done the night before—the first she had done for over a year—and by a largely sleepless night. But it was a headache that needed to be willed away, not coddled. He was dead, she told herself quite deliberately as she arranged her wide-brimmed bonnet far back on her head, as was the fashion, and tied the ribbons beneath her chin.

Richard came running at her knock on the cottage door and immediately began prattling to her about a frog he had seen the day before at the edge of the pond while Flora came up behind him.

"Let Lady Cardwell at least come inside, sweetheart," she said, laughing. "Do come in, Rebecca."

He looked like David with his narrow face and dark hair, though his eyes were gray, not blue. It always angered Rebecca that the child must grow up to cope with the stigma of bastardy when he should be the acknowledged son of a viscount, grandson of an earl. He should be Richard Neville, not Richard Ellis. There was no reason at all why David should not have taken the consequences of his actions and married Flora. She was, after all, a gentlewoman, even if she was not of such exalted rank as one might expect the wife of a viscount to be. That did not seem to matter as much as it had used to, anyway. One had only to consider the case of Louisa, for example. And there were all sorts of aristocrats who were marrying into the families of wealthy traders and industrialists.

Flora was personable enough. Beautiful even, with her very dark hair and eyes and her voluptuous figure. And intelligent and good-natured. Rebecca often wondered about the passion that must have flared between her and David for Richard to be conceived. Flora showed no bitterness over what had happened, or what had not happened. She rarely mentioned David, never in connection with herself.

"Oh," she said now, "you are wearing gray, Rebecca."

Rebecca looked down rather self-consciously at the plain, full-skirted dress and jacket bodice she had had made a few months before but not had the will or the courage to wear until today. She had worn black for so long.

"It is very becoming," Flora said, "and fashionable. Come into the kitchen if you don't mind. I shall make some tea."

Richard told Rebecca again about the frog and how it had hopped away each time he had tried to pick it up, refusing to be caught.

"Frogs need to be free," she said, running her hand over his soft hair. "Just like little boys."

Her own elder child would have been just a few months younger than Richard, had it lived. Sometimes it seemed a strange irony that Flora's illegitimate child had survived to birth while her own much-wanted children, within matrimony, had not. But she never dwelled long on that thought. Life had altogether too much pain to drag one down—if one allowed it to. She had allowed pain to ruin almost two years of her life.

Besides, Richard was not unwanted, at least by his mother. She doted on him.

"David is home," Rebecca told Flora. She could not resist watching her friend rather closely as she spoke.

"Yes." Flora's hand paused for a moment as she set the kettle over the fire to boil. "I had heard. How is he?"

"Thinner," Rebecca said. "Older. His eyes are older. He has sold out."

"Yes," Flora said. "I had heard."

"He was with Julian when he died," Rebecca said. "He told me how it happened."

"Oh?" The cups and saucers that Flora was lifting down from a dresser rattled against one another.

"He was being foolish and reckless," Rebecca said. "He was leading a charge and got shot through the heart. He was dead by the time David reached him and turned him over. And then David was wounded. Strangers buried Julian. I suppose it didn't matter, did it? He was dead."

"Yes." Flora arranged the cups slowly and deliberately on their saucers. "It must have happened so quickly, Rebecca. He would have felt no pain."

"That has been my consolation overnight," Rebecca said. "I have often had nightmares, wondering."

"Yes," Flora said. "Yes, I can understand that." The kettle was beginning to hum on the fire.

"And so I put him to rest," Rebecca said firmly, smiling down at Richard who was holding a book and looking up at her hopefully. She lifted him to her lap. "Overnight I have put him to rest, Flora. I have to get on with my life—without him. I have indulged myself too long in mourning. Nothing can bring him back after all. And I shall always be able to remember that while he lived everything was perfect between us. I have had that in my life at least. So—I move on. And hence the gray dress. No more black. It is about time, isn't it?"

"Yes," Flora said, bending over the fire to test the heat of the kettle with her hand, though it was obvious that it was nowhere near boiling yet. "I am glad, Rebecca. Glad for you. You do not have to humor Richard, you know. He has had that very story read to him twice this morning already, haven't you, sweetheart?"

"But I like humoring him," Rebecca said, opening the book and feeling suddenly and unexpectedly light-hearted—and almost guilty at the feeling.

She wondered later, as she left the cottage and began the walk back to the house, if she should have said more about David. She wondered if Flora was starved for news of him or if hearing about him was painful to her. They had never discussed him. She wondered if David would call at the cottage. Surely he would want to see the three-year-old son he had fathered. The child had been little more than a baby when he left for Malta and the Crimea.

She resented him again and the fact that he had had a lovely woman he had refused to marry and a live son whom he had refused either to acknowledge or to make legitimate. And the fact that he had survived the war to return and continue to shirk his responsibilities. While Julian . . . But no, she would not think about it anymore. Bitterness would hurt only her in the end. It was time she started to live again. She had made that decision the night before as she had dried her tears. And she had committed herself to it this morning. No more gloom. No more self-pity. No more bitterness. She was going to find something to make life meaningful again. She deliberately put something like a spring into her step.

And then she saw David walking toward her along the path she was taking. There was no possibility of turning into another path to avoid him. He had seen her. All her newly made resolutions fled and she felt her spirits plummet. And yet it was David, she thought, walking determinedly on, who had been her salvation. He had brought her the truth and set her free. He had enabled her to set Julian finally to rest.

David had come to a decision overnight. He supposed it was one that had been hovering at the back of his mind for a long, long time, though he had never until now made it a conscious plan. After all, he had not seen Rebecca and did not know either how she was taking Julian's death or how she was coping with life without him.

He only knew that he realized her predicament. Her mother was living with a sister. Her brother had a wife and at least five children that David knew about. Rebecca was living at Craybourne with his father, who was not even in reality her father-in-law. And his father had a new wife, a woman only a few years older than Rebecca— and a woman who most awkwardly had been Rebecca's paid companion before the marriage. She could not live alone—Julian had not been a particularly wealthy man, and his estate had passed to another relative since Rebecca had no sons.

She must feel that she belonged nowhere.

Of course she was young. And extraordinarily beautiful. Perhaps she had recovered from Julian's death and was already engaged in an active social life again. Perhaps she had suitors or would have soon. Perhaps she would be married again soon. Those were the thoughts that revolved in his head for the last several months.

Perhaps he had no responsibility to her at all.

But he had seen the truth last night. He had seen that she still mourned deeply, that she still had not adjusted. He had seen that she had not yet learned to cope with life after Julian. And he had seen that she was living in a house where she must feel out of place, especially under the particular circumstances of his father's remar-

riage. And clearly Louisa was very much mistress of
Craybourne, a position Rebecca herself must have held
when she first came there from Southampton.

Rebecca's life must seem empty and useless. Yet as a
woman there was very little she could do to change matters. She had been brought up to expect life as a married
lady and mother and as mistress of her husband's home.

Through a sleepless night David had felt the weight of
his responsibility toward her. He had made a certain decision a few months before her marriage and thereby en-
sured that she did marry Julian. He was responsible for
the fact that she had married a man who was unfaithful
to her, who, had he lived, would probably have brought
her ultimate unhappiness. But he had not lived. David
had killed her husband and destroyed the whole fabric of
her life.

And of course there was the fact that he loved her, had
always loved her even when he was a boy and she was
just a quiet, happy little girl, golden-ringleted and hazel-
eyed, gazing worshipfully at him and smilingly at Julian.
The worship had died as he had got more and more into
trouble over the years, like the time when he had taken
the blame for locking the head gardener's two daughters
in a toolshed on a hot day and forgetting them there until
they had been discovered all of six hours later. Rebecca
had wept over those little girls and had gazed at him
reproachfully when he had confessed to having been the
masked bandit who had committed the crime. She had
dropped her gaze when his father had led him away for
a thrashing.

Her smiles for Julian had never stopped.

His love for Rebecca complicated matters. There was
always the chance that what he felt and was deciding to
do was more self-indulgence than duty. And perhaps, he
thought, he would not have killed Julian if he had not
loved Rebecca. Perhaps he would not have been so out-
raged at the affair Julian had been involved in. Perhaps
it was that outrage that had caused him to aim for the
heart rather than for an arm or a leg.

It was a ridiculous thought, of course. He had acted
with the instinct of an officer during that moment of time.

He knew that he ought not to let guilt distort his memories of what had happened.

However it was, he came to a decision overnight.

He discovered in the morning that Rebecca had had a light breakfast in her room, as she often did, and had gone out.

"She must have gone into the village," the countess said. "Or more likely to Flora Ellis's. She usually asks me if I want to go with her when she goes to the village. Do you know where Flora lives?" And then she flushed, and he knew that she had just remembered what Flora Ellis was supposed to be to him.

"Yes," he said. "I'll go to meet her."

He came upon her about halfway to the cottage. He noticed the gray of her clothing immediately and the elegance. Her hair shone gold in the sun, exposed by the bonnet worn fashionably far back on her head. He wished suddenly that he could turn back, change his mind, give himself more time to think.

"Good morning, Rebecca," he said.

"Good morning, David." She did not smile.

"You have been visiting Flora Ellis?" he asked. A poor beginning. Her lips tightened.

"Yes," she said. "And Richard. Is that where you are going?"

"No," he said. "I came to meet you. Would you care for a stroll?" He offered her his arm.

"I suppose so," she said, taking it.

"Is this the first time you have worn gray?" he asked.

"Yes." She looked up at him fleetingly. "I owe you an apology, David, for rushing away last evening. It was such a relief, you know, to discover that you were there, that you saw it happen, that it was quick and painless, that he died instantly." Her smile was strained. "That he really was a hero. I needed to be alone for a while."

"Yes," he said. "I understood that, Rebecca."

"He died," she said, "almost two years ago. It is time I put him to rest. My maid is taking all my black clothes away this morning."

It was a little better than he had expected. She had given him the opening he needed.

"What will you do?" he asked. "Have you thought of your future?"

She stared ahead of herself for a while. "Women have so little control over their future, David," she said. "I hate living here though it seems very ungrateful to say so. Your father is as kind to me as if Julian had really been his son, and Louisa has continued steadfastly to be my friend. But you cannot imagine how out of place I feel."

"Yes, I can," he said.

"Can you?" She glanced up at him again. "I could go to Horace's I suppose. At least he is my real brother. I don't believe they would turn me away, though they are rarely at home. But they have never invited me, you see. I don't think Denise likes me particularly. I can't go there. I really can't."

"No," he said. "I think it would be unwise."

"I could live very modestly on the settlement Julian made on me at our marriage," she said. "Many people manage to live quite comfortably on less. But when I mentioned it, your father became quite angry. I have never had him angry at me before. I am reluctant to broach the subject again."

"He sees you as a daughter," he said. "Julian was with us from the age of five, you know. He was as much a son of the house as I was."

"I know," she said. "And he loved the earl and called him father. And he loved you, David."

"Yes," he said, his heart feeling like a stone in his chest, as it so often did. "We were like brothers. So my father could not see you going into relative poverty, you see."

"And that rules out my taking employment too," she said with a sigh.

"Have you thought of marriage?" he asked.

She closed her eyes. "No." She drew breath. "Had you asked me that question yesterday, David, I would have replied that I am already married. But I am not, of course. I am a widow and have been for almost two years. No, I have not thought of marriage. It is the only way a woman can change the state of her life, though, isn't it? I will have to think of something."

"I am going to Stedwell at long last," he said. "It has been mine all my life, yet I have never done more than pay it fleeting visits. I intend to make it my home and to make the running of the estate my job. I sent there this morning to warn the housekeeper that I am coming. She will need to make some preparations and hire more servants. I sent word that I will be coming in a month's time or so."

"I think you are wise," she said. "You would not feel at home here any longer, David. Not now that your father has remarried. They are happy, you know. If you have feared as I did that . . . Well, I don't believe it is true."

"Yes," he said. "I was a little worried, but I can see that I need not have been. She is genuinely fond of him, I believe—and he of her. I am taking on a huge task at Stedwell. The house is rather shabby, I believe, and the gardens have been kept tidy but nothing more. I know nothing about my tenants and laborers or about the efficiency or lack of efficiency with which things have been run. I know none of the neighbors."

"It will be an adventure," she said. "But you need something to keep you busy, David."

"To keep me out of trouble?" he said, looking down at her. She flushed but did not reply. He knew that she had never approved of him. But he could not allow that to stop him.

"I am going to need a wife," he said.

"Yes," she agreed. "She will be able to take charge of the house and gardens while you concentrate on the farms. You will not have any problem finding someone willing, David. You are young, and I am sure you know you are handsome too. Have you had a chance to choose anyone yet?"

"Yes," he said and waited for her to look up. "I want you to marry me, Rebecca."

She looked at him blankly for a while. "Me?" she said at last. "You want me to marry you?"

"We could both solve a problem by marrying each other," he said.

"No." Her voice was incredulous.

"You would have a home of your own," he said. "Not

only that. You would have a definite purpose in life. You would be very much needed.''

''You are proposing a marriage of convenience?'' she asked him. They had stopped walking and she had dropped her arm from his. ''We would marry just because I need a home and you need a helper?''

''Not entirely,'' he said. ''We are not strangers, Rebecca. I am fond of you and I think you are perhaps a little fond of me. It would not be quite as cold-blooded as a marriage of convenience.''

''I am not fond of you.'' Her eyes were wide. She flushed deeply after the words were out, but she would not retract them. ''Julian loved you and so I suppose I felt a certain bond with you. But I was never fond of you. I have no wish to marry you, David, either for convenience or fondness. Thank you but no.''

He felt rather as if he had been slapped across the face. But she had told him nothing that he had not known already. He could not retreat. He had heard too much of the loneliness of her situation in what she had told him a few minutes ago, although she had spoken without open self-pity.

''Think about it,'' he said. ''Think about a home and position of your own, Rebecca. Think about being able to move away from here and not having to contemplate living with your brother or with your sister-in-law, who would perhaps resent having you. Think about the fact that I need a wife.''

Her dark eyes blazed up at him suddenly and her nostrils flared. He could not remember seeing Rebecca angry. ''You need a wife?'' she asked him. ''You have one, David. It is just that you have neglected to marry her. And you have a son.''

''No,'' he said.

''Go and ask Flora to marry you,'' she said. ''Have you even thought of calling on her today? Have you even thought to see how your son has grown in your absence? He has your dark hair, you know.''

''Flora has dark hair too,'' he said.

''So you are going to deny your paternity?'' she said. ''I despise you for that, David. I despise you more than I can say. Everything else you ever did I could put down to the wildness of youth, but not that. How could you beget a child and desert the mother?''

''I did not desert her,'' he said, ''or the child. They are safe and warm and have all their needs provided for, don't they?''

''By you?'' she said. ''Or by your father?''

''Both,'' he said.

She turned from him and gazed across the wide lawn on which they had been strolling toward the distant line of trees.

''She would not have accepted marriage with me,'' he said quietly.

''I don't believe you,'' she said. ''And by your very words you are admitting that you never asked her. You did not even try to do the decent thing.''

''Ask her,'' he said. ''I believe she will tell you that she would not have married me even if I had asked. We had an understanding.''

''Oh, yes,'' she said. ''Money and a home in exchange for silence and docility. And so your son is a bastard, David. He will have to live his life with that stigma.''

''Yes,'' he said. ''But he will be well cared for. Marriage between Flora and me would have been impossible, Rebecca. Ask her.''

She began to walk in the direction of the distant house. ''Marriage between you and me would be even more impossible,'' she said. ''I cannot think why you had the gall to ask.'' She stopped again and turned to look full at him. ''I am Julian's wife. Julian's widow, if you will. Do you think I could marry you after being his, David? Do you?''

He could think of no answer to give her.

''I have tried,'' she said, and her eyes were tormented suddenly, ''not to wish it were Julian coming home and not you. It would be a cruel wish, wouldn't it? But I have wished it nevertheless. And I wish it now, God help me. If it had to be one or the other of you, then I wish it were Julian standing there and you in the grave in the Crimea. And I hate you for forcing me to make that admission out loud. Don't follow me. Please.''

She hurried away across the lawn, holding up her full

skirt in front so that she would not trip over it in her haste.

He stood looking after her, feeling as if she had plunged a knife into his stomach and twisted it. But it was natural, of course. How could he expect her to wish anything different?

And he had the same wish as she. He wished it could be Julian there at Craybourne with her, and himself in that grave on the Inkerman Heights. She would be happy—for a time—and he would be at peace.

He wished it profoundly.

5

The countess was to attend a meeting in the village after luncheon to arrange a prize-giving and fete at the school. Rebecca would normally have gone with her, but she made an excuse of her headache and retired to her room.

Much as she had felt awkward about living at Craybourne after Julian's death, especially during the past year, she had never felt afraid to leave her room. She was afraid now. She did not know where she might safely go. She did not know where David was. At luncheon he had said nothing about his plans for the afternoon.

She had been appallingly rude to him. She could not remember ever treating another human being with such discourtesy. She could not remember speaking deliberately to hurt on any other occasion.

If it had to be one or the other of you, then I wish it were Julian standing there and you in the grave in the Crimea.

She could hear herself speaking the words, wanting to hurt him. Feeling quite vicious in her need to wound.

And you in the grave in the Crimea.

Yes, she hated him for forcing her to say those words. She hated him.

How dare he ask her to marry him! And in such a cold-blooded manner. Merely so that she could get his house in order for him. How could he possibly have expected her to say yes when she had been married to Julian? He knew what that marriage had been like. He knew how close they had been, how deeply they had loved each other. Had he seriously expected that she would be willing to make a marriage of convenience after knowing that? And with him of all people?

I am fond of you, he had said. Was he? Yes, he probably was. He had been fond of Julian for all his wildness, and she had been Julian's wife. And he had always been tolerant of her as a child even though she was four years younger than he—and a mere girl.

And I think perhaps you are a little fond of me. He was wrong about that. She was not fond of him at all. And yet Julian had loved him. And yes, there was something of a bond. She closed her eyes and remembered Southampton and her final wrenching parting from Julian. She had hugged David there and felt a terrible dread for him and begged him to keep himself safe—even though all her mind had been on Julian and the fact that she must next turn to him and take her leave of him.

Forever, as it had turned out.

Yes, she felt a little fondness for David, she supposed, though it had been drowned out by dislike. By that one unforgivable fact about him. He had fathered Flora Ellis's child outside of marriage—the very thought could make Rebecca's cheeks grow hot with shame—and had refused to take responsibility for his actions afterward. He had refused to marry Flora. Though she would not have accepted him anyway, he had said. That was difficult to believe. Any woman in such circumstances would gladly marry even if she did not love the man. And how could Flora have done what she had done if she had not loved David?

Ask her, he had said.

Did it matter to her? Was it any of her business what had passed between those two former lovers and why they had made the decisions they had made? Was it of any personal concern to her whether David had treated Flora as shabbily as it had always appeared or whether Flora had not wanted marriage? They had an agreement, David had said—whatever that meant. It was really not her concern, Rebecca thought, unless she planned to marry him. She did not plan any such thing. The idea was absurd.

And yet when she sat down to write a letter to her mother, she dipped the pen in the inkwell three separate times but could think of not a word to write. Except "David is home." But she could not begin a letter with those words. It would seem that the fact of his homecoming was of immense significance to her. It was not. She set the pen down and got to her feet with a sigh after ten minutes when the paper was still blank.

She glanced through the window. Clouds had covered the sky since morning. It looked chilly. It would be more comfortable to stay inside where it was warm. She had nothing to go out for. She had made her visit that morning and had got enough air and exercise for the day. It was too late to go with Louisa. She would stay in.

And yet a scant two minutes later she had hurried into her dressing room and was tying the ribbons of her bonnet resolutely beneath her chin. She wrapped a shawl about her shoulders—she would need it this afternoon.

She was going to have a word with Flora.

David had not followed Rebecca back to the house. Instead he had turned and walked back the way they had come together and the way she had come alone. He had been to Flora Ellis's cottage only once, with his father. It had been before the birth of her son.

He knocked on the door and then looked down as it was opened almost immediately by a small boy. Yes, the child was dark, like himself—and like his mother. He had Julian's gray eyes.

"My lord?" Flora Ellis came up behind her son and curtsied awkwardly. She looked startled.

"Flora?" he said. "May I come in?"

She drew her son out of the doorway and motioned for David to come inside. She led the way into a small yet cozy parlor, snatching a book off one chair and some sewing off another as she went. She asked him to be seated.

"May I offer you some refreshments, my lord?" she asked.

He had forgotten how lovely she was, how voluptuous her figure. How very much Julian's type, physically speaking. He had loved Rebecca, of course. There could be no doubt about that. But Rebecca was a lady and a refined one at that. Julian had always needed more than beauty and refinement and love.

"No, thank you," he said. "Flora, how are you?"

She might be voluptuous to look at, but she was a lady

too. She had been a happy, high-spirited girl, as often in trouble with her straitlaced father as he ever was with his.

"I am well, my lord," she said, "as you see. And you? I am glad you came back safely from the war. I was happy to hear that you were coming home."

"Thank you," he said. He looked at the little boy, who was standing beside her chair, clinging to her sleeve and staring at him. "You have a beautiful son."

"Yes." She smiled at the child. "He is my pride and joy."

"You are managing, Flora?" he asked. "You have enough of everything?"

"Yes," she said hastily. "I am very well blessed, thanks to you and his lordship. We have everything we need."

"He will go to the village school?" he said. "We will talk about further education when he is older. And about a suitable career for him."

"Yes," she said, "thank you. You are most kind."

He looked at her broodingly for a few silent moments and at the child. "I want Rebecca to marry me," he said and watched her eyes widen. "She wants to know why I did not marry you."

Flora blushed. "I said at the time it was madness," she said. "I said it would come back to haunt you. I should have insisted on the truth being told, I suppose, but at the time I was in no state to make sensible decisions. I allowed you to talk me into something I should never have agreed to."

"At the time," he said, "it seemed the only thing to do. The wedding was all arranged and the guests had all been invited. There would have been a dreadful scandal. And you said yourself that you realized Julian would never marry you."

Flora bent over her child suddenly and whispered in his ear. "You may go and take a biscuit from the jar if you wish, sweetheart," she said. "Sit at the table nicely to eat it."

"Two?" he asked, holding up two fingers.

She smiled. "Two, then," she said. "Just this once. No crumbs, mind." She waited for him to dart from the room. "Why do you not tell her the truth now?" she asked.

"She loved him," he said. "She will always love him."

"And yet you want to marry her?" She flushed at the forwardness of her question.

"Yes," he said.

She frowned. "I don't know why," she said, "when you deserve so much more. But it is impertinent of me to say so. You would let her marry you, then, thinking this of you? You would do that rather than sully her memory of him."

"Yes," he said.

She looked down at her hands. "You always did love her, didn't you?" she said. "You were always ten times the man he was. And so often the scapegoat, by your own choice. I was one of the few people ever to realize that, I think. Rebecca never did, did she? But then that last time you did it for her. It was not for him, was it, or for what the scandal would have done to him. It was because she would have been hurt and you loved her." She sighed.

"Flora," he said, "she may come here asking questions. If she decides to give any consideration to my proposal at all, she may come. And she needs a husband. She needs a home of her own and a purpose to her days. She could find them with me."

"I will answer her questions with care," she said.

He leaned forward in his chair. "But you will not tell her the truth?"

"I promised," she said. "Before your father gave me this cottage, before we knew he would be so kind. When you and Julian came to make arrangements for my support, I promised that I would never tell anyone who Richard's father is. *Was.* I was a fool, perhaps, but I promised and I will not break that promise now if it is your wish that I keep it. I owe you more than I can ever repay."

He searched her eyes before nodding, satisfied, and getting to his feet. "I will not keep you longer," he said, "or the biscuit jar will be empty."

He led the way into the hall. But he paused with his

hand on the door latch and turned back to her, hesitating for only a moment.

"He died well, Flora," he said quietly. "And instantly. He could not have felt pain."

"I know," she said. "Rebecca mentioned it earlier." There was a sudden rush of tears in her eyes and she bit her upper lip. "Thank you," she whispered as he opened the door and let himself out.

Rebecca found Flora and Richard, not at the cottage, but beside a rather neglected lily pond a short distance away. It had not been much frequented since the far larger lake had been constructed east of the house. But Flora would not take her son there, where they might encounter the earl or countess at any time.

"Are there any frogs today?" Rebecca called as she approached.

"Only fish," Flora said with a smile while Richard poked intently at the water with a stick and called to Rebecca to come and see.

They strolled onward a few minutes later, along the wooded path that would take them back eventually to the cottage. Richard ran on ahead.

"I came back this afternoon for a reason," Rebecca said abruptly.

Flora looked at her inquiringly.

"What happened with David?" Rebecca blurted. "Did he ever ask you to marry him? Was there ever any question of marriage?"

Flora drew a deep breath. "We discussed it," she said, "and decided mutually against it. He was very honorable and kind."

"Honorable?" Rebecca said with scorn. "Kind? To bring such trouble on you, Flora, and then *discuss* taking the consequences? It was only right that he do so. Did he make it so obvious to you that he did not want to?"

"I did not want to marry him," Flora said. "It would have been quite the wrong thing—for both of us. Neither of us loved the other. He would have been doing it out of nobility and I would have been doing it merely out of fright and desperation."

"But he had fathered your child," Rebecca said. "Did he not owe you marriage?"

Flora did not answer for a while. "Sometimes," she said, "people get carried away by passion. I know you would find that hard to understand, Rebecca. You have such strong moral principles and standards of behavior and I must honor you for that. But it does happen nevertheless. Trying to put right that wrong with another wrong does not solve anything. It would have been wrong of me to marry Lord Tavistock."

"But if you did not love him," Rebecca said, "how could you have . . ." She flushed. "Pardon me, it is really none of my business. Do forgive me."

"Passion and love do not always go hand in hand," Flora said. "Not always. Have you blamed Lord Tavistock for not marrying me? Don't. He would have done so, I believe, but I made it clear that it was not what I wanted. He did no wrong."

"He is responsible for Richard," Rebecca said, tight-lipped.

"Do you think I would be without him?" Flora asked. "Can you look at him and say he should not exist, Rebecca? That he is somehow wrong? What I did was wrong. I knew it then and I know it now. But I cannot be as sorry as perhaps I should. I have Richard, you see. And so I am not really sorry. And I don't want anyone else feeling responsible, though I must confess that I am grateful for the support both Lord Tavistock and the Earl of Hartington give me."

Rebecca was silent. Yes, looked at that way, it was hard to see matters in purely black-and-white terms. She could not understand the talk about passion. Love she knew, but passion was something beyond her experience. It suggested something irrational, something beyond one's control. Something she had no wish to experience.

But she would not judge. She had never condemned Flora for something she herself could not understand. And how could she say that what Flora and David had done was wrong when there was Richard? Sometimes it was not so easy to decide what was right and what was wrong. Sometimes life was not easy.

"I'll not come inside," she said as they approached

the cottage. "I just needed to ask those questions, Flora. He wants me to marry him."

"Lord Tavistock?" Flora asked.

"I could not do so, of course," Rebecca said. "I do not even like or respect him. And I cannot consider a second marriage yet. It is too soon."

"It is almost two years," Flora said.

"It sounds like a long time," Rebecca said with a sigh. "It does not seem long, Flora. I still feel married. I am having to tell myself quite firmly that I am a widow and have been for almost two years. Does that make sense?"

"Yes," Flora said quietly.

"What I need to ask," Rebecca said, "though it is foolish to do so when I have no intention of marrying him now or ever. What I need to ask, Flora, is whether you would mind. Whether you would be hurt."

"If you married Lord Tavistock?" Flora asked. "No. Oh, no, Rebecca, you must not think I would. That is all long in the past. Over. You must not hold back on my account. He would make you a wonderful husband. I know it. He is a wonderful man."

Rebecca laughed without amusement. "And yet you do not love him?" she said. "Or want all these wonderful things for yourself?"

Flora flushed and then bent down to take the bunch of dandelions and daisies that Richard had picked for her. "Thank you, sweetheart," she said. "How lovely they are." She straightened up. "No," she said. "No, I don't, Rebecca. And I mean it. But I do not hate or even dislike him. I can see clearly that he is a good man."

Rebecca sighed again. "But I am not in search of a husband," she said. "Certainly not David."

She took her leave and walked back toward the house, her head down.

You would have a home of your own, he had said. *Not only that. You would have a definite purpose in life. You would be very much needed.*

Whereas she was hurrying toward a home that was not really hers, a home in which she had no clearly defined function. A place where she had to find her own amusements with which to fill the long and empty days.

But not David. She could never marry David.

* * *

Sunshine returned the following day and the earl announced at breakfast that all other activities must give way to an afternoon walk to the lake.

"You can play Lady Bountiful tomorrow again, my dear," he said, patting the countess's hand, "and Rebecca too. Today you must please the men of this family and walk with us."

The countess suggested a ride instead, but the earl insisted that a walk would be quite strenuous enough exercise. She pulled a face at him and smiled.

"Oh, very well, then, William," she said. "A walk it will be at whatever sedate pace you care to set."

"You have to humor my advanced age," he said, and she laughed at him outright.

No one had ever teased or laughed at his father in David's memory. And yet, stern as his expression was, he did not look angry or even displeased. David shifted his glance to Rebecca. She was wearing gray again, a lighter shade than she had worn the day before. He wondered if she had gone back to Flora Ellis's yesterday, if she was still angry with him, if she was still adamant in her determination to refuse him.

He wondered if since the morning before she had been tempted by his offer. If she ever could be tempted. She was eating her breakfast with lowered eyes, though she had talked with some animation with Louisa for a while about an elderly cottager who liked to be visited. They had half planned to call on him that afternoon. Their visit would have to be postponed now.

He walked with her when the four of them set out for the lake after luncheon. She took his arm without protest, and they had soon outdistanced his father and Louisa, who were walking rather slowly despite Louisa's protests.

"The sunshine is back," David said.

"Yes," Rebecca said. "Yesterday it looked as if we were in for a spell of rain."

They lapsed into silence.

"Did you speak with Flora Ellis?" he asked at last.

"Yes," she said. It appeared at first that she did not

want to talk about it, but she continued after a while. "You spoke the truth. I have misjudged you all this time. I am sorry."

"How much am I forgiven?" he asked. "Will you marry me?"

"No," she said hastily. "No, David. I think I made myself clear on that. I should never have said what I did. And I did not mean it quite as I said it. I have never wished you dead. I have only wished Julian alive."

"I understood," he said. "I am not asking to take his place, Rebecca."

She looked up at him. "What then?"

"I know you will always love him," he said. "I would never expect or ask you to give that up."

"And yet you wish to be my husband," she said.

"Yes."

"If I married you I would have to give him up," she said. "I would owe everything to you—loyalty, obedience, affection. That is what marriage is, David. There can be no half measures."

"And you could not in all conscience give me those three?" he asked. "Even though love would be withheld? Affection is a desirable ingredient of any relationship. I believe a marriage can exist quite well on mutual affection. Can you not feel that for me?"

"I don't know," she said. "I honestly don't know, David. But if I could not offer my heart, I could not offer my whole loyalty. I would feel that I had cheated you, that I had been unfaithful to you. I could never offer you my heart. It is dead and buried in the Crimea."

They had reached the lake. They stood on the bank for a while, looking across to the trees at the other side. But he turned with her to stroll around it. He was not ready yet to be joined by his father and Louisa.

"If I were prepared to take you without your heart?" he asked.

"It would not work, David," she said. "Believe me, it would not. Julian and I loved each other dearly, and yet even so there were certain things. . . . There were . . . It had to be worked on. Constantly. It was not easy. Not for either of us. It was only our love and our—our commitment to that love that held us together until the end. Even though we were apart for the last seven months of our marriage.''

"If you can never again love," he said, "if your heart is really dead with him, Rebecca, must you remain widowed for the rest of your life? Will you never again be able to consider marriage?''

She stared up at him, her eyes not quite seeing him. He knew he had put a new and rather frightening idea in her mind.

"I don't know," she said at last. "I don't know, David.''

"Or is it just me?" he asked. "Is it just that you cannot marry me because I came home and he did not?''

"You were like brothers," she said. "I could not marry my dead husband's brother.''

"But we were not brothers," he said.

"David," she said. "I couldn't. Please, I couldn't.''

He had to leave it. She was neither crying nor distraught. Rebecca was far too disciplined a person to show much open emotion in public. He knew that her behavior on the night of his return home was not typical of her. But he could see from her eyes now that she could be pushed no farther. She would not have him. At least at the moment she would not. Perhaps tomorrow he would try again, after she had had time to consider what they had talked about today.

But he did not think she would have him. Some other man eventually perhaps. But never him.

And so none of the burden of his guilt could ever be lifted from his shoulders. He would never be able to do anything to help and protect the woman whose husband and lover he had killed almost two years before. She would not be helped.

"Let's wait here for a few minutes, shall we?" he suggested, and he could feel her relief. "My father and Louisa should come up with us soon.''

The earl, when they did, frowned at the end of the lake where they stood and expressed his concern over the reeds that were growing out of the water.

"Any boat venturing down to this end could get stuck fast," he said, "and never get free. It would be quite dangerous to swim here. I'll have to have it cleaned out.''

"But the reeds give a lovely wild, picturesque aspect to the lake," the countess said. "Don't you think so, David? It does not have to be a pleasure lake, does it? Can it not merely be a pleasure to look at?"

"My gardeners would love to be within earshot now," the earl said dryly. "You would be offering them a wonderful excuse to be lazy, my dear. We would have wild nature to the very doors."

She laughed. "Now that is not what I said at all, William," she said. "Is it, Rebecca? Men will persist in thinking us foolish creatures by hearing only what they think we say instead of what we actually do say. Let's walk ahead and talk sense to each other, shall we?"

He was not sorry, David thought, as they strolled back the way they had come, to be with his father for the return walk.

"What do you think?" the earl asked. "Shall I have the lake cleared out, David? Or shall I please your stepmother?"

"I would not touch those questions with a thirty-foot oar," David said, chuckling.

"Well, I suppose if it is just the one end that is clogged and picturesque, there is no great harm," the earl said gruffly. "Those who want can still bathe and boat at the other end. But I am not going to allow the whole lake to get quite overgrown, you know."

The explanation for the walk rather than a ride and for the slowness of the walk came at tea after they had all arrived back at the house. The countess stood behind her husband's chair after pouring the tea, and set a hand on his shoulder.

"Shall we tell them, William?" she asked him.

He covered her hand with his and then patted it. "I said yes when you asked me the same question earlier, my dear," he said. "Go ahead."

She flushed deeply. "But I feel so very embarrassed," she said. "David is twenty-eight years old."

David raised his eyebrows.

"You are going to have a brother or sister," she said. "A halfbrother or halfsister, that is. Will you mind?"

For a twenty-eight-year-old man he must be incredibly naive, David thought. He had not really considered it as a possibility. The idea of his father begetting a child at the age of fifty-two seemed incredible to him. And yet his shock was laughable. His father was *only* fifty-two, after all. Louisa was only thirty.

A brother or sister? At his age? He got to his feet.

"Will I mind?" he said. "I am delighted," He shook his father by the hand, noting with interest that he looked as embarrassed as Louisa. And he pulled Louisa into his arms and hugged her tightly. "I am pleased for you," he said. "Why would you be embarrassed to tell me?"

"I don't know," she said. "I am also very happy. And immensely proud of myself. Aren't I, William?"

But the earl was getting to his feet and holding out his arms to Rebecca.

"Father," she said, going into them, "I am delighted for you, And for you too, Louisa."

And then the two women were hugging and Louisa was laughing. Father and son looked self-consciously at each other over their heads.

Perhaps all was not lost after all, David thought.

6

At breakfast the following morning, Rebecca and Louisa made arrangements to spend the afternoon visiting the elderly Mr. Maynard and one or two other cottagers who had been ill. But Rebecca had the morning to herself and took a book out to the rose arbor beside the house. She always found it a haven of peace and beauty with its neatly clipped shoulder-high hedges and stone arched entrance, with its wrought-iron seats and marble statues. And of course its roses.

She opened her book but did not even try to read. A breeze fluttered the edges of the pages but was not strong enough to turn them.

She kept remembering his asking if she would remain forever a widow since her heart was buried with Julian and she could not contemplate marrying without being able to give her heart. Just a few days ago she would have answered unhesitatingly. The answer would have been yes. How could she marry again when she was already married to Julian?

She was not so sure of her answer now. She could never love again, it was true. But life would be so empty of meaning if it were never to hold anything more than she had now. She realized that for a long time she had been waiting—waiting for the next phase of her life to begin. Waiting for Julian to come back. But he was not coming. Ever. Could her own life stop just because his had? At one time she had wished the answer could be yes. She knew that for almost two years she had wished unconsciously that she were dead too.

But she was not dead. And life was reasserting itself. Slowly and painfully, but undeniably. She had willed it so just a few days before. And she had put aside her black clothes and donned gray as an outer sign of her return to life. And yet the future yawned empty and rather frightening. She was lonely.

But not alone. Someone was coming through the archway. She looked back over her shoulder and saw without surprise that it was David. She had been half expecting him, she supposed. Nothing had been settled between them. She had said no, adamantly and on both occasions when he had asked. And both times he had given up pressing the point. But she knew nothing had been settled. She knew that he would ask again. And she knew that her final answer had not been given yet.

They did not greet each other. He sat quietly beside her on the seat she had chosen. It was strange that greetings were not necessary, she thought. It seemed that they were communicating beyond the medium of words. He was waiting for her to speak. Not impatiently. But he knew she would say something. He knew she had something to say.

She closed her book. And her eyes for a few moments.

"I am happy for them, you know," she said. "It is not that I am not happy."

He said nothing. Perhaps because he did not know what she was talking about, though she felt that he did.

"I don't think I can bear to be here when the child comes, David," she said. "They will be more of a family than ever. I will feel more out of place than ever."

Still he said nothing. He took the book from her hands and set it down on the seat on the far side of him.

"I wanted both of those babies," she said, her eyes closed again. "You can't imagine how much I wanted them, David. It was hard for Julian. He was so very pleased and then so upset both for his own loss and for my pain. But it was harder for me. They were inside my body. Part of me. It hurt dreadfully to lose them."

She felt his fingers rest lightly against the back of one of her hands for a moment.

"They would have made our happiness complete," she said. "Just as this child will make your father's and Louisa's. I really am happy for them. But I dread being here."

He spoke at last. "Come with me, then," he said.

She was so very tempted. For the first time she was tempted. And yet all through the night and the morning she had known that he would ask again. She had steadfastly held her mind away from making a decision. She had convinced herself that there was no decision to make. She could not marry him.

"David," she said, opening her eyes to look down at her hands. She swallowed convulsively. "David, I don't love you."

"I don't ask for your love," he said. "I ask merely for your help and companionship, Rebecca. And perhaps for a little affection if I prove to be a good husband to you. I don't ask for what you cannot give."

"But as your wife," she said, "I would feel honor-bound to give all."

"All you can," he said. "And your loyalty. That is all I ask, Rebecca. It is what I offer you."

She clenched her hands and then spread them over her lap.

"How would you feel," he asked, "if you came to Stedwell with me and found it as shabby and even as derelict as I suspect it is?"

She thought for a moment. "I think I would feel invigorated," she said. "There would be so much to do."

"There would be no one to help you," he said. "Except me—and the servants, of course. But I would be busy with the farms, which will need my attention after all these years."

"I would not ask for help," she said. "It would be wonderful not to need help, to have a free hand in accomplishing such a large task. To be needed." She stopped suddenly, realizing what she was saying.

"You would be needed, Rebecca," he said. "I need you."

But she could not. He was David. She had never even liked him—or not since childhood anyway. And especially not since—since Flora. She could not use him now for her own convenience.

"Is it a marriage in name only that you are proposing, then?" she asked him, feeling herself flush.

"No," he said. She knew he was looking steadily at her even though she could not bring herself to turn her head to meet his eyes. "It would have to be a marriage in every sense of the word. I don't believe we could live together in the same house otherwise."

"But I couldn't . . ." she said, clasping her hands tightly together in her lap. She could not face the intimacies of marriage with a man she did not love. Even with the man she had loved it had been difficult. Duty of course was what forced a woman to submit quietly—her whole upbringing had prepared her for that—but she did not think she would have found it possible without her deep love for Julian, her earnest wish to please him. It was unpleasant for a woman, even when there was love. Without it, it would be quite repugnant.

"I would not be trying to take Julian's place, Rebecca," he said.

He did not understand. Men did not, it seemed. Julian had always found it pleasurable. He had come to her almost every night, except when she had been with child and when she had been having her monthly periods. She had never minded because she had loved him and because she had been his wife. She did not believe he had ever realized that it had not been as pleasurable for her as it had been for him.

"Come with me," David said. "Marry me and come with me."

She turned her head to look at him for the first time. "David," she said, "we both know why it might be in my interest to marry you. I am lonely and adrift and need a husband and home. But what about you? Why would you wish to marry me when you might marry whomever you choose? You don't love me."

It was a question that had deeply disturbed her since he first asked. He knew she did not love him and never could. And yet he was prepared to marry her? It made no sense at all.

I want to start my new life at Stedwell without delay," he said. "After all these years of neglecting it, I can't wait to begin. I need a wife now. I don't want to waste more precious time going about trying to meet someone suitable. *You* are suitable. I know you. You need me. We need each other."

It still made no sense. Could he be so cold that he felt

no need of love? Or was he naive enough not to believe in love just because he had never yet encountered it for himself?

"But perhaps you would find love if you waited awhile," she said.

He shook his head. "I believe in affection more than love," he said.

"Perhaps you would fall in love with someone else after our marriage," she said, "and it would be too late."

"I would make you certain vows on our wedding day," he said. "I could not take marriage vows lightly, Rebecca. All my devotion and fidelity would be pledged to you—for the rest of my life and yours."

It seemed somehow cold and unfeeling even though he mentioned devotion. As if devotion could be willed. And as if there were no real emotion involved. And yet it was all she would ever be able to give a second husband. Perhaps it could work. Perhaps her first marriage was not the only kind of marriage that could succeed.

And yet, she almost said aloud, *you did not remain either devoted or faithful to Flora.* But then he had made no vows to Flora. She wondered how many other women there had been since Flora. There must have been others, surely. She had heard that soldiers, the officers anyway— the unmarried ones—often lived lives of wild debauchery when they were able. It was the inevitable result of the constant threat of death that was a way of life to them, she supposed. David must have had many women. He was such a very handsome and attractive man.

She was aware of his attraction for the first time since his return, of his handsome features and very blue eyes, of his broad shoulders and well-muscled physique. She had fought her attraction to him as a girl, suffering dreadful pangs of guilt whenever she had caught herself gazing at him appreciatively or daydreaming about him. It was not seemly to think of a man in physical terms, especially when one could not like or admire the man himself. She had always turned with renewed adoration to Julian, who deserved her love, and whose whole person she loved.

And now David could be hers. She felt breathless suddenly, as if she had been running hard. It was wrong to be attracted to a man's body. The physical did not matter. It was unimportant in life. She had heard that so many times at church and from her parents and her governess when she was growing up that it was deeply ingrained in her very being. Besides, she knew from experience that the physical side of love was not even pleasant for a woman.

It was a duty. It was the price a woman paid for a home and a place of her own in the social order. And for companionship and love and that feeling of oneness with the beloved. And for children if only one could bear them to term. It had been such a small price to pay for Julian. A few minutes of discomfort each night in exchange for long days of his love and for what she had hoped would be a lifetime of companionship.

"Rebecca," David said, breaking the silence, "I would be unhappy at Stedwell, thinking of you pining away alone here. I want us both to have a new life. The roses will be dying soon, won't they? Soon it will be autumn and then winter. But spring will come again. It always does. When the roses bloom again, you could be mistress of your own home. You could have a new and meaningful life. You could have something to replace the grief and the emptiness. For Julian's sake I want to give you security and a chance at least for contentment."

"For Julian's sake?" she said. "Is that what this is all about, then, David?"

"And for mine," he said. "I need you."

That was what did it finally, that repeated assertion that he needed her. It was so long since she had been needed, since she had felt that her existence mattered to at least one other person. Julian's all too few letters from Malta and Varna had been filled with love and longing, but he had not needed her enough to send for her. That was unfair, of course. He had denied himself and insisted she stay at home because she had just miscarried and had not fully recovered either her health or her spirits before he left. But she had searched his letters for need, for some sign that he could not live without her, just as she could not live without him. She would have gone at a moment's notice.

And since Julian's death? Louisa had needed her, at

least financially, for a while. But no longer. The earl had been kind to her. But he did not need her. No one had needed her for a long time.

"David—" she said.

But he would not let her finish. He took one of her hands in his and squeezed it tightly. "Rebecca," he said, "I need you. I need you to say yes more than you can possibly realize." Just as if he knew what argument would finally tell with her.

She looked up into his eyes. They gazed back intently and—anxiously? He really did want to marry her, she realized. And she thought of how it must be for him to be home in England again, alive and safe after the horrors of one of the worst wars in English history. She thought of how eager he must be to put it all behind him and start the new life he had decided upon. A new life in which he would undoubtedly need a woman's help. She could understand his impatience, his unwillingness to look about him for the uncertain advent of love. And for the moment she gave in to the temptation to block from her mind the knowledge that he should cultivate patience, that he should give himself the time to choose with greater care.

He needed a wife. And he needed one now. He had chosen her because he knew her and felt a certain degree of affection for her. And because of Julian. But most of all because he needed her.

"You need not fear that I will pine for him or talk of him or even think of him," she said. "When I become your wife, David, you will have all of me. As it should be. As it must be in marriage." She was not sure if she was offering the impossible.

"*When?*" he said. "Are you saying yes?"

She nodded.

He squeezed her hand a little more tightly. "I'll see the vicar this afternoon," he said, "and have him begin calling the banns next Sunday."

"Yes," she said. "I'll see the dressmaker and have new clothes made. It would be disrespectful to you to wear even half-mourning after our marriage." She looked down at her hand when he released it and drew off her wedding ring, teasing it slowly over the knuckle it had not passed since Julian has put it there on their wedding day. She dropped the ring into the pocket of her dress, aware of David's eyes on her. Her hand felt suddenly and appallingly naked. Her finger was white and dented where the ring had been.

"Thank you, Rebecca," he said quietly.

She smiled fleetingly at him. He was a serious and stern man, as his father had always been. As her father had been too. Though there had been that strange wildness in David too—all the more disturbing because it never seemed quite to fit his outer aspect. It almost seemed that he must be two people. She could not quite picture him with Flora. . . . He would not be easy to live with. He was her betrothed, she thought suddenly. In less than a month's time, once the banns had been called, he would be her husband. She felt panic claw at her stomach. What had she done? David? David of all people?

But she would not retract. Her word had been given. He needed her, and heaven knew she needed him too, or the life he could offer her anyway.

He was going to be her husband.

"I'll leave you to your thoughts and your book," he said gravely, handing it to her and getting to his feet. "You would like to be alone, wouldn't you?"

It was an unanswerable question. "Thank you," she said, taking the book.

"I'll see you at luncheon," he said. "Shall we tell my father and Louisa together then?"

Her stomach lurched. It would be real, irrevocable, once someone else knew. "Yes," she said. "You announce it, please, David."

"Until later, then," he said.

When he was gone, she lifted the book with both hands against her mouth and closed her eyes. She could not stop herself from remembering that when Julian had proposed marriage to her and she had accepted, he had whooped with delight and very improperly lifted her off her feet and twirled her about until they were laughing and dizzy. And then he had kissed her. . . .

"I would like a word with you, David," the earl said when he rose from the luncheon table.

The two men had said very little during the past ten minutes, since David had announced that Rebecca was to marry him and remove to Stedwell with him in one month's time. Louisa had scarcely stopped talking—and sparkling with excitement. She was talking animatedly about bride-clothes to Rebecca when the earl got to his feet. And then she flushed and scrambled to hers.

"I am so sorry, William," she said. "I forgot myself."

"David would probably not believe that you are normally very quiet, my dear," the earl said.

"Have I been talking too much?" Her flush deepened. "So many happy things have been happening in the last few days. David's coming home and my discovery that he is not an ogre after all; my visit to the doctor and his confirmation of my hopes; and now Rebecca betrothed— to David. Why isn't everyone prattling?" She laughed.

"David?" the earl said.

The countess laughed again. "It takes a woman to appreciate a wedding," she said. "Rebecca, do come to my room and I shall have tea brought up." She linked her arm through Rebecca's.

The earl's manner was not so festive. He crossed to the window of the library a few minutes later as David closed the door behind them, and stood looking out, his hands clasped at his back.

"David," he said, "have you considered carefully?"

"About my marriage?" David said. "Yes, Papa. Very carefully."

"Why are you doing this?" the earl asked. "Is it for Julian's sake?"

With his father at least he did not have to dissemble— or not entirely so anyway. Yes, it was for Julian's sake. Or at least for the sake of what he had done to Julian. But the reason was simpler than that—and far more complicated. And that at least he could admit to his father.

"I love her," he said.

The earl turned from the window, his eyes hard. "Oh, yes," he said. "I know that, David. I've always known that. She was intended for you, you know. That was the reason for all those visits as the two of you were growing up. But she chose Julian instead. Marrying her now is the last thing you should be doing.''

''Because she chose him rather than me?'' David asked. He had not known that Rebecca had been meant for him. It was a new and rather painful realization.

''Yes, because of that,'' the earl said. ''And because of the reason she did, David. She was besotted with him. She has not even begun to recover from his loss yet. She is unhappy and lonely and upset now because of Louisa's condition.''

''Then I will soothe her unhappiness and loneliness,'' David said, ''and give her a child of her own.''

The earl frowned. ''You do not know much about life, David,'' he said, ''for all your years and your experiences as a soldier. Your love and concern are not going to make her forget Julian. They will only make her feel resentful. She will come to hate you.''

Perhaps he did know more about life than his father thought. He knew the risk that he ran. He had already felt all the fears that his father was voicing. But his father did not know the other reasons for his marriage. It was something he had to do even if she did come to hate him eventually. He had to care for her, look after her, keep her safe. He had to somehow make up for letting her marry Julian in the first place and for taking Julian away from her in the end.

''I want her,'' he said. ''I need her.''

His father passed a hand over his eyes. ''My son,'' he said, ''I wanted you to be happy. All I have ever wanted for you is happiness.''

''I'll be happy, Papa,'' David said. ''I *am* happy. Rebecca is going to marry me.''

''And so they lived happily ever after,'' his father said wearily. ''I loved Julian as a son, David, and always treated him as one—or so I thought. But perhaps I deceived myself in believing that. I always loved you more. And your life was ever blighted by him. Now it seems that he is reaching out even beyond the grave to cloud your happiness. You will not be happy with Rebecca.''

''I thought you loved her too,'' David said quietly.

''I do,'' the earl said, ''and will continue to do so after

she is your wife, David. She is a good woman and the soul of honor. If she has agreed to marry you, then I know she will do her best to make you a good wife. But I am not sure that her best will be good enough. Not for you, my son. You need more than she can give.''

"I have told her that I do not expect her love,'' David said. "I have told her that I understand about Julian. I know she will always love him.''

"Then you are a fool,'' the earl said, seating himself heavily in the chair behind the desk, "or an innocent. You will never step free of his shadow, will you? The stronger dragged down by the weaker?''

David stared at his father.

"Did you think me so very blind and so very stupid?'' the earl asked. "Did you not realize that I always knew, my son? Knew that nine out of every ten thrashings I gave you as a boy were given to the wrong son? I suppose we both loved him unwisely and too well. You shielded him from my wrath because he was not my son as you were, and I punished you instead of him to show him that I loved him no less than I loved you. And now this, David. You would marry the widow who should have been your wife because she is lonely and heartbroken— because of Julian.''

David could think of nothing to say.

"Well.'' The earl got to his feet again. "There is nothing to be done about it now, is there? Your offer has been made and accepted. Honor must take you to the altar now. I will hope for your happiness, my son. And I will pray for it fervently.''

"Thank you,'' David said.

"Brandy?'' the earl asked, setting out two glasses on a sideboard before picking up the decanter. "I will have to hope, I suppose, that there will be no Julian to be playmate to my new son or daughter. And yet I loved him, David. One would have had to try very hard not to love Julian. He always meant well. He was just weaker than you. We both felt the need to protect him.''

"Yes,'' David said.

"He died well?'' the earl asked. "The story you told Rebecca was at least close to the truth?''

David drew a slow breath. "He died well, Papa," he said.

The earl nodded and handed him his glass. "I notice that you have not answered my second question," he said. "But we will let it rest. And what about Richard Ellis? You have seen him since your return home?"

"Yesterday," David said. "He seems to be a sturdy and happy little lad."

"He looks not unlike you," the earl said, sitting down again and looking keenly at his son. "Except for his eyes."

"Yes," David said.

"You will continue to provide for your *son?*" the earl asked, putting a little extra emphasis on the last word.

"Of course," David said. "He will go away to a good school when he is older, as I assured Flora yesterday, and I will see to it that he is prepared for decent employment."

"Yes," the earl said. "I would not expect you to forget your obligations, David, even after your marriage and after the birth perhaps of legitimate offspring."

"I will not forget," David said.

The earl nodded. "Louisa is going to take this wedding right out of your hands," he said. "She is ecstatic, as you doubtless realized at luncheon. There will be guests galore and flowers and decorated carriages and wedding breakfasts and numerous atrocities I cannot even dream of at the moment. The mind winces away from the very prospect. But she is to be humored, David." He frowned rather ferociously as if he expected to have to deal with stiff opposition. "Do you understand me? She is to be allowed to do all that is proper for you and Rebecca."

David grinned. "I can subscribe to the theory that a wedding is a festive occasion," he said, "especially my own. I was rather ecstatic too, you know, Papa, until you started to talk gloom and doom to me. I will aid and abet Louisa in any way I can."

"Oh, my son," his father said, looking suddenly and unaccustomedly wistful. "All I wish for you is that you may some day know the great happiness of married love."

They were words David would never have expected to hear from his father's lips. He felt a deep dread and a great stabbing of longing suddenly as he looked down to swirl the last drops of brandy in his glass. It was something he supposed he would never know.

7

Craybourne, August, 1856

The earl's prediction proved quite correct. His countess
approached the coming nuptials with energy and delight.
Her own wedding the year before had been a modest
affair, the earl still having been in mourning for his godson at the time and his son having been still at war. But
there were to be no restraints on David's wedding and on
her dear Rebecca's.

Neighbors for miles around were invited to attend the
morning service in the village church and the wedding
breakfast at Craybourne afterward. Invitations were sent
to Rebecca's mother and aunt in the North, to her brother
and sister-in-law in London, to the earl's three sisters and
their families, and to a few of David's friends, officers of
the Guards.

Rebecca was to have a wedding dress and a trousseau.
But the village seamstress would not do for such an important assignment. Indeed she would not be able to handle such a large order in time. Rebecca must be taken to
London for a week or so.

Rebecca did not object but went along meekly, traveling up by train with Louisa, their maids, and a foot-
man, putting up at a hotel since her brother was out of
town. She did not object because she wanted the month
prior to her wedding to be so filled with activity that she
would have no time to think. She did not want to think.
There was terror hovering somewhere in the direction of
thought.

And she made no objection because she realized the
necessity of buying a trousseau. For almost two years she
had worn nothing but black. She had had a few gray
dresses made some months before, but even those would
be inappropriate to her new life. She had meant it when

she had told David that it would be a discourtesy to him to carry her mourning for her first husband into a marriage with him.

She could not marry as a half-measure. She could never, of course, offer David her love. There was none left to offer. But she would give him everything else. She could not in clear conscience marry him if anything was withheld. Hence the terror that constantly hovered at the edge of her consciousness. It had been easy to give everything to Julian. There had never been any thought to holding anything back—even that which she had never really enjoyed giving. It had been all his— her body and her whole self. It was not going to be easy with David.

Everything had to be new. The clothes Julian had bought for her, the ones she had worn before his death, had all been packed away into boxes and were in the attic at Craybourne. Most of them would have been out of fashion anyway, but even those that were not would stay in the boxes. Eventually she would ask Louisa to have them distributed among the servants and the poor. She would not take anything from her first marriage into her second.

She had given her wedding ring to the earl and asked him if he would keep it somewhere safe.

Thinking of Julian as dead and gone, putting him firmly into her past, living a present, and planning a future—it all brought a yawning emptiness with it that was in many ways worse than the grief had been. At least then there had been some emotion to sustain her. Now there was none. Hence again the terror that she pushed firmly away from the thoughts that occupied her day-to-day life.

She kept reminding herself that she had decided before agreeing to marry David that it was time to live again. And that was what she was going to do. Perhaps she had made a mistake in accepting him—she dared not dwell on that possibility—but there were positive things to look forward to. She would have her own home for the first time in her life and plenty of responsibilities there. It would be a new start. She would be too busy to dwell on memories that could do nothing but sap the energy from her life. There was some excitement in being able to look ahead again. Louisa's exuberance was somewhat infectious. If she could just ignore the terror, Rebecca thought, there was much to be thankful for.

She attended church with David—and with the earl and countess—each Sunday except the one she spent in London, and heard the banns being read. She sat with him—and them—at meals and walked with him and rode with him and spent evenings in the drawing room with him. But they were almost never alone together. They almost never spoke directly to each other. The only times she ever touched him happened when she took his arm to be escorted from place to place.

The festive mood that pervaded the house when the wedding drew close and the house guests began to arrive surprised her. Louisa's excitement she had grown accustomed to, but it seemed strange to see her mother and her aunt both smiling and crying as they hugged her on their arrival—and they had traveled such a long way just for her wedding. Her brother too hugged her and kissed her affectionately and told her how happy he was for her. Even her sister-in-law seemed pleased for her. David's relatives and friends filled the house with boisterous noise and laughter.

She had not expected her wedding to be such a festive occasion. It was all rather as if Julian had never been. Yet the very thought made her realize how foolish she was to have expected that they would all be sober-faced out of respect for his memory. Julian was no more than that—a memory. He was nothing to most of the guests gathered for her wedding and David's. Even to David and the earl he was nothing more than a memory.

Was he more to her? Was he still more than that? Her heart was buried with him, but surely the rest of her could go on without him. Must go on. She was about to make a new marriage.

And so she awoke on the morning of her wedding, saw sunshine beyond the still-drawn curtains at her windows, and smiled determinedly. This was her wedding day and she was about to give herself to David for the rest of her life.

Soon she was forced to smile, whether she wanted to or not. It seemed that no sooner had she stepped out of an early and sweet-smelling bath than her dressing room was filled—with her maid, with her mother and her aunt, with Louisa. And later with Denise, her sister-in-law, and inexplicably with Louisa's maid. Everyone seemed to be talking at once. There was a great deal of laughter.

Rebecca talked and laughed along with them.

She was not to wear white. She was no virgin bride, after all, but a widow. She wore a dress of royal blue. She had given in to fashion and had a hooped petticoat made in London. She agreed now that it was a far more comfortable garment than the several layers of petticoats she usually wore, and left the legs free to move. Her skirt looked fuller and swayed pleasingly when she moved. The neckline of her dress was lower than usual and trimmed with a collar of broderie anglaise. The sleeves were wide and open-mouthed, flaring at the wrists in a pagoda shape. Her white undersleeves matched the collar. There was to be no bridal veil. She had bought a bonnet to match the dress. But Louisa had other ideas.

"I have had a bouquet made for you," she said. "It should be here at any moment. It is mostly of pink roses—your favorites, Rebecca."

"But I am not . . ." Rebecca began to protest.

"Oh, yes, you are," Louisa said briskly. "You most certainly are a bride."

"And you must carry flowers, Rebecca," Denise agreed.

"Oh, yes, dearest," Rebecca's mother said.

So she would look like a bride after all. She still could not quite believe that she was one. It all seemed so very different from the last time. But she resolutely closed her mind to those particular memories.

"And I have had a matching garland made for your hair," Louisa said, clasping her hands to her bosom and gazing admiringly at her friend. "Oh, you do look lovely, Rebecca."

"A garland?" Rebecca looked at her in some distrust. "I am no girl, Louisa. I shall wear a bonnet."

"Oh, not all about your head," Louisa said. She laughed gaily. "Were you picturing something like Ophelia? Just a small one to twine about your braids. It will be very becoming. And it will show your glorious hair to advantage. I would cheerfully kill for your golden hair.'' She laughed again.

"It would look very pretty, dearest,'' her mother said.

"Let's try it, mum,'' her maid suggested as a knock on the door heralded the arrival of the flowers.

Rebecca sat meekly on the stool before the mirror. There was color in her cheeks, she noticed. She was used to seeing herself looking pale. But the room was hot with so many people in it. And now it was filling with the smell of roses.

Her hair, dressed à l'Impératrice, folding back over softly rounded pads from a center part to reveal her temples and ears, did not look greatly different after her maid had finished her task. Mere wisps of leaves and petals showed in the mirror like a delicate, colored halo. She had to turn her head from side to side to catch glimpses of the garland.

"Oh, dearest, you look beautiful,'' her mother said, leaning over her from behind and hugging her, careful not to touch her head. "And you have a gloriously sunny, warm day for your wedding. You are going to be happy. I know it. I have always had a soft spot for David.'' There were tears in her eyes.

There was a time when both her mother and her father had told her that it was David she should encourage, not Julian. There had been an understanding between them and the earl for years to encourage such a match, they had said. She had been surprised that they would even consider David for her, given his wild reputation, though he had seemed to mature and get into less trouble as he grew to manhood. It had been before the time of Flora's disgrace. But of course, in her parents' eyes he had been—and still was—a viscount and heir to an earldom, whereas Julian had been a mere baronet.

Well, her mother was to have her wish at last. Rebecca turned on the stool, smiling, and got to her feet. And found herself being hugged and kissed by all the ladies present, while the two maids smiled their approval.

Rebecca held on to her smile. Everything was beginning. Everything—a whole new life. The ladies were all leaving, summoned away to the carriages that were waiting to take them to church. And Horace, her brother, was standing in the suddenly empty doorway of her dressing room, smiling at her, holding out his hands to her, kissing her on both cheeks, and telling her how lovely she looked.

"With hands like ice," he added.

"Being a bride is nervous business," she said. "I look all right, Horace? The flowers do not make me look ridiculously girlish?"

"You look good enough to eat to me," he said. "Besides, Rebecca, if that roomful of women approved of your appearance, then who am I to contradict them? Mama always has an eye to what is right and proper. So does Denise. Are you ready?"

She nodded and reached for the small bouquet of roses.

"We'll be on our way, then," he said. "We don't want to keep a churchful of people waiting, do we?"

No, they certainly did not want to do that. What might be excusable in a blushing young bride would seem in poor taste for a mature widow. Besides, there was no point in delay. There was a new life to be begun and one part of her was eager to begin it. Eager to outdistance her doubts and that niggling feeling that she was betraying a man who was long dead.

In some ways, she thought after she had been handed down from the carriage outside the church and entered its cool porch on her brother's arm, it must be easier to be a bride than a groom. Everything began as soon as the bride arrived. There was no time for last-minute doubts and jitters. And the bride entered the church from behind everyone, though it was true that everyone turned a head to see her come. It must be hard to be the groom, standing at the front of the church for an uncertain number of minutes before his bride's arrival, the eyes of everyone focused on him.

She wondered how long David had been waiting.

He looked wondrously handsome in formal morning dress, with gray trousers, silver embroidered waistcoat, white linen, and dark blue frock coat. He was not at all outshone by the Guards' officer at his side, resplendent in scarlet-coated dress uniform. She noticed for the first time that David did not follow the current fashion for heavy mustaches. He was clean-shaven. She was glad of it.

He stood still and tall, his feet slightly apart, his hands at his back, watching her approach. Her bridegroom. At her last wedding he had been standing where the officer was standing now. He had been Julian's best man. Rebecca felt her smile slip and did not readjust it though she pushed the memory firmly from her mind. At least—thank God—it had been in a different church, the church at her father's home.

She did not smile again. Could not smile. It was all so real. Dear God, it was so very real. The organ music was coming to an end, the hushed murmur of voices was reverting to expectant silence, and she was turning with her groom to face the vicar.

She heard the words of the service no more than she had the first time. But for different reasons. Then she had been borne along on the euphoria of the occasion. Julian had been at her side. Her love for him had glowed through her and her longing to be walking away from the altar with him. His wife. Walking into the happily ever after. Now she felt paralyzed by the responsibility she had taken on, by the necessity of giving what she had not even been conscious of giving the first time. By the necessity to forget.

One could not forget by the mere effort of will. It was not going to be easy to forget. Perhaps it was going to be impossible.

She watched David's hand as it clasped hers, a strong, long-fingered, capable hand—Julian's had been smaller, blunter-fingered. She listened to his voice as she watched his hand, not quite hearing what he said, and she heard her own voice repeating what the vicar said to her, not quite aware of what she said. She watched David's other hand place a ring over her finger—the finger where Julian's ring had always been—and slide it on, easing it past her knuckle. It was a little wider than Julian's ring, and very shiny and new.

It was the ring that jolted her out of her stupor. The ring did not belong there. It was not hers. It was a usurper, just as he was. She looked up into his eyes.

Blue, intent on hers. Pained. They were the eyes he had brought home from the Crimean War.

". . . man and wife."

She scarcely heard the vicar's voice, though she felt the sense of his words.

Her husband's eyes.

He bent his head and kissed her lips, his own light and cool. No man except Julian—and probably her father during her childhood—had ever kissed her lips. But David had the right to. He was her husband.

Her husband.

Julian was her husband.

David was her husband.

She was aware suddenly of sounds—a murmuring among the congregation, someone's muffled sobs, a distant cough. And of smells—roses, David's cologne. And of the reality of the moment. She tried to smile and was not at all sure that she succeeded. But there was a look in his eyes that made the pain disappear for a moment— relief? Was he relieved that she smiled? Had he not expected her to?

Some time later—she lost all track of time—she was walking back down the aisle of the church on his arm and saw all the faces that he must have been forced to look at before her arrival. Smiling faces. Happy for her. And for him. For them. She smiled back.

"Rebecca." He covered her hand on his arm with his free hand and drew her to a stop on the church steps. There was a moment—only a moment—before their relatives and friends began to spill out of the church and around them. "You look beautiful."

She was surprised. She had not expected him to say anything so personal. Yet what could be more personal than a wedding? It was more the tone of his voice, its pitch low, the words for her ears only. A portent of things to come. They would be alone soon and together, the two of them, for the rest of their lives.

He had said the same words, she remembered with a jolt, at her wedding to Julian. He had set his hands on her shoulders, smiled into her eyes, kissed her on the cheek, and spoken them. "You look beautiful, Rebecca." And she had laughed back into his eyes and thanked him. She had felt beautiful.

But this time there was no Julian to turn back to.

She had no chance to return the compliment and tell him how very handsome he looked—she must be the envy of every woman present, she thought. They were surrounded by smiling well-wishers.

"Welcome, daughter," the Earl of Hartington said, squeezing her hand and kissing her cheek before standing back so that his countess might greet her more effusively.

"Lady Tavistock," David's best man said, grinning cheerfully at her, "may I?" And he too took her hand and kissed her on the cheek.

Daughter. Lady Tavistock.

Julian. For the first time she realized that she was no longer Rebecca Cardwell. She was Rebecca Neville, Lady Tavistock. Oh, Julian!

She smiled back at everyone.

"You are comfortable?" The words *my dear* stuck in his throat. It was how he had planned to address her after they were married. But he could not say the words after all.

"Yes, David." She smiled at him. "Train travel is so much more comfortable than carriage travel, isn't it? And faster. We will be there in two hours? Aren't we fortunate to live in this modern age?"

He settled beside her in their private compartment, their relatives and friends who had come to the station to wave them on their way having long disappeared from view.

"Yes," he said, "and a little unfortunate too, perhaps, to be seeing the end of a more leisurely and far cleaner era."

"And a less comfortable one," she said. "When I look back on the past forty or fifty years, or even on the portion of them that I can remember personally, I marvel that so much change is possible. Will it continue, do you think? Will our present world seem unrecognizably backward even twenty years in the future? Are further changes possible? Some people say we are just at the beginning of a wholly new age."

It was their wedding day. They were alone together at last after a busy morning at church and at Craybourne. They had not had a moment to themselves—until now. Under different circumstances he would have set his arm about her shoulders, drawn her against him, kissed her with slow thoroughness, and talked love nonsense to her all the way to Stedwell. She was his bride, his wife. No, only his bride. Tonight she would become his wife.

She sat straight-backed beside him, looking extremely elegant in her dark green traveling suit. Looking breathtakingly beautiful, as she had all day. His breath could still catch in his throat as he remembered his first sight of her at church that morning, regal and lovely—and smiling—on her brother's arm.

She was making conversation with him, careful to choose a topic that could occupy them for a while. Not the weather. Conversation about the weather usually died very quickly.

"I think they are probably right," he said. "Fortunately we will live through those twenty years a day at a time and will have ample chance to adjust ourselves to all the changes as they occur. Unless we stubbornly bury our heads in the sand, that is, and refuse to acknowledge that anything is different."

"Like Mr. Snelling," she said. "Wasn't he foolish, David, when he said at breakfast that he would not come to the station with us because he does not believe in trains? As if they are a figment of the collective imagination."

"It is more fun, I suppose," he said, "to be pushing carriage wheels out of muddy ruts."

"Especially when one has servants to do it for one," she said.

They smiled at each other in shared amusement, but the emptiness of the compartment, their aloneness after all the noise and bustle of the morning, set their smiles to fading and the conversation to faltering. She turned her head to look at the scenery rushing past the windows, and he did likewise, so that they were looking in opposite directions.

He wished he had taken her into his arms as soon as the train had drawn away from the platform. He wished he had established the fact that they were a bride and groom leaving for their new home and their new life together. He had intended to do that, had planned it. But it was too late now. It would seem foolish and just too damned embarrassing to lunge for her now, out of the blue.

He wished his father's voice would not keep echoing in his mind. *You will not be happy with Rebecca*. He would be. She was his bride. He would have her with him for the rest of their lives. He would have the chance to take care of her for the rest of his days. It was all he had ever wanted. He would not ask for her love. He would be happy just having her for his wife.

You need more than she can give. He did not. All he needed was what she had already given—her hand in marriage. Rebecca was the soul of honor, as his father had admitted. She would do her best to be a good wife to him and to give everything but what was not hers to give—her love. He did not need her love. Only a little affection. He would earn her affection. It was all he needed.

But he wished he could forget that confrontation with his father. He had always valued his father's advice and opinions. He had always respected his wisdom.

"Don't expect anything wonderful," he said now, turning his head to look at Rebecca. "Stedwell is going to look very shabby after Craybourne. Perhaps I should have taken you somewhere else for a week or two." *For a honeymoon,* he had been going to say before changing his mind.

"I would be disappointed if I found something wonderful," she said. "I am counting on finding it very shabby indeed, David. I want the challenge of making a lovely and comfortable home for you. It is why I married you, remember?"

To make him a lovely and comfortable home? Or to find a challenge in life? Her meaning was not clear. But he knew the answer. It was both. It was for the latter reason that she had finally accepted his offer. But she would work for the former. Being Rebecca, she would devote most of her energies to being his wife.

And all the time she would love Julian. She would

never talk of him, never think of him after their marriage, she had promised him. And he did not doubt that she would keep her promise or at least try. But beyond thought, in that part of a person's being that was uncontrolled by the will, she would love Julian. Never him. Always Julian.

He saw Julian suddenly, turning toward him, surprise in his eyes, before pitching forward across George Scherer—the face and the expression and the action that most often occupied his nightmares, and sometimes even imposed themselves on his waking consciousness. And he felt deep resentment. Julian had deserved to die—he had been about to kill an unarmed man. A man he had been cuckolding for several months. David had done what any other officer who had arrived on that spot at that moment would have done. He had shot Julian. He resented the fact that he must endure the nightmares and carry around the load of guilt for the rest of his life.

This was his wedding day—to Julian's widow.

Damnation!

Rebecca was watching him. "I am sorry," she said. "Were those words hurtful? I did not mean them to be. I want to be a good wife to you, David. I must learn how to please you. You must show me how."

The words from another woman might have been provocative. From Rebecca they were not. They were meant quite literally, he knew. They did not refer specifically to their sexual relationship, though they would apply to that too.

"You please me by being," he said, taking her hand in his and squeezing it. He could feel his ring on her finger. His, not Julian's. He kept her hand in his although they resumed their separate study of the scenery beyond the windows.

She was his, he thought, knowing that he could keep her hand in his for the rest of the journey if he wished. No longer would his touches have to be brief and infrequent. Tonight he would have her in his bed. He would hold her and make love to her. Sleep with her.

Sleep with Julian's wife.

He felt sick to his stomach.

He tried not to see the surprised eyes. He tried not to feel the pistol in the hand that now held hers. He tried to tell himself—as he had done thousands of times for almost two years—that he had nothing to feel guilty about.

8

Stedwell, August, 1856

David had expected a carriage to be waiting at the station since he had informed his housekeeper of the exact day and time of his arrival. And sure enough it was there, a shabby, ponderous old coach drawn by four horses that looked as if they might feel more at home drawing a farmer's cart or even a plough. The coachman looked as if he might be a gardener playing an unfamiliar role.

What David had not expected was the small crowd waiting on the station platform and the large white bows tied to its pillars. The Reverend Colin Hatch, the village rector, stepped forward to make himself known, though his clerical garb would have done that anyway, cleared his throat importantly, and in the clear ringing tones that were peculiar to the Anglican clergy read a formal speech of welcome to the viscount and viscountess and of congratulation on their marriage. He understood that they had entered the bonds of holy matrimony that very morning? The words were phrased as a question and accompanied by a bow.

There was a smattering of self-conscious applause from the rector's wife, the innkeeper and his wife, the doctor and his wife, the schoolmaster, the trademen and their wives gathered there, and a few people whose clothing and bearing suggested that they were important enough socially to have secured a place with the welcoming committee.

David smiled. Good Lord, he had not expected this. If he had, he would have rehearsed a suitably gracious reply. As it was, he had to rely on smiles and simple thanks and handshakes all around. Rebecca, he noticed, rose to the occasion without fuss or confusion, moving easily amongst the small crowd, talking and smiling as she went. But he would have expected no less of her. If a suitable viscountess and hostess was all he wanted of marriage, then he could have done no better than marry her.

Outside the station more people were gathered, people whose position in life had not merited them a place on the platform. They too applauded. Two children waved white handkerchiefs. Someone whistled and there was some laughter. David raised a hand in acknowledgment of the welcome and smiled again before handing his bride into the carriage. He noticed that she did the same.

He looked at her in some amusement when the door closed behind them and the carriage lurched into motion. "That was unexpected," he said.

"But pleasant," she said.

"Those people should all be familiar to me," he said. "Stedwell has been mine since birth, and I am almost twenty-nine years old, Rebecca. They should have met me with hisses and boos. I deserve no better. I feel guilty for having neglected my responsibilities here."

"The people will grow familiar," she said. "And there is never any real point in feeling guilt for what is past, David, unless there is something one can do about it and is not doing it. You are doing something—you are here."

"I suppose you are right," he said, frowning at the almost threadbare upholstery of the carriage. No, there really was no point, he thought. Not unless one could do something about it. Some events of the past were irrevocable. Feeling guilt was pointless.

Except that guilt about some things was not something one could shrug off at will.

There was a general air of neglect about Stedwell. The massive gateposts were surmounted by stone lions—or had been. One lay in the grass beside its flat-topped post and looked as if it had lain there for a long time. The iron gates stood open. The square lodge was empty. One window, devoid of glass, was boarded up. Grass grew long on the banks of the river they had to cross to reach the house, almost obscuring the water. The grass stretching before the main house was tidy, but more in the way one might expect a spring meadow to be tidy than a lawn. Daisies grew in gay profusion. Trees to the west of the house had been allowed to crowd too close to it. Branches obscured some of the long western windows. Grass was growing in several places amongst the gravel of the terrace fronting the house.

And yet the house itself looked as sturdy and as picturesque as David remembered it. Only a hundred years old, it had been built of gray stone in the best style of the eighteenth century. The central section had been designed in imitation of a Roman triumphal arch, its four massive columns topped by classical deities apparently striding forward to victory. Long-windowed wings stretched to either side with a second story above. Wide stone steps led up to the front doors.

The marble hall, two stories high, was clean and tidy, though David was not permitted a good look. Mrs. Matthews, his housekeeper, was there to greet them and to present the staff, most of them newly hired, all lined up stiffly to greet their new master and mistress.

David would have nodded and smiled pleasantly at them and moved on, but Rebecca had other ideas. She approached the line of servants and moved along it, smiling and exchanging a few words with each servant. Frightened looks from the younger ones turned to smiles as she moved along. David followed her example. Oh, yes, he thought, he needed a woman in his home to teach him something about gracious living. There had been no woman at Craybourne while he was growing up.

His lordship and her ladyship would wish to see their rooms and refresh themselves before a late tea in the drawing room, Mrs. Matthews said as she led them through the stairway arch and up the broad stairway at last. The carpet on the stairs was faded and worn, David noticed. Dinner would be served at seven, the housekeeper explained, if that met with her ladyship's approval. The chef was new and had been brought from London at a moment's notice. He came well recommended.

Seven o'clock would do very well, Rebecca assured Mrs. Matthews.

Rebecca's bedchamber was extremely shabby and gloomy despite the fact that it faced the front of the house and late-afternoon sunlight slanted through the window.

Curtains and bedhangings that had once been blue were now a nondescript gray. So was the carpet. But that was not the worst of it.

"I am afraid the mattress was found to be mildewed with the damp when we came to ready it for you, my lady," Mrs. Matthews said, trying to coax the curtains wider at the window in order to dispel more gloom. "There was no time to replace it. I have prepared another room for you, my lady, just in case, but—" She glanced significantly at David.

But this room connected with the master bedchamber and they were newlyweds, her look said.

"It does not matter, Mrs. Matthews," he said. "My wife will instruct you in the days to come on changes to be made. In the meantime she will be sharing the master bedroom with me." He spoke matter-of-factly and crossed the room to look down on flat lawns and ancient trees and the river beyond with a three-arched stone bridge that had been hardly noticeable as they had crossed it a short while ago in the carriage. It felt strange calling Rebecca "my wife." It still seemed unreal.

"It is a well-shaped room," Rebecca said calmly from behind him. "It will be cozy in time, Mrs. Matthews. Does this door lead to my dressing room?"

"Yes, my lady," Mrs. Matthews said, opening it. "There is warm water on the washstand, and your trunks will have been carried up already. The other door leads into the master bedchamber."

David followed them through the dressing room to the room he had occupied on the few occasions when he had visited his home. It was large—twice as large as Rebecca's room—with wine-colored draperies, gold-and-wine bedcovers, and a Turkish carpet. All looked as if they had seen better, brighter days. But the mahogany furniture gleamed, and there was a fire burning in the grate despite the fact that it was a warm August day outside. Obviously there had been dampness to dispel here too.

"Thank you, Mrs. Matthews," Rebecca said. "Tea will be served in the drawing room?"

"Whenever you are ready, my lady," the housekeeper said, inclining her head and turning to leave.

David watched his bride as she waited for Mrs. Matthews to leave. He had intended all along that they would occupy the same bedchamber. He had never thought that the custom of a husband and his wife occupying separate rooms would suit him. He had never pried into the bedroom habits of his relatives and acquaintances and did not know, for example, whether his father slept all night with Louisa. He did not know what Julian had done or what Rebecca had expected.

Was she shocked, he wondered, at the turn of events that apparently gave them no choice? Embarrassed? Upset? Accepting? Was it what she expected anyway? One could not tell with Rebecca. She was always—almost always—so thoroughly the lady that it was impossible to know what her feelings on any matter were just by looking at her.

"I'll wash my hands and face, David," she said, turning to him with the calm dignity that almost never deserted her. "I'll not change my dress if you will excuse me since it is already rather late for tea. Will you knock on my door in ten minutes' time?"

"Yes," he said. He wondered if she was as aware as he that they were a bride and groom alone together for the first time in their bedchamber. If she was, she did not show it.

"Tea will be very welcome, won't it?" she said as he strode past her to open the door into her dressing room.

"Yes, very," he agreed and closed the door again behind her.

Perhaps if she hurried, Rebecca had thought at first, she could be out of her dressing room and decently in bed before David appeared. But though she had undressed and washed and donned her nightgown—decently high-necked and long-sleeved—in something of a hurry, she had lost time over her hair. She always wore it loose to bed even though it was more than waist length and would be easier to comb in the mornings if she kept it confined; but it was more comfortable to wear it loose.

She had always worn it loose during the nights of her first marriage. She had never thought of doing otherwise. She did not know why she had given the matter a thought now except that she watched herself absently in the mirror as she brushed through it—she had dismissed her maid—and saw herself suddenly through someone else's eyes. Through a man's eyes. She looked—wanton.

She could not go to David with her hair hanging loose down her back. She would feel—naked. The thought made her flush painfully and she dropped her brush in order to gather up her hair and start braiding it. It was not easy to braid such thick, long hair when she could not stand behind herself to do it. It took three tries before she had it plaited to her satisfaction.

And so by the time she opened the door into the master bedchamber, turning the handle slowly and pulling the door quietly toward her as if she thought that quietness was going to help anything, he was there before her, standing at one of the windows looking out, wearing a brocaded dressing gown. She felt deeply mortified that she had not thought to put one on herself.

It was a situation very new to her. Julian had always come to her in her own room, always after she was in bed. She could not remember a time when he had come to her before. She busied herself with closing the dressing room door as quietly as she had opened it, while David turned from the window toward her.

She did not know what to do. She did not know whether to cross calmly to the bed, without even looking at him, and climb in—but which side was to be hers?— or whether to stay where she was and await instructions. She felt gauche and embarrassed. She felt like a virgin bride again.

And how was she to sleep beside him all night? Julian had never been in her bed for longer than ten or fifteen minutes at a time.

Fortunately she did not have to make any decision or even reveal her indecision. He came striding across the room toward her. Oh, dear God, it felt wrong to be in a bedroom with David, both of them in their nightclothes. Where was Julian? Her mind actually thought the thought in one blank moment of panic.

"Rebecca." He took both her hands in his—she had not realized how like ice they were until they were in his warm ones. He raised them one at a time to his lips.

"You will not regret today. I will see to it that you will not regret the decision you have made."

She already regretted it. Had regretted it from the moment when she had given in to temptation and said yes. And yet the alternative had been emptiness and dependence. It would be all right, she told herself. Just let the next few minutes be over with so that she could know she had twenty-four hours in which to adjust her mind to her new role and responsibilities before it was all to face again tomorrow night. And the next and the next.

Really it should not be so bad. Not painful. Only a little uncomfortable and humiliating. But it was her main marriage duty. And she had married him quite freely that morning. She looked into his eyes.

"And I will do likewise for you, David," she said. Should she now release her hands and cross to the bed? She wished she were there already so that she could have calmed her breathing before he came to her.

"You are nervous," he said, releasing her hands for her and setting his own on her shoulders. "You do not need to be, Rebecca. I'll not hurt you."

His eyes were very blue. She had not had to tip her head so far back to look up at Julian. She felt very helpless. "I know you won't, David," she said. "But I think it is natural to be nervous. Forgive me."

He lowered his head and kissed her. She was taken by surprise. Kissing was something that she and Julian had done in places other than the bedchamber. It had been part of their love and romance, the sort of physical closeness she had enjoyed. Bed had been for something else. It had been for his enjoyment alone. Her first instinct now was to pull away in bewilderment and fright. But David was her husband and she did not want to compare. She must not compare. He had a right to do with her what he wished.

His lips were warm and slightly parted, their pressure light. They moved caressingly over hers. She realized suddenly that her hands were touching the smooth brocade at his waist. She could feel the fabric too with the tips of her breasts and with her thighs.

"Isn't the braid uncomfortable when you lie on it?" he asked.

She stared dazed into his eyes before the meaning of his words penetrated her mind. "I don't usually braid it at night," she said before she could think of a more suitable reply.

"Just for your wedding night?" His eyes smiled briefly.

"I did not know what you would wish," she said.

His mouth touched hers again, unmistakably open this time, as his hand came behind her head and the labor of the past half hour was undone in seconds. She felt her hair fall loose and felt his hands twine in it.

"Rebecca," he said, not taking his mouth quite away from hers, "this is what I wish." He lifted his head. "Come to bed."

She calmed herself by looking at the clock on the mantel. Twenty-five minutes past ten. By twenty-five minutes to eleven, twenty to at the latest, it would be all over for tonight. She would be able to settle for sleep on her side of the bed, knowing that she had done her duty, that she had allowed him his conjugal rights without shrinking.

She lay flat on the bed, drawing deep breaths and letting them out silently through her mouth as he removed his dressing gown and turned out the lamp. There was still light from the fire, which had been built up to counter any damp that might still linger after the long inoccupancy of the room.

He lay down beside her instead of pushing up her nightgown and coming immediately on top of her as Julian had always done. But she would not compare. She must not compare. And she must not—oh, she must not think of Julian now. All men must have different ways of taking their pleasure. She must not expect it to be the same. She must learn to accept David's way.

Ten minutes. Only ten. Probably less. It was usually less. Ten minutes at the outside.

He raised himself on one elbow and leaned over her to kiss her again. His mouth brushed hers, opened over hers, deepened the pressure. She spread her palms against the mattress as she felt his tongue press lightly against the seam of her lips and then push through and curl up behind her upper lip. There was a great gush of sensation that had her almost clawing at the bed. His tongue brushed back and forth across her clamped teeth until she realized in sudden shock that he expected her to open her mouth.

She kept herself calm. Nine minutes. Perhaps even eight. He was her husband. He had the right. It was her duty to submit. She opened her mouth with slow reluctance. And felt his tongue slide inward and out again. He moved his mouth to her chin and her throat.

Let it happen quickly, she pleaded silently. *Let it be over with. Let him raise my nightgown soon and come on top of me. Let it be over soon. Let my courage hold.*

It was almost a relief to feel his hand grasping her nightgown and easing it up her body. Soon now. Soon. And then the minute or two of discomfort. Then the end.

But he did not move onto her immediately when her nightgown was to her waist. He spread his hand over her abdomen and held it lightly there while she waited, tense.

"Relax, Rebecca," he said against her ear.

She was deeply shamed. To have to be told such a thing. To have to be told that she was not pleasing him, that she was resisting him. She relaxed instantly. And had to fight not to tense again when his hand moved upward beneath her nightgown, up through the valley between her breasts and around to cup one of them. Julian had never . . . She pushed the thought away. David was David. He was her husband.

"Relax," he murmured against her lips. It was not an admonition this time.

She could feel his thumb brushing against the tip of one breast and could feel the nipple growing taut. And there was that rush of sensation again. She fought the need to squirm, to push his hand away. It was wrong. He should not . . . She should not . . .

Please, oh, please let it be over with.

And then his hand was moving down once more, down over her stomach, over her abdomen, down between her legs. She bit down on her lower lip. This was worse . . . This was far worse . . . But she had known it would be. She had loved the first time. She did not love this time.

His fingers were parting her and stroking her. And then something he did with his thumb, something she did not consciously feel at first, sent that sensation stabbing through her again, upward inside her from the place he touched through her womb and her breasts, past her throat and up behind her nose. A totally raw pain that was not pain. She turned blindly into him, seeking escape.

And finally—oh, thank God, finally—he was going to do what was familiar to her. Only the brief discomfort now and then it would be finished for tonight. She went gratefully over onto her back again, his hands beneath her, and spread her legs obediently astride the pressure of his. She drew a slow breath and set her hands flat on the bed on either side of her.

There was no pain, no discomfort. That was her first relieved thought. But it was only momentary. He was sliding into wetness. She could both feel and hear it. The embarrassment and humiliation had her losing control, panting for breath, pushing at his chest, before she could take herself in hand.

"Easy," he murmured. He was up on his elbows, looking down at her. She wanted to die of humiliation. There was nowhere to hide her face. "Easy, Rebecca."

He was deep. Much deeper . . . Much larger . . . But she would make no comparisons. She spread damp palms against the mattress, pressed them down hard against it.

His mouth came to hers. "Easy," he said into it. "I'll not hurt you."

It did not hurt. She was too wet for discomfort or pain. She listened to the wetness as he began to move and waited for the swift pounding that would bring the humiliation to its familiar end. Only a minute now.

He moved slowly, withdrawing almost completely before sliding deep inside again. The movements, the sounds, became gradually rhythmic. And she found after all that she was able to relax, to hold herself open to him, to give him what he wanted and needed without resistance. She tried not to listen to the sounds. She wondered how disgusted he was with her.

She forgot time. This was what it felt like to be David's wife, she thought after the rhythm of his loving had relaxed her and there was leisure in which to think and feel. He was making prolonged, deeply intimate use of her body. Their marriage was being very thoroughly consummated. She knew that she would feel sore and throb-

bing when he had finally finished with her. That she
would feel very much his wife.

Was that what he intended? Did he mean to banish any
lingering ghosts once and for all? Put the strong stamp
of his possession on her from their wedding night on?
Dare her ever to feel that she was still another man's
wife? She did not feel it. She was David's. She had made
herself his by her will and her words in church that morning. He was making her his tonight by the deep rhythmic
pumping of his body into hers.

But even if she had not already put the past determinedly behind her in order to make herself undividedly
this man's wife, she would have been his wife now. She
felt thoroughly possessed, thoroughly known. Her body,
opened and in use, held no secrets from him. Her soul
felt as if it were pinned open to his gaze and his possession.

But after all it was not so difficult. It was not even
entirely unpleasant—despite the fact that it had continued
for much longer than she had expected it could.

And then his hands were gripping her shoulders and
he stilled inside her, thrust deeply once, twice, three
times more, and sighed against the side of her face. She
felt with a stab of surprise the hot release of his seed.

She felt damp and cool when he lifted himself away
from her and lay at her side again. He drew her nightgown down with one hand and the bedclothes up over
her, keeping his arm across her when he was finished.
She turned her head and looked into his eyes. One lock
of his dark hair was down over his forehead. His hair
looked thoroughly rumpled. He was David, she thought
in some wonder. David, of course. He was her husband,
the man she had married just that day. But even so—
David! Her mind felt dazed with the knowledge that what
had just happened, the consummation that had been so
far different, so much more—*carnal* than she had expected, had happened with David.

She wondered if it had been proper. Were husbands
allowed to use their wives so? An absurd thought, of
course. Anything was proper within marriage—anything
that the husband initiated. Husbands were allowed to take
their pleasure of their wives in any way they pleased. A

wife must submit herself—but not enjoy it. It would be unseemly for a wife to enjoy anything that was of the body. She had been taught that as a girl.

She had not enjoyed it. She had only found it—well, not unpleasant. Less unpleasant than she had ever found it before though it had been far more carnal and had lasted a great deal longer.

She closed her eyes at the betrayal of that final thought. Julian had loved her. He had treated her as a lady. David did not love her. That was why he had treated her . . . But he had a right to treat her as he would.

Julian. She could not after all put him from her mind. It was so final now. So very final. She was another man's wife in every sense of the word. David's. And she had promised David that she would not even think of Julian any longer. She would not think of him, then. It would be disloyal to do so. She would not.

She was David's wife.

She felt him lean over her and then his lips were brushing hers. "Thank you, Rebecca," he said softly. "Sleep now. It had been a long and tiring day for you."

Yes. Ages and ages long. And bone-wearying. Soul-wearying. She did not open her eyes or reply. Some time later she slept.

9

David did not sleep for long. It felt strange to be sharing his bed. He had slept all night with women before, but it had been different. The main purpose of such nights had been sexual. Sleep had been taken in snatched intervals between bouts. The main purpose now was to sleep, to make love first and then to sleep. To set a pattern for the rest of their married life.

It felt strange. And to be lying with Rebecca. He could hear her breathing quietly and deeply. She was lying on her back, her head turned toward him. Her hair spilled over her pillow and over the covers. She looked different—not the quiet, disciplined, always proper Rebecca he had known for much of his life, the unattainable Rebecca of his dreams, but a woman, voluptuous and relaxed after sex.

She was his wife. In every sense of the word she was now his wife. He would be content with only what she was able to give, he had told her. He would be content with her help and companionship and perhaps her affection. Never her love. He closed his eyes and tried to will sleep to come back. It seemed years since he had had a good night's sleep. A lifetime.

He had planned his wedding night with care. She had known love and a lover. She had been married to Julian for almost three years. She knew all about passion and sexual fulfillment with a man she loved with all her heart. He could not hope to compete. He could not hope to arouse passion or joy in her. And yet he had known that he could not be satisfied with mere brief, dispassionate exercises of his rights at night. Their marriage would stand little chance if there was not at least some physical tenderness between them.

He would love her with his body, he had decided, and take whatever she could give in return. But he was very aware that she was a lady, that he must love her with some restraint. It would have been different for her with Julian—she had loved him. She did not love her new husband. He must love her with restraint.

He was not sure now that she had been able to give him anything except her acquiescence. Rebecca would always give that. It was her duty as a wife, and duty would always come above everything with Rebecca. She had been repelled by his touch. He had touched her only enough to prepare her body, to ready it for penetration. He knew from an early manhood experience with an outspoken prostitute that it was uncomfortable, even painful, for women to be mounted when quite unaroused and dry. He had learned on that occasion—and practiced it ever since—how to make the passage wet and comfortable for his woman. And pleasurable for himself.

Rebecca's body had responded. She had not. Duty had had to fight with repulsion. Duty had won—of course. She had relaxed completely after he had mounted her and established a rhythm in her. But she had been utterly passive. Her hands had not even touched him.

She must have been making comparisons, he thought. It must have been dreadful for her. It must have seemed to her that she was being violated. A war must have been raging in her mind—all the time he had worked in her—between duty and protest. And he knew that she would have fought not to remember, not to make comparisons. She had made him the promise that she would not even think about Julian after her new marriage.

And yet David had stubbornly kept to his planned course. He could have finished swiftly in her. Heaven knew that touching her had aroused him enough. But he had wanted the consummation of their marriage to be something quite decisive, something that would establish beyond question the new physical bond between them.

In the process he had probably given her a lasting disgust of him and of what her duty to him was going to involve.

He wondered if he would have the courage to go on. Not that there was any going back now. She was his wife.

And she was awake, staring at him with rather vacant eyes. Looking for Julian? Soon there would be the awareness in her eyes that it was he, David, not Julian.

"Comfortable?" he asked.

She was more than half asleep still. "Mm," she said, and her eyes fluttered closed again.

She was going to have a stiff neck in the morning. He moved a little closer to her, slid one arm beneath her neck, and turned her onto her side against him. She was all soft, relaxed heat. Her hair smelled of soap, but there was a more enticing smell about her—the smell of woman. It was a smell he had encountered before but had never associated with Rebecca. But then he had always been careful during those four years to keep his mind out of Julian's marriage bed.

Her eyes were open again, he saw when he looked down at her. But she had still not stiffened into full wakefulness. He kissed her. Her mouth was relaxed and yielding.

"Your head was at an awkward angle," he explained. "Your neck would have been stiff in the morning."

"Oh," she said. She lay still in his arms, but it was the stillness of acquiescence now. She knew that something was to come between this moment and a return to sleep. He could feel the awareness in her, though no part of her body tensed.

That had not been his intention. One might take a whore for one's pleasure as many times in the course of a night as one had energy for. One did not demand as much of a wife. He had had Rebecca once and had taken his time over it. He had intended to allow her to sleep after that. She had had a busy and emotionally exhausting day. And what had come at the end of it had not been a pleasure for her.

He ran one hand lightly down her back, feeling the curve of her spine. He could feel her breasts resting against his chest, her thighs brushing his. And she was right, of course. Her body had picked up the message even before his brain was aware of it. He kissed her again, tasting her lips with his tongue. He could feel the silkiness of her hair over his arm.

He eased her nightgown and his night shirt up between

them and touched her lightly, his hand flat against her. She was still warm and moist. He ran two fingers downward, parting her, and reached them up a little way inside her. Her body was ready for him. The sounds of wetness enflamed him, sending his temperature suddenly soaring.

And then she was pressing her head against his shoulder and going rigid with tension. "I'm sorry," she said, her voice high with distress. "I'm so sorry."

"Sorry for what?" His hand stilled against her. Sorry that she just could not do it? Could not be his wife?

"I'm so sorry," she said again. "I feel so humiliated."

He understood suddenly. It was because her woman's body was responding to his man's touch although her heart could feel nothing for the man himself. God, he thought. Unbidden, he remembered his father warning him that she had not even begun to recover from the loss of Julian.

"Because of the wetness?" he said. "I deliberately induced it, Rebecca, so that you would not feel pain with my possession. Would you have preferred it otherwise? Did I hurt you? Are you sore?"

There was a lengthy silence, during which he felt some of the tension drain away from her. "No," she said at last. "There was no pain. I am sorry, David. I am determined to be a good wife. It is just—difficult. I do not know what pleases you or displeases you."

"You knew," he said, "that the marriage was to be a real one. I do not wish to hurt you or overexert you. But this part of our marriage is important to me, Rebecca."

"Yes, I know," she said. "It always is to men."

He frowned. Yes, he understood that it was true. Men wanted it while women did not. He wondered when moral standards and accepted patterns of behavior had dictated that it be so. When had it become a necessary requirement of being a lady to find sex distasteful? And yet, to be fair, it was only sex without love that was an ordeal to Rebecca. Things must have been vastly different with Julian—a thought he had no wish to pursue.

"You will please me," he said, "by relaxing and not worrying about pleasing me. Is it very abhorrent to you?"

''No,'' she said, her voice shocked.

''Would you tell me if it were?'' he smiled rather ruefully into the darkness. Of course she would not.

''How could it be?'' she said. ''You are my husband, David.''

Ah, yes, a shield. He began to have a glimmering of an understanding of what life with Rebecca was going to be like. He would have the perfect wife. He had no doubt about that. Her behavior would be above reproach. But he would never get beyond that. He would never know her.

But her body was against his now and they were both naked from the waist down. She had relaxed again. Even her mouth was relaxed when he kissed her. She would make sure that she learned fast what pleased him. She had learned earlier that he liked tongue play. He slid his tongue inside her mouth briefly, but her own lay still beneath it.

God, but he wanted her. Her body, yes. Oh, yes, he wanted her body and would have it too. She knew that and had accepted it and he was past stopping. But he wanted more. He wanted her—all there was of her. He wanted to be inside her body, inside her mind, inside her soul. But all he could ever have of her was her body and her dutiful loyalty. It might perhaps have been different. If she had known as they were growing up . . . If she had known three months before her wedding to Julian that Flora . . . If she had known what had gone on even after her marriage and in Malta and the Crimea . . .

But she had never known and never would. Only over his dead body. Julian had been the love of her life and still was. And she, David thought, gentling his kisses, which had become fierce, was the love of his life. Nothing was going to destroy her memories. Nothing. Certainly not his needs.

He lifted her top leg and brought it snugly up over his hip, easing her into position against him before pushing slowly and firmly into her. He held her steady with one hand spread behind her.

''You see?'' he murmured to her. ''The wetness makes it easier for both of us.''

''Yes.'' He heard her swallow.

"It is the way a woman's body prepares for and adjusts to what is to happen to it," he said. It seemed strange to be giving instruction to a woman about her own body, especially to a woman who had known love and passion for more than two years. But then passion would have made the act of sex an instinctive thing for those two years. She would not have noticed then what embarrassed her now.

"Yes," she said.

He loved her slowly and gently, not turning her onto her back so that he might drive more forcefully into her. He let himself revel in the feel of her, the soft heat that sheathed him without clenching around him. Her inner muscles were relaxed. She was relaxed and quiet.

"You please me, Rebecca," he said, setting his mouth against hers again. "Never doubt that you please me."

"David," she said, "it is not abhorrent to me. I don't want you thinking that. It is not."

He could feel himself coming. He just wished that there were something to share. He wished that she could meet him there in the world of shared ecstasy beyond passion. But it had never been part of the bargain or part of his expectations. He would receive sexual satiety; she would receive his seed. There would be no real sharing at all.

But he was coming, pushing more slowly and deeply into her until the blessed moment when he felt the gush of release and sighed against the side of her face. She lay pressed against him, her leg hugging his hip, quiet and still.

When he had recovered from the spasms of his release, he straightened her leg down beside the other again and held her close, allowing the delicious relaxation that was the aftermath of sex to pull him downward toward sleep. He should release her, he thought drowsily. He should remove himself from her body and ease his arm out from beneath her head so that she would be free to move and find a comfortable position in which to sleep.

But she felt so very good where she was. And he was very close to sleep. Perhaps he would sleep the rest of the night away without waking and without dreams. It would be a rare luxury. He did not want to move and perhaps push sleep away altogether.

She smelled so very good. Better than the most expensive and alluring of perfumes.

He slept.

Rebecca spent her first morning at Stedwell inside the house. She was so busy that there was not a spare moment in which to set foot outside to appreciate the warm sunshine. But it was not an unhappy morning.

She spent a short while after breakfast conferring with the chef on the day's menu. He was dissatisfied, it seemed, with the lack of variety of foods that could be obtained from the kitchen garden and from the village. He was equally dissatisfied with the help he had in the kitchen, declaring that he must have more professional assistance from London if he was to do justice to his culinary arts. Rebecca smiled and made soothing noises and assured him that both she and his lordship would be happy with plain foods well prepared. She was aware as she left the kitchen behind that she had ruffled the man's professional pride.

Mrs. Matthews spent the following hour with her, showing her from room to room of the house until she felt familiar with it. Every room and corridor gave the same impression of faded splendor, shabbiness, and damp neglect. The task of restoring it to a cozy home seemed daunting indeed.

And yet the very hugeness of the task made Rebecca feel thoroughly invigorated. She could make a difference here. She really could. She could be busy for a year and there would still be more to do. She would transform David's house—and her own—into a home, and she would watch the pleasure her efforts gave him.

David. The lower part of her body still throbbed with a feeling that was not quite pain. Last night she had learned the differences there could be between two men. Oh, not just the physical differences. Most of those had been obvious enough and they were relatively unimportant anyway. But differences in what they expected in the marriage bed and what they did there. She felt all over again this morning like a young bride who had just learned the secrets of physical intimacy.

But she would not think of such things. There was

quite enough and more to think about in what she saw around her. David was master in their marriage bed as he was in every other aspect of their life. She would grow accustomed to her duties there just as she had before, though the circumstances were so vastly different.

She had never had a real home with Julian. She felt a moment's regret but put it firmly from her. Perhaps it was just as well. At least her treacherous mind could make no comparisons in that direction. She dismissed the housekeeper, choosing to revisit each room alone and at her leisure so that she could stand quietly looking about her and assessing what needed to be done.

There was so much to be done—in every single room. Ceilings and walls needed to be regilded and repainted; carpets needed to be replaced as did curtains and some furnishings; other furniture needed to be reupholstered; paintings needed to be cleaned. Fires needed to be lit daily in almost every room to get rid of the general feeling of dampness. The list could go on and on. She ended up in the morning room, seated at an escritoire with one leg slightly shorter than the other three, making lists— dauntingly long lists of what she would like to do with every part of the house.

It would cost a fortune, she thought, looking back through her lists when they were made. A huge fortune. But David was a wealthy man. She would have to compile estimates for his approval. And then they would have to bring in workmen.

She smiled when the luncheon bell rang, and tapped the pile of papers into a neat stack. She had not even been outside yet. She would be able to spend a second fortune in the garden, she was sure. She wanted flower gardens, a rose arbor as at Craybourne, a lake. . . . There was an excitement in her, a sense of energy that she had not felt for years. Perhaps ever. There had been very little really to occupy her even during her first marriage. They had always lived in military billets, she and Julian. She had longed for more—for a home. She had forgotten until now the disappointment she had felt when he had announced his intention of buying a commission just before their marriage. And she had forgotten the boredom she had often felt during the long days while he was away, living for the moment when he would be back with her.

She shook her head. It had been a perfect marriage. But this one need not be a disaster. Indeed she was quite determined that it would not be. She was mistress of Stedwell, a dreadfully shabby and neglected house and park with all the potential for beauty and splendor. She would make it beautiful and splendid. She and David together.

She got to her feet. David had spent the morning with his steward in the main office downstairs—the only room that Rebecca had not visited. They had been closeted there all morning. She did not doubt that her husband had been as busy as she.

Her husband. Her stomach lurched a little as she made her way from the morning room to the dining room. Yes, her husband, she told herself firmly. That was the way it was. She glanced down at the unfamiliar green of her dress and twisted the shiny, unfamiliar ring on her finger. And she felt again the unmistakable physical awareness that she had been with him the night before.

Strange, she thought. She still half expected to wake up and find it all a dream. But then she had felt the same way for months after the news of Julian's death had reached her. This was real just as that had been. It was more than time that she anchored herself in reality.

David was in the dining room before her and stood to help her seat herself. It was a strange feeling looking at the man with whom she had been intimate for the first time the night before. He was looking so very correct and handsome and elegant.

"Have you had a good morning, David?" she asked, straightening her shoulders so that she would not slouch against the back of her chair. A governess had once made her sit absolutely still and silent in the schoolroom for two whole hours with her arms about a backboard because she had rested her back against her chair during a reading lesson.

"An enlightening one," he said. "My property has been in good hands with Quigley. He has managed it well and it has prospered. I knew that, of course, from the brief reports he had always sent me, but this morning I could examine the books and see for myself. It seems that my task here will be an easy one."

"You will just allow Mr. Quigley to continue as before?" she said.

He nodded. "Though I intend to make everything much more personal. Tomorrow I shall start paying calls on my tenants and all those dependent upon me in any way. And how about you, Rebecca? You have been busy?"

"I wish there had been someone as efficient looking after the house over the years," she said. "Or perhaps I don't either. There would be less for me to do. It is indeed shabby, David, just as we expected and just as we saw last night from the few rooms we were in."

"You have seen everything?" he asked.

She nodded. "I have long lists of what needs to be done. I shall show them to you when you have a moment. You must decide whether we are to go ahead and do everything at once or whether we should do a little at a time."

"Everything at once, I would think," he said. "We might as well have one great upheaval and get it over with. What about the garden?"

"I have not had a chance to go out there yet," she said. "I want some flower beds, David. Apart from the daisies, everything looked very bare as we approached yesterday."

"Those trees must be cut back from the west side of the house," he said. "They are dangerous during a storm, and they must cut out a great deal of light from the rooms in that wing. Perhaps we can step outside together for a while after we have finished eating if you have no other plans."

"Only to go outside and look around," she said. "We might as well do it together. I shall hear your ideas and then try to draw up some plans. I can present them to you with those for the house some time tomorrow or whenever you have a free hour."

Her marriage was little more than twenty-four hours old, Rebecca thought as she came back downstairs some time later, ready for the outdoors, and yet already she was beginning to feel that perhaps after all she had done the right thing. She had enjoyed the morning almost as a child enjoys a new toy, and she had enjoyed the thoroughly businesslike conversation she had had with David at luncheon. There was going to be so much to do over the coming months and even years that there would be little time to brood.

Perhaps by the time everything had been set to rights they would have settled to a comfortable amity. She would hope that his wildness was all behind him. After all, he was almost twenty-nine years old. It was almost five years since he had disgraced Flora. Since then he had fought in the Crimean War as one of Her Majesty's officers and had distinguished himself to the extent that he had been awarded a Victoria Cross. He had been severely wounded on two separate occasions. She hoped that he was now changed. She hoped it fervently. She had always hated it when some new perfidy of David's had come to light. If there had ever been an air of mischief about him, maybe it would have been different. But he had always seemed so quiet and respectable.

Anyway, for the time being she was feeling almost happy. Certainly happier than she had felt for long ages—since before the day she had discovered that Julian's regiment was bound for Malta without her, she supposed. And even before that there had been the agony of her second miscarriage. She had something to do now and she owed deference to no one except David. She was mistress of Stedwell. There was something marvelously exhilarating in the thought.

Something certainly did need to be done about the trees west of the house. At the very least, branches needed to be cut away. They were both agreed on that.

"Perhaps some of the trees should be taken out altogether to make room for my rose arbor," she suggested.

"Rose arbor?" He looked down at her. "Yes, it will suit you, Rebecca. Plan for it, then."

They spent an hour taking the air, enjoying the wide views from the house in most directions, admiring the three-arched stone bridge that they had ridden over and not noticed the day before, discussing what might be done to make the gardens more picturesque.

"Rebecca," he said at last, "you are not daunted at the prospect of so much to do?"

"No," she said. "It will give my life purpose to be so busy, David. You realized that when you were persuading me to marry you. You were quite right."

"You are not sorry, then?" he asked, "But it is a little soon to ask such a question, I suppose. And perhaps it would never serve any useful purpose to ask it."

"I am not sorry." She looked at him, curious again to know exactly why he had married her when it seemed that he had so much less to gain than she. "I made a commitment yesterday, David. To you, not just to restoring this house. I took you as my husband and vowed to make you a good wife. Such vows are always challenging, I think. They were . . ." She stopped in some dismay. She had vowed never to talk of Julian. "Well, they are challenging. Committing yourself to someone else's happiness is not easy. But I have made that commitment."

He stared at her broodingly and she wondered if she had made a mistake. She wondered if he wanted or expected such a commitment. Perhaps all he wanted was a companion and helper—and someone to satisfy his needs in bed. She flushed at memories of the night before. It had been so very different from what she had expected and from what she had once been accustomed to.

He stared off over her shoulder suddenly. "We are about to have visitors," he said. "I suppose it was to be expected. We have neighbors to grow familiar with, Rebecca."

A carriage was making its way up the driveway.

"Yes," she said. It was a pleasing thought. To be mistress of her own home. To be the leading lady of the neighborhood, socially speaking. To be about to make new acquaintances, perhaps new friends. "And other responsibilities to be taken on. I wonder what they will involve altogether?"

"We had better stroll back so that we are on the terrace by the time that carriage arrives there," he said.

"David," she said impulsively, "it feels good to be mistress of my own home. Thank you."

"I hoped it would," he said quietly. "And it feels

good to have a mistress for it, Rebecca, not to be here alone. It would be lonely.''

As he had said, they both had something to gain from the marriage. It was not going to be bad after all. Provided she could keep on tucking her memories firmly into the past, she could expect a measure of contentment at least from the future. Perhaps in time it would even be possible to give David the affection he had asked for. She would try, she resolved. She would try very hard.

10

Three sets of visitors arrived before the afternoon was out. At one time they were all in the drawing room together and everyone was very merry. Including Rebecca. Her neighbors had come calling with the obvious intention of doing more than just making her acquaintance and David's.

"Stedwell has been unoccupied altogether too long," Mrs. Appleby said over tea. "Of course, my lord, we understand that for many years you were a mere boy living with your father, the Earl of Hartington, and that more latterly you have been serving Her Majesty and our country in the Crimea. We were all proud to bursting when we heard of how you distinguished yourself there. Weren't we, Gregory? But it is truly wonderful to have you home at last and with your lovely new bride. Isn't it, Mrs. Mantrell?"

The lady referred to, middle-aged like Mrs. Appleby, and as thin as the other was plump, agreed. "Our only hope is that you are here to stay now, my lord," she said. "It seems such a waste to have a large estate like Stedwell uninhabited. There is no leadership, if you will forgive my saying so, though we all do our part to do the best we can."

"Our intention is to make this our home, ma'am," David assured her. "I have been dreaming for several years of settling here and my wife has been looking forward to having a home of her own."

The ladies were satisfied and were quite content to let the gentlemen begin their own conversation about hunting and shooting and crops and stocks and shares—all those dull topics that would make a lady yawn merely to think of. Mrs. Mantrell wanted to assure herself that the new Lady Tavistock was going to take up her position as lady of the manor and leading lady of the neighborhood.

"Even though you are a new bride and have other duties too," she added, smiling and nodding in a manner that set Rebecca to blushing.

There were various committees with which she was expected to involve herself, Rebecca discovered, among them the church flower committee, the ladies' missionary aid committee, and the school committee.

"Not that the school committee's task is a very onerous one these days," Mrs. Appleby remarked, "there being very few pupils attending school any longer. But then I always have said that teaching the poor to read and write is a waste of time when they will spend their lives in the fields."

And Rebecca would be expected to sponsor the spring flower and baking show, the summer fair, and the children's Christmas party.

"My mother used to talk about the Stedwell summer picnics," Lady Sharp said, introducing the topic with such a determined tone to her voice that Rebecca realized that doing so had been the main purpose of her visit. "Involving all the leading families, Lady Tavistock. There used to be sports and food in the outdoors during the day and a dinner and ball during the evening."

"It would be truly wonderful if you and his lordship were to revive the custom," Mrs. Appleby said. "I can remember my father talking about the cricket. It was the grandest event of the year, according to him. I was a mere child when the last one was held."

"It sounds like a wonderful tradition to be renewed," Rebecca said, smiling. "Next summer we must begin it again. Are there usually many parties and balls here?"

It seemed that her neighbors all did their part to keep the social life of the countryside active. There were dinners and musical evenings and dances as well as afternoon calls.

"But no real balls, Lady Tavistock," Miss Stephanie Sharp said wistfully, speaking for the first time. "No one hereabouts has a real ballroom, but only drawing rooms. And there is never an orchestra, but only pianoforte music."

"Sir Gordon and I will be taking Stephanie to London next spring to be presented, Lady Tavistock," Lady Sharp said. "She will be almost twenty, which is a little old, I am sure you are thinking. But she is our only daughter, you see, and we have been reluctant to have her taken off our hands."

The girl was rather lovely, Rebecca thought, smiling at her. She was small and slim, with dark ringlets arranged in fashionable clusters at the sides of her head and a healthy, rosy complexion. She had been staring, rapt, at David through much of the visit. It struck Rebecca suddenly that if he had come to Stedwell a single man, Stephanie Sharp would have been an eligible match for him. There might have been all the excitement of a courtship in the neighborhood and a connection that would have bound David more closely to Stedwell.

But now was not the time to remind herself that the time might come when David would regret his dispassionate, loveless marriage with her. She glanced at him as he talked with the men, and saw him as he must appear to Stephanie—young, wealthy, elegant, and handsome to a fault.

And he was hers. She almost lost the thread of the conversation for a moment as she remembered just how he had become hers the night before.

"The Stedwell ballroom is large," she said, "though it has an air of neglect about it as most of the house does, I am afraid. We will have to restore it to splendor by next summer and have a magnificent ball there—with a full orchestra. But by that time, Stephanie, after a Season in London, it will appear very commonplace to you."

Mrs. Appleby clasped her hands to her bosom. "How wonderful all this is, Lady Tavistock," she said. "So wonderful to see Stedwell about to be restored to its original glory and to have the viscount and his lady in residence. But we have stayed long enough." She got firmly to her feet. "The men will talk until dinnertime and not even think of breaching etiquette. Come along, Gregory, do. We have been here far longer than half an hour."

Everyone left together with a great deal of bustle and cheerful farewells and assurances by Rebecca that they would return the calls within the next few days.

She smiled at David when they stood alone together on the steps at last, the three vehicles all on their way down the driveway. "Were you just conversing politely with the gentlemen?" she asked. "Or were you being organized as I was, David? I gather that I am already on about six different committees and that I am to be a leading light at annual fetes and flower shows and children's parties. Oh, and there is to be cricket and croquet and a picnic tea out here one day next summer and a grand dinner and ball in the evening of the same day. An ancient tradition, I gather. It is all planned."

"Rebecca," he said, "you are the Viscountess Tavistock, you know, and must not let yourself be manipulated."

"I know," she said. "But oh, yes, I will, David. This is wonderful. I feel already that I belong. I am quite sure that idleness and boredom will be the least of my worries for the next ten years or so. In fact, I may even have to give up sleeping at night."

She spoke lightly from a welling of excitement the visits had brought her. She had done the right thing, she thought. She had put the past two years behind her and wrapped up the memories of the love and happiness that had preceded them to keep in a secret part of her memory where they could no longer cause her raw pain. She had replaced it all with a life that was going to bring her practical satisfaction. It was the sort of life she had been brought up to live. The sort of life she had always wanted to live—with Julian. But no—no, she would not spoil what had been a surprisingly happy day with that thought.

"Give up sleeping?" David said, turning to lead her back inside the house. "I think not, Rebecca."

She felt herself flushing scarlet. And even that, she thought, did not seem so dreadful.

Rebecca's lists were almost complete. She had not yet shown them to David, but doing so was merely formality. He had promised her a free hand in the changes to house and gardens. She was longing to see a start being made, to see that she somehow made a difference in someone's life.

But the following morning she decided to accompany

her husband on his ride to visit some of his tenants. She was, after all, responsible for their well being and was eager to meet them all and discover their needs.

"Though I suppose your tenants are quite independent, aren't they?" she said. "It is your laborers who will probably be more in need of my help. There may be some elderly people who will appreciate visits or some sick people who will need medicines."

"This is going to take several days," he told her. "Apart from the accounts Quigley has been sending me and the books I examined yesterday, I know nothing of my estate, Rebecca. The human element is totally absent from my knowledge."

"But all is prosperous?" she said. "Your people must be happy, David. Do we dare canter over these fields? We are moving at a very sedate pace."

They gave themselves up to the enjoyment of fresh air and sunshine as they took their horses at a faster pace toward the cottage of one of the tenants.

Mr. and Mrs. Gundy did not seem particularly happy to see them, though they were perfectly polite. Mr. Gundy stayed outside the house with David while his wife invited Rebecca inside and offered her tea.

"This is a pretty house," Rebecca said, smiling at two young children, who were standing in a doorway, staring at her.

"Yes, my lady," Mrs. Gundy said. "Except when it rains and the roof leaks."

"Oh, dear," Rebecca said. "That must be uncomfortable. Has Mr. Gundy been too busy to repair it?"

Mrs. Gundy busied herself with preparing tea and did not answer.

"Do the children go to school?" Rebecca asked.

"No, my lady," Mrs. Gundy said. "They are needed here to help with the farm."

"At their age?" Rebecca said. "Are they not a little young?"

"We need the help, my lady," Mrs. Gundy said, rather tight-lipped. "It can come only from our own family."

Her questions were resented, Rebecca realized. Obviously Mrs. Gundy was a proud woman who did not like having the lady of the manor prying into her business. It was quite understandable. And Rebecca had really not come to interfere. For the rest of the visit she talked on safe topics, concentrating on establishing some sort of easy amity with her husband's tenant.

She was not sorry when the visit ended.

"That was not too successful, I'm afraid," she said after David had helped her into the saddle and they had ridden away from the cottage. "The roof leaks and the children cannot go to school because their labor is needed on the farm. And Mrs. Gundy hates the fact that her husband smokes a pipe in the house. I do believe she also resented the fact that I came calling."

David was looking severe and uncommunicative.

"Was Mr. Gundy more amiable?" she asked.

"His rent is too high," he said shortly. "It has been raised sharply year by year despite the near-impossibility of his paying it. One more raise and he will be forced to leave."

"To go where?" Rebecca asked. "He has a wife and two young children."

"And the traditional help from the manor with things like repair of the barn and of the house roof has been withheld," David said. "It seems that I cannot afford the expense."

"But I thought you were prospering," Rebecca said.

"So did I." He looked grim. "I hope Gundy's is an exceptional case. It will be easy to rectify if it is."

"You have promised him help and a reduction in rent?" Rebecca asked.

"I have promised nothing," he said. "I have some investigating to do first."

It was not after all a good morning. The first visit was a mere harbinger of the four that followed it. It seemed that everyone's rent was exorbitantly high. Every penny earned that was not going to pay the rent was being spent on mere survival. There was no money to spare for essential repairs and improvements. And there was no help from Stedwell. Only constant demands for more money. Very few of the children were attending school. They wanted their children to attend, one vocal wife explained to Rebecca. They had ambitions for them. But what could they do? Their help was needed at home.

"It's amazing, David," Rebecca said when they were finally riding home, rather tired and dispirited, "that they were as civil to us as they were. They must hate us with a passion."

"They do not do so," he said, "only because they believe we are suffering along with them. They have seen the condition of the house and grounds at Stedwell. And they know that I was in the army, fighting in the Crimea. A viscount does not do such a thing unless he is in great financial straits—or so the theory goes."

"And yet—" Rebecca said.

"And yet," he said vehemently. "There are a few things I need to have explained, Rebecca. I think perhaps you had better not accompany me on tomorrow's visits. Or on any visits for a while."

"Why not?" she asked.

"I have the feeling that none of them will be any more pleasant than today's," he said. "You might as well stay at home."

"David," she said quietly, "we are in this together. I did not marry you for a pleasant life of ease, remember? You promised me challenge. You promised that I would help you. Don't try now to make an ornament of me."

He gazed steadily at her for a few moments. "Perhaps there is an explanation," he said. "Perhaps we just visited all the wrong people this morning."

They rode the rest of the way home without further conversation.

David came awake with a surging of terror and relief. He was suffocating, his body wet with perspiration. He flung back the bedclothes before remembering that he was not alone as he usually was when the nightmare came. He turned his head to look at Rebecca. She was sleeping quietly on the other side of the bed, turned slightly away from him.

God! He sat up on the edge of the bed and rubbed his hands over his face. His heart was still pounding like a hammer in his chest.

Always the same nightmare. It had come to him first at Scutari and had followed him back to the Crimea and home to England. It was not fading with time, as he had told himself at the first that it would, but was getting more frequent and more vivid. Sometimes it came to him more than once in a night. Sometimes he fought exhaustion to stay awake merely to avoid it.

He got to his feet and crossed the room to stand at the window, looking out into darkness. The terrifying thing about dreams, he had discovered, was that they could distort time horribly. In the dream it always took him what seemed like ten minutes to pull his pistol free of its holster and fire it, though he knew that in reality it had taken only a split second. In the dream there was time for all sorts of strange things to happen within that split second.

In the dream he always knew what he was about to do. He always knew the alternatives and the consequences. He had time to debate with himself whether he would fire merely to get Julian to drop his sword or whether he would shoot to kill. He had had enough of Julian, of always covering for him, excusing him, expecting him to grow up and become a responsible adult. Nothing would ever change. It was time he got rid of Julian from his life. It was time he killed him. If he killed him, perhaps he would have a chance with Rebecca. There would never again be any need to blacken his own name in order to protect Julian. His willingness to lie and take punishment in order to protect Julian had always been his greatest weakness. No more weakness. He was going to be strong.

And so he always shot to kill. Quite deliberately. Quite cold bloodedly. He always hated Julian in the dream. He felt no love for him at all. Only the overwhelming desire to kill him.

God! David closed his eyes and rested his forehead against the glass of the window. He was sweating again. His waking self could never shake off the dream. What if the dream was the reality? What if the dream had merely uncovered what his conscious mind denied? What if his killing of Julian had had nothing really to do with George Scherer? What if he had killed Julian because he hated him and wanted him dead? Because he wanted Rebecca?

And now he had Rebecca. She lay asleep in the bed behind him. He had made love to her only a couple of hours ago. She was his wife. But why had he married her? Only because of the responsibility he felt toward the widow of the man he had killed? Or because he had cold bloodedly planned to have her for himself?

He shivered in the coolness of the night air. Another thought always haunted him during this waking part of the nightmare, though it had no part in the dream. What if Julian's actions had been in self-defense? What if George Scherer had been trying to kill him and Julian had had no choice but to defend his own life? What if it had been a kill-or-be-killed situation? And yet Scherer had had right on his side—he was a wronged husband. Would that have given him the right to kill Julian, though? And in the midst of a battle in which they were both supposed to be killing the enemy and defending their countrymen?

The questions were academic if David's initial reaction to the scene before his eyes had been the correct one. But what if it was not? Even then, could he have stood by and watched Julian run a fallen man through with his sword?

The dream, terrifying as it was in itself, always gave place to a waking nightmare that was many times worse.

"David?" A light hand touched his arm.

He whirled around to find Rebecca standing beside him, looking at him in some concern. God, she was the last person he wanted to see at the moment—his wife, in her nightclothes and with her hair loose down her back, in their bedchamber. All the intimacy of a domestic scene. Julian's wife.

"Go back to bed," he said harshly. "You should be sleeping."

"Are you all right?" she asked. "Is something wrong?"

"Nothing is wrong." He glared at her. "Get back to bed."

Her hand fell away from his arm. "You were breathing heavily," she said. "I thought you were in pain."

"A little insomnia," he said. "I suffer from it occasionally. It is nothing you need concern yourself with, Rebecca."

"*Stay out of my life,*" she said so softly that for a moment he was not sure what she had said. "This is the way you have always looked and sounded when something was wrong and one might have offered you some sympathy, David. *Stay out of my life.* I had forgotten that it was that as much as anything that used to make me dislike you.''

He sucked in air slowly. ''Go back to bed,'' he said, his tone more controlled. ''I appreciate your concern, but I would not keep you awake too, Rebecca. It would be unfair.''

''Was it a bad dream?'' she asked.

His fragile control snapped again. ''Yes, goddammit, it was a bad dream,'' he said. ''It is no great matter. It was a bad dream, that's all. Do you want to tuck me back into bed and smooth a hand over my brow and assure me that there are no ghosts in the cupboards after all?''

He watched her jaw harden in the dim light from the window, though she did not turn away. ''I used to have them too,'' she said, ''I used to wake up crying and sometimes screaming. Is it the war, David? Is it war memories that trouble you?''

''Yes,'' he said curtly. ''There was so much death and horror and so much suffering, Rebecca. Is it any wonder that a man's dreams become haunted?''

''No,'' she said.

He turned back toward the window. He wished to God that she would go away. It was impossible to explain that it was not so much the dream as the wakefulness following the dream that was most to be dreaded. He did not want her of all people to step into that wakefulness.

''Do you dream of *him*?'' she asked abruptly.

''Yes.''

''Is it guilt you feel, David?'' Her voice was no more than a whisper.

''God!'' He closed his eyes very tightly and clamped his teeth together. He felt bathed in sweat again. He willed her to give up and move away from behind him.

''Do you keep imagining that you might have saved him?'' she asked. ''That if you had held him back or gone forward instead of him you might have saved him? But he might still have been stopped by another bullet. I don't know what battle is like, David, but I do know that thousands of men died just on that one day. Besides, you could not watch out for just Julian. You were responsible for the lives of all your men. Don't blame yourself.''

He rounded on her again suddenly. ''You are right, Rebecca,'' he said through his teeth. ''You know nothing of what battle is like. Don't mouth platitudes at me. And I thought it was agreed that he not be mentioned between us. I thought you promised that he would not. It is not to happen again, do you understand me? Julian is dead. Let him go.''

Her eyes were huge with shock.

''Go back to bed,'' he said.

She turned away, but he grabbed for her wrist and spun her back around to face him. What had he done? But words of apology could not force themselves through the turmoil of his mind. He hauled her against him and lowered his mouth to hers.

It was not a tender kiss. Ghosts were clawing at him and he fought to banish them, to impose the reality of the present on the dreams and horrors of the past. She was his wife. They had married less than three days before. This was their honeymoon.

She was clinging to him when he lifted his head again, her body arched in to his, held there by all the strength of his arms. But she made no protest. She should have slapped his face—hard. Instead she was playing the part of dutiful wife, as he suspected she always would. His anger intensified. He hated her in that moment. He stooped down, scooped her up into his arms, strode across to the bed, and tossed her down onto it.

He leaned over her, hauling her nightgown with one pull of both hands up beneath her arms. He lifted himself over her, pushing her legs wide with his knees and kneeling between them. He held her nightgown up to her chin with both hands while he lowered his head to one of her breasts and took it into his mouth, sucking inward, laving the stiffening nipple with his tongue.

He heard her sharp intake of breath and felt its ragged expulsion. And he felt her fighting for control as he moved his mouth to her other breast, and winning. Her body began to relax beneath him. She was becoming as always the submissive wife. She would allow him his will, no matter what indignity he had planned for her.

"Damn you," he hissed at her, lifting his head and glaring down into wide eyes. "Fight me. Respond to me."

She shook her head slowly. He could feel her bewilderment and it infuriated him. She lay spread-eagled on the bed, her hands palm down against the mattress.

"You wanted to comfort me," he said with quiet fury against her mouth. "You wanted to banish my nightmares. Then banish them. Banish the memories. Give me some of what you used to give Julian."

She whimpered as he pushed his tongue into her mouth. He withdrew it. He slid his hands beneath her, cupping her buttocks, holding her steady as he lowered his weight onto her and thrust into her. He worked fast and deep, his head buried against her hair, his eyes tightly closed. *Banish the memories. Banish the memories, Rebecca. My love. Put your arms around me. Hold me.* His teeth were clamped together. The words were not spoken aloud.

He shouted out his release and relaxed down onto her. And realized as sleep was about to envelop him what he had done. And remembered some of the words he had spoken. *Damn you. Give me some of what you used to give Julian.*

And his father's voice—*now it seems that he is reaching out even beyond the grave to cloud your happiness.*

He lifted himself away from her and off the bed. He stood beside it, his back to it. "I'm sorry, Rebecca," he said. His voice sounded abrupt, stilted. He searched his mind but there were no other words. And she said nothing, of course. He crossed to his dressing room, let himself in quietly, and closed the door behind him.

He spent most of the rest of the night standing on the triple-arched bridge a short distance from the house, staring downward into black, fast-flowing water.

It was one of the hardest things Rebecca remembered doing to leave her dressing room to go downstairs to breakfast the next morning. She had lain awake all through the night after he had left, unable to sleep, afraid that he would return. Afraid that he would not. She did not feel alert enough now to face what had to be faced. Though she did not know what that was.

She was afraid of him. Terrified. He was no gentleman. He was wild as she had always known he was beneath the quiet, almost austere veneer he presented to the world. He had not changed at all. No gentleman would have treated his wife as she had been treated during the night. Her face burned with the memories of the passion he had unleashed on her. She had been almost naked. And he had touched her—with his mouth.

She was afraid of him. Perhaps most of all because she had been excited by it. Repelled, horrified, terrified—and excited. *Fight me,* he had ordered her. And she had wanted to fight. She had wanted to strike him for what he was saying to her and to lash out with fists, legs, and body for what he was doing to her. But she had been terrified of where it might all lead. Terrified of the unknown.

Besides, a woman's role was to be a lady at all times. In control at all times. Submissive to her husband at all times. And yet he had commanded her to fight him, to respond to him. He was no gentleman at all, commanding the impossible. She had been right to dislike him all their lives. Control had never been so hard to hold on to as it had been last night. But she had held. She had lain quiet and still beneath his assault. She had been obedient to her upbringing and training and in the process she had been disobedient to her husband.

She did not know how she would face him. And she had been feeling so complacent for two full days, she thought bitterly. She had been so convinced that they had settled quickly into a perfectly amicable business arrangement. No, more than that. She had thought perhaps they were even settling into what might after all be an affectionate relationship. She had been feeling almost happy.

She descended the stairs slowly, but with steps that refused to falter. *Give me some of what you used to give Julian.* She almost lost her footing. What had he meant? Was he demanding her love after all?

He was in the breakfast room, seated at the table. She had hoped that perhaps he had breakfasted early. But this was as well. He had to be faced some time. She stiffened her spine and schooled her features to show nothing but a calm morning face. His own face was shuttered and grim.

"Good morning," she said.

"Good morning." He got to his feet to help her to her place. The perfect gentleman again. The civilized being again.

They conversed steadily and courteously through breakfast, planning out their day's activities. Everything they said was spoken for the benefit of the servant who stood at the sideboard.

"I would take a moment of your time if you can spare it, Rebecca," David said at last, when they had both finished eating and risen.

"Of course," she said.

He led her in silence to his office and closed the door behind him before speaking.

"I owe you an apology, Rebecca," he said, raising his eyes to hers and holding them with a steady gaze. "I make it with all sincerity. My behavior was unpardonable."

"I am your wife, David," she said quietly.

But the words did not please him. She watched his jaw harden. "That fact does not excuse me," he said. "In the future when I have the nightmare, I shall leave the room and so protect you. I warn you that I am best left alone at such times."

"I beg your pardon," she said. "I thought to help."

He held her eyes, his expression unfathomable. "He was an important part of both our lives," he said. "I don't believe we can go through the rest of a lifetime without ever speaking his name, Rebecca. You made me a promise before our marriage that I did not demand though I did last night. I release you from both the promise and the obligation to obey the command. You must speak of Julian whenever you feel the need."

She swallowed.

"I wish I could make it easier for you," he said, turning from her abruptly.

"David," she said, "I want to keep myself busy with

this new life of mine. There is so much to do. I have no wish to brood.''

''Well, then.'' His voice brisker. He stood with his back to her, his hands braced on the desk. ''We had better get on with it. Visits to some laborers' cottages this morning and the hope that what we observed yesterday does not apply to them at least. They do not pay rents after all. How soon can you be ready to leave?''

''Ten minutes?'' she said.

He nodded and turned to walk past her to hold the door open for her. His face was an impassive mask, one she was familiar with from the past. Much as she had disapproved of his boyhood pranks, she had always been willing to show him some sympathy after he had emerged from a confrontation with his father, which had inevitably involved a thrashing. He had never allowed her sympathy or anyone else's. He had never allowed anyone in. David had kept David very much to himself. And so over the years she had come to dislike him. The night before she had seen the wilder, crueler side of David for the first time and had even been a victim of it. Now this morning he was his incommunicative self. And yet there had been more than cruelty the night before—she had glimpsed pain in him. It had been pain that had caused the violence. But he still would not let her in. He would leave their bedchamber in the future when he had the nightmares, he had said. He would keep his pain to himself.

He would keep himself to himself.

She hurried upstairs to change into her riding habit.

11

It was all far worse than he had ever dreamed, David found over the next few days as he gradually visited every laborer in his employ and every tenant who rented from him. Indeed he had not expected to find anything bad at all. The reports he had received over the years had indicated growing prosperity on his estate. The only negative fact he had known about it was that the house was falling into neglect—but that was only because he had never seen the need to keep it up.

What he was now finding was an estate that had grown rich on the exploitation of its workers and renters. The laborers' cottages were hardly fit for habitation. His men and their families were thin and listless from malnutrition—it seemed that he could spare them no land about their cottages on which to grow their own food and their wages would buy them only the bare necessities. There was much sickness, especially among the children and the elderly.

He had wondered at the shortage of older children and young people until someone explained to him that they usually left home as soon as they were able to search for work in the industrial towns. Most of them were successful, but they lived as desperately there as their parents did at home. There was rarely any money to spare to send back.

Some of his workers seemed resigned to their lot. They were, after all, very little different from most other agricultural workers they knew about. Times were bad for those who lived off the land. That was all there was to be said about it. Some were bitter. Their parents and their grandparents and generations before that had lived comfortably on the land. Were they now, and their children, to be forced into the towns, where they had no desire to be?

None seemed mutinous. Their master, after all, was suffering through hard times too. There was no money anywhere.

Only David seemed to feel any deep emotion. He was furiously angry. He did not confront his steward until his visits had been completed, but he did so eventually, hoping that he could hold on to his temper sufficiently that he would not punch the man in addition to dismissing him.

And yet he did neither when it came to the point. Quigley had after all been an excellent steward. His job over the years had been to see to it that his absent master's estate prospered and earned him wealth. In that he had been eminently successful. The fact that he had shown no compassion for the human agents of that success was really irrelevant to the situation. It was not his job to show compassion.

That was his master's job.

But his master had been away, living his own life, accepting the reports from Stedwell at face value, quite careless of the fact that several hundred people were directly or indirectly dependent upon him for their very survival. He had been too busy since reaching adulthood carving out a career for himself in the Guards. A career he had undertaken so that he could get away from the woman he loved but could never have.

He could have begun a career as owner of Stedwell and done better. Julian would not have followed him to Stedwell except as an occasional visitor. David would have had no occasion to kill Julian at Stedwell. He could be living there now, perhaps alone, perhaps with a different wife, but certainly with a clear conscience.

Now he was weighed down by conscience. Guilt attacked him from all quarters.

''Thank you, Quigley,'' he said when the interview was over, staring through the window of his office, ''that will be all for now. I intend to remain at Stedwell now that I have finally come here and will be taking over the actual running of the estate. But I will need your knowledge and expertise and your skill at bookkeeping. Perhaps you will find your job less onerous from now on.''

''It has always been a pleasure to serve you, my lord,'' the steward said with all sincerity.

David continued to stare out the window after the man had left. He had Rebecca's lists in a pile on his desk. He had been through them with her a couple of days ago. She had estimated the costs of some items; he had done the same for others. Some things neither of them had any idea about but had costed at what seemed slightly above a reasonable estimate. The house and grounds would be magnificent when all was done. As he had expected, she had an unerring eye for what was needed.

It had been the prospect of transforming his house into a home fit for a viscount and viscountess which had finally swayed her to accepting his marriage offer. He knew that. She would not have married him if she had not had the prospect of something useful with which to fill her days. He had promised her a free hand. The presentation of those lists for his approval had been a mere formality, but of course one that Rebecca would always observe. To her he would always be master for the simple reason that she had married him.

His jaw tensed as he clamped his teeth together. He walked purposefully to the bellpull beside the fireplace and told the servant who answered his summons to ask her ladyship to join him in the study if it was convenient to her.

She came within five minutes.

''Rebecca,'' he said, ''sit down. We need to talk.'' He indicated a comfortable armchair before the desk, waiting for her to be seated before he sat down himself behind the desk. ''About these lists.''

''David,'' she said, ''these people need food and medicine. I am sending someone to town tomorrow with a list of the medicines I will need. The food can be taken from the gardens here or bought at the village and some of it can even be cooked here. I shall deliver it myself.''

''Of course,'' he said. ''That is all part of your domain, Rebecca. You do not need my permission if that is what you are asking for.''

''I do want your permission to dismiss the chef,'' she

said. "With a good reference and perhaps a month's salary. He will have no trouble at all finding another position in London. He does not fit in here, David. He is contemptuous of the rest of the staff and has inspired their dislike. And though his dishes are magnificent, they would not be suitable for food baskets. He is making a great fuss over my requests for plain food."

"You must dismiss him, then," he said. "The servants are your responsibility, Rebecca."

"Thank you," she said. "The woman who used to cook here is living in the village with her sister. She has no other employment. The servants all agree that she was a good cook, but Mrs. Matthews thought that her dishes would not please our aristocratic palates. People are foolish. I wish to rehire her. The job should be offered locally anyway. These people need jobs."

"I will expect you to handle the matter," he said. "And no, I will not mind plain dishes, Rebecca, provided they are well prepared. I spent years with the army, remember. About these lists."

"I am going to start knitting socks for the children," she said. "Did you notice how many of them were barefoot, David, with autumn just around the corner? Perhaps some of the women can knit. If I provide the wool for them, perhaps they can get busy on scarves and gloves—and shawls for the elderly. I am going to see what can be done, anyway."

"It sounds like a good idea," he said. "I will leave you to organize it, Rebecca."

"I plan to visit the school tomorrow," she said. "It is under your patronage, David? I want to see if it has all the necessary supplies and if it is equipped to take more pupils if I can persuade more parents to send their children. Mrs. Appleby told me that it is poorly attended."

"Rebecca," he said, "I wish to speak to you about these plans for renovation." He set a hand on top of the pile of her lists.

Her eyes rested on his hand for a moment before she got to her feet, apparently in some agitation. "David," she said, "I can't . . . I know it was why you needed a wife. I know it was why you married me. And I promised." He heard her draw breath and expel it. "Well, I married you and now you are my husband. What is your will, then? What have you decided?'' She turned and sat down quietly again.

He felt some of the dread and tension ease from his body. He might have known. Of course, she was Rebecca. He might have known.

''Which items on these lists are absolutely necessary?'' he asked.

She clasped her hands in her lap. He could see the whiteness of her knuckles. She thought for several moments. ''The chimneys need sweeping,'' she said. ''It seems to be generally agreed among the servants that there is danger of a fire in them if they are not swept soon. Mrs. Matthews should have seen to it before now.''

He waited for more but she seemed to have finished.

''It must be done immediately, then,'' he said. ''Before winter. You will see to it?''

''Yes, David.'' She looked up into his eyes.

''Those cottages have to be made habitable before winter sets in,'' he said.

She nodded.

''And their wages need to be raised so that they can buy wholesome food,'' he said. ''They cannot rely wholly on charity from the house.''

''No,'' she said. ''I was a little concerned about that. I thought they might come to resent me if I arrive too often with baskets. I understand that people's pride is sometimes more important to them than comfort.''

''And I am going to have to reduce the rents,'' he said. ''To last year's levels at first, I think. And more later if it is possible. I am going to have to help with outstanding repairs.''

''Yes,'' she said.

He looked away from her and stared down broodingly at the pile of neatly penned plans and estimates. ''I brought you here under false pretenses, Rebecca,'' he said. ''I offered you a secure life of luxury as my viscountess. I offered to allow you to create that luxury for yourself.''

''I do not remember the word *luxury* being used,'' she said.

''Did it not go without saying?'' he asked. ''I warned

you of the shabbiness of Stedwell, but I promised that it would be only temporary.''

"I married you so that there would be a sense of purpose in my life," she said. "I think I am getting far more than I bargained for, David. My duties as your viscountess are threatening to quite overwhelm me. I have more enthusiasm for the future than I thought it would be possible to have ever again.''

He raised his eyes to hers once more. "There just will not be the money for all the work of restoration if I am to set right the wrong of years with my people," he said. "Not at present anyway. Perhaps next year.''

"Besides," she said, "it would be criminal for us to be seen setting up a life of luxury when your dependents are barely subsisting, David. I have never particularly thought of it before. It is rather criminal, isn't it?''

"We must live the life we were born to," he said. "And try to do it at peace with our consciences.''

"But we might as easily have been born in one of those cottages," she said. "We did nothing to deserve our life of privilege, did we?''

"You will not mind, then," he said, "if we put these lists away for a while?''

She shook her head. "It is such a relief," she said. "I thought you might not understand. I am sorry, David. You do have compassion for those in your care. Thank you.''

He got to his feet, embarrassed and absurdly pleased with her praise. "It must be teatime," he said. "Shall we go up? Is this the first afternoon we have had no visitors?''

"People have been very attentive," she said. "We returned those first three calls but have five more to make. We already have two dinner invitations—to the Sharps' and to Mr. Crispin's.''

He set a hand at the small of her back as they left the room. She felt warm and feminine despite the restricting stays she wore. Such dispassionate touches were all he had allowed himself of her in several days—since that disastrous night when she had walked into his waking nightmare, in fact. He offered her his arm when they reached the staircase.

It was an enormous relief to know that she had accepted his decisions concerning Stedwell. He had been very much afraid that he would have to deal with sullenness at best, tantrums at worst. And yet his fears seemed absurd now. He could not imagine Rebecca either sullen or in tantrums.

She was the perfect lady. The perfect lady of the manor.

It was the reason he had made the sofa in the library his bed for the last three nights. Although he had apologized to her and made his peace with her, he could neither forgive himself nor trust himself close to her again. He had used her to punish his own conscience.

Give me some of what you used to give Julian. He could still hear himself saying the words. He could not rid his mind of them. They had never yet invaded his dreams, but they were there like a constant nightmare in his waking mind.

He was still jealous of Julian. He would never put his ghost to rest. And he could not after all be contented with only what she was able to give. She gave that—without hesitation or complaint. Even when he had assaulted her so cruelly she had given her body without shrinking.

But it was not enough. He had fooled himself ever to think that it would be. His father had seen it, but he had refused to. He had wanted her so badly that he would have taken her on any terms. And of course he had needed to marry her, to offer her the protection of a married name and a home.

He was glad at least that they seemed to be in harmony over their duties as lord and lady of Stedwell. That was one small comfort in a largely comfortless existence. But he knew that there could never be anything more personal between them. If he was to put her interests first— and for a long time it had been the focus of his life to do that—then he must give her the comfort of a home of her own and all the activities that went with it but leave her to her memories of a perfect, love-filled marriage. Perhaps he owed Julian the ultimate victory. Perhaps. Though he always felt an impotent sort of fury when he thought of how fickle Julian's love had been.

They conversed during tea, as they always did, like polite and not unfriendly strangers. He let his eyes feast on her as they talked—the only part of him that he would now allow to do so. He had always been fascinated by her very disciplined deportment. Her spine never touched the back of any chair on which she sat but was always ramrod straight. The high-necked bodice of her dress molded her corseted figure and ended at a small waist. Corsets must be dreadfully uncomfortable, he thought, and were quite unnecessary. Whose idea had it been, he wondered, to imagine that men would find a caged figure enticing?

And yet Rebecca looked enticing. Her full skirt was arranged neatly about her. Her golden hair was in its usual smooth style. He could remember how it felt spread over his bare arm, and how it smelled. She could be incredibly voluptuous if she chose to be. But then, of course, she would not be Rebecca. It was her very discipline and neatness and even primness that he had always loved.

He had tried so hard to impress her during his boyhood. But Julian had kept on doing thoughtless and sometimes even cruel things, and it had been impossible to break the childhood habit of taking the blame himself so that his father would not turn Julian off—foolish child that he had been ever to have feared that that might happen.

And so she had never been impressed with him. Perhaps he should have done things differently from the start, been more concerned with his own reputation and future prospects. But then he could not go back. It was useless to wish that he could.

They had fallen silent without his even realizing it until he saw her flush and her cup rattled slightly against the saucer as she set it down.

"David," she said, "I should have thought of it in your study earlier when you asked. Perhaps there is one other matter that is urgently in need of doing."

"Yes?" he said.

"Perhaps we should have a new mattress purchased for my chamber," she said. "I have already instructed Mrs. Matthews to throw the other one out. I would be able to move into my own room if it were replaced. Would it be too much of an expense at the moment?''

"You have a room," he said. "The master bedchamber."

"But it is yours," she said. She hesitated. "Where have you been sleeping? Have you made sure that the bed is well aired?''

He got to his feet. "It does not matter where I have been sleeping," he said. "In the library actually. I do not need much sleep. I am restless at night. And I often have bad dreams. I'll have Mrs. Matthews prepare another room for me. Perhaps you would care to see to it?''

She had stood up too. "Yes," she said quietly. Again the hesitation. "David, have I done something to displease you?''

He closed his eyes briefly. Yes, she would see it that way. She did not enjoy sex—with him. She found it repugnant although she had denied doing so. He had felt her steeling herself for the ordeal. And yet she saw it as her duty to provide him access to her body for his pleasure. She had probably been brought up to see that as her most important marriage duty.

"Nothing," he said, forcing himself to walk toward her. "Nothing at all, Rebecca.''

"If I have," she said, "please tell me. I did not mean to upset you the other night. I thought perhaps it would help you to talk. It won't happen again, David. Now that I know you prefer to be left alone, I will not interfere. I know that sometimes it is hard to adjust one's life to the loss of privacy that marriage brings. Marriage is not easy. I can understand that sometimes you would rather be alone. I am trying to learn your ways and your preferences as quickly as I can.''

"And I have no obligation to learn yours?'' His voice was harsher than he had intended it to be.

She bit her lip.

"Marriage is all give by the wife and all take by the husband?" he said. "It makes for a very smooth relationship, I suppose, and a very satisfactory existence for the man.''

She swallowed.

"I do not need to have you debasing yourself for my

sake,'' he said. ''You must have ways and preferences and opinions and feelings too, Rebecca. If you disagree with something I say, then say so. If I tread on your toes, stamp on mine. If I am angry with you, as I am now, yell back at me. Slap me. I have no business being angry with you. You have merely expressed the wish to please me.''

Anger had taken him completely by surprise. There was no cause for it at all. He was quite bewildered by it. It seemed almost that the very qualities for which he had always loved her—her quiet, ladylike submissiveness—were now causing him fury. He wanted her angry with him. He deserved her anger. Perhaps he would feel better if she lashed back at him.

Better about what?

''You have always been difficult to understand, David,'' she said. ''I knew that living with you was not going to be easy, but I thought that after I had married you and taken on the relationship of wife to you it would be a little less difficult. I would know my role and my duties and responsibilities, I thought. But I seem incapable of pleasing you. I am sorry.''

''You are sorry.'' He grabbed her wrist. ''Goddammit, Rebecca. Don't ever be sorry about anything. If it is commands you want from me, then heed that one. Don't ever be sorry. You have nothing to be sorry about.''

''I think,'' she said quietly, ''that you are carrying around terrible demons inside you, David. But I cannot ask what they are. You find it impossible to reveal yourself to anyone else, don't you? Least of all to me.''

''Why least of all to you?'' He released her wrist.

''Because I was Julian's wife,'' she said, ''and you cannot stop blaming yourself for his death, can you? You cannot stop thinking that there must have been some way you could have saved him. I know now why you married me. It puzzled me since you could have waited for love. You might have had almost any woman you wanted. But you married me because you felt guilty about Julian. You thought you owed him something. You thought you owed me something.''

His face was turning cold as if all the blood were draining out of his head. The air he breathed in felt icy.

"Well, it is an accomplished fact now," she said. "You have paid your imagined debt to both Julian and me. We are married. Julian is dead and you and I are married, David. If you do not like having a wife who is determined to live up to her duties, I am sorry. I cannot change to the extent that you ask. I cannot learn to answer you back or to fight with you. I can only be what I have been brought up to be."

God. Oh, God!

"You were a dutiful wife to Julian," he said.

"Yes, I tried."

"And are now a dutiful wife to me."

"Yes, I am trying."

"With one essential difference," he said.

She bit her lip again. "Don't David," she said, her voice pleading. "Please don't. We have been married only a week, but I have held nothing back from you. I am not brooding on the past. The past is gone. I want to be a good wife."

He lifted a hand and cupped one of her cheeks with it. He ran a thumb lightly across her cheek. "You are a good wife, Rebecca," he said. "Far better than I deserve." He laughed softly without feeling any amusement. "It is just that I am a poor husband. I have had less practice than you and I am not sure that even when I have had more I will be better at it."

She leaned her cheek into his hand.

"We have a great deal of work ahead of us," he said. "Both of us. Far more than we expected and far more important than we expected since it involves people rather than things. Let's throw ourselves into it body and soul, shall we, and put off more personal matters until a later date?"

She was silent for a while. "If you wish," she said.

"I do wish," he said. "See about having that room made up. For me. You will continue to occupy the master bedchamber, where you belong."

"If you wish," she said again.

He lowered his hand and crossed the room to the door. "May I escort you to your room?" he asked.

She nodded and came toward him.

"Rebecca," he said, pausing with his hand on the knob

of the door, "it is not because you have done anything to displease me. I don't want you thinking that."

Her nod was almost imperceptible.

She began to find it hard to sleep at night. Sometimes she lay awake simply staring up into the darkness. Sometimes she stood at the window where he had stood that night, until the chill of the room drove her back under the covers. Sometimes she wandered through to her own bedchamber in the darkness, wondering if she would find it easier to sleep there if there were only a bed to sleep on. It was not David's room after all.

She should have been happy. She was after all having the best of both worlds. She had all the advantages of marriage without the single unpleasantness. If David meant what he had said in the drawing room, they were to sleep separately for some long indefinite period. Perhaps forever. It should seem like a dream marriage.

Yet she was not happy. They worked well together in the daytime and even seemed to share something resembling a friendship. They spent a good deal of time in each other's company and never found conversation difficult. But there was nothing to give a personal dimension to their marriage. They were more like business partners than a married couple. It should not have mattered, but it did.

It would not have mattered with Julian, she thought. If Julian for some reason had decided to stop coming to her bed, she would not have fretted. There had been so much closeness during their days, so much love, so much sense of being married. What had happened nightly in her bed had not been necessary to her happiness. Indeed she would have welcomed its absence.

But it did matter, curiously, with David. It was all that bound them together as man and wife. There was no love and no real closeness. She sensed and had occasionally glimpsed the turmoil and the pain that seethed beneath the rather grim surface of David's being, but he would not allow her to come close. The only closeness there had been was the physical union that had happened between them during the first three nights of their marriage.

She had not enjoyed it. But in some strange way, she

realized now that it was no longer happening, she had welcomed it for the bonding it had begun between them. A bonding was needed. Friendship—if there was friendship between them—was not enough. She was not sure it even existed, anyway. Sometimes she thought he hated her. She could certainly provoke him to anger without even doing anything.

She needed it, she realized in some surprise. She needed the reassurance that his lovemaking would bring. The assurance that she was needed, that he did not regret marrying her.

And she did not find it unpleasant. She could not explain to herself why she did not when she did not love him as she had loved Julian and when he took so much longer doing it than Julian ever had. It was not that she enjoyed it at all, but—oh, she found that she missed it after that night when he had left her bed never to return.

Her cheeks burned when the truth finally formulated itself in her conscious mind. She wanted her husband's body. In hers.

She closed her eyes and concentrated on falling asleep—in the large, very empty bed that was David's.

12

Stedwell and London, Autumn, 1856

Life became busy—blessedly so. There were tenants to be visited again and decisions to be made about what repairs were in urgent need of doing and what could wait until at least next spring. There were extensive repairs to be done on the laborers' cottages and the decision to rebuild three of them completely. They would all have to be rebuilt over time—perhaps he would need to make a five-year plan, David thought.

There were rents to lower and wages to raise and adjustments to be made for his projected income during the coming year. Quigley could at least be trusted to deal with those inanimate matters. There were a few growing children to worry about. They were at the age of being able and ready to work but were being forced to go elsewhere to seek employment. David could not take on an endless number of workers for whom there would not be enough to do.

A partial solution came when he looked regretfully at his overgrown gardens one day and realized that if the regular gardeners had extra help with the day-to-day business, like cutting the grass, then they could perhaps deal with some of the more pressing problems. Three sturdy lads were hired from the laborers' cottages, and the regular gardeners began the task of cutting back branches from the trees to the west of the house.

Rebecca did her part. She rehired the former cook, as she had promised, and a young girl to help her and to learn the skills of cooking for a large household. She increased the staff further by hiring three more young girls. The house would look less shabby, she decided, if it were cleaned far more thoroughly than it had been for many years. The three girls were promised that if they

worked hard, they would be recommended for jobs elsewhere in domestic service if and when they were no
longer needed at Stedwell.

Four of the tenants hired older boys to help with the
harvest, able to afford such a luxury with the lowering of
their rents. Their own young children were sent to school.
Rebecca had found the schoolhouse very dilapidated and
the schoolmaster quite demoralized. She had ordered new
supplies and had promised to spend two afternoons a
week at the school, helping with reading classes and with
music and needlework.

She was paying regular calls on the sick and the elderly
and frequently taking baskets of food to the laborers'
cottages. A few of the women began to knit with the
wool she provided. She too spent many of her evenings
at home knitting. She even tried the experiment of getting the knitters together in the schoolroom on the occasional evening, herself included, so that they could
enjoy one another's company as they worked. The women
all seemed to enjoy the novelty of being able to go out,
as their husbands did more often. Once they relaxed more
in her presence, Rebecca found that she learned a great
deal about their lives and dreams and worries.

Other evenings were taken up with visiting or being
visited. They were fortunate enough to have friendly
neighbors. Soon they were dining out, playing cards,
dancing, singing—Rebecca sang, proving to her husband
that she had not lost the voice that had delighted him as
a boy. He went fishing or shooting some afternoons with
one or two of his neighbors. Rebecca often went walking
or driving with some of hers. Stephanie Sharp, in particular, seemed fond of her and liked to admire her fashionable clothes and to copy her regal bearing.

Rebecca and David were busy almost constantly,
sometimes together, more often separate, but always in
harmony with each other. They had become almost
friends after two months of marriage, except that friends
spoke to each other from the heart. They spoke to each
other only about day-to-day concerns.

He wondered about her sometimes. Rebecca carried
her discipline and her dignity about with her like a shield.
Always calm and dignified, always the lady, always busy

and concerned about others—it was impossible to know if she was happy or unhappy or something in between the two extremes. He wondered if she hated him or was indifferent to him or even perhaps was growing to like him. He wondered how deeply she still grieved for Julian.

Sometimes he thought himself a fool for putting an end to the physical side of his marriage and making her into no more than a business partner. But whenever he considered going back to her at nights, he would remember her carefully controlled revulsion and his inability to be content with only what she had to give. Dutiful submission was not enough, he had discovered during those brief nights. If he could not have her love, or at least her affection, then it was better to deny himself his rights altogether.

Besides, there were the dreams. He could not risk any repetition of the strange surges of anger that he had turned against her on two occasions. She had done nothing to deserve his anger. Nothing at all.

He could not ask for a more dutiful wife.

Except that that was not what he wanted.

"I need to speak with you, David," she said one afternoon when they had come back inside the house after waving the rector and his wife on their way from a visit.

He tried to anticipate what it was that was troubling her. Was she going to ask again if she had displeased him? And if she did so, would it be because she wanted him? Or because she felt that duty compelled her to offer herself?

It was not about business. He sensed that immediately. Her back seemed even straighter than usual, if that were possible. Her face looked rather as if it had been carved of marble. He was reminded forcefully and unwillingly of the way she had looked in the shadow of the stairs at Craybourne on his return from war.

She stood still just inside the doors of the library while he closed them carefully. She clasped her hands at waist level.

"What is it?" he asked. He crossed the room to set his back to the fireplace. He was accustomed to talking business with her. He braced himself to treat this—

whatever it was—as one more business dealing. After all they had nothing of a marriage. Only a work relationship.

"I am expecting a child," she said quietly.

He heard each separate word but could not for a few moments connect them into a meaningful whole.

"I wanted to be sure before telling you," she said. "I am sure now. Perhaps I will be able to present you with an heir, David."

"A child." The words scarcely made it past his lips. He remembered telling his father that perhaps he could give her a child. But he had been with her so few times. He had not really thought of it since his marriage.

"And perhaps not." Her face was paler. "If you are pleased about it, don't hope too much, David. I miscarried in the fourth month both times before. I think perhaps it is impossible for me to have children."

He saw her suddenly with eyes that had been deliberately clouded over for almost two months but had been cleared by the few words she had spoken. He saw Rebecca, his love, his wife. Rebecca, womanly and ladylike and elegant in her high-necked, long-sleeved, full-skirted dress. He remembered the feel of her, warm and soft, and the smell of her. He remembered each separate occasion—there had been six in all—when he had planted his seed in her. Including the last.

"Rebecca." He realized that he was whispering and cleared his throat. "Are you all right? Are you well?"

"I am always well," she said. "I do not have to suffer nausea as many other women do. I am fortunate in that. I tire easily, but that is natural."

"You have seen the doctor?" he asked.

"Yes."

He stared wordlessly at her. His seed had taken root in her womb. His child was growing in her—now. His eyes strayed down her body. There was going to be a child that was of both him and her. A new person. Theirs. A child of their marriage. After all it was a real marriage. It had been consummated and it was to be fruitful.

He was going to see his baby at her breast. Perhaps.

"Are you pleased, David?" she asked.

His eyes snapped back to hers. "Pleased?" he said. "Yes."

"Just be prepared," she said. "I may not be able to do this for you. I don't want you to be too disappointed if I miscarry."

I may not be able to do this for you. For a moment he felt a flash of the old anger. She did not want to do it for herself? For them? But it was not a time for irritation. Now that the first shock was passing, he was beginning to feel terror.

"Would you be disappointed?" he asked.

Every part of her remained the same except her eyes. But in her eyes, before she directed them downward toward the carpet, he saw sudden pain that seemed almost to be despair.

"Yes." The one terse word. But she continued after a short pause. "I want a child more than anything else in the world."

A child. Not his or theirs. Just a child.

"I try not to want it too much," she said. "It is a sin to want something too much. I think I must have committed that sin the first two times. I don't expect too much this time. But I felt obliged to tell you, partly because you have a right to know, and partly because you will need to know what is happening when . . ."

"I want you to have expert advice and care," he said harshly. "What did the doctor say?"

"He agreed that there is danger of the same thing happening again," she said, "since it followed the same pattern both times—everything fine until the fourth month and then . . . He advised me to pray. I did not need that advice. I have been praying both morning and night—and every hour of the day, since I began to suspect. But I try not to want it too much."

"I am going to take you to London," he said. "I am going to take you to the best physician. We will leave the day after tomorrow. Tomorrow I will send to warn the servants at Hartington House to prepare it for us. Tell your maid to pack your things."

"David," she said, "we can't leave now. There is so much to do. And there are invitations we have accepted."

"I'll have everything taken care of tomorrow," he said. "You have had a busy afternoon, Rebecca—first the visit to the school and then the rector calling here. You must be tired."

"It is a natural part of my condition," she said. "I don't like to give in to it, David. There is too much to do."

"You will go to your room now," he said, "and lie down until your maid comes to dress you for dinner. And you may close your mouth and leave the words unsaid. That is an order."

She closed her mouth and looked calmly at him. God! He could remember calling on her a few days after her second miscarriage. If that was what she had looked like a few days after, how must she have appeared while it was happening and immediately after? Through the careless taking of his pleasure—and once through the abusive display of his anger—had he forced her to have to go through that again?

She wanted a child more than anything in the world, she had said. Was he to raise her hopes again only to have them dashed by the cruelty of a miscarriage? He clamped his teeth together and felt his jaw harden.

"Yes, David," she said and turned quietly to leave the room. He had to dash across it in order to open the door for her.

"I'll take you up," he said, offering her his arm.

"Thank you,' she said.

Rebecca had miscarried twice. His mother had died in childbed. He felt terror rush cold into his nostrils as he led her silently up the stairs to the door of the room that was no longer his.

They took the morning train for London. Rebecca forced herself to relax and watch the passing scenery. The work at Stedwell would not collapse because they were to be away for two weeks. As David had explained to her, Mr. Quigley and Mrs. Matthews were both loyal and capable servants and would do an exemplary job now that there were definite directions for them to follow.

But she did not like leaving Stedwell behind. She felt

as if she really belonged there. She had never had a
chance to feel a sense of belonging during her first marriage since Julian had so impulsively followed David into
the Guards and they had had no fixed home. He had
needed her, of course. He had often told her that he would
not be able to live without her. She had belonged to him
and had felt wonderfully needed.

It was a need that was not there in David. He needed
her for Stedwell but not for himself. He had shown that
in two months of marriage. There was no closeness, no
union. Not even the affection he had once told her he
hoped for. There had to be some sharing of selves in
order for there to be affection. David shared nothing of
himself. She glanced at him seated next to her in the
railway carriage, reading his newspaper. He was always so controlled, so austere. He had permitted her
only rare glimpses of the man within—and none vol-
untarily.

He felt her eyes on him and looked up. "You are all
right, Rebecca?" he asked.

She nodded and smiled.

"You are not cold?" he asked. "Or tired? Would you
like to lie down?"

"I am fine, David," she said.

His eyes stayed on her for a few moments and then he
returned his attention to his paper.

He had refused to allow her to deliver food baskets the
morning before and had insisted that she lie down for an
hour after luncheon and again for an hour before they
went to the Mantrells' for dinner. She hated being idle—
there had been so much idleness in her life. But she had
been touched by his concern. And by this—taking her to
London to consult a physician when there was a doctor
in the village at Stedwell.

She had thought in the first rush of bitterness after she
had got up the courage to break the news to him that
perhaps his concern was not so much for her as for his
unborn child. It might, after all, be a son and he must
want a son as heir to both Stedwell and Craybourne after
him. Heir to a viscount's title and eventually to an earldom. But she had admitted to herself almost immediately
that the thought was unworthy of her. David had been

unfailingly courteous to her from the start—with two memorable exceptions. Besides, she was convinced that what she had said to him that afternoon in the drawing room almost two months before was right. He had married her because he blamed himself for Julian's death and felt he owed her his protection.

Yes, his concern was as much for her as for his child. Her health would be of some concern to him.

But she still felt as bitter now as she had felt two days ago. She could remember Julian's reaction on the two occasions when she had given him similar news. He had been boyishly overjoyed, lifting her off her feet the first time and spinning her around until they were both dizzy and laughing helplessly, hugging her to take her breath away the second time.

David had not moved from his position in front of the fireplace until it was time to escort her to her room. His expression had neither softened nor changed. She had had to ask him if he was pleased. He had said yes, and he had shown concern for her health—to such an extent that he was bringing her to London for a fortnight, perhaps longer if the physician felt it necessary for her to stay. But—oh, there had been so much missing.

She had not realized until she was alone in her room—in what should have been his room—just how much she had hoped that her news would break down some of the barriers between them. She had longed for him to smile, for those blue eyes of his to warm, for . . . Yes, foolish woman that she was, she had even longed for him to take her in his arms and tell her without any prompting at all how pleased he was about the baby, how pleased he was with her.

She had wanted him to see her terror about miscarrying. She had not even tried to hide it. She had needed his arms then. But all she had got was his voice, sounding almost harsh, dealing with the possibility as a practical problem. She appreciated his concern. But at that moment it was the emotional problem she had wanted dealing with. She had needed his arms, and his voice against her ear, assuring her that it would not happen, that he would not let it happen. She had wanted comfort and make-believe.

And then she had been alone in her room, escorted there by her husband with the command to rest—and abandoned at the door. Did he have no feelings? No understanding of how much she had needed him to stay with her? If he had lain down with her and held her in his arms . . .

What a very foolish idea, she thought. David? David holding her in his arms? Tenderness between her and David? It was not David she needed. The thought came to her on an unaccustomed wave of self-pity, and guilt stabbed at her at the same moment. It was Julian she wanted. Julian's arms.

Julian!

She closed her eyes and swallowed several times. She fought guilt. She had promised not to think of him, and though David had released her from the promise, she had tried to keep it to herself. And yet she was aching with grief again. She focused her thoughts on the child growing in her womb. Not Julian's child this time. David's. But much-loved and much-wanted anyway. Oh, very much wanted. *Please,* she prayed silently. *Please, please. Oh, please.*

She was in the pleasant drifting world that preceded sleep when an arm slid behind her neck and drew her head down against a broad and firm shoulder. She snuggled into it gratefully without opening her eyes or letting go of the drowsiness that her pregnancy was making so insistent these days.

She was sleeping by the time David turned his head and kissed her temple.

Sir Rupert Bedwell was reputed to be the best ladies' physician in London. It was to his offices that David took his wife by appointment two days after their arrival in London.

It was his opinion, Sir Rupert told them after subjecting Rebecca to a thorough examination, that Lady Tavistock's womb was of the rare type that rejected an unborn child at a certain size and weight, usually from some time late in the third month to the end of the fourth. It would not be easy to extend a pregnancy beyond that time, but if it could be done, then all would probably be well.

"And how might it be done?" David asked. His wife was pale and silent. He guessed that the physical examination which she had just endured had been a humiliating ordeal for her as well as this conversation about her body and its functions.

The doctor shrugged. "I would not fill either of you with false hope," he said. "I am afraid the chances are high that Lady Tavistock will miscarry this time as she did twice before. If that happens, I would not advise further pregnancies, though they are not always easily avoided."

Rebecca's face was suffused with color suddenly. David clenched his teeth.

"There is nothing to be done, then?" he said. "Beyond praying, as our local doctor has advised?"

"Lady Tavistock's best hope," Sir Rupert said, "is to minimize the downward weight of the unborn child during the danger period. Complete bed rest, in other words. And a great deal of rest and little exertion even before that."

"But still the danger is high." Rebecca spoke for the first time. It was not a question.

"Yes, my lady," Sir Rupert said.

"Thank you for your candor," she said.

"Perhaps," he said, rising as she and David did, "I might have a word with you, my lord? I will keep him for but a moment, my lady."

He closed the door after Rebecca had stepped out into the reception room. "I would advise, my lord," he said, "that you forgo exercising your conjugal rights until your lady is safely delivered of a child or until she had had two or three months during which to recover from a miscarriage."

David drew a slow breath. "I understand," he said. "Like my wife, I thank you for your candor."

"After all," the doctor said, smiling in sympathy, "there are alternatives, aren't there, my lord?"

"Are there?" David, his voice and eyes cold, resisted the sudden urge to plant his fist between the man's smiling eyes.

There were a few brief shopping trips during the coming week and one short visit to the National Gallery. There were several visits with Lord and Lady Meerscham, Rebecca's brother and sister-in-law, since they happened to be in town. They attended the theater one evening after dining with a colonel of the Guards and his lady. But David had no intention of involving Rebecca in a social whirl. If their child was to be saved, then he would do all in his power to see that it happened.

By the time they were within four days of returning to Stedwell, they had entertained several afternoon callers. But they were alone after tea on the afternoon the butler brought in yet another card on a tray.

David held it in his hand and felt himself grow cold as he read the name.

"Who is it?" Rebecca asked.

"Yet another Guardsman," he said. "Now sold out, like me. I will entertain him alone if you wish to go upstairs to rest, Rebecca."

"No," she said. "I like meeting your former comrades. I know so little about that part of your life. Have I met him before?"

"No." He nodded to the butler to admit their guest. "He was with the Coldstreams, not the Grenadiers." He felt horribly out of control of the moment.

Sir George Scherer came striding into the drawing room a minute later, beaming cordially, one hand outstretched. He had put on weight. His complexion seemed even more florid than it had been. "Major Tavistock," he said. "I could hardly believe my luck when I heard just this morning that you were in town. I have been meaning to look you up. I came around as soon as I could extricate myself from another engagement."

"Scherer," David shook his hand. "Rebecca, I would like you to meet Sir George Scherer. We served in the Crimea together."

"Your wife?" Sir George asked as Rebecca inclined her head to him and smiled. "I am charmed, ma'am. Your husband deserves such beauty, I must say. I owe my life to him. Has he ever told you? It was at Inkerman. We . . ."

"My wife," David said very distinctly, "was Captain Sir Julian Cardwell's widow. You may remember him."

Sir George's mouth remained open for a moment before he recovered himself. "Cardwell?" he said, his eyes narrowing. "Yes, of course. He was killed at Inkerman, wasn't he? My condolences, ma'am, though it was a long time ago."

"You knew him?" she said. "You were at Inkerman too, Sir George? Perhaps you . . ." She flushed. "David saved your life?"

"I had a Russian's bayonet at my throat," he said. "Your husband shot him through the heart as cool as you please, ma'am. On the slopes of the Kitspur it was in the middle of a dense fog. I was never so glad to see a British greatcoat in my life." He laughed heartily.

"The Kitspur," she said. "It was where—my first husband was killed. Where he is buried."

"Yes, ma'am," he said. "He was a brave man. He held the heights according to orders after most of the rest of us had broken ranks and gone down, and then he brought his men down to rescue us. He gave his life in the process."

"Yes," Rebecca said into the silence that followed his words. "I had heard that he was a hero."

David felt as if he could not have moved or spoken to save his life. If Scherer was going to invent a story, could he not have checked with David first?

"Lady Scherer and I would be delighted to have you both dine with us tomorrow evening," Sir George said. "If you have no other engagement, that is. I came to invite Major Tavistock alone, but this is altogether better. Cynthia will be delighted to make your acquaintance, ma'am."

"My wife has been indisposed," David said.

"Oh, but I would love to go," she said, looking at him, her cheeks flushed, her eyes bright. "May we, David?"

He inclined his head. The nightmare was intruding into the real world again. It could no longer be held behind the boundaries of sleep. "Thank you, Scherer," he said. "You will give me your direction before you leave."

"May we offer you tea or other refreshments?" Rebecca asked.

But Sir George knew that his call had been made after teatime and apologized for coming so late. He had done so merely to issue the invitation. He did not stay beyond a couple more minutes.

By the time he had seen Sir George to the door, David found that Rebecca had retired to her room for her usual rest before dinner.

13

Rebecca dressed carefully for the visit to the Scherers, wearing a green silk evening dress she had had made for her trousseau and had worn for only one dinner and dance at Stedwell. There was something exciting about meeting a man who had known Julian and fought with him. There were a thousand questions she wanted to ask Sir George Scherer, though she knew she was going to have to be discreet. She must not show an overeagerness to hear about Julian in David's presence—or out of it, for that matter.

And yet her hands stilled as she clasped a string of pearls about her neck. Julian? David had been in the Crimea too. She was hungry for knowledge about that time in his life. Apart from what he had said on the evening of his return to Craybourne, when she had been too preoccupied with her own pain to listen attentively, he had shown a marked reluctance to talk about the Crimean War. It was understandable, she supposed, especially in light of the fact that he had nightmares about his experiences there. But she longed to know more. If she only knew what he had lived through during those years, she sometimes thought, she would have the key to knowing him and understanding him. Though she had never known or understood David, even when he was a boy. He had never allowed her to.

"You saved Sir George Scherer's life?" she asked him at the dinner after the baronet's visit.

He had shrugged. "I probably saved a hundred men's lives," he had said, "and a hundred men probably saved mine. Fighting a war is a communal effort, Rebecca. Men look out for their comrades as well as for themselves when every moment can and does bring death."

And yet Sir George had seemed to feel particularly indebted to David. She longed to discover that David had been as much of a hero at the Battle of Inkerman as Julian had been. She had always been so intent on seeing Julian as a hero that she had somewhat ignored David's efforts in the same battle. And yet he had been gravely wounded there. She wanted him to have been a hero there too as he had been later, after Julian's death.

And yet there was something strange. She frowned into the dimness of the carriage that was conveying them to Scherers' leased house on Portman Place. David's tone at dinner had been so dismissive that the topic had died a quick death. And today he had left home after breakfast and not returned until a couple of hours ago. He had commanded her to spend the day quietly at home and she had done so, despite the fact that she had been planning to call on Denise during the afternoon.

He sat beside her now, looking morose. He did not want reminders of that time in his life, it seemed, even pleasant ones, and out of sheer instinct she almost stretched out a hand toward him. But she stopped herself in time. One did not do such things with David.

They were the only dinner guests of the Scherers. Sir George was as effusive in his greeting as he had been the day before. Lady Scherer was a great deal more reserved—and very beautiful. Rebecca admired her petite figure in a dark wine red evening gown, and her very dark hair and eyes.

"Lady Tavistock, you will remember I told you," Sir George said to his wife, looking down into her face, "was married to Captain Cardwell. You remember him Cynthia."

"You knew Julian too?" Rebecca asked, her eyes widening.

"Yes, we had an acquaintance," Cynthia Scherer said.

"You went abroad with your husband," Rebecca said, the envy in her voice unmistakable. "How fortunate you were. I would have given anything in the world to go too, but Julian did not believe my health would stand it. I have always regretted those lost months."

She was aware suddenly of David standing silently beside her. She smiled at Lady Scherer and hoped that someone would change the subject. But she ached with the longing to ask question upon question. It was a relief when Sir George moved away to pour them drinks and Lady Scherer began a polite discussion of the weather.

But the conversation moved inevitably back to the Crimea during dinner. At first Rebecca welcomed the fact. She drank in every detail, trying not to ask questions, trying not to make obvious her thirst for knowledge. But Sir George seemed to sense it.

"Tell Lady Tavistock what you remember of Captain Cardwell during those months, my love," he instructed his wife. "Another woman can probably remember details that would escape the memory of mere males. Eh, Major?" He laughed heartily.

"I scarcely knew him," Lady Scherer said. "I do remember that he was very popular with both his fellow officers and his men. He seemed to possess the rare gift of being always cheerful."

"Yes." Rebecca leaned forward, forgetting everyone else at the table for the moment. "He was always like that, even as a boy."

"And he was charming to the ladies," Sir George said. "Come now, you must admit that, Cynthia."

"Everyone always loved him," Rebecca said. She turned her head sharply suddenly. "Didn't they, David?"

"Rebecca and I are partial, of course," David said. "Julian and I grew up as brothers. Rebecca was his wife. You sold out of the army after being wounded, Scherer? How has civilian life been treating you?"

"Oh, it can be a little tedious at times," Sir George said. "Cynthia misses the excitement of army life, don't you, my love? Some wives do, Lady Tavistock. It gets into the blood, you know."

"You were fortunate that your husband survived," Rebecca said, smiling at Cynthia Scherer. "What a great relief that must have been to you."

"Thanks to your husband," Sir George said, raising his wineglass. "My wife owes my survival to him. We must drink a toast to Major Tavistock, my love. Will you join us, Lady Tavistock?"

Rebecca lifted her glass and smiled at David. "He tells me that saving lives is commonplace in battle," she said.

"Modesty, Lady Tavistock," Sir George said, laughing. "Your husband is too modest by half. That sword had already incapacitated my right arm—I will carry the scars to my grave—and was within a second or less of piercing my chest. Your husband shot the blackguard through the heart. He was dead before he hit the ground. A steadier aim I have never seen."

"I think," David said, "that the ladies would prefer a more cheerful topic of conversation."

"Modesty, you see, Lady Tavistock?" Sir George said, laughing. "It embarrasses him to be proclaimed a hero. Cynthia never ceases to sing his praises, do you my love? Let's drink that toast."

David's eyes remained on his plate as they lifted their glasses to their lips and drank.

Rebecca did not like Sir George Scherer. She had at first and could not quite understand why she did not now. He was jovial and friendly and kept bringing the conversation back to topics she craved to hear talked about. David had saved his life and he was obviously brimful of gratitude. But there was something.

There was an atmosphere. As if the three of them were privy to some secret that she knew nothing about. In reality, of course, it was just that she felt like an outsider since the three of them shared experiences and memories that were denied her. That was all it was. But that was not it either. Not quite. There was an atmosphere.

David and Lady Scherer rarely spoke. Or smiled. They never either looked at each other or spoke to each other, Rebecca realized at last when they had all moved to the drawing room for coffee. But then they had had little chance. Sir George Scherer was the type of man who liked to dominate the conversation. All the rest of them needed to do was to respond on cue.

That must be why she disliked him. And why the others disliked him too—she realized in some shock that it was so. Even his wife disliked him. It was difficult to like a man to whom others were nothing more than an audience. Not people to be understood and listened to, but anonymous members of an audience. There were such men—and women too, probably—and Sir George Scherer was one of them.

Yes, that was it. It was a relief to have analyzed what was wrong with the evening and with herself and her three companions. She was glad of the chance to stroll across the room with Lady Scherer to admire a display of china and to become involved in a purely feminine conversation about fashion.

But the respite did not last long.

"How wonderful it is to see you making friends so easily, my love," Sir George said to his wife. He had come up behind them, David with him. "My wife is rather shy with other ladies, Lady Tavistock. Perhaps it is because her father is in trade, though I have assured her more times than I can recall that such a fact means nothing nowadays. Or perhaps it is because she spent so many years surrounded by men. I sometimes believe she finds it easier to be with men than with women."

He was also vulgar, Rebecca thought. He could have phrased that last sentence differently. A gentleman would have chosen his words with more care.

"We have been deciding that the crinoline is a silly fashion," she said lightly. "We have decided that if we had our way we would return to the days of the Regency and wear those lovely loose, comfortable dresses."

Sir George chuckled.

"Ladies enjoy talking about fashion," Rebecca said firmly before he could launch into a speech. "Don't we, Lady Scherer?"

"You must call my wife Cynthia," Sir George said. "You must see more of each other during the coming days."

"We are here for only a brief stay," David said. "We will be returning to Stedwell soon."

"Stedwell," Sir George said. "In Gloucestershire?"

David inclined his head.

"Cynthia's father lives in the city of Gloucester," Sir George said. "Not a stone's throw from the cathedral. We often visit, don't we, my love? We must call on you one of these times."

"You will be very welcome," Rebecca said, smiling at Lady Scherer.

"Thank you," she said. "We do not go often."

Sir George chuckled. ''You see how wives make liars of us, Major?'' he said.

It was a great relief to Rebecca when she and David were finally in the carriage on the way home. It had been a mistake, she thought, to look forward to hearing more about that missing part of Julian's life. And a mistake to try to pry into David's heroism when he had not wanted to talk about it himself. The evening had been far from successful.

But she felt amused more than anything now that it was all over. She wanted to turn to David and laugh with him over the strange character of Sir George Scherer. She wanted to ask him if he had ever regretted saving the man's life. But she realized, as she turned her head to look at him in the darkness of the coach interior, that the joke would be in very bad taste. Perhaps he would not see it as a joke at all. He was looking grim enough.

And that atmosphere was back again, though they were away from the house on Portman Place and were alone together on their way home. That quite indefinable atmosphere that filled her with unease. And so she said nothing at all about the evening. They traveled most of the way through the streets of London in silence.

''I want you to stay in bed all morning tomorrow, Rebecca,'' David said quietly when they were close to home. ''We will take the afternoon train back to Stedwell.''

''Tomorrow?'' she said. ''I thought we were not going until Friday.''

''I want you at home,'' he said, ''where you can relax properly. There is nothing further to stay here for.''

''Horace and Denise are coming to dinner tomorrow evening,'' she said.

''I will send our excuses,'' he said. ''They will understand. They both know about your condition. We will go home tomorrow afternoon—after you have had a good rest.''

''Yes, all right, David,'' she said.

She was enormously relieved. Suddenly she wanted to be back home. At home there was so much to do. At home there were no silences with David. There was always something to be discussed. At home they were friends. Yes, it was not an exaggeration. They were—friends.

She felt desperate to be away from this atmosphere. It was just London, that was all. City life did not suit them. There was too much idleness there, not enough to do. That was all that was wrong. And now that dreadful man had accentuated it all. The atmosphere would be gone once they had left London behind.

"It will be good to be home," she said.

He looked at her for the first time. "Yes," he said. "Yes, it will."

She wanted him to take her hand in his. But of course he did not.

It was amazing how quickly a place could come to feel like home. Stedwell had been David's all his life, but he had lived there for only the past two months. Yet when he stepped from the train with Rebecca and found the same shabby, old-fashioned carriage waiting for them as had met them on their wedding day, it seemed to David a wonderful homecoming. And his heart lifted even further when he had his first sight of Stedwell and it looked unmistakably like home—still with its neglected air, except that branches no longer obscured the western windows and there were no daisies blooming in the grass beyond the river and the bridge—and the lion had been put back on its pillar at the gateway.

He felt bruised and battered after less than two weeks away. The doctor had been unable to give them either the reassurances or the cure he had hoped for. It appeared that Rebecca was almost certain to lose her child again. The thought was an agony to him. He felt a fierce longing for this child, the only really personal link between them, the only remnant of an intimacy they had shared all too briefly. And he felt an even more fierce longing to see Rebecca happy. He could not forget how her eyes had looked when she had told him that she wanted a child more than anything else in the world.

He felt a huge relief to be away from London and the dreadful unease it had brought. To have encountered George Scherer of all people! Just one sight of the man's face had brought it all flooding back. He had remembered the last sight he had had of that face. And Cynthia Scherer with whom Julian had amused himself in Rebecca's absence!

It had been ghastly. He had hoped never to set eyes on them again. He supposed now that he had always been aware of the possibility that their paths would cross. But if he ever had considered it, he had assumed that Scherer would be as reluctant as he to have any memories dredged to the surface again. The man had to live with the memory that his wife had been unfaithful to him.

Yet Scherer had seemed anything but reluctant. It had become quickly obvious to David that the man's motive in inviting him and Rebecca to dinner was to humiliate and punish his wife. If he did feel deep gratitude, it had been somehow swallowed up in something else once he had met Rebecca and learned of her relationship to Julian. It was clear too that Cynthia Scherer had not been spared the truth as Rebecca had. She knew that he had killed her lover and saved her husband's life. She was being punished with him too during that ghastly evening.

He and Rebecca had not referred to it since.

They fell gratefully back into the pattern their days had followed at Stedwell since their marriage, except that he would no longer allow Rebecca to go about as much—and soon she would not be able to go about at all or rise from her bed for longer than a few minutes at a time. He intended to be adamant about that, though he did not believe that he would have to be. Although they did not speak about it, he knew that they were both determined to do everything possible to save their child.

"I am going to have to find something with which to occupy my hands and my mind," she told him at luncheon one day after she had been lamenting the fact that she had had to watch the cook's assistant set out with food baskets for four of the cottages during the morning before retiring to bed herself. "I feel very useless and restless, David. Would it be a good idea to make curtains for the schoolroom, do you think? It looks very stark and bare as it is. I could do that, couldn't I?"

"Yes," he said, "until it comes time to lie down completely." He was pleased that she was not willing to give in to boredom, though he wondered how she would cope with a whole month spent in bed—if the whole month proved necessary. He did not want to pursue that thought. There were numerous neighbors, of course, who would be only too pleased to come and keep her company. They all soon knew of her condition.

And so she sent for material and set about her task with a will. But it did not stop there.

"David," she said to him at tea about a week later after he had arrived home to find Lady Sharp and Stephanie about to leave and had escorted them downstairs and seen them on their way, "I have had an idea. I think it will work and it will solve several problems. It will involve a little expenditure, though."

Rebecca always seemed to hate broaching the subject of money, just as if she believed them to be paupers after the rental reductions and the raise in wages.

"Is the tea cold?" he asked, pouring himself a cup. "What is the idea?"

"Probably not cold, but thoroughly stewed," she said, looking with distaste at the dark brown liquid in his cup. "I shall ring for more, David."

But he held up a hand when she would have got to her feet. "What expenditure?" he asked, helping himself to sugar.

"I thought," she said, "that I could gradually start replacing some of the shabbier curtains in the house. They will not cost so much if I make them myself. Though they will cost a little more if I employ a few of the women and girls to help. Miriam Phelps, for example. She is always bemoaning the fact that there is no employment for women in these parts, David, except for the few jobs at the house here. So many of the girls end up in towns where there are factories. It is a dreadful life for them. I could keep a few more of them employed at the house here for a long time, and they would be learning a skill."

He thought for a moment but could find no flaw with her plan.

"And I would enjoy the company," she said, "just as I have enjoyed my evenings with the knitting group. Just for a few mornings a week, David?"

"Afternoons," he said. "You have heard my opinion on your being up and about in the mornings."

"For a few afternoons, then," she said. "Perhaps I could begin with the smaller windows upstairs."

"That," he said, "is your domain. I shall leave all the plans in your hands. The new cottages are almost finished—in good time before winter. They look remarkably cozy. I must have three more put up next year, I think."

He sat down with his cool, overstrong tea and they settled into a familiar and thoroughly comfortable pattern of conversation. If he could just keep his thoughts under control, he could consider himself quite contented, even happy.

But thoughts, of course, cannot be so easily controlled. He wondered unwillingly how she and Julian must have behaved together during her two pregnancies. They had never behaved any differently than usual in public, of course. They had both been too well-bred for that, especially Rebecca. But in private they must have shared their dreams and hopes for the child that would be theirs. They must have shared their fears the second time. Their love must have been deepened by their knowledge of her condition.

Except that Julian had slept with other women during Rebecca's pregnancies—as the doctor had hinted that he, David, might do. He felt a flash of the old fury against Julian.

Nothing was changed between him and Rebecca. He wanted to talk about the baby, about the excitement but he could not dare give rein to it. He wanted to hear about the fears he knew she had bottled up inside her unfailingly calm exterior. He wanted to hold her and comfort her even if there was no real comfort to give. He wanted them to share the hopes and the agonies.

But all they could talk about was the building of new cottages and the sewing of new curtains.

"David," she said, "that tea must taste quite dreadful. You should have let me order more."

She was quite right. He set down the half-empty cup and got to his feet. "Time for your rest," he said.

"It is always time for my rest." She smiled at him.

She stood up and took his arm. It had become a daily ritual for him to escort her to the door of her room after tea. He wondered suddenly how she would react if he stooped down and lifted her into his arms to carry her upstairs. He would take her right into the bedchamber and set her down on the bed—the bed where his child had been conceived. And he would draw the covers over her and kiss her warmly on the lips before leaving her to her sleep.

He walked quietly up the stairs, her arm through his, and opened the door into the master bedchamber for her. He closed it behind her, just as he always did.

Rebecca awaited the coming of the end of November with dread. She would be going into her fourth month. And she could no longer even begin to pretend that it did not matter greatly to her, that she would not be able to mourn too deeply a life that had never existed independently of her body.

The fact was that it did exist. Inside her. Dependent upon her. Deeply, deeply loved. It took on more reality as the dreaded fourth month approached. There was movement, and her stomach and abdomen became soft and a little flabby. She had not lost her figure the other two times, but this time she was beginning to feel and look pregnant already. Her breasts were larger and tender to touch. She tried not to imagine what it must feel like to have a baby suckling them.

She took the unprecedented step of leaving off the tight stays beneath her dresses and hoping that the fact would not be too noticeable. Soon it would not matter. Soon she would be in bed and would not need to dress.

Her need for David's arms became a physical torment. But the more she felt it, the more resolutely she kept herself from giving him any sign. He had married her so that she would help him, and she had married him on that understanding. She had wanted to be needed, not to need. She drew comfort from the fact that he was even more insistent than she thought necessary that she rest. She drew comfort from being obedient to his every command even when it meant leaving her girls and women to work alone on the bedroom curtains twice a week while she worked with them and directed them on two other afternoons. If he considered that even sewing was too much of an exertion for her, then she would not sew.

But she dreaded the fourth month. She dreaded those first signs and the growing certainty and the birth that was not a birth but only its opposite. She dreaded the death of her child. She wondered how far along into the fourth month it would be before it happened. Would fate tease her and withhold it until almost the end?

She was not sure she would not be able to go through the month without revealing her need for comforting arms. She wondered how he would react if she crumbled.

Please, dear God, let me not crumble.

Please, God. Oh, please. Just this once. Just this once. Please.

When she came downstairs at her usual late hour one morning, the butler directed her to the study, where his lordship was waiting to have a word with her.

"Louisa is coming," he told her after he had seated her. He handed her a letter from the desk. "I was not sure her own condition would allow her to travel, but I asked anyway. Papa is bringing her tomorrow. They will stay for a few weeks, perhaps until Christmas."

"You asked her to come?" she said, looking up at him in wonder.

"You are going to need company," he said. "Someone you feel comfortable with and can confide in. Someone who can be at the house all the time. You and she were close friends. You must stay in bed soon, Rebecca. Starting the day after tomorrow, in fact."

"Yes," she said. She held the letter against her bosom. "Thank you, David. You are very kind."

He looked at her, a frown on his face. He looked as if he was about to say something, but he changed his mind. He walked over to the desk and busied himself with the papers on it, his back to her.

"Louisa will be company for you," he said.

Yes, she would. Rebecca felt a rush of longing for the next day to come quickly. It would be wonderful to see her friend again. To have someone to talk to, not just about business matters.

She would scarcely see David during the coming month, she thought suddenly. He never came into the master bedroom. She gazed at his back as she got to her feet to leave the study. Just a few months ago she had dreaded seeing him again. She had found it hard to stop herself from wishing that it had been he who was dead rather than Julian. Just a few months ago she had disliked him and thought it would be quite impossible to marry him and live the rest of her life with him.

It seemed a long time since she had felt that way. She could never love him, of course. She could never feel the bliss of married love that she had felt with Julian. But she would not reverse her decision now if she could. She liked being married to David. If only it were a real marriage. If only he had thought of giving her his own company instead of Louisa's.

But she felt gratitude nonetheless. He was not completely insensitive to her emotional needs.

"You will be happy to see your father again, David," she said.

He turned to look at her. "Yes," he said. "I want to show off all that we have accomplished in three months, Rebecca. Clean chimneys and new curtains in several of the bedrooms." He gave her one of his rare smiles.

A smile that left her feeling unexpectedly happy as she went to consult the cook about a special menu for to-morrow's dinner.

14

Rebecca did not know quite what she would have done without Louisa in the coming weeks. The month of her confinement to bed coincided with a return of energy, the tiredness of the early months having quite passed into history. It was akin to torture to lie in bed all day long and then all night long.

Louisa was seven months pregnant when she arrived at Stedwell with the earl. Although she insisted on walking outside for at least half an hour each day, leaning heavily on her husband's arm, she assured Rebecca that she felt heavy and lethargic and that it was no sacrifice at all to spend hours of each day sitting in the latter's bedroom. She busied herself with various needlework projects while she did so.

At Louisa's suggestion the women and girls who were working on the new draperies brought their work to the bedroom on a few occasions. Rebecca read aloud to them while they sewed, something she had done occasionally downstairs after discovering that they were eager to listen to stories. The arrangement worked well after Rebecca's initial embarrassment at being seen in bed by the woman had passed together with their giggling self-consciousness. Her knitting group also appeared on occasion, bringing with them a shawl for her they had all helped knit, and some little cakes Mrs. Shaw had baked.

The neighboring ladies all came to call, some of them more than once. They brought her news of her various committees and of the school and church. The schoolchildren were preparing a Christmas play and concert and were disappointed to know that Lady Tavistock would be unable to play the pianoforte for them. Louisa offered to take her place.

The earl came to tea on several afternoons.

David came twice a day, to Rebecca's surprise and delight. He came after breakfast each morning to stand beside the bed for a few minutes while he inquired after her health. And he came before dinner in the evening and sometimes sat talking for half an hour or longer. He kept her informed of what was going on in the house and on the estate, with the result that she felt less out of touch than she might otherwise have felt.

She was very fortunate, Rebecca concluded. But even so the days were long and the nights endless. There were inevitably long hours when she was alone with herself and her thoughts. And her fears. Long hours in which to wonder if it was all going to be worth it. She hardly dared hope that it might.

She read a great deal. But even the pleasures of reading could pall when there was little else to do night or day but read. She found herself staring upward for much of the time, her thoughts ranging over topics that her self-discipline normally kept locked away from her conscious mind. She had not even realized that she did such a thing until the thoughts surfaced and she found herself frightened yet unable to suppress them again.

Julian had led the charge down the Kitspur hill, David had said. He had been a great hero, a mere captain going out ahead of a major and perhaps officers of even higher rank. Julian had held the line at the top of the hill, Sir George Scherer had said, and gone down the hill only later to rescue those who had participated in the charge. Who was right? David or Sir George? Perhaps what David had meant was that Julian had led the rescue. Perhaps he had deliberately made it sound as if Julian had been more heroic than was in fact the case. He had wanted to comfort her.

It did not matter anyway. All must have been confusion during the battle. Perhaps both men believed what they had said, and really their stories were not vastly different. Anyway, Julian was just as dead no matter who was right. Except that she would prefer to believe David's story. And so she tended to believe Sir George's. But it did not matter.

But thinking about the discrepancies between the two

stories set her to thinking about that evening at Sir George Scherer's, an evening she would be just as happy to forget. She was not particularly sure why. She had not liked Sir George himself, but he had been perfectly amiable as had Lady Scherer, and the food had been good.

But there had been that atmosphere. It made Rebecca uneasy even now, weeks later. There had been something, something she had not been able to put her finger on at the time. Something she had not wanted to understand, maybe. But something she could not leave alone now that she had thought of it again.

Lady Scherer did not like her own husband. Rebecca had sensed it though there had been no outer sign. What she realized only now when she looked back on that ghastly evening was that Sir George did not like Lady Scherer either. He had called her "my love" several times, but in reality he hated her. Rebecca frowned and slid a pillow out from beneath her head to try to shake a greater softness back into it. Where had that idea come from? What had made her think that Sir George hated his wife? *Hated?*

There was no evidence at all. She was becoming fanciful. What she should do was try writing a story or even a whole book so that her imagination could run riot and produce a fictitious tale that would harm no one. A Gothic romance, maybe.

David and Lady Scherer had felt very uncomfortable in each other's presence. They had scarcely looked at each other or exchanged a word all evening. Rebecca had noticed it at the time and had carefully locked away the memory from her conscious mind. Why would they feel such an awkwardness? They had met before and should have had some common experiences to use as a basis of conversation. Even if they had never met and had had nothing in common, each had had experience in making polite conversation with strangers.

No, there had been an awareness between them. A discomfort caused by the added presence of her husband and—his wife?

Yes, there it was, Rebecca thought at last, grasping the pillow again, yanking it out from beneath her head, and tossing it to the floor. Now she had done it. She could not leave well enough alone. It was none of her business. It had all happened long before she and David married or even thought of doing so. It had happened probably while Julian was still alive.

David and Lady Scherer had been lovers.

She had no evidence whatsoever for the conclusion she had just drawn and despised herself for jumping to it so hastily. But she knew it was true. Because she did not want it to be true, she knew that it was. She had never wanted bad things about David to be true, but they always had been.

He had had an affair with another man's wife.

Rebecca wondered if Julian had known and how he had reacted. He had always made light of David's iniquities, telling her that David was good at heart and she must not judge him on a few little incidents that were really of no consequence at all. Except that some of them had been of great consequence. Like Flora Ellis's pregnancy.

Had Julian tried to remonstrate with David, tried to get him to give up Lady Scherer?

It did not matter, Rebecca told herself firmly. What David had done before he was her husband was really none of her business. Besides, she did not know for sure. The evidence on which her conviction was based was fragile at best. Perhaps she was doing him a great injustice. But she knew she was not.

She picked up a book and waited impatiently for Louisa's return from her daily walk.

But the poisonous thoughts would not leave her alone. She woke up in the middle of one night so suddenly that she held her breath and waited in some alarm for the pain and the pushing sensation that she had been expecting and preparing herself for ever since she first suspected that she was with child. But there was no pain.

Sir George Scherer hated David too. That was the thought that had woken her up? It was a stupid thought. It must have woven itself into one of those dreams that have no relation to reality at all. Sir George owed his life to David and made no secret of the fact. He had called on them and invited them to dinner so that he could express his gratitude.

Rebecca turned over onto her side, running her hand down over the unmistakable swelling of her abdomen and trying to keep her emotions detached from the child that was growing inside her. She closed her eyes and tried to duck down beneath the cover of sleep again.

He hated David, nevertheless.

He knew.

He had invited them to dinner so that he could taunt both David and his wife.

David had said that it was commonplace for soldiers to save one another's lives during battle. There was nothing extraordinary about the fact that David had shot the Russian soldier who had been about to bayonet Sir George. Sir George had made it seem extraordinary only so that he could bring David and Lady Scherer face-to-face again under uncomfortable circumstances.

It was ridiculous, Rebecca thought impatiently. How foolish she was, making up a story in her head that was pure fiction and yet that maligned real people.

But it was true. She felt that it was true.

It was all in the past anyway. It was none of her business. She must forget it. But she could not get back to sleep for a long time. And then just when drowsiness was finally taking a welcome hold of her mind, her eyes popped open once more.

It had been a bayonet in the first telling. The Russian had been a soldier with a bayonet, Sir George had said— a private soldier. In the second telling the would-be killer had been wielding a sword—an officer. There was quite a difference between the two versions. Even allowing for the confusion of battle, there was quite a difference. Anyway, over time one of the versions would surely have become ritualized in the retelling so that Sir George would not say one thing one day and another the next.

Unless the whole thing had been a recently fabricated story.

Had it been? Had there been no lifesaving incident at all? Or had the whole thing been quite different from the way it had been told? Just as what had happened to Julian might have been different from what either David or Sir George had said. But there was no connection between the two incidents, of course. Except that they had both happened during that brief episode on the Kitspur. David had saved Sir George Scherer's life—or not saved it—and Julian had died as a hero—or not as a hero—all within a few minutes. And David had been a part of both incidents.

Rebecca felt rather sick. There was no connection between the two events. What malevolent night spirit was trying now to suggest that there was? It was horrible. Horrible! She hated the suspicions that were crowding into her mind, without any basis in fact at all. And the terrible unease. She hated the unease.

There probably had been no affair, she thought firmly, and both David and Sir George Scherer had told the truth as best they remembered it from all the confusion. There had been no awkwardness between David and Lady Scherer beyond a certain reserve in both. And Sir George did not hate his wife or David. On the contrary he was grateful to David for saving his life. And he called his wife "my love."

There. That was the truth of the matter. There was no secret, no mystery.

But the mind is not as easily controlled as the will. What had really happened on the Kitspur? she wondered as she sought in vain for a return of sleep and oblivion. Had there been any sort of three-way connection there among David, Julian, and Sir George Scherer?

That last thought was the most fantastic of all and the one least founded on any evidence whatsoever. It was also the most frightening for a reason that Rebecca could in no way fathom.

Rebecca did not feel well the following morning. She had a headache from lack of sleep, and she felt so depressed that she found it difficult to greet David with her usual cheerfulness after breakfast and assure him that she had a good night and was feeling well.

He looked closely at her. "You are pale," he said.

"Well," she admitted. "I did not sleep too much, David. I woke in the middle of the night and could not go back to sleep again."

"You must sleep this morning, then," he said. "I shall tell Louisa not to come too early."

It was in vain to protest that she looked forward to Louisa's morning visits—and she could not say that today of all days she needed the distraction of Louisa's conversation. When David had that set look on his face, she knew there was no arguing with him.

"Very well," she said at last. "I shall try to sleep, David."

"You are sure you are feeling well?" He was looking down at her broodingly.

She nodded and closed her eyes. "Just a little tired still," she said. "At your insistence I shall be lazy."

Looking at him, she thought, keeping her eyes closed, it was impossible to believe him capable of any of those old wrongdoings. It was impossible to believe him capable of impregnating Flora—and then callously refusing to marry her. It was impossible to believe him capable of having an affair with another man's wife.

He seemed so very respectable.

But perhaps he was not guilty of that last wrong. She had no evidence except the strong feeling that she must be right.

She fell back to sleep.

And woke to an empty room an indeterminate amount of time later in a sweat and a panic. She lay very still, her eyes closed, until the pain came again and the urge to push—both very faint. Both very possibly a figment of the imagination or part of a leftover nightmare. She lay still again, afraid to move even to ease stiffened legs. She tried to relax and breathe evenly. She tried to sleep.

The next faint wave of pain was subsiding as Louisa entered the room, bright and cheerful as she usually was, armed with embroidery and knitting and conversation.

"Oh." She dropped her bundles onto the nearest chair and hurried over to the bed. "What is it, Rebecca?"

"Fetch David." Rebecca pressed her palms against the mattress and tried to hold on to sanity. She failed dismally. "Fetch David," she wailed. "Fetch David."

Louisa moved quickly for one who had grown so bulky. She disappeared even as Rebecca drew breath noisily into her lungs and stared wide-eyed into hell.

He came running no more than a minute or two later. "Rebecca?" he said. "Trouble?"

She did not notice the paleness of his face or the harshness of his voice as he came up to the side of the bed. She clawed at him, wailing horribly, all control lost. "Hold me."

He knelt on the bed, gathering her close with his arms.

"I don't want to lose the baby," she wailed into his shirtfront. "I don't want to lose it."

"You are having pains?"

"Yes," she said. "I think so. I don't know. David, hold me. Oh, please, hold me." She was too distraught to be embarrassed by her noisy sobs and the flood of tears that followed as she clung to him, trying to climb inside him for safety.

He eased her downward until she was lying down again, her head on his arm, her face and her body along the length of his. He held her close and cried with her. Some detached part of her mind was aware that he cried too.

Somehow he had got beneath the bedclothes with her so that he was able to pull the blankets up warmly about her ears. She was cocooned in warmth and began to feel the hysteria drain away. She relaxed gradually against him.

"Any pain now?" he murmured to her after a few minutes.

"No."

He ran a hand up and down her back, circling it slowly so that she relaxed further to its rhythm. She began to realize that David was lying fully clothed in bed with her—he was even wearing his boots, she could feel with one bare foot—holding her close to him, massaging her back through her nightgown. He was doing what she had longed for months for him to do. And it felt even more wonderful than she had imagined.

He had made the pains go away. There had been none since he had come. He had cried with her, she thought in some wonder. Their child was as important to him as it was to her. And surely she meant a little more to him than just a business partner and almost-friend. He might have just sent for the doctor and held her hand—or sent Louisa back to her—until the man came. Instead he had

climbed into bed with her, boots and all, to hold her
because she had asked to be held.

Very soon now, she thought drowsily, she was going
to despise herself for showing so little discipline and for-
titude. Soon she was going to be embarrassed for having
shown him that she needed him—she had even sent
Louisa running for him. But not yet. If she felt those
things too soon, she would have to push away from him
and assure him that she was quite recovered, thank you
very much. She did not want to be quite recovered yet.

Did it matter that she mean more to him than a friend?
she wondered through the fog of returning sleep. Did she
want to mean more when she knew so many unsavory
things about him? And when she loved . . . But she refused—she positively refused to consider such thorny
matters at this precise moment.

"Mmm," she said sleepily against his shirt as his hand
circled her lower back and comforted the ache there.

He waited until she was deeply asleep before easing
himself slowly and carefully out of bed and leaving the
room. As he half expected, his father and Louisa were
waiting in the corridor outside. Louisa had been crying.
He was suddenly aware that the traces of his own tears
were probably still visible and that he must look horribly
disheveled. He did not much care.

"She is sleeping," he said. "I think perhaps it was a
false alarm. Or perhaps things are just getting started. I
know little about these matters. I never had cause to discuss them—last time."

"The nearest brandy decanter is in the drawing
room?" his father asked sternly. "We will take ourselves
there without further delay, my boy. If you think you can
walk that far."

"I'll send Rebecca's maid to sit with her until she
wakes," Louisa said quietly. "We were planning to return home tomorrow, David. But William agrees with me
that we should stay. Perhaps we should spend Christmas
here after all, as you suggested."

"I hope," David said, "that there will be something
still to celebrate."

"Whether there is or not," she said, taking his arm

and squeezing it, "I think we are needed here, David. By both of you. And it really does not matter if William and I are here or at home for Christmas. We have each other and that is all that really counts."

David was ashamed suddenly that he had ever suspected his stepmother's motives for marrying his father. Their obvious affection for each other, despite the age difference, showed up the emptiness of his own marriage. He wondered if they had noticed that he and Rebecca were very nearly estranged even if there was no open hostility between them. But how could they have failed to notice? His father's silence on the topic was evidence enough that he knew his fears had been well-founded.

But she had needed him, David thought. For a few minutes, in her panic, she had needed him and sent Louisa running for him. Louisa had come bursting into his study, where he had been discussing some financial matters with Quigley, without even knocking on the door first.

He had not even realized fully how much he needed to be needed until Rebecca had reached for him, her eyes wild with panic, demanding to be held. Her panic had drawn an answering response from him, and for a few minutes he had been lost in pain and tears of his own. But the wonder of being needed, of having his empty arms filled again, had aroused a pain of a different sort. He could have held her forever. Only the knowledge that his father and Louisa would be waiting anxiously for news had sent him reluctantly from her bed when she was fast asleep.

Even through the thickness of his frock coat and trousers he had felt the slight swelling of her pregnancy. The memory of the feeling brought an ache back to his throat as he took his glass of brandy from his father's hands. His own, he noticed in some surprise, were shaking slightly. Louisa had gone to give instructions to Rebecca's maid.

"Drink it before you disgrace your manhood and faint," the earl said gruffly.

David drank.

"I fainted when word was brought that you had been

born,'' his father said. ''I was too numb to faint when your mother died with your sister. Be thankful, David, that at least you do not have cause to feel numb. There is still hope. And she will survive at this point even if the child does not.''

David swirled the remaining contents of his glass and downed them in one gulp.

''I am terrified,'' his father mumbled, taking David quite by surprise.

He watched the earl drink his own brandy and smiled ruefully. ''I have been very selfish, haven't I?'' he said. ''Acting all these weeks as if I am the only anxious expectant father. Forgive me, Papa?''

''She must need you,'' the earl said, pursing his lips and acting as if he had not for a moment revealed weakness. ''If she sent for you like that—Louisa said all she could say, over and over again, was to fetch you—she must need you. It's something, my son. It's something.''

''Yes,'' David said, almost afraid to believe. But his thoughts were interrupted by the arrival of the doctor, whom he had yelled out for as he had raced up the stairs earlier and whom the earl had sent for. They sent him away again after giving him a drink and after David had directed him to return in the afternoon.

But in the afternoon, when she finally awoke, Rebecca declared that she was feeling better and that there had been no recurrence of the pains. She gazed at her husband with eyes that he sensed only barely hid anxiety and the need for reassurance. She still looked unnaturally pale.

''Relax and try not to think of it,'' he said, sitting on the edge of the bed instead of on the chair as he usually did. ''Louisa and Papa are going to stay for Christmas. Perhaps you will be able to come downstairs for a few hours on Christmas Day. The month will be over.''

It seemed somehow the right thing to do to speak as if there was hope.

''It will be wonderful to be up again,'' she said. ''You would not believe how idle I feel, David. I may have forgotten entirely how to work.''

''I'll have to crack the whip again then,'' he said and was pleased to see a half smile on her pale lips. ''But not for a while. I'll carry you downstairs for Christmas and back up again.''

''It will be wonderful,'' she said. ''Is the downstairs still there? I have been wondering.''

He almost reached out to cup one hand about her cheek, but he could not make up his mind to risk wiping the near smile off her face.

''I am going to be sleeping here at night for a while,'' he said abruptly and watched the smile disappear after all to be replaced by a wary look. ''You need someone close by, Rebecca.''

Just in case. The words hung in the silence between them.

But he was not sure his decision was not just an excuse. An excuse to be close. Perhaps to touch. Perhaps to be needed again. He had not realized until that morning just how starved he was.

She did not argue, as he had half expected she would. But then, of course, Rebecca would not argue. She was his wife. It was her duty to receive him into her bed whenever he chose to put himself there. He would read no more into her acquiescence than that.

''Thank you, David,'' she said.

15

Rebecca came downstairs for the first time on Christmas Eve, a day earlier than David had promised. The earl, Louisa, and David had dined in her room with her since it was a special occasion, and then had left her to rest. They were planning to go to church later. Rebecca tried not to feel depressed to be left alone. Indeed, there was everything to put her in just the opposite mood. Tomorrow was Christmas Day and she was to go downstairs for the first time in a month. And that was the most significant and wonderful fact of all. A month had passed, the dreaded fourth month, and she was still pregnant.

If she could just get safely past the fourth month, Sir Rupert Bedwell had said, then she would probably be able to carry her baby to term. And she was about to enter the fifth month. Oh, no, she decided, closing her eyes and spreading both hands lightly over her abdomen, there was no reason at all to feel a little low in spirits merely because she had been left alone during the evening of Christmas Eve. She would not be so foolish.

And then the door opened again and she turned her head to see David come inside. She gazed at him wistfully and wondered if he realized how dependent upon him she had grown in the last month. His visits were the high point of her day though they rarely talked about any topics other than strictly impersonal ones. Sometimes she wondered if she had invented that memory of him holding her and crying with her, but she knew she had not. It had been one of the very rare chinks in the armor he had always worn so carefully to shield himself from other people's view.

She wondered if he knew how dependent on him at night she had grown. She doubted if she would be able to sleep at night if he were not there beside her. It was so very tedious to lie in bed for twenty-four hours each day. He never tried to touch her or kiss her, but there was the warmth of his presence beside her and the knowledge that she was not alone, that he was there if she needed help. Sometimes she awoke during the night to find that they were snuggled up close to each other, though she never knew who had snuggled up to whom. Sometimes she edged away from him self-consciously. At other times she was too warm and comfortable to move but merely closed her eyes and went back to sleep.

"Did you forget something?" she asked.

"The carolers are here," he said. "A great army of them, Rebecca. They almost fill the hall. And they want you. I did not think it would be quite the thing to bring them up here."

She laughed.

"I think it would be easier to take you down," he said. "Are you feeling up to it?"

"Downstairs?" she said. She felt rather like a child being offered a rare treat. "Now? But look at me."

"You had your hair neatly braided for dinner," he said. "It still looks tidy. I'll fetch your dressing gown and then wrap you up in a big blanket. But only if you want to, Rebecca. I'll tell them you are just not up to it if you don't. If I leave the door open, you will hear them singing. I didn't exaggerate when I said there was an army of them."

"I want to," she said hastily, sitting up and throwing back the covers. "It's Christmas. I always used to love Christmas more than any other time of year. It seems years since I celebrated it properly. It was in London with Jul—"

"I'll fetch your dressing gown and a blanket," he said, disappearing into her dressing room.

It had been in London with Julian. Noisy celebrations with large numbers of his fellow officers and their wives. She had not really enjoyed it. She would have preferred to be alone with him or with a small group of close friends. But Julian had always loved large gatherings. It had been a few days before her miscarriage. Perhaps it had happened because she had danced and danced over

Christmas though she had not wanted to. Julian had insisted that she enjoy herself. She was going into the mopes, he had said when she had tried to take life quietly out of fear that she would miscarry as she had done the first time.

"Here," David said and helped her into her dressing gown as she sat on the edge of the bed. "No, don't stand. I'll wrap the blanket around you like this and pick you up like this. Comfortable?"

"I must weigh a ton," she said. "I have done nothing all month but lie here putting on weight."

"A mere feather," he said.

He really had not exaggerated. She could hear the babble of voices as he carried her down the stairs, and it seemed when they reached the doorway into the hall that it was filled to overflowing. She saw Miriam Phelps and some of her knitting and sewing ladies at a glance, though there seemed to be a bewildering crowd of faces. She smiled.

Everyone clapped at the sight of her and then cheered. A few of the men whistled. They were all clearly in a merry festive mood already. Rebecca felt an unexpected rush of tears to her eyes and had to turn her face into David's shoulder for a few moments. The earl and Louisa, she noticed when she looked up again, were standing beside one of the large fireplaces. A huge log fire was burning in each. An oak settle had been drawn close to the heat.

David seated her on it and sat beside her, his arm still about her shoulders. Everyone lapsed into near silence.

"Carolers?" Rebecca said. "Don't carolers go singing from house to house? Are there any houses left that are not empty?"

There was a general burst of laughter.

It had been someone's idea, it seemed, to go caroling at Stedwell since the house was inhabited for the first time in a long while. And everyone knew that the viscountess was confined to her bed and would not be at church. The idea had caught fire and almost everyone had come—everyone from the laborers' cottages, many from the village.

"The question is," Rebecca said, "can you sing?"

There was another roar of laughter.

But many of them could and did sing and those who could not joined in anyway so that it did not matter that some sang too loudly or too hoarsely or too far off-key. It really did not matter at all. Rebecca joined them, and she could hear David's voice close to her ear. Louisa was singing too, she saw when she looked her way. The earl was looking his usual stern self. But his foot was tapping.

Carolers usually sang three or four carols before taking some refreshments and going on their way. These carolers sang on and on until after about twenty minutes when David signaled to their butler, and a few minutes later the cider and the mulled wine were carried out by footmen and trays of mince pies and cakes by maids. The sounds of music gave place to jovial chattering voices and laughter.

"Are you tired?" David asked quietly. "Shall I take you back up?"

"Not yet," she said, turning to look at him. "Just a little longer, David."

He nodded and set a mince pie on a plate for her.

Their people were too shy to come to speak to them personally, but there were several jokes made for the general amusement of all. The most popular was made by Joshua Higgins, one of the young men who had helped in the garden during the autumn.

"What's this, then?" he said when there was a lull in the general noise as everyone seemed to be preparing to leave. His voice was bewildered. "Where did this come from? How did it get in my pocket, eh? Who put it here?" He drew a little sprig of greenery from the pocket of his large coat.

"Looks like mistletoe to me, Josh," another of the men said. "P'raps Miriam put it there. P'raps she was telling you that you're too slow by half."

There was general laughter and blushes and loud protests from Miriam. Joshua moved toward the fire as if to drop the wilting little plant into the flames, but he turned at the last moment, a grin on his face, and the laughter swelled and was accompanied by whistles.

Oh, dear, Rebecca thought, it was above her head. He

was not going to kiss her, was he? Well, she would not become flustered. It was Christmas, after all.

And then her husband's arm tightened about her shoulders and his free hand cupped her chin to turn her face toward him, and he kissed her. Lightly, on the lips. As he had kissed her at the altar on their wedding day. A public kiss. A Christmas kiss. The whistles became piercing.

On her wedding day she had been oppressed by the knowledge that he was David, that she had freely married him, that she owed him all of herself for the rest of her life. She had been terrified by the thought of intimacy with him. And now . . .

And now? He was David. He was her husband. She had given herself to him and was carrying his child within her womb. She was his for the rest of her life. Nothing had changed. Except the terror. And the sense of oppression. It felt good—oh, it felt so very, very good to belong. To belong to this house and these people. To belong to a man again. To be living in renewed hope of being able to have a child of her own.

They were going to be a family. A real family.

Suddenly the past seemed no longer painful, no longer to be pined for. Suddenly the present seemed very good and the future something to be anticipated with hope and pleasure.

"Happy Christmas, David," she said quietly when he raised his head.

He made a short speech of thanks to the carolers for coming and giving such a lovely start to their Christmas. Then he announced he was going to carry his wife back upstairs before they opened the doors and let all of winter inside. Rebecca smiled at them all and would have cried, she felt, if it had been a suitable thing for a viscountess to do. She noticed suddenly new scarves and mittens—a few new woolen caps—and directed a special smile at Miriam, who was now standing beside Joshua.

They were silent on the way up to her room. She felt all the anticlimax of leaving such a warm gathering. And a little embarrassed to be alone with David when he had just kissed her. The last time he had kissed her had been on the third night of their marriage, after he had had that nightmare. She both hated that memory and was fascinated by it. It seemed hardly possible that it had really happened. That perhaps it was then their child have been conceived.

He sat her on the edge of the bed and unwrapped the blanket from about her. He stood in silence as she removed her dressing gown and handed it to him. She was lying down when he returned from her dressing room.

"I'll send your maid to brush out your hair," he said. "We will probably be late back from church. I'll try not to wake you when I come to bed."

"David," she said and then did not know what she wanted to say to him. It was not words she wanted to speak. She wanted . . . Oh, she did not know what she wanted. It was Christmas and she had been infected with that longing Christmas always brought for something wonderful, something lasting, something beyond imagination.

"Yes?" He stood looking down at her, his hands clasped behind him, waiting. Such a very elegant, correct, stern-looking gentleman, she thought, with his black frock coat and starched linen.

David. She had always yearned to know him, had always been hurt by his aloofness and puzzled by his cruelties, had always disliked him because she could not understand him. Because he was unknowable, beyond the realm of her experience. And now he was her husband and the yearning was becoming rather painful.

"It was lovely of them to come, wasn't it?" she said.

"Yes," he said. "I think you have found a way into their hearts, Rebecca. I think I did a wise thing indeed when I married you. Good night. And happy Christmas."

Tears came when he had gone. Tears of happiness. Tears of frustration. Tears of . . . She did not know why they came. And she did not know whether she felt happy or sad. Perhaps both. Was it possible to feel both? *I did a wise thing,* he had said. What a very typically dispassionate thing for David to say. Wise. Because she had won the hearts of their people? Had she? Had he not exaggerated a little? She had not done a great deal for them after all.

Were tears spilling over onto her cheeks because he saw her that way? Because he thought he had done a wise thing to marry her? Were they tears of happiness? Or was it because he had not said he was glad he had married her? Because he had not thought to kiss her good night when they were alone together? Because those blue eyes of his had not smiled at her?

She wished she could know him. She wished he could let down the barriers and let her see him as he was. She wished that the affection he had spoken of could grow between them. She would like to see affection in David's eyes.

He had cried with her once. Because he had thought his baby was dying? Or because she had panicked and he knew she was suffering? She had thought the latter at the time. She still thought it. But one never quite knew with David.

She had always known with Julian. Julian had always worn his heart on his sleeve. She felt a stabbing of longing for the openness of the love they had shared. An openness like that with David—how lovely it would be. And then she opened her eyes wide. There could never be anything like that with David, or with any other man. Only with Julian could she ever have felt such closeness. Julian had been the love of her life. She felt a sudden fear that perhaps time would dim the memory of that love. She had loved him with a love that could happen only once in a lifetime. She did not want to forget that.

It was not that she wanted with David. She wanted friendship and affection with David. And the security of a home and a family with him. Not love. Not that all-pervading emotion that had held her to Julian—that would always hold her to him in the depths of her heart.

He would try not to wake her when he came to bed, he had said. Rebecca smiled. Did he not realize that she would not sleep properly until he did come?

Louisa had supervised the decorating of the house with greenery, at David's request. It was his first real Christmas in a long while too. Rebecca's last one had been spent in London with Julian, she had said. He had spent the same Christmas with his father at Craybourne. He had been in the hospital at Scutari the year after.

Christmas excited him this year. For the first time in his life he was to spend it in his own home. His father and his father's wife were to spend it with him. And his own wife. She was to come downstairs on the afternoon of Christmas Day—for tea and the exchange of gifts. And for something else too though that was to be a surprise for her.

He helped decorate the drawing room himself, most notably the Christmas tree, an item that had his father frowning and Louisa laughing. A Christmas *tree*? A whole tree? But yes, he had said, had they not heard of such a thing? Prince Albert, the queen's consort, had introduced the custom to England several years ago. David filled a pail with soil himself, planted the tree in it, and decorated it with bows and bells and candles. He wanted something special for Rebecca to see when she came downstairs.

Rebecca. It would be their first Christmas together as man and wife. And things were going well, he thought. She was past the danger time, though he still suffered from anxiety. She was going to be able to have her child. They were going to be a family of three. She was already quite noticeably pregnant, though not nearly as large as Louisa, of course. Sometimes he woke during the nights to find her cuddled in against him. Unknown to her he often turned toward her on those occasions so that he could feel the swelling of her abdomen against his stomach. He found the feeling wonderfully—oh, not erotic. Definitely not that. Tender. He found it wonderfully tender.

She seemed almost happy despite the tedium of the month in bed and the anxiety she must have felt every single moment—it had erupted dreadfully during that terrible morning when she had thought she was miscarrying again. Last night she had seemed happy—happy to be taken downstairs, happy to be at Stedwell, surrounded by their people, sharing Christmas with them.

And he was happy. Everything he had hoped to accomplish when he came home from the Crimea seemed to have been accomplished. He had persuaded her to marry him, he had been able to offer her a life of security and usefulness, even though the house still looked woefully shabby when one took a good look at it, and now it seemed that she was going to have a child.

He had atoned, he sometimes thought cautiously. He had given something worthwhile back to her in place of the invaluable something he had taken away. And in the process he was being healed. His wounds had not bothered him for months. And his other wounds appeared to be filming over too. He still had the dream, but not so frequently. When it did come, he simply got up from bed and left the room so that he could recover from it in private without involving Rebecca should she awake.

He knew that he had had no choice but to kill Julian. He knew that he had killed him only because he had had to. Not because he had hated him. Not because he had wanted Rebecca. He knew that he loved Julian. Despite everything. He knew that love is unconditional, that he had not stopped loving Julian merely because Julian had weaknesses of character and had been married to the woman David loved. He knew that he had nothing really to feel guilty about.

He waited patiently for full healing, for the time when he could forget and could look at Rebecca without even the smallest twinge of guilt. The time would come, he told himself.

In the meantime there was Christmas to be celebrated— the birth of the Christ child and now the promised birth of his own child.

Rebecca had dressed—for the first time in a month— in a new deep blue dress that was of a far looser fit than her other dresses. Her hair, smooth over her head, shone gold. Her waist had disappeared; her breasts looked larger; her face was fuller. She looked unbelievably beautiful to the husband who went to carry her downstairs early in the afternoon of Christmas Day.

"You look beautiful," he told her, picking her up as he had the evening before. He spoke the simple truth, though he did not hug her and kiss her as he ached to do. He was trying very hard to treat her with quiet affection, not to make any demands on her emotions that she might find disturbing. He always remembered with some horror the passion with which he had once used her.

The Christmas tree delighted her. When he would have set her down in the most comfortable chair beside the fire, she begged him to set her down in the one opposite it so that she could gaze at the tree.

"It is magical," she said. "What a wonderful idea, David. Was it yours?"

The first surprise was the arrival of all the neighboring gentry for tea. All of them had gatherings and parties of their own to organize and attend, but all had been so concerned for Rebecca's health that he had persuaded them to come just for an hour so that she would know that she had been missed, that she was now an accepted and valued member of a community.

He would not allow her to move from her chair, and of course this gathering was far quieter and more refined than last evening's in the hall had been. Even so, he looked anxiously at her when everyone had left and the earl had brought a stool for her feet, despite her protests that she was no invalid. He hoped that his plans for the day would not overtax her strength.

The children arrived a short time later—all the pupils from the school with the schoolmaster. All of them were frightened and excited and gazed about them in awe. They had performed their concert two days before, but this afternoon they were to do it again for the exclusive pleasure of the Earl and Countess of Hartington and Viscount and Lady Tavistock. Mostly for the viscountess, who had spent many hours at the school helping them with their reading and sewing, teaching them that singing could be fun. The Countess of Hartington, of course, was to accompany them with some of their songs, as she had at the school two days ago.

There was singing and dancing and reciting—and of course the Nativity play. Christmas had somehow never seemed quite so precious to him, David thought, sitting in a chair from which he could watch both his wife and the children's performance. There was a warm smile on her face. He wondered treacherously if she had done any more thinking about that last wonderful Christmas with

Julian she had begun to speak of the evening before, but he pushed the thought away.

David had bought each of the children a ball. He handed them out after the Nativity play was over, while the earl distributed coins among them. Rebecca gave only smiles and praise and thanks to them—and the schoolmaster—for their kindness and generosity in giving up part of their Christmas Day for her pleasure. David wondered if she realized that for the children, who were about to be herded into a salon for a lavish tea, this was probably the high point of all the Christmases they could remember.

She did not protest when he carried her back upstairs after the children had been led away by Mrs. Matthews.

"You must rest awhile," he told her as he set her down on the bed, still clothed. "The fourth month is only just over."

"Yes," she said. "But it is over, David. The fifth month is just beginning."

She usually looked at him with calm self-possession. It was usually impossible to know quite how she was feeling on any matter. Only occasionally did her eyes allow him a glimpse into what was going on beneath the exterior. Her eyes were luminous now—slightly anxious, slightly hopeful. She wanted him to talk about the fifth month rather than the fourth.

"Yes," he said. "It is beginning. Just as a new year will be soon. But you must continue to rest as much as possible."

"Yes, David," she said. The submissive wife again.

He wished he dared try to get through to the hidden Rebecca, the one she kept to herself behind the dignity and the training of years. But he was afraid of what he might find there. Perhaps the veneer was better than the reality would be.

"Thank you for my gift," he said before turning to leave her.

"A silk shirt made by my own hands?" she said. "It seemed a sorry gift when a tailor might have done a far better job, David. But I have not been able to buy you anything. Thank you for mine." She fingered the single diamond pendant on a gold chain that she wore about her neck.

A single diamond unadorned by others or by a fancy setting. It did not need embellishment. Just as she did not. He wondered what she would say if he told her that.

"If you are feeling strong enough," he said, "I'll come back after dinner with Papa and Louisa. Perhaps we can play cards. Would you like that?"

"Yes, David," she said.

Would she rather be left alone—with her memories, perhaps?

"Very much," she added.

He nodded and left the room. She meant it. It had been a far more wonderful Christmas than any he could remember. Next year there would be a child in the house. Perhaps.

He wondered if it would be tempting fate to admit to himself that he was happy. He was. Almost. He had the rest of a lifetime during which to make her happy too— to help her to forget the worst of her grief, to help her relax into a relationship of affection, to make their marriage a full reality again, to give her perhaps another child or two. Though just this one would bring more happiness—to both of them—than he could possibly imagine at the moment.

Yes, he thought, going downstairs to discover that Louisa too had been banished to her room for a rest, he was happy.

Almost.

16

Christmas would have been perfect—for both of them, though they did not speak of it openly to each other. For both it was wonderful because the spirit of Christmas had been recaptured again after several lost years. And because they had found it together even if neither quite knew that the other did too. But it was not quite perfect after all.

The earl and Louisa left for Craybourne on Boxing Day. They were both anxious to get home since the time for Louisa's confinement was drawing closer. David accompanied them to the station and stayed with them in the relative warmth and comfort of the carriage until the train could be heard steaming along the track. Then they moved onto the platform.

Several passengers got off the train. David had kissed Louisa's cheek and helped her aboard and had turned to shake his father by the hand before he was hailed by the hearty voice of one of the new arrivals. Sir George and Lady Scherer had decided to break their journey home from Christmas in Gloucester in order to call on their dear friends, the Tavistocks.

Hasty introductions were made before the guard's whistle blew and the train departed on its way. Louisa smiled warmly at Lady Scherer.

"Rebecca will have company for a little while longer," she said. "She will be so glad."

"My wife is suffering through a rather difficult confinement," David explained quietly to his newly arrived guests, hoping that perhaps at the last possible moment they would change their minds and jump aboard again. But a small mountain of luggage had already been deposited on the platform close to them. "She will be pleased to see you."

He did not know if she would or not. She had wanted to dine with the Scherers in London, and perhaps from her point of view it had been a pleasant evening. Certainly Scherer had given them a hearty welcome and Cynthia had been quietly friendly—to Rebecca. They had never talked about the evening.

For David it had been torture. He had never particularly liked Scherer, with his loud, brash manner. Under any circumstances he would have been less than delighted to be forced to spend an evening socializing with him. But he certainly needed no reminding of how his life had somehow become linked with the man's. And he had no wish at all to be in Lady Scherer's company, knowing the part she had played in the whole terrible drama of those events in the Crimea. The thought of Rebecca having to be with Cynthia, not knowing, had filled him with impotent rage.

But it seemed he had no more choice now than he had had then. Scherer, for reasons of his own, was choosing to treat him as some sort of hero. The man did owe his life to him, David supposed. But at the same time Scherer should remember how close he and Julian had been. He should be sensitive to the fact that David did not want to remember that day in his life. But sensitivity seemed to be something George Scherer lacked.

How could Scherer force his wife to remember? And to face the man who had killed her lover? And the widow of that lover? But perhaps that was Scherer's intent. David had the uneasy suspicion that the man hated his wife.

And so when he returned from the station and went up to his bedchamber to bring Rebecca downstairs to tea, he took also the news that they had visitors for an indeterminate number of days.

They stayed for only two days. It seemed more like two months to Rebecca. After Boxing Day she stayed in bed during the mornings at David's insistence, but she came downstairs in the afternoon, walking on legs that felt alarmingly weak and unsteady, and did not retire again until after dinner.

Sir George Scherer was as friendly and as hearty and as talkative as she remembered him from London. His wife was as quiet. Rebecca set herself to entertaining them, determined to be gracious, determined to like them if she possibly could. She felt rather ashamed of some of the wild imaginings she had indulged in during her month upstairs. That evening in London could not possibly have been as sinister in tone as she remembered it.

But the atmosphere she remembered there returned.

"Do a lot of shooting, do you, Major?" Sir George asked David after dinner on the second evening.

"Not a great deal," David said. "And I have not been a major or of any other military rank for half a year, you know."

Sir George laughed. "But I always think of you as Major Tavistock," he said. "It was fortunate for me that you were, eh? He should shoot frequently, Lady Tavistock. He would keep your larder full. I have never seen such a deadly accurate shot in my life as the one that killed that Russian."

Rebecca smiled and asked Lady Scherer if she played the pianoforte. Lady Scherer did not.

"Do you still have that pistol?" Sir George asked. "The one that killed him?"

"Yes," David said. "Perhaps you would like to play for us for a short while, Rebecca, if you are not tired."

"You do?" Sir George said. "Fetch it in here, Major, if you please. It would be a pleasure to see it again. Cynthia would like to see it, wouldn't you, my love? The gun that saved your husband's life and shot the villain who would have killed him?"

Lady Scherer said nothing. He was tormenting her, Rebecca thought. But how? And why? Was he reminding her that her lover had saved her husband's life so that he could go on tormenting her? Was that it? But she had put those thoughts behind her. She did not want to be thinking them.

"I consider bringing a gun into the presence of ladies to be in rather poor taste," David said, getting to his feet and holding out a hand for Rebecca's. His eyes were cold, she saw.

"Quite so," Sir George said. "But I wish you could have seen it happening, my love. Right through the heart with no time at all to take aim. That was some shooting. But pardon me, Lady Tavistock. I should not be conjuring such images before your eyes, should I? It will only serve to remind you that your first husband too was shot—in the same battle, at that. Right through the heart too, was it not? But you can comfort yourself with the knowledge that he died a hero. A great hero, ma'am."

What was he saying? Dear God, what was he saying? Rebecca set her hand in David's and looked up into his cold, cold eyes.

"This is almost the first day my wife has been downstairs for an extended period of time," he said. "I am afraid she is overtired. The music must wait until tomorrow. Come, Rebecca, I'll take you up to your room."

Though she had walked down the stairs, leaning heavily on his arm, and they had agreed that she would move from place to place in future on her own feet, he lifted her up into his arms.

"I am sorry," she said, turning her head to look at their guests. "Please excuse me."

"And I am doubly sorry, Lady Tavistock," Sir George said, on his feet, a look of contrition on his face. "Here am I talking war talk when Cynthia keeps reminding me that everyone wants to forget the war. And you more than anyone must wish to forget. Do forgive me, ma'am."

"Good night, Lady Tavistock," Lady Scherer said quietly.

It was a long time before David came to bed. Rebecca had even fallen into an uneasy sleep by the time he came. But she had lain for a long time staring up into the darkness. What had he meant? The Russian David had killed had been shot through the heart. Julian had been shot through the heart.

What had he meant? What had he been implying? Anything? Had he been implying that there was somehow a connection between the two shootings? There could be no possible connection. Her mind stopped just short of making one—it would be too nightmarish to move her thoughts even one step closer. She stared upward.

The following morning David asked George Scherer to leave. He took him riding early, while the ladies were still in bed.

"What I did in the Crimea," he said abruptly once they were away from the stables, "I did because I had to. Not because I wanted to. It would have hurt to be forced to kill any fellow officer. To have to kill Julian Cardwell was an agony to me, as I am sure you must realize, Scherer. We grew up as brothers. I do not argue that you had a legitimate quarrel with him. That was not my concern. But losing him—by my own hand—hurt and still hurts more than I can possibly describe in words. I would have expected you to understand that."

For once George Scherer had nothing to say.

"My wife loved him dearly," David continued. "It is painful for her to be reminded of his death and of the manner of his death. I don't want her reminded, especially at this time. She is preparing to give birth and has not had an easy time of it."

"No," George Scherer said, none of the usual heartiness in his voice, "I don't suppose you do want her reminded, Major. Especially of the manner of his death."

David frowned. "Having you here," he said, "can only serve to remind us both of what is best forgotten. Inhospitable as it sounds, Scherer, I must ask that you do not prolong your visit."

"I wonder," Sir George said as they turned their horses for home again after a very short ride. He did not say for a while what it was he wondered. "You married Lady Cardwell very soon after your return from the Crimea, Major."

It was as he had begun to suspect, David thought. The man had not come out of gratitude at all.

"I begin to wonder," Sir George said so quietly that he might have been talking to himself, "for whose sake you shot him, Major."

David sucked in his breath. "There is a train leaving this afternoon, I believe," he said. "At the same time as the one you arrived on the day before yesterday."

"Cynthia and I will be on it," Sir George said, chuckling and looking his old self again. "We would stay longer, Major, but we would not tax Lady Tavistock's health. A short Christmas visit seemed in order, though. Cynthia has talked of little else. 'We simply must call on the Tavistocks without whom you would not be alive and here with me, George, dear,' she has said to me more times than I can count since we decided to go to Gloucester for Christmas. And so we came. This afternoon we will resume our journey. We will call again when your wife is in better health. Perhaps for the christening of your son? I will pray that it is a son. Every man likes to have an heir."

David said no more. He did join Lady Scherer briefly in the breakfast room when he discovered her there alone, but he did not stay. She froze when he tried to talk with her. She knew the full truth, obviously. She knew that he had killed her lover. He wondered briefly if she had loved Julian, if after all it had not been mere boredom that had led her into the affair. Perhaps she had loved him.

Whether she had or not, it must be difficult for her to make polite conversation with the man who had killed him and prolonged the life of the husband who hated and probably abused her. He wondered if George Scherer had always been the same, or if he had treated her thus only as a result of her infidelity.

But he did not want to wonder. He did not want Cynthia Scherer to become a person in his mind at all. He wanted only to forget. And so he took his leave of her after he had exhausted the topic of the weather, and saw her only once more, when he and Rebecca were taking a formal leave of their guests that afternoon. David did not accompany them to the station.

And so the magic of Christmas was gone. And with it some of the closeness they had both been feeling. Rebecca mourned her loss through a tea and a dinner and an hour in the drawing room, during which they discussed in great detail and with some animation what they would do at Stedwell once spring came and work could resume.

But she could no longer keep everything bottled up inside as she had done until now. Questions, suspicions, fears gnawed at her like a toothache, making it quite impossible to think of anything else or talk of anything else or sleep without their constant intrusion.

What had he meant?

"David," she asked when he came to bed, late. She rather thought he was displeased to see that she was still awake. "Did you ask them to leave?"

He busied himself poking the fire, which did not need poking. "He is the sort of man who lives on war memories," he said. "He will probably bore everyone he encounters for the next fifty years with them, if he lives so long. You don't need to listen to those stories, Rebecca."

Why? The question was on her lips. But she did not have the courage to ask it.

He crossed the room toward the bed and dimmed the lamp before lying down beside her. He never did touch her, but tonight he seemed more distant, more silent than usual.

"David?" she said. But it was a question she could not ask. A lady did not ask such questions. And really she did not want to know the answer.

"Yes?" His voice was tense.

"Was Lady Scherer your mistress?" She could hardly believe the words had been spoken. She would do anything in the world to recall them, she thought. She did not know what she was unleashing.

There was a short silence. "Why do you think she was?" he asked.

"I don't think he feels gratitude at all," she said. 'I think he hates you, David. And I am sure that he hates his wife. You and she never look at each other, never speak."

"And so," he said, "he must be bringing us together to taunt us with a former indiscretion—and in front of you."

"Yes," she said unhappily. "I am sorry, David. I should not have asked. It is not my business. It happened before our marriage."

"But it would make a difference if it had happened since?" His voice was harsh.

"Yes," she said. "Oh, yes, it would, David. Infidelity is the worst possible sin within marriage. It is, isn't it? I cannot think of anything that would be more calculated to make the other partner feel unloved and worthless. I would . . ."

"You would . . . ?" he prompted.

"I would want to die, I think," she said. "Though that is probably a foolish exaggeration. I think I would want to die, though. If you did that to me. If Jul—"

"If Julian had ever done that to you," he completed for her.

"I wish I had not started this conversation," she said. "I wish they had not come, David. Does it make you feel dreadful seeing her again and having to face him?" She drew a deep breath. "She is beautiful."

He surged over onto his side to face her. She could see him quite clearly in the dancing light of the fire. His face was taut with anger or with some other powerful emotion.

"Rebecca," he said, "nothing can be served by digging up the past. Believe me, nothing can. Only misery for us both. Only a strain on a marriage that is imperfect to start with. I married you. I made the same commitment to you that you made to me. I have seen you make every effort since then to live by that commitment. I have done the same. And I shall continue to. Let's make a pact to leave the past where it belongs. Shall we? Please? I'll not allow those people here again."

There was comfort in his words—somewhere. He was committed to their marriage. Yes, she had seen that. He had put his past self behind him when he married her. He had changed. Yes, there was comfort in that. She might always have liked David if there had not been those flashes of cruelty—and the total reticence. She might even have fallen in love with him. Though that would have been impossible, of course. She had fallen in love with Julian.

"Yes," she said. "What you were in the past is none of my concern, David. You have been a good husband to me. I wish—" She sighed. "I just wish memory could be cut off at will. I'll try. I'll not ask you such questions again."

He did something then that he had never done before. He reached out a hand and spread it lightly over the swelling of her pregnancy. "How have you been feeling?" he asked.

"Well," she said. "I feel very well, David. And so full of energy that I want to go running all around the estate."

"You had better not," he said. "Not if you don't want to suffer the worst tongue-lashing of your life."

She closed her eyes, hoping that he would keep his hand where it was. But he did not.

Only misery could come of digging up the past, he had said. And a strain on their marriage. Would misery and strain have come from a simple yes to her question? If she already knew about Flora, could knowledge of Lady Scherer make that much difference?

Or had he meant something else?

Both the Russian soldier and Julian had died from a bullet through the heart. No! There was no connection. None.

A marriage that is imperfect to start with. Yes, it was imperfect. But not impossible. There had been happiness at Christmas—just a few days ago. But it was not a marriage that could withstand much strain. The link that bound them together was very fragile.

He was right. The past was best left where it was. But then she had been right too. The past could not be forgotten at will. Especially when one did not know quite what the past had entailed.

He knew as soon as he surged upright in bed, bathed in a cold sweat, that it had been a different dream. And somehow more terrifying. He had become accustomed to the other and knew how to handle it once he had pulled himself free of it. This one was new.

Julian had been standing at the foot of the bed. God, it had been so real. He had been standing there.

"Dave," he said with his sweetly charming smile, "you had better tell her, old chap. Do you think she will never find out? Scherer will tell her. He will, Dave—to spite me because he could not kill me himself and to spite you because you saw his humiliation. He'll tell her.

Better to do it yourself. Just don't tell her about Cynthia and me. It meant nothing, Dave, but Becka would be hurt. You won't tell her that, will you? But you had better tell her the other.''

Lord God. No hatred. No accusations. No raging over the fact that he had married Rebecca and was lying in the bed with her. Just the sweetness and the charm—and the reluctance to have his own weakness known. It had been so damned real. As if he really had been standing there.

David looked over his shoulder. She was looking at him. He could see her eyes despite the darkness. She would be afraid to intrude upon his nightmare after that last time.

"I'm sorry," he said. "I woke you."

"David," she said softly. "If you ever want to talk about it, I am here. You don't have to bear it alone unless you wish to do so. I want you to know that."

He stared down at her. *I killed Julian.* Three words. He tried to hear himself saying them. He tried to picture her reaction. He tried to feel the burden fall away from his shoulders—onto hers. He would never say the words, he knew. Even if he could convince himself that it would be the right thing to do—for her as well as for him—he could not do it. Because those three words would have to be followed by an explanation.

She would be hurt to know the truth about Julian. That was what Julian himself had just said in the dream. Hurt? She would be destroyed by the knowledge. She would want to die, she had said. She would want to die even if it were he who was unfaithful to her. Just because he was her husband. How would she feel if she knew that Julian—the love of her life—had been unfaithful to her? No, there was no way on this earth he could ever do that to her.

"Thank you," he said.

He should get up as he usually did when he had the dream—the other dream—and go somewhere else for the rest of the night. Perhaps it would come back and he would end up hurting her. But he did not want to get up. He wanted more than anything to unburden himself to her—to the last person he could allow himself to speak to.

He lay down again beside her, turned toward her, and saw that she had turned her head to watch him. Oh, God, how he loved her. How he wanted everything down between them—all the barriers, all the silences, all the armor. Even if there was nothing left at the end of it. Just so that he could see her as she really was and she could see him. So that for once they could gaze into each other's eyes and see through to the soul.

But there was no way of revealing himself without destroying her.

He did something he had wanted to do for months. He slid one arm beneath her shoulders and set the other about her waist and drew her against him. He held her there, not tightly, but firmly, fitting her against him, pregnant womb and all, and settled his cheek against the top of her head.

"Are we going to have a boy or a girl?" he whispered to her.

"A child," she said, turning her head to rest a cheek on his shoulder. "A living child, David. We are going to have a child."

"Yes," he said fiercely. "We are going to be a family, Rebecca. We are going to have a future."

17

The Honorable Charles William Neville was born late in the afternoon of a day in mid-May, one week earlier than expected, and hours sooner than either the doctor or mid-wife had predicted when they were first summoned to Stedwell. The labor was short and intense, the delivery fast.

It all happened so quickly that David himself knew nothing about it until he arrived home from one of his tenant's farms, where he had been helping to build a barn. His wife had refused to have him sent for, having been assured that it would be well into the night or perhaps even the next morning before she would be delivered.

His son was born a scant hour after David arrived and long before his anxious pacing of the drawing room had worn a path in the faded carpet.

For Rebecca it had not seemed either a short or an easy time. She had been in pain—with very little respite between bouts—since shortly after David had got up from bed. Though by the time she was quite sure of what was happening and rang for her maid, he had already left the house. She would not send after him.

She had heard that pain and exhaustion were quickly forgotten when one finally heard one's baby cry for the first time. She smiled and even heard herself laughing as pain and pressure all disappeared in a rush and someone was crying with lusty protest at such cruel treatment.

"You have a son, my lady," the doctor said, and she felt tears running down her cheeks, though she continued to smile and even laugh.

"Oh," she said, "let me see him. Where is David? Send for David."

But a husband, it seemed, was not to be allowed to

enter the room until all evidence of blood and sweat and pain had been erased.

Her son was blood-streaked and fat-cheeked and pug-nosed and slit-eyed and bald as an egg. His mouth was a pink hole in his face and was roaring his rage. Rebecca gathered all his beautiful, wonderful humanity into her arms and wept and laughed for joy.

"Hush, sweetheart," she crooned to him. "Oh, hush. Mama has you all cozy and warm. Shh." She gazed in wonder at her son. For so long he had been real, moving and kicking and punching inside her womb, swelling her so large that David had commented just the week before that he was preparing his mind for the arrival of triplets. The child had been real, but not this real. This was the baby that had been inside her? This very real person?

"Shh," she said as her son finally paused to consider the fact that he was warm again. "What will Papa say if you are howling like that when he comes to visit you? You have to be on your very best behavior for Papa."

The baby was quietly surveying the world through unfocused eyes. He had been very rudely disturbed, but he had found comfort again. And the voice with which he was familiar again. But this was too bright a world for him to open his eyes wide just yet.

He did not like being taken by alien hands a few minutes later and unwrapped and washed. He did not like it at all and was not shy about letting the world know his feelings. But finally, clean and dry and wrapped snugly, he was where he wanted to be again and that voice close by was lulling him. He stopped his crying.

The doctor, leaving the room with the midwife, promised to send David up. Rebecca gazed at the sleepy child snuggled into the crook of her arm and kept glancing at the door. What was keeping him?

But in reality he came less than a minute after the doctor's departure. He closed the door quietly behind his back and stayed where he was, looking rather fearful, Rebecca thought. She felt a rush of emotion, seeing him standing there. Her husband. The father of her son. A rush of deep tenderness and contentment. Almost of love.

"David," she said, "we have a son."

"A son." He looked dazed. "No one would tell me. They said you should be the one to do that."

"Don't you want to see him?" she asked.

She watched his eyes move to the bundle in her arms. She watched him swallow and finally leave the sanctuary of the door to cross the room toward the bed.

"He is rather pink and patchy," she said anxiously. "It will be a few days before his head takes its proper shape." The child was still gazing through the slits of his eyes.

She so wanted David to be pleased. Pleased with her. Pleased with his son. She looked up into his face when he said nothing. He was crying, his eyes brimming with tears, some trickling down his cheeks.

"He is beautiful," he said. "Our son." He reached out a hand toward the baby but dropped it to his side again. "Our son, Rebecca."

"Touch him," she said. "Hold him."

But he took one step backward.

"Hold him, David." She picked up the little bundle.

He took it from her gingerly, the look of terror on his face giving way gradually to wonder. "Our son," he said, his eyes softening. "You had better be good to your mama, young lad. She has suffered for you."

The young lad listened quietly.

Rebecca watched her husband talking nonsense to their son. He was David, she told herself. The David she had known most of her life. The David she had still disliked just a year ago. A year ago he had not even returned from the Crimea. A year ago she could not have pictured this scene even in her most bizarre dreams.

It was hard now to cast herself back to see him and think of him as she had done then. And as she had done the day of his return, when she had resented so much the fact that he had returned while Julian had not. And the days after his return, when he had taken her so much by surprise by asking her to marry him. It was hard to remember her indignation, her revulsion at the very idea. And her wedding day and the fear that she was doing quite the wrong thing.

Now she could see him only as David, the man with whom she had lived for almost nine months. The man with whom she had grown familiar and comfortable. And more than that. The man of whom she had grown fond. Even that sounded tame. She felt a warm tenderness for him. He was holding the son he had begotten in her on their wedding night or the night after or the night after that, the son she had been delivered of less than an hour before.

It was a strong bond that was between them. As strong as love.

"You must be tired," he said, setting the baby back down in the crook of her arm. "Was it bad?"

"Dreadful," she said. "But it might have been very much worse according to all I have heard. It was very short in comparison to many labors. And our son was worth every moment. What are we going to call him?"

"Do you have any ideas?" He looked wary, even tense suddenly.

"Charles?" she said. "He has been Charles to me for several months—or Charlotte. Unless you would prefer to have him named David. Or William."

"Charles William," he said, "is going to sleep, I think."

She smiled.

"Which is where you should be going too," he said. "You look tired. The doctor warned me you would be. I'll leave you to rest."

She realized for the first time just how tired she did feel.

"Rebecca," he said before turning to leave, "thank you. Thank you for my son."

Charles lay snug and warm—and awake—in his father's place beside his mother after she had fallen asleep, a smile on her face and tears on her cheeks. On the whole his new surroundings did not seem nearly as bad as they had at first. The slits of his eyes gradually closed and stayed closed.

The bells of the village church rang for a whole hour on the day an heir was born at Stedwell. They rang again on the day of his christening, when the viscount had declared a holiday for his laborers and most of his tenants too had taken the day off. All had been invited to enjoy

the gardens of Stedwell after the church service and to
make free with the long tables of food and drink set out
on the terrace. All the families of higher social standing
had been invited to the house for the celebrations. The
Earl and Countess of Hartington had come for the occasion with their new daughter, born three months before
her nephew.

Everything was very good, David decided in the two
months following the birth of their son. He had come
home to England a little less than a year before buoyed
by hopes and oppressed by dread. He had hoped to forget, to find healing, to begin a new and meaningful life.
He had dreaded having to face Rebecca, to see the signs
of the suffering he had caused. He had dreaded having to
face her, knowing that he had killed her husband, her
beloved Julian. And then when he had faced her, he had
felt all the weight of his responsibility toward her and
had dreamed up his scheme of offering her a future.

It seemed hard to believe that that had all been less
than a year ago. Everything had worked out remarkably
well—with a few notable exceptions. His house still
looked rather down-at-heel, though even it looked more
splendid now that it had had a thorough clean and new
draperies—and now that it looked and felt unmistakably
lived in. There were still all those barriers between himself and Rebecca, and always would be. A marriage, he
had realized, could never hope to thrive when one of the
partners must keep a dark secret from the other. And
there was always the fear—yes, he was afraid—that Sir
George Scherer would show up again with his strange
hatreds and sly insinuations. And of course there were
the dreams, rarely now the one of the shooting, almost
always the one in which Julian stood at the foot of the
bed.

Oh, yes, there were imperfections that could cloud his
happiness when he stopped to brood on them, as he did
more often than he liked. But there was happiness too.
His first year at home had brought far greater contentment and peace than he would have dreamed possible
during his voyage back to England.

Rebecca, he believed, had recovered from the worst of
her grief and was almost happy with her new life. It was

never possible to know for sure with Rebecca. The quietness, the discipline, the obedience could mask either happiness or unhappiness. But he had lived with her for almost a year. He could sense contentment.

She had resumed her duties about the house and many of those beyond it. She went to the school two afternoons a week. She attended committee meetings. She was beginning to organize a grand picnic, dinner, and ball for some time during the summer—involving everyone of both the upper and lower classes, just as they had done for Charles's christening. She had brought a dressmaker down from London on the understanding that she would set up in the village and employ three or perhaps even four of the local girls and train them. Rebecca was convinced that there were enough customers in the neighborhood to keep a really good seamstress and several assistants busy. And three or four more girls would be saved from having to move into one of the industrial cities.

Most of all she was contented with her new motherhood. Wholly absorbed in her love of Charles. If he had done nothing else for her, David thought, he had done that. He had given her a child of her own. He had given her a sense of completion as a woman. He had given her someone on whom to lavish all the love that had lain dormant for more than two years.

He knew that she was embarrassed the first time he went into the nursery to find her nursing the baby, singing softly to him as she propelled a rocking chair gently with one foot. But he stood and watched anyway, a silent spectator, a little apart, not quite within the circle of love, but warmed by it anyway because he had caused it. He had given her that. He had put that child in her arms.

He came back often until she became accustomed to his presence and relaxed. He liked to watch his son sucking greedily at her breast, his curled fist pressed into the soft warm flesh. He liked to watch her cradling arms, her eyes heavy with love.

He liked to watch his whole world there in the rocking chair. The peace he had craved. His wife. And his son.

She did not try to shut him out. Part of him had feared that she would. Since she did not love him anyway, he had feared that he would become quite unimportant to her once her baby was born. But it did not happen. And of course it would not. Not with Rebecca. Rebecca would always do what was correct. He was her husband and head of her family. She would always include him. But he liked to think that it was not just duty that motivated her.

She often handed him the child when he was sleeping, sated with his meal. She set herself back to rights, her eyes lowered.

It was always a joy quite beyond words to describe to hold his son. He would have kept coming to the nursery just for that. He kept coming for another reason too. They were a family there, the three of them. The world could somehow be held at bay there. The world that threatened him. Because it held a secret that would shatter everything if it was ever revealed to her.

"He is going to have your hair," he said to her once when he was holding the baby, "if he ever decides to grow any."

"My lovely golden-haired boy," she said, smoothing her hand over the fine, almost invisible down on the baby's head. "With beautiful blue eyes like his father's."

He could almost imagine that her tone of tenderness was meant for the father as well as the son.

After two months she would have recovered from the birth. He still shared a bed with her. He had not made love to her for almost a year. During three nights he had made love to her, six times in all. He did not know what was going to happen at the end of the two months. He longed for her and dreaded the time of decision. And the decision would be his to make, he knew. She would do her duty. But as passively and as stoically as she had done it on their wedding night and the nights after?

He could expect no more of her.

It was all he had asked of their marriage.

Fool that he had been!

Sometimes he remembered unwillingly what his father had said to him on the day he and Rebecca had announced their betrothal. *You will not be happy with Rebecca. You need more than she can give.* He did not want to remember. Everything was going well. He was almost happy. She was almost happy.

But he did not know what was going to happen at the end of the two months.

They were outside together, standing in the middle of the rose arbor—or what would be the rose arbor next year. This year there was a young hedge and a trellised arched entryway with no roses, a fountain with no water, and rose bushes with no blooms.

But next year the roses would bloom.

Next year . . .

It was pleasant, Rebecca thought, so pleasant to be able to look forward. Next year Charles would be toddling around, doubtless getting under everyone's feet and into every imaginable mischief. She did not think she would be able to have him confined to the nursery with a nurse. She wanted to spend every possible moment of his upbringing with her miracle child. Perhaps her only child.

"Well," David said, "what do you think? A little dreary?"

"Oh, no," she said. "Just think of what was here when we arrived here late last summer. Overgrown trees that were cutting light from the windows. And now we have the beginnings of an arbor. I am so glad you decided to employ those boys again this year, David. They would not enjoy town life."

"When the roses bloom," he said, "it will be quite beautiful here. Your own special corner of the garden, Rebecca."

"When the roses bloom . . ." she said. "You said that last year too. Remember?"

When the roses bloom again, he had said, *you could be mistress of your own home, Rebecca. You could have a new and meaningful life. You could have something to replace the grief and the emptiness.*

"Yes," he said. "They have not literally bloomed here—yet. But they will—next year. I promised you a new life and new meaning, didn't I? Have you found them?" His voice sounded rather stiff.

"There has been so much to do here," she said, "and

still is. I think we have made a little difference in some people's lives, David. And as you promised, I no longer have that feeling of not quite belonging or of not having any meaningful function in life. And I have Charles.''

''You are happy?'' he said. ''Contented?''

Contented, yes. Happy? Was she happy? Sometimes, when she did not really think about it, she felt that she was. But perhaps not. She had told herself after Julian's death that she could never be happy again. And there was too much that she had to hold beyond her conscious mind. She could never relax into total happiness. There were Flora and Richard—she had seen them both at Katie's christening and had been pleased to find that her brother's new tenant was showing some interest in Flora. There was Lady Scherer and all the mystery surrounding that missing part of David's life—and Julian's. If there was a mystery. She had decided to let it go, not to think about it.

''Yes, David,'' she said quietly, fully aware that she had not made it clear which question she was answering. And not really knowing herself.

''You saw the doctor this morning,'' he said.

''Yes.''

''All is well?'' he said. ''With Charles? With you?''

''He howled with outrage,'' she said. ''He was not at all amused at having his sleep interrupted. Yes, we are both well, David.'' She drew a slow breath and pulled off a leaf from the hedge that had escaped the clippers.

There was a silence during which she wondered if only she felt a tension. She was afraid to look up at him.

''Rebecca,'' he said, ''it was always meant to be a real marriage between us, wasn't it? It was agreed that an incomplete relationship between us just would not work.''

He was the one who had decided that. Though he was right. She had felt it after their marriage, when he was sleeping in another room, before she had become aware of her pregnancy.

''Yes,'' she said.

''I want it to be a marriage again,'' he said. ''If you can bear it.''

She looked up at him at last. ''I am your wife,'' she

said. "I have no right to refuse. I never did refuse you, David. It was you who . . ."

"I don't like to be served merely out of duty," he said. "Not by my wife, Rebecca."

It was not just duty. It was more than that. Perhaps at the start . . . But it was more than that now. She remembered how she had wanted him, and felt somewhat ashamed of the fact, when he first stopped coming to her bed. How she had grown dependent upon his presence there during her pregnancy and since. How she wanted now to be touched, to . . .

She had always hated it with Julian. And yet she had loved him totally. She could not understand why now it seemed important to her—to be totally married, to be one with him in body if not in everything.

"Not if it is something you have to steel yourself for," he said.

"I want to be your wife, David," she said. She could see from his eyes that her words were ambiguous to him, that he still did not know if she was speaking from duty or desire. But she could not speak more plainly to him. Not about such matters. She could feel herself blushing.

"Very well, then," he said, his voice abrupt.

18

She had fed Charles. Sometimes he slept almost through the night. Almost as if he knew that it was his father's turn now to disturb her nights. David waited, standing at the window of their room as he had done on their wedding night. Feeling a flutter of anticipation and apprehension as he had done then. One just never knew with Rebecca. But it had to be a real marriage. He knew that nothing less than that would do.

As she had done on their wedding night, she came quietly into the room, closing the door into her dressing room as if there were a sleeper she did not wish to disturb, hesitating there as if she did not know how to proceed. As on that occasion he went to her.

"I am going to have to teach my son table manners," he said. "He sucks loudly and greedily."

"Only at first," she said. "Once he realizes that his meal is not going to be snatched away from him, he settles down to enjoy it more delicately."

"He is going to get fat," he said.

"He was fat when he was born." She smiled.

He liked to see her smile. She did so far more often these days than she had done at first. He liked to see her smile now. It meant that she had relaxed somewhat. It really was almost like a wedding night all over again, he thought. It had been almost a year, and even then there had been only three nights. He lifted a hand and brushed the backs of his fingers over her cheek. Her smile faded.

Her lips were soft and warm, closed and unmoving against his. He cupped her face with both hands and kissed it softly, letting his lips linger on her eyelids, her cheeks, her chin, letting her feel his mouth open over hers, his tongue trace the outline of her lips.

There was neither response nor lack of response. She was warm and relaxed and yielding.

Don't expect too much, he told himself. *Don't think of Julian.*

"Come to bed," he said, releasing her face and setting an arm about her shoulders. She leaned into him. She did not flinch away.

He wanted to see her. But he dimmed the lamp before getting into bed beside her. He did not want to embarrass her. There was no fire to give light.

She lay relaxed while he kissed her. She opened her mouth eventually to the probing of his tongue and allowed it to come inside. He tasted heat and moistness and sweetness. He felt himself harden with desire, with the urge to press onward to the act his tongue was simulating in her mouth. He imposed control on his mind and his body.

She lay relaxed while he raised her nightgown and moved his palm lightly up her body, beneath the gown to her breasts. He circled them lightly, caressing them with his fingertips as he kissed her again. So much the lady outside her clothes, so much the woman beneath the stays and the decent, concealing fabrics. He wanted her now. But he forced himself to prepare her with methodical patience.

He would not touch her nipples. For the present they were for his son. He moved his hand downward again, feathering it into the shapely hollow of her waist, over the womanly flare of her hip, down her smooth, warm thigh, around to the heated inner thigh and up.

She lay relaxed while his fingers parted her, smoothed between the folds, circled the entry to her. But her body responded as he worked and when he touched the one spot with the pad of his thumb and pulsed lightly against it. Her body prepared itself for penetration.

She lay relaxed as he lifted himself over her and lowered his weight, spread her legs wide with his own, and positioned himself to unite them. He could feel her drawing deep steadying breaths as he pushed firmly inward. He could feel her body tense even so. He lay still, deeply sheathed in her, as she brought herself under control and relaxed again. She was not touching him with her hands.

Her arms were spread wide on the bed. He set his own on top of them and spread his hands over hers.

He had caught her before she could school herself to total duty and obedience. Her hands were rigid. Her fingers were digging, clawlike, into the mattress.

He kept his hands where they were while her own flattened and relaxed. He rested his forehead against the pillow, above her shoulder, and felt sick. Quite physically sick. He was making love to a woman who found his touch repulsive. A woman who would allow him the use of her body because he was her husband.

Nothing had changed. Not a single bloody thing. Only him and his expectations. He drew himself out of her body, lifted himself off her and off the bed, and went to stand at the window. Desire died in him and hope and all faith in the future. He had tied himself to this for life. And he had tied her.

There was silence behind him for a long while. And then a rustling. He wished he had left the room immediately. He would go back to the one he used for a while after their marriage. He would have his things taken there from his dressing room tomorrow. Somehow he would have to learn to live with a marriage that was not a marriage. With a business partner. The mother of his son.

"David?" He had not realized that she had left the bed and was standing just behind his shoulder. Her voice was trembling.

He swallowed.

"What did I do?" she asked. Her voice was higher-pitched than usual. She sounded on the verge of tears. "I tried. I tried so hard to please you. I don't know what else to do. I don't know what you want."

He braced his arms on the windowsill, closed his eyes, and lowered his head. He wished to God he had left the room as soon as he had got out of bed.

"What do I want?" he said. "I know what I don't want, Rebecca. I don't want to rape you. It is not a pleasant feeling."

There was a short silence. "I'm your wife," she whispered at last. He could hear the shock in her voice. "You can't—"

"Possessing a body that cringes from mine feels like

rape," he said. "I'll not touch you again, Rebecca. And you need not feel you have failed in your duty. I choose not to touch you again."

"I did not cringe from you." Her voice was aghast.

He laughed. "No, not quite," he agreed. "You did try hard, Rebecca. Very hard. You have very good control over yourself. That is your greatest strength, I believe, isn't it? But the forced relaxation, the deep breaths, the stillness do not fool me, you know. And your hands gripping the mattress. Do you think I can take any sort of pleasure from raping a woman who has to so school herself to overcome revulsion in order to receive me?"

"I was not repelled," she said. "Oh, David, it was not that."

He turned away from the window at last to look at her. He tried to get a grip on his temper. "Then suppose you tell me what the hell *was* going on," he said. "It is late. I want to get some sleep and you are going to have to get up early to feed Charles."

"I was not repelled," she said. "You are not to think that. It is just that I felt ashamed. It is not right. Women are not supposed to . . . It is vulgar. And sinful. I didn't want you to know. I didn't want to disgust you. It won't happen again, David, I promise. It is just that it has been so long and I . . ." She drew a deep breath. "I wanted it to be good for you. I wanted to be totally submissive, but I failed. Give me another chance. Please? Don't go away. Please don't go away again. It won't happen again."

He gazed at her fixedly. He had rarely seen her so close to being distraught. "Women are not supposed to what?" he asked.

"It won't happen again," she said.

"What won't?" he asked.

He could see from the dim light of the window that she was biting her lower lip.

"What won't?" he repeated.

"It felt so good," she whispered. "It has been so long. Forgive me, David."

"For wanting me?" he said softly.

"It won't happen again," she said.

"It had better," he said, "if this marriage is to continue."

She stared at him mutely.

"It is a dreadful age we are living in," he said. "I don't believe it has been so through the rest of history. Are women—ladies—really taught that pleasure to their bodies is sinful, Rebecca? That sex is wrong?"

"Not wrong," she said, swallowing. "It is for a husband's pleasure. And for children."

He caught himself just in time from uttering an obscenity that she probably would not have understood anyway.

"There is to be no pleasure for the wife?" he said.

"Pleasure in giving pleasure," she said. "And in bearing children. And in suckling them. David—"

He pressed a finger firmly against her lips. "You want to give me pleasure?" he asked. "You see it as your duty to do so?"

"Yes," she said. "It won't—"

But he pressed his finger back in place.

"You will give me pleasure by taking it," he said. "It is your duty to allow me to pleasure you, Rebecca, and to show that pleasure quite openly."

"It would be unseemly—" His finger pressed more firmly.

"God made us with bodies as well as souls," he said. "And he created male and female to live together, to love together, to procreate together. He did not decree that the man enjoy and the woman endure. Preachers in our own century have done that. He created man and woman to be equal."

He felt her lips move against his finger. He did not remove it.

"I cannot use you as my wife if you merely submit, Rebecca," he said. "I don't expect your love. It was never a part of our bargain. But I do want us to draw equally from this marriage. Equal comfort, an equal sense of purpose, equal companionship and affection. Equal pleasure. I will use you only if you will use me." He dropped his hand back to his side.

"I want what you want," she said carefully.

"No," he said harshly. He would not fill the silence

that followed. It was up to her. Their future was up to her.

"I need you," she whispered at last. "Please, David. I need you. Don't' go away from me. I can't stand the emptiness, the loneliness."

"Neither can I," he said. "We will be together from mutual need, then, shall we? Neither one of us giving or taking more than the other?"

She nodded.

His heart turned over. As he lifted his arms to touch her, he was not sure that he was not getting in far deeper than he had ever thought to go. Far deeper than he could bear to go. For he was committing everything to her and she to him when neither could possibly give everything.

He put all thought firmly from his mind.

She needed him. Oh, God, she needed him.

She was not at all sure what she was agreeing to. She felt deeply uneasy. And entirely on unfamiliar ground. She had admitted to a need. She had all but begged him to stay with her, to make love to her. The idea that a woman's needs were of no account was deeply ingrained in her.

She was to be his equal, he had just said. They were to be equal in everything. He could not be her husband if she was a submissive wife. But she did not know how to be a different sort of wife. And it was wrong. Except that he had said it was not. He had told her what her duty was. And she was to obey him. She had promised that in all earnestness at their wedding. A wife's first duty was to be obedient.

Her nightgown buttoned down the front, the buttons extending from the high neck all the way down to her navel. At first when his hands kneaded her shoulders and then moved to undo the buttons she assumed that he intended to undo only the top ones. So that he could kiss her throat, perhaps? But he did not stop.

She realized what was going to happen when he lifted the fabric away from her shoulders and took her arms to straighten them at her sides. She was deeply mortified as the nightgown slid down her arms and over her breasts, past her waist and her hips and all the way to the floor.

Their eyes had become accustomed to the darkness, and light from a bright moon and stars was streaming through the window. She was facing the window. She did not want him to see her. She closed her eyes tightly as he took a step back.

And then he took both her hands in his and raised them to the top button on his nightshirt. No. She tried to pull her hands away.

"Yes," he said fiercely. "Yes, Rebecca."

She kept her eyes closed. Her fingers felt as if they were ten thumbs. She paused when she had opened the bottom button. But she knew what he wanted, what she must do. Drawing air into her lungs became a conscious effort.

His shoulders were warm to her touch, firm and muscled. But the fingers of her left hand brushed over a hard ridge. His scar. She opened her eyes as he shrugged out of his nightshirt and let it fall to the floor. Ah. Ah, dear Lord, he was beautiful. So very beautiful. She thought she might cry, and bit her lip.

He touched only her head, one hand cupping the back of it, the other raising her chin so that he could kiss her. She opened her mouth without waiting for the demand of his tongue and consciously resisted the instinct to quell the feeling, to school herself to be submissive. She allowed herself to feel. To feel the soft warm moistness of his mouth against hers. To feel the hardness of his tongue invade the cavity of her mouth and circle her own tongue before stroking over the sides of her mouth and the sensitive roof. The rawness of the sensation it created terrified her for a moment. She heard herself moan.

And then his mouth was moving down over her chin and along her throat to nuzzle the racing pulse at its base. His hands circled her breasts lightly, like the lick of flames. He held them cupped in the dip between his thumbs and forefingers and lifted them.

She let her head fall back. It felt so good. So very good. And she did not have to fight the feeling. He did not want her to. And he was to be obeyed. He had said it was not sinful. Man and woman were created with bodies. What God had created could not be bad.

She felt his lips against one nipple and then his tongue.

She gasped. And then cried out with shock and desire and clutched at his hair as he sucked hard. She felt a gush of milk to both breasts. And panted with embarrassment.

"Yes," he said. "Ah, yes." And he moved his head to the other breast and sucked gently. "Ah, yes." His face was over hers again and he kissed her wide-mouthed. She tasted the sweetness of her own milk.

"I want you," he said, straightening his arms down along his sides and drawing her against him at last. "Tell me you want me too. Say it."

"I want you," she said. Her need for him was pulsing between her thighs and deep inside her.

"Where?" he asked fiercely against her mouth. "Where do you want me?"

She could not answer him. She could not say the words aloud. Or even think them.

"Where?" he insisted. "Tell me."

"Between my legs," she said. "Inside me."

"Yes," he said exultantly. "Yes. Come then."

She was pulsing with longing, sore with the aching of desire. She was beyond either embarrassment or horror at her utter wantonness. She did not know how she would wait a moment longer. She did not know how she would bear the pain of his entry into such aching soreness.

He laid her down on the bed and came immediately on top of her. She spread her legs and arms without waiting for him to do it for her.

"No," he said, finding her mouth with his. "Touch me, Rebecca. Touch me."

She brought her arms about him, rubbing her palms hard over his shoulders and back, feeling the muscles, feeling all the masculinity of him. She could feel him poised and hard at her entrance and felt aching and empty and ready to explode with longing. Her hands moved downward, trembling.

"Please." She knew it was her own voice, sounding drugged, sounding utterly wanton. But she was beyond the point of being able to control it even if he had not commanded her not to. "Please. Give it to me. Give it to me, David."

He reached down to hook his hands beneath her legs and lift them over his own. She twined her legs about his powerful thighs and felt them open wider and push upward.

"This?" His voice was low against her ear. "This is what you want?"

She was frightened suddenly. She was utterly defenseless and wide, wide open. And tilted so that she knew there would be nothing to hold back. Nothing that would not be touched.

"Yes." Her voice was a gasp. "Yes. Oh, yes."

There should have been pain, he was so deep. There was pain. One that would surely drive her mad. There was no drawing back from it, no avoiding it. Her legs were imprisoned about his. He was holding her buttocks with strong, spread hands.

"And this?" He withdrew slowly and pushed in hard and deep again.

She could hear sounds, whimpering sounds, which she was powerless to control.

"And this?"

It became an agony. There was nowhere to hide. No part of herself into which to withdraw. It was too late for that. And there was nothing gentle about the endlessly repeated inward thrusts or about the speed at which they pounded at her central pain. He showed her no mercy at all. Only the demand that she give all. And—more terrifying—that she receive all.

And then she was clawing at him, drawing blood from his back, though she did not know it. Something was happening. Something was going to happen. Something so alien to her experience that she fought it with blind terror.

"No!" She tore at him. "No!"

"Yes." His face was above hers, his eyes heavy-lidded and intense with a passion that compounded her terror. "Yes, Rebecca. All of it. All of it."

The pounding had stopped but he would not withdraw completely. He would have no mercy. Always, slowly, relentlessly, came the deep inward push again and again and again, and the prolonged pressing against her pain until the last vestiges of control vanished and everything broke apart.

Everything.

She cried out.

He was saying something against her mouth.

And moving firmly and deeply again.

And sighing and murmuring into her mouth.

But everything had broken apart and body and soul were flung into a free fall beyond her control and beyond her caring. She let herself fall and cared nothing for the landing. Only the freedom mattered and the abandonment to something beyond herself. It did not matter when she landed or where or whether the jolt of the landing would kill her or merely bruise her. The fall was everything.

She fell, locked with the body of the man who was falling with her.

"It can be beautiful, you see," he was saying sometime later—maybe a few seconds, maybe a few hours later. "Not just when there is love, but even when there is not, provided there is affection and commitment. There is both with us, Rebecca, isn't there? There is affection."

He had removed himself from her body though he had kept his arms wrapped about her so that when he moved to her side she turned with him and lay against him. They were both damp all over and both still panting. He pulled a sheet and blanket up over them even though it was a warm summer night.

She was too lethargic to answer him. Too drowsy to think about what had happened and how it had shattered all that she had been taught and had experienced in her twenty-five years.

Affection? Was this what affection felt like? And commitment? Was this what committing oneself was like? Was this what being married was all about?

With my body I thee worship. She could hear his voice repeating the words after the vicar at Craybourne Church.

She felt worshiped. Carnal and frightening as it had been, she felt worshiped.

And drowsy.

And exhausted.

And wonderful.
She slept.

Sometimes when she was alone she would go off into deep thought. Or sometimes when she was busy, even when she was with other people, she would pause in what she was doing and go off into a dream that would take her beyond her surroundings.

What had it been like with Julian? she wondered. What had their courtship been like? And their marriage? Sometimes it frightened her a little that she could no longer remember quite clearly. All she could remember was a dream of love and a dream of perfection. Though she had never had a proper home with him. Or anything useful to do with her time. Or a child. And she had never enjoyed their conjugal relations.

And yet there had been the love and the feeling of perfection. And the conviction that life could not go on without him, or if it did because life could not come to an end just because one willed it to, then life could have no further happiness to offer. No further love.

Sometimes she felt uneasy and guilty about the happiness life had brought her not so very long after Julian's death. And she was happy. She could no longer deny it. There was Stedwell and all the busy routine of daily life there. And all the busy preparations for the picnic and dinner and ball in August, on their first wedding anniversary. There was Charles, her little bundle of joy. The bald and blue-eyed son who could and did make her heart ache with love.

And there was David. She never tried to put her feelings for him into words, even in her mind. She knew only what she did not feel for him. But he was important to her. Oh, far more than that. He was central to her new life, to her contentment, to her happiness. Without him it would all crumble. Without him there would be no one with whom to share the joy of a life she had not expected to find again after Julian.

David was her companion, her assistant, her advisor, her friend. Her child's father. Her lover.

Julian had been her love. David was her lover. She sometimes worded it that way in her mind. There was a difference though she did not analyze what it was. She did not want to know. She felt a little afraid to know though she did not stop to analyze the fear either.

David was her lover. The companionship and friendship were made personal and precious by the physical bond between them. What happened between them in their bed at night was something secret, something that only they shared, something that she had stopped feeling guilty about. It was her duty to please her husband. She pleased her husband by being pleased herself.

She allowed him to please her. She learned actively to please him.

And in the process she discovered the wonder of her own sexuality. And the wonder of focusing that sexuality on one man. On her husband.

Julian had been her love. She would always remain loyal to that knowledge. Her heart would be his for as long as she lived. Part of her would always be buried with him on the Inkerman Heights in the Crimea.

But David was her lover. And David was alive and warm and wonderful. She no longer thought about his past. His past was not her concern. He was her husband now, in the present, and would be for the rest of their lives.

Now, in the present, he was her friend and her lover.

She gave in gratefully to the temptation to be happy.

Until the day of the picnic.

19

Only the older people could remember the picnic and ball at Stedwell, though at one time it had been an annual tradition. But in the past it had always involved only the members of the gentry. This year, in reviving the tradition, the viscount and viscountess were also renewing it, making it an event for everyone.

There were to be outdoor games for the energetic—croquet, cricket, tennis, bowling, quoits, races for the children. There were to be canoe rides on the river. Those less energetic could stroll about the lawns or sit viewing the other activities or even wander indoors. Tea was to be served on the terrace.

In the evening there was to be a grand dinner—in the dining room for the gentry, in the ballroom for the lower orders. Later there was to be a ball. David and Rebecca had rejected the idea of having dancing outside for the lower classes. It was time everyone learned to mingle for certain events, they agreed.

Extra gardeners, cooks, and house help were hired for the week or so prior to the big day. It was a busy and anxious time—anxious because the weather could not be made to order and it had been a summer of unsettled weather. Alternative activities in the ballroom had been planned, but it would not be nearly as much fun to have everyone crammed in there during both the daytime and the evening.

But anxiety was put to rest when the morning dawned cloudy and dry but with the promise of opening out into a beautiful day. Rebecca sat in the rocking chair in the nursery, feeding Charles, who was sucking with his usual enthusiasm and gazing up at her, wide awake and serving notice that he had no intention of going back to sleep for a long while.

"Slow down," she told him. "Papa says you are getting fat. Just look at those cheeks." She tapped one of them with her forefinger.

Her son paused long enough in his breakfast to favor her with a wide and toothless smile. He sucked for five more minutes before deciding that he was full but very ready to play. There was a great deal to do, Rebecca thought. There would be precious little time to spend with him. She set him on her lap and bent over him to rub her nose against his until he smiled again.

"Here comes Papa," she said, hearing the door open behind her. "Have you saved any smiles for him?"

David set a hand against the back of her neck—a characteristic gesture—while he leaned over and tickled his son beneath the chin.

"I suppose you ate your breakfast to the last drop," he said. "Those cheeks are going to burst one of these days."

Charles gazed solemnly up at him before grinning widely at the joke.

"Happy anniversary," David said, turning his head to look down at Rebecca. "A present for you." He set a small parcel in her hand and then lifted the baby from her lap.

She had bought him a new watch chain, but it was still in her dressing room. There were small diamond earrings in the box, a perfect match for her Christmas pendant. "How lovely," she said. "Thank you, David. It seems longer than a year, doesn't it? Life is so different."

She knew that he would not have to ask if it was better. Though they never talked directly from the heart, they had both relaxed into the contentment of their life together at Stedwell. He had lost the tight, grim look that he had brought back from the Crimea. His eyes no longer looked as if they were accustomed to witnessing horrors and death. He seemed happy—except for the frequent times when he got up from bed during the night and she knew that he had been having nightmares again. She hoped they too would disappear with time.

"You were a good boy and slept all night again," he

said, turning his attention to their son, "What are your plans for today? Are you going to lead Nurse a merry dance? No, don't suck Papa's collar. It is clean and freshly starched."

It was a wonderful day on which to hold the picnic and ball, Rebecca thought, relaxing for a few moments more in the rocking chair and gazing down at her gift. Their first wedding anniversary. She felt a deep contentment— and then got determinedly to her feet. There was so much to do that the very thought of it all made her dizzy.

A team of David's laborers was playing a team of his tenants at cricket, though the outcome was a foregone conclusion, Mr. Gundy complained loudly and good-naturedly since the rival team had Joshua Higgins and everyone knew that he had only to show his bat to the ball and a six bounced right off it. Mr. Crispin and Mr. Appleby were rowing women and girls on the river. Stephanie Sharp and some of the other girls were playing tennis. Mrs. Hatch, the rector's wife, assisted by Miriam Phelps, was organizing the children's games and races. A few other ladies were playing croquet. It was almost time for tea.

David strolled from group to group, his son on one arm, looking about himself with interest. Charles had just woken up from a long sleep and was to favor his father's guests with his company for a short while. He was instantly popular with the ladies and girls. Rebecca was nowhere to be seen at the moment. David guessed that she was in the kitchen making sure that the tea was ready to be brought out.

The day was going to be a great success. Looking about him, he could not think of anyone who was not there. And he could not see anyone who was looking bored or dissatisfied—except for one small lad who set up a sudden wailing and was swept up for comforting by Miriam.

He should have done this years ago, David thought. He should have come home as soon as he reached his majority. He might have been saved a great deal of grief if he had. But then one could never know how life might have turned out if one had made different choices in the past. One had to accept the present for what it was and make an earnest attempt to prepare for a contented future. Both the present and the future were looking good to him at the moment.

But his pleasant musings were interrupted by the sight of a plain carriage—a hired one from the village—approaching along the driveway. He must have forgotten about someone, he thought, when he had just made a mental inventory of everyone in the neighborhood. He made his way up to the house in order to greet the late arrival.

But the smile that had been on his face all afternoon, and the words of welcome that had hovered on his lips died an instant death when the carriage came to a halt and Sir George Scherer stepped out and greeted him heartily before turning to hand down his wife.

"Major," he said, "we were passing through again and lamenting the fact that we were cooped up inside a train on such a lovely day. Cynthia remembered you, didn't you, my love, and insisted that we stop off to see you. I was afraid that you might be away or else busy with other matters, but you know what women are like once they get something into their head. It is easier to give in to them. It looks as if we have chosen an opportune time to come. This looks like a rare party."

"Welcome," David said involuntarily, shaking his hand and turning to Lady Scherer, who was as silent and grave as ever. She ignored his outstretched hand. He felt a sense of deep foreboding. He wondered if he should be bluntly rude and tell Scherer that in fact he was not welcome at all. He had a vivid memory of telling Rebecca that he would never again allow them in his house. But it was easier to imagine oneself doing such a thing than actually to do it especially on such a public occasion. Besides, there was no other train until morning.

"Your child?" Sir George said, smiling broadly at Charles. "Lady Tavistock was safely delivered, then. Your anxieties went for nothing, my love. A boy, I hope?"

"A boy, yes," David said. "He was born three months ago. We are having a picnic, as you can see. Tea is to be served any minute. I'll have you shown to a guest room. Perhaps you would like to freshen up before joining us.

You will join us for dinner too? There is to be a ball this evening.''

Rebecca had come up beside him. She greeted their unexpected and unwelcome guests as he fully expected her to greet them—with cool and competent graciousness. She took them into the house herself. But David, knowing her rather well after a year of living with her, could feel the coldness and tightness in her.

She thought he had once had an affair with Lady Scherer, he remembered.

Charles, who had been perfectly contented until his mother had come up beside him and totally ignored his smile and his expectation of being transferred to her arms, opened his mouth and bawled.

Perhaps, Rebecca thought during tea and the hours following it while she changed for the evening's activities and then during dinner, if they had had to come at all it was as well that they had chosen today by coincidence. Sir George was cheerfully sociable and seemed content to find an audience with the neighboring gentry. Even his wife seemed less reticent than usual and mingled with the ladies to whom she had been introduced.

Perhaps they would stay overnight and resume their journey on tomorrow's train and no one would be any the worse for their visit. Perhaps it was mean of her to be so displeased to see them.

And yet the knowledge that they had come affected her mood. They were a reminder to her again of the past that she had put firmly behind her. David's former mistress was there at their house, participating in the celebrations that coincided with their first wedding anniversary. And Sir George Scherer, who liked to taunt both her and David, was there too and one never knew if he was satisfied now or if there was more to come.

Why would he keep coming to the home of the man who had cuckolded him? The question chilled Rebecca as she smiled and tried to continue to enjoy herself. It could not after all be that he had come for an innocent visit, could it?

She wanted them gone. The happiness that she and David had found together was such a very fragile thing.

She had always known that. There was something between them, she knew, that perhaps would not bear the
light. Something that might make it very difficult even
for them to go on as they were. She did not want to know
what that something was.

She was afraid to know.

She and David began the dancing at the ball. It was a
waltz. They had danced together before since dancing
was one of the favorite activities of their neighbors. But
tonight there was a full orchestra and a full-sized ballroom, which had somehow lost its shabbiness behind
banks of flowers and greenery. This should be the happiest moment of a happy day, Rebecca thought, trying to
persuade herself that it really was. David looked magnificent in his black-tailed coat and trousers with crisp
white linen. His hair needed cutting—the way she liked
it best.

"You look beautiful," he said.

She had had the new seamstress and her assistants
make her a gown of shimmering gold silk, its bodice
unusually low for her, its hooped skirt ridiculously—and
exhilaratingly—huge.

She smiled, aware of eyes on them. Most people were
allowing them to dance alone before joining them on the
floor.

"I wish they had not come," she said and then wished
she had said nothing. It would have been better to say
nothing.

"I will make sure they leave tomorrow," he said. His
answer was so prompt that she knew their visit was
weighing heavily on his mind too.

Perhaps, she thought, the very best course of action
would be for the four of them to get together and have
everything out in the open. Perhaps only that way could
ghosts be exorcised and forgotten about. And perhaps
only that way could lives be destroyed. But how? They
had had an affair. It was over. Perhaps Sir George bore
a grudge, but she did not. It had happened long before
she married David.

But perhaps . . . She shut her mind to the frightening
notion, always there at the back of her mind, that there
was something else. There was a ball to be enjoyed and

a wedding anniversary to be celebrated. And guests to entertain.

Later in the evening Rebecca found herself beside Lady Scherer at the punch bowl. She smiled. "I hope you are enjoying yourself," she said. "And I hope you are not feeling neglected. It was a strange and happy coincidence that you came on this of all days."

"Oh, it was no coincidence," Lady Scherer said, her voice so low that Rebecca had to bend her head closer. "He knew. He knows everything about you."

Rebecca felt her stomach lurch uncomfortably.

"He knew about the picnic and ball?" she said. "Then I am glad you decided to join us."

"And that it is your anniversary," Lady Scherer said. "And that your son was born on May 15."

Rebecca stared at her, but Lady Scherer was looking coldly down into her glass.

"Watch out for him," she said. "He hates you. All three of you. He will harm you if he can. Sometimes I think he is deranged."

Rebecca's eyes widened and her thoughts focused on Charles, in the nursery upstairs with his nurse.

"I suppose you have guessed at least part of the truth," Lady Scherer said, looking up at her at last. Her voice when she spoke again was low and fierce. "I just want you to know that it was not sordid. To me it was not. And I have hated you too though totally without reason, I must admit. I loved your husband, you see. And I persuaded myself that he loved me."

She turned and walked into the crowd surrounding them, taking the ambiguity of her words with her. An ambiguity that she doubtless had not intended and that Rebecca did not even recognize.

It was impossible to avoid dancing with Sir George Scherer when he asked. Rebecca was talking with a group of neighbors and could have refused no one without seeming very ill-mannered, least of all the house guest who had arrived unexpectedly just that afternoon.

"Thank you," she said, setting her hand on his arm and allowing him to lead her onto the floor.

"I can hardly believe our good fortune in choosing this of all days to call upon you, Lady Tavistock," he said.

"It was a happy coincidence," Rebecca said.

"You must be very proud of the success of your party," he said. "It is your wedding anniversary, I understand?"

"Yes." She smiled at Sir Gideon Sharp and Mrs. Mantrell dancing past them.

"You were fortunate to make such a happy marriage," Sir George said. "I understand that Major Tavistock and your first husband grew up almost as brothers."

"Yes," she said.

"And that you were quite a close neighbor." He laughed heartily. "It must have been difficult to make your choice between them. But as it turned out, you were to be given a chance to choose both."

Only her upbringing kept her quiet. How dare he! What was he insinuating?

"Or perhaps," he said, "it was the major who wished to see to it that you could make a second choice."

"It was not a matter of choice, sir," she said, stung. She knew even as she spoke that it would be far better to keep her mouth shut. "I had always loved Julian."

"Ah, quite so," he said. "Young love, Lady Tavistock. I know all about it. Cynthia and I married as young lovers. We have lived happily ever after since our wedding day. You were not given so long."

Rebecca concentrated on the steps of the dance.

"But then," he said, "you were given a second chance with his brother and seem quite happy."

Would the music never end? But it had just started. She smiled at Stephanie Sharp.

"I'm glad of it," he said. "Glad for the major's sake. I owe my life to him, you will remember, Lady Tavistock."

"Yes," she said.

"It is strange, that memory, though," he said. "But then memories can be strange, can't they? Sometimes after a while one cannot decide what is real memory and what has been imagined. Have you ever noticed that, Lady Travistock?"

"I am sure you are right, sir," she said.

"Sometimes," he said, "when I remember that Rus-

sian soldier, Lady Tavistock, I see him with a scarlet coat
beneath his greatcoat. Now is that not ridiculous? Only
we British wore scarlet coats. Why would a British soldier be brandishing a sword in my face? And why would
the major be shooting him? Right through the heart it
was. A very strange memory, would you not agree?''

''Yes.'' She should not have had the ballroom decorated with flowers. Or not with so many anyway. There
was no air left. She could not breathe.

''But I should not be talking of such matters, should
I?'' he said. ''I always forget that it is distressing to some
ladies to be reminded of the war. Especially when they
lost husbands there. In just the same way, too, in your
particular case. Your husband was shot through the heart
as well, wasn't he? Are you all right, Lady Tavistock?''

''Yes,'' she said. But his voice was coming to her from
very far away. Everything was very far away. There was
a buzzing in her ears. The air she was breathing was
suddenly very cold. She was very cold.

''It's all right,'' someone was saying—from very far
away. ''She merely needs air. It has been a busy day for
her. Appleby, signal to the orchestra to start playing
again, will you?''

She was being lifted from the floor by strong arms and
carried out into fresher air and up the stairs. She was
sitting on a hard chair, and a strong hand was at the back
of her neck, forcing her head downward toward her
knees.

''Just relax,'' David said. ''There is no hurry. You
fainted, that's all.''

She was in her dressing room, she realized as the world
started to come back.

''How foolish of me,'' she said. ''Whatever will people think?''

''That the room was too warm and the excitement too
much for you,'' he said quietly. ''Just keep your head
down for a while. I'll fetch you a glass of water.''

''I can't imagine doing anything more embarrassing,''
she said, lifting her head after a minute or so and taking
the glass from his hand. ''And I can't think what brought
it on. I never faint. We must go back down, David.''

He set the glass down on the washstand after she had

taken a few sips. "What was he saying?" he asked quietly.

"Oh, the usual," she said. "About you saving his life. About Julian getting shot through the heart. I'm afraid I am rather squeamish about the thought of such things. It was the wrong time and the wrong place."

"He said nothing more?" he asked.

"No," she said brightly. "Just the usual. But the trouble is, David, that now I know what to expect him to say and it is even worse. It is not the sort of conversation one wants to listen to at a ball."

"They will be on the morning train," he said.

"I am sure he means no harm," she said. "But his conversation is distasteful. I am ready to go back downstairs. I feel so embarrassed."

"Lean on my arm," he said. "Stay close to one of the windows. Signal me if you feel faint again."

"I won't," she said. "I am so sorry, David, to have caused such a commotion."

A redcoat, she thought as they walked downstairs and she tried desperately to think of something else. Three redcoats. Three British officers—the third man too had carried a sword. No Russian at all. Two of them in conflict over a woman—the wife of one of them, the lover of the other. And the third one—the one in the middle, the peacemaker—getting shot. And killed.

"You are sure you are well?" David asked as they approached the ballroom doors. He set a hand over hers.

She felt instant panic. She wanted to snatch her hand away. But it was no time for hysterics. No time was good for hysterics. The self-discipline of years would not allow her to go all to pieces.

Merely because she was walking with her husband, her husband's murderer.

"Quite well, thank you," she said. "It was very foolish of me to faint. I am quite recovered."

She smiled, hiding embarrassment as many people turned her way, concern on their faces, when she stepped into the ballroom again on David's arm.

He should have had the strength of will to turn them away on their arrival, David thought. He had, after all, asked Scherer to leave the last time. The man had known he would be unwelcome.

But he had not turned them away. And Scherer had said something to make Rebecca faint. It was nothing in particular, she had said. Only the usual. The usual was bad enough. Reminding her in the midst of a ball that Julian, whom she had loved so dearly, had died with a bullet through his heart was more than enough to make her faint.

David wondered again why Scherer hated him so much since he had undoubtedly saved the man's life. If he had shot one second later, Scherer would have been dead with Julian's sword embedded in his chest. David had saved his life.

But the reason was not so hard to discover, as he had realized before. It would be humiliating to a man like Scherer, as to many men, to know that he had had to be saved from the sword of a man who also had been sleeping with his wife. It would be as easy to hate the man who had saved him as to feel gratitude toward him.

And David knew that Scherer was wondering about his motive for killing Julian in light of his seemingly hasty marriage to Julian's widow on his return home. Scherer was wondering if his motives had been as selfless as they might have appeared at the time. Scherer's suspicions were echoing David's nightmare—that he had killed Julian out of hatred and jealousy, that he had wanted the field clear so that he could marry Rebecca himself.

It was also clear that Scherer hated Rebecca. Because he suspected that she had been unfaithful to Julian as his wife had been to him? Or merely because she had been Julian's wife? It was an eye-for-an-eye hatred, perhaps. Julian had made him suffer. Now he would make Julian's wife suffer too.

For Rebecca's sake David cursed himself for not turning them away. He hated the thought that they were in his house for the night, that they would not be on their way until the morning.

It was a mistake to try to make love to Rebecca after the ball. She was tired, and Charles had woken up and demanded a late and leisurely feed. She looked dispirited when she finally came to bed. She was suffering a feeling of anticlimax after such a busy day, perhaps. And the leftover distress of her fainting spell. She was upset over whatever it was Scherer had said to her. And David was upset and agitated for all the same reasons. And because he had neglected to protect his wife from distress.

She was the old Rebecca when he touched her, stiffening at his first touch, then imposing deliberate relaxation on her body. She was totally silent and unresponsive. Only submissive. He persevered, touching her and kissing her in ways and in places that he knew from the experiences of the past month could arouse her to passionate frenzy. And yet finally he had to admit defeat and mount her unaroused.

Except that he could not do even that. At the last moment he found himself humiliatingly impotent. He moved to her side and lay staring up into the darkness. He did not turn his head to see if she did the same or if she had fallen asleep.

But he knew she was not sleeping.

He fought panic and despair. It was just that they had both had a busy day and were tired. And they were both upset at the unwelcome arrival of their house guests. Tomorrow they would be alone again. Tomorrow they would be able to rebuild what had fallen apart today.

It was such a fragile thing, their happiness. So near to the brink all the time. But tomorrow they would recapture it.

He wondered with a dull ache of the heart exactly what George Scherer had said to her.

20

It was a dreadful thing indeed, Rebecca found over the coming months, to have deep, dark suspicions bottled up inside. No longer suspicions that could be put firmly behind her because they did not really concern her. These concerned her very much indeed.

And yet they were suspicions that were totally unfounded. They rested entirely on the malicious insinuations of a spiteful, wronged man who wanted any revenge that he could wreak, no matter how innocent or guilty his victims. Even his wife had admitted that she sometimes thought he was deranged.

They were ridiculous suspicions. Wild. Insane. Nightmarish.

Terrifying.

She knew as the days and then weeks and even months passed that she should have acted decisively at the start. She should have told David as soon as she recovered from her faint what Sir George Scherer had said. She should have looked him in the eye and explained what she thought he had been insinuating. She should have asked if it was true.

Of course it was not true. David would have looked at her with incredulity and laughed. They would both have laughed—not entirely with amusement but with relief. He would have admitted that he had indeed had an affair with Cynthia Scherer and that now Sir George was trying to destroy David's marriage as David had destroyed his.

There would have been guilt. It was not a pleasant thing David had done. But relief too. It was in the past. It was something he had put an end to. And it really would not have touched their own marriage at all. It had all happened long ago.

That was what she should have done, Rebecca told her-self. But she knew that she could not have done it. For there was always the chance that he would not have looked at her with incredulity and he would not have laughed. There was always the chance . . .

No! There was no chance at all.

Sometimes during those months Rebecca suspected that she must be pregnant again. Certainly she felt queasy enough much of the time and sometimes vomited in the mornings. And she was frequently tired and lethargic. But she was not pregnant.

They still worked together and discussed business to-gether. They still shared an active social life. They still spent a great deal of their time with their son, often together. And they still shared a bed and made love— sometimes with a fierce intensity. But the contentment, the happiness had gone. There was too much mutual awareness of the barriers that divided them. And too much reluctance to admit that they existed. And no willingness at all to bring them into the open to discuss them.

She was terrified to confront the barriers.

And so she remained locked up inside her mind with the unwilling and terrifying suspicions. And watched the grim, shuttered look come back to his face and the bleak look to his eyes. Sometimes she wondered why he did not ask the questions if he did not have anything to hide more serious than the affair with Lady Scherer. She had already confronted him with that, after all.

And the wondering would bring on yet another wave of nausea.

Spring was not too far off, David thought when they were returning to Stedwell after spending Christmas at Craybourne. Perhaps things would improve once they could be outdoors more and all the work of the year be-gan again.

Rebecca had Charles on her lap in the train compart-ment and was making him laugh helplessly. It was not difficult to make him laugh. He was a sunny-natured child and adored his mother. Rebecca was barking like a dog and pretending to bite his stomach—and then laughing with him.

But the quiet, poised self-discipline had returned to her dealings with everyone except their son. The signs of contentment and even happiness had disappeared. Even when she responded to his lovemaking, as she sometimes did, it was with a fierce sort of desperation rather than with the joyous wonder she had been learning with him for a while.

The changes could be dated exactly, of course. Scherer had not been dealing out the usual to make her faint on the night of their ball. It had been something else. He should have acted decisively right then, David realized now. He should have forced her to tell him. He should have forced it all into the open.

Except that he had not the courage.

What if she knew?

How would they go on if that ever came into the open between them? Would they be able to go on?

And yet, he thought now as Charles, tired of the dog game, crawled off Rebecca's lap and onto his to pull at his watch chains, wouldn't anything be better than this constant tension between them? This constant awareness of all that was unspoken between them?

Perhaps it would be better to force the issue even now. Perhaps it was not as bad as he feared. Would she have been able to go on at all if Scherer had told her the truth? Perhaps Scherer had told her only about the affair between his wife and Julian. Perhaps that was what was eating away at her. He would be able to comfort her over that—perhaps. It would be a dreadful thing for Rebecca to know that. But he would be able to assure that it had happened because Julian was lonely, because he desperately missed Rebecca. He would be able to tell her about Julian's sense of guilt, about his longing to be home.

He would not even have to tell many lies.

He drew his watch out of his waistcoat pocket to hold against Charles's ear and chuckled as his son turned his head to see what he could hear and try to put it in his mouth.

David knew he would not talk to her. He was too much

of a coward. There was too much to lose. Even what they had now was better than nothing.

And yet, he discovered when they returned to Stedwell, silence between them was no longer possible.

Charles was cross by the time they arrived home, having refused to fall asleep in the train and so having missed his afternoon nap. David carried him up to the nursery and Rebecca went along too to change the baby's nappy before turning him over to his nurse's care.

"Mrs. Matthews said tea was being sent to the drawing room immediately," David said as they left the nursery. "Let's go straight there. The fire and a cup of tea will be very welcome, won't they?"

"It is chilly outside," she agreed. "Perhaps it would warm up a little if it would only snow. We haven't had any this year yet."

Someone had set the post that had arrived during the week of their absence on a salver beside the tea tray. David flicked through it while Rebecca poured the tea. Thus it was that they both looked together at the Christmas card that had arrived too late to be opened before Christmas.

The handwriting was large and bold. "Cynthia joins me in sending our greetings for a very merry Christmas," Sir George Scherer had written. "We sincerely hope that the two of you and your son have enjoyed your week at Craybourne."

It was a perfectly conventional greeting for a Christmas card. Except perhaps that a man who had been a stranger to Stedwell and its inhabitants since August should not have known about the weeklong visit to Craybourne. And yet it was, when all was said and done, a quite innocuous Christmas greeting.

David set the card back down on the tray without comment and accepted his cup of tea from Rebecca's hands. She took her own, and they seated themselves, as they usually did when they were without company, on either side of the fireplace with its blazing fire. Neither took any sandwiches or cakes from the plates on the tray.

Conversation eluded them. There was so much they could have talked about—the week they had just spent with his father and Louisa and Katie, the Christmas party they had held before they left for Craybourne, their plans for the spring, their son, but neither spoke.

The crackling of the flames and the clinking of cups against saucers became oppressive.

Rebecca set her cup and saucer down on the table beside her. Her tea was unfinished, but she knew she could not raise the cup to her lips even one more time. Her hands were beginning to shake. Without looking up she was aware of David setting his own cup down too.

She knew at the same moment that the time had come. That there could be no more putting it off. Even so she tried.

"How did he know," she asked, her voice falling toneless into the silence, "that we were going to Craybourne for a week?"

"A lucky guess perhaps." His voice was taut with tension.

"He knew about the picnic and ball," she said.

"A coincidence," he said.

"No." She pleated the fabric of her dress between her fingers. "His wife told me that he knew everything about us. He even knew that Charles was born on May 15."

He said nothing.

She could feel her heart hammering, not only in her chest but in her throat and in her ears and against her temples. She knew she was going to ask it. The unaskable.

"David." Her voice came out as a whisper. "How did Julian die?"

She waited without hope for the reassertion that it had happened as he had described it on the evening of his return from the Crimea. She knew it would not come.

"What did he tell you?" he asked.

"Nothing," she said. She leapt to her feet suddenly as if she thought there was somewhere she could run, realized there was not, and turned away from the fire and away from him. She fixed her eyes on the pianoforte at the other side of the room. "And everything. He said nothing. He implied everything."

There was a long silence. More than once she heard

him draw breath as if to speak and shut her eyes very tightly. But the silence stretched.

"What is everything?" he asked at last. "What do you suspect?"

"That you killed him." The nightmare words had been spoken. There was no recalling them. And still the silence stretched. There was no instant shocked denial. Just the silence. "Did you?"

A moment's silence could be an eternity. An eternity during which one knew life was forever changed, the past forever gone.

"Yes."

The single word. The single knife wound. The ending of everything.

She heard herself drag breath noisily and painfully into her lungs. It came shuddering out of her again.

"The bullet was intended for Sir George Scherer," she said. "You were shooting at him and Julian got in the way. That's how it happened, isn't it? You did not shoot deliberately at him. You didn't, did you? Tell me you didn't. Tell me it was an accident that you killed him."

"Rebecca—" She could tell that he had got to his feet. His voice came from just behind her.

She spread her hands over her face.

"I loved him," he said. "He was as close as a brother to me. I wish it could have been the other way around. I wish I could have died and sent him home to you."

"It should have been the other way around." She wondered if there were any possibility that she would wake up and find this to be a vivid nightmare. But she knew it was not. She knew it was really happening. "You were the one who deserved to die, David."

She could feel him standing very still behind her. He said nothing.

"Why were you shooting at Sir George?" she asked. "Was it self-defense, David? Was he trying to kill you for what you had done with his wife? And was Julian trying to act the peacemaker? In the middle of a battle? Did it really happen in the middle of a battle? Why did no one else see?"

"There was a heavy mist," he said, "and all the smoke from the guns."

"So there were just the three of you." She could feel herself swaying for a moment but imposed an iron discipline on herself. If she stumbled or fell, he would touch her. "Was it self-defense?"

"It was a kill-or-be-killed situation," he said. All tone had gone from his voice.

"Over Lady Scherer," she said. "Her husband had just discovered the truth and was incensed."

"Yes."

"And Julian got caught in the middle," she said. "It was Julian who saved Sir George's life, not you. Julian took the bullet that was meant for him. My husband was taken from me because you could not keep your hands off another man's wife."

He said nothing.

"And so," she said, "you came home and married me." She laughed suddenly. "I was right about that, wasn't I? You felt guilty that you had not done more to save him, I said. How very comical. I was far more accurate than I dreamed when I said that, wasn't I? You married me to make up for the fact that you had murdered Julian." She could not seem to stop laughing. And her laughter suddenly seemed more horrifying, more grotesque than anything else that had happened in the past few minutes.

"Rebecca—" he said.

"Oh, don't worry," she said. "I am not going to do you any great injustice, David. I know that you did not rejoice in doing it and that you have carried around the guilt of it ever since. Your eyes and your face have told me from the moment of your return that you have suffered greatly. It must be a terrible thing to know yourself a murderer, however inadvertently it was committed. It must be a terrible thing to know that Julian died for your sins." She closed her eyes.

"Yes." There was despair in the single word.

She turned at last to look at him. His face was ashen, almost the color of his shirt. And if she had thought his eyes bleak before, now she would not have been able to find the word to describe them. Hell was mirrored in his eyes.

"We have been friends," she said. "Lovers. We have had a child together."

"Yes."

"Yet you killed Julian."

"Yes."

"I married my husband's murderer," she said.

His answer was a long time coming. "Yes," he said at last.

"I wanted to die, you know," she said, "when your father called me into the library and they gave me the news, he and that soldier who had come to bring it. I didn't know how I was to live without Julian. But death will not come just by willing it. I wish I had died. I thought there could be nothing worse than learning that he was dead. I was wrong."

He closed his eyes and lowered his head.

"Death in battle seems so pointless," she said. "But there is a certain logic to it. He died for his country. He died a hero. He died leading his men. There is very little comfort in such thoughts, but there is some. I have hugged it about me ever since his death. But his actual death was worse than pointless. He was twenty-four years old. He would have been not quite twenty-eight now. I was twenty-two. Two innocents destroyed by a sordid incidence of adultery. But I don't suppose you need my accusations to sharpen your guilt, do you?"

He shook his head without opening his eyes.

"It all must have happened so quickly," she said. "And I know you did not mean to kill him. I think perhaps, David, the time would have come when I could have forgiven you. Perhaps. I don't know. But I'll never be able to forgive you for marrying me."

He looked up at her.

"I am married to the man who killed Julian," she said. "Charles's father. How can I forgive you for that?"

"Charles is a baby," he said, speaking at last in more than a monosyllable, "and in no way to blame for the fact that he is a product of my seed. He has no involvement whatsoever in all this, Rebecca. Your feelings toward him must not change in light of what you now know about me."

Her eyes widened. "Charles is my child," she said

fiercely. "I bore him in my womb and delivered him in pain. He is the sunshine in my life. My love for him could never ever be diminished."

They stared at each other wide-eyed. The passion of her words had broken something in the atmosphere. They both realized with sudden blinding clarity that they were in a real situation with no apparent resolution.

"What do you want me to do?" he asked. "Where do we go from here?"

"I don't know," she said. She thought for a moment. "I don't know. He has had his revenge, though, hasn't he?"

"Scherer?" he said. "Yes, he has made our marriage as hellish as his own. Is it to be a marriage, Rebecca? Do you want me to send you away and settle you and Charles in another home elsewhere? Is that what you want?"

Was it? She stared at Julian's killer and saw David. And thought of leaving Stedwell and their neighbors and friends. She thought of giving up all her involvement in community affairs and all her responsibilities as lady of the manor. She thought of taking Charles away and bringing him up in a fatherless home. And of leaving David, of perhaps never seeing him again except very briefly and very formally on special occasions in Charles's life.

It was too late to go away. They had been married for a year and a half. Their lives were bound up together. He was her husband. Perhaps she really would never forgive him for marrying her, but they were married.

"I am your wife," she said.

"Duty and submission and obedience." There was a hardness about his jaw, bitterness in his voice.

"Yes," she said. "You will always have them from me, David, because I can live only as I have been taught to live and as I have vowed before God to live. I am your wife and will be dutiful and obedient to you as I was to Julian before you. Our marriage should never have happened, but it did, and it has existed for a year and a half. We have a child who needs us both." Her tone was as bitter as his.

"We continue on, then?" he asked.

"We have no choice," she said.

"As man and wife?"

"That is what we are, David."

There was something strangely anticlimactic about the moment. Something dreadfully wrong about it. There should be no possibility of their going on. He had killed her husband and then come and married her himself. She had lived with and conceived a child with the man who had deprived Julian of his life and marriage and children. And now she was agreeing to continue their marriage.

Because there was no choice.

Because they were married.

And because there was Charles.

He reached out a hand and touched her arm tentatively. Her first instinct was to draw back in horror, but she was looking into his eyes—into his suffering eyes. And he was David. She did not move. He raised his other hand and curled them both about her arms. He drew her against him and set his arms about her. Her face rested against his shirtfront.

"I could say I'm sorry, Rebecca," he said. "But the words would not begin to convey my sorrow and would sound like a glib insult. I can only say that though I loved him in a different way from the way you did, I loved him just as deeply."

"Yes," she said. "I know."

She tilted her head back after a while and looked up at him. "David," she said, "I know that you wronged Sir George Scherer, but he has let hatred poison his life and his marriage. I don't want to let him extend that hatred and that poison to ours. There is nothing left hidden between us now, is there? We have touched the depths and can only stay there or move onward and upward."

"Onward and upward, then," he said, his eyes sadder than she had ever seen anyone's.

"There *isn't* anything left hidden, is there?" she said.

He gazed into her eyes for a long moment. "Nothing," he said.

"It is terrifying to see the pit open at one's feet," she said. "But it is better after all than knowing it is there and being afraid to look. We have both known for a long time that it is there. Now we have seen it. It is better so, isn't it?''

''Yes.'' He closed his eyes and lowered his head to set his lips, closed, against hers. ''It is better so.''

And yet, Rebecca thought, closing her own eyes and leaning her weight against him, she did not know quite how they would go on.

Except that they had no choice.

She did not know how she could bear to let him touch her.

Except that he was David.

David had always wondered as a boy if it was a strength or a weakness in his character that made him cover up for Julian's misdemeanors and bear the punishment himself. It had not been easy to see disappointment in his father's face and to put up with the pain of thrashings he had not deserved. And sometimes he had felt horribly used despite Julian's gratitude.

Was it strength or weakness? He had concluded at the age of seventeen that it was weakness and had put an end to it—until Flora Ellis. After once more agreeing to be the scapegoat, he had come to the same conclusion. He had helped Julian out, but at the same time he had kept from Rebecca what she had a right to know before taking the irrevocable step of marrying Julian. Julian's subsequent behavior had shown David that she should have known. She should have been given the chance to make a decision based upon truth.

The truth was always best, he had concluded on that occasion. He had been weak to agree to hide the truth from her.

And this time?

There was nothing that remained hidden, he had assured her. Everything was at last in the open between them. They had touched the depths and were now ready to move onward and upward again.

Once again he had allowed himself to be the scapegoat. She had put what he agreed seemed a perfectly logical interpretation on past events, and he had allowed her to go on believing it. It was he who had had the affair with Cynthia Scherer, she believed, and he had not denied the charge. It was he and George Scherer who had been involved in a death struggle and Julian who had come along to interrupt them. He had allowed her to go on believing that.

He had taken Julian from her. All she had left were memories of what she had thought was the perfect marriage. He had not taken that from her as well. He could not. It was all she had.

He was not sure that matters would have been better for him anyway even if he had told her the full truth. He really had killed Julian. Perhaps the truth would be worse. The truth was that he had aimed at Julian, not Scherer. Even if the decision had been made in a split second and without any conscious choice, he had quite deliberately aimed at and killed Julian.

Would it help anything to protest his innocence of the lesser charge? To deny the affair with Lady Scherer? The only way he could convincingly do so was to accuse Julian—and so destroy something else in her, the most precious memory she had. He could not do it. *Would* not do it.

Was it weakness? Or strength?

It did not much matter, he supposed.

Incredibly their lives carried on much as usual. They continued with their work, dined and danced with their friends, played with their son. They even loved. He was tempted on that first night to seek out a bed elsewhere, but he knew that if he once did it he would not find the courage to return to her. And they had the rest of a lifetime to live through together. For a while he lay silently beside her, but when he turned to reach for her, she received him with neither the old submissiveness nor the more recent passion. She loved him with tightly closed eyes and a quiet sort of tenderness.

As if she felt and understood his pain.

As if she longed to forgive him.

As if she wanted to be forgiven for not turning him off.

Almost as if she had grown to love him despite everything.

By the end of January he was not at all sure that they could go on as they were, that they could ever put the past finally behind them and move on into the future. He did not know if it was love or despair that was between them, holding them somehow together. Were they at the beginning of the future? Or at the beginning of the end? He did not know.

But at the end of January the letter came. The Earl of Hartington was summoning them to Craybourne in an unusually formal manner. It was a matter of great urgency. They must come immediately—both of them.

21

Craybourne, 1858

After a short consultation, they decided to take Charles with them. But of course it was a foregone conclusion that he would go too. They could not possibly go anywhere for longer than a day without their son. But under protest he traveled in a compartment with his nanny and his mother's maid and his father's valet. David and Rebecca traveled in a compartment alone, worried and speculating on the reason for the abrupt summons.

"It must be that Father is ill," Rebecca concluded for surely the dozenth time since the day before. It was the only reasonable explanation, though why he had written instead of Louisa if he were ill they could not understand. Unless the illness was a lingering one that was going to kill him slowly. They did not mention that possibility though it always hung in the silence between them.

Perhaps it was Louisa who was ill. Perhaps it was Katie. Or perhaps it was not an illness at all. Perhaps . . . But they had exhausted all the possibilities, likely and otherwise, and really there was no way of knowing. They might as well not even try guessing but talk about other matters. They had guessed themselves in circles.

"We will soon find out," David said and put an effective end to the discussion. Soon they would be at Craybourne.

Rebecca thought about their last visit there as the carriage the earl had sent to the station approached the house. It had been only a few weeks ago—at Christmas. Everything had changed since then. Everything and nothing. She wondered if they would appear different to David's father and to Louisa. She wondered if they *were* different. Life was much as it always had been between

them. That brief month of happiness last summer had
been exceptional. And yet it had created—or revealed—
a bond between them that was proving surprisingly enduring.

For better or for worse they were married and she could
not quite persuade herself that she was sorry he had
tricked her into marriage, playing on her vulnerability,
hiding the truth of what had happened in the Crimea.
She should be sorry, she knew. Knowing what she now
knew, she should find being married to him quite insup-
portable. But she did not. She had discovered a depth of
fondness for him that had taken her by surprise during
the past weeks.

The house looked normal, she thought, gazing out of
David's window as he set his own face close to the glass.
Whatever it was, it was nothing that was obvious to the
eye. The carriage drew to a halt.

"I'll take Charles up to the nursery and get him settled," she said. "You can find Father and set your mind
at rest, David. Or he will find you. He has probably been
watching for the carriage."

But it was the butler who met them in the hall, looking
as dignified and as grave as he had ever looked. Perhaps
the nurse would take the child upstairs, he suggested. His
lordship wished to see Lord and Lady Tavistock in the
library without delay.

Rebecca handed an overtired and cross Charles to his
nanny and exchanged a glance with David. It was all so
very formal. She remembered how the earl had come
into the hall to greet David on his return from the Crimea. Even at Christmastime he had been there, with
Louisa and Katie.

And now he wanted to see both of them in the library?
Not just David? Rebecca found that her heart was beating
with uncomfortable rapidity. She saw her own anxiety
mirrored on David's face as he set a reassuring hand
against the back of her waist and guided her toward the
library doors, which the butler was opening.

The earl was standing with his back to the fire, opposite the door.

"Father," Rebecca said, smiling and taking a few steps
toward him. But something stopped her. He really was

ill, was her first thought. He looked deathly pale and stood unnaturally still. No, it was Louisa, was her second thought. Louisa was dead.

She did not know what caused her head to turn sharply toward the large window to her left. The sudden awareness, perhaps, that there was someone else in the room. Someone standing in front of the window, the light behind him, just as still and silent as her father-in-law.

She could not see his face. But she knew him instantly. There are certain people whom one identifies more through the emotions than the senses. She could not see him clearly and he said nothing. But she knew him. Even if her rational mind had been able to tell her that it was not he, that it could not possibly be, that it was someone else of the same height and build and coloring, her heart would have told her without any hesitation at all that it was indeed he.

She looked at him, strangely calm. But of course time and place and reality have no part in such moments. She had lost touch with all three. She took two steps toward him, stopped, and found herself suddenly released from the spell that had bound her.

"J-U-L-I-A-N!" She flew across the room, wailing his name, and was caught up in a bruising hug and twirled around and around. She continued to wail, her face buried against his shoulder, while he laughed and tried to squeeze all the breath out of her.

Just like Julian. So very typical of him.

"Becka," he said against her ear, his voice full of laughter. "Becka my darling."

Her hands were grasping his shoulders. Her whole body was touching his. She could feel his arms tight about her, could hear his voice talking to her and laughing at her. Flesh and blood. Warm. Alive. He was alive. She drew back her head and looked up at him, her eyes wide with wonder.

"Julian?" Her voice was a whisper. She touched one of his cheeks with trembling fingertips. "Julian?"

"Alive and well," he said, smiling the old charming smile, looking and sounding so shockingly familiar that her eyes widened further, "and home. And discovering that I was reported dead and buried at Inkerman instead of just captured there and carried off into Russia to an endless captivity. I've come home, Becka.''

''Captured?'' She spoke as in a dream. ''You did not die?''

''Very nearly.'' He chuckled. ''I came within a whisker of a whisker, but it seems my time was not up. it took them a year to bring me back to life and then they couldn't bear to part with me for several more years. But here I am at last with only a rather ugly purple hole above my heart to show for it all. I came home two days ago.'' His smile faded. ''To find myself facing one hell of a mess, Becka.''

It was only then—how long had it been since she had turned her head toward the window?—it was only then that reality came rushing back. She was in Julian's arms—Julian's!—in the library at Craybourne. Her father-in-law was in the room too and so was David. *And so was David.* Charles was upstairs in the nursery.

Rebecca gazed at Julian. She could not have turned her head to save her life. *One hell of a mess.* His words rang in her head and echoed in the room.

He kept one arm tightly about her waist and turned her. ''Hello, Dave,'' he said. ''I didn't send word ahead. I thought I would just turn up and create a sensation. I didn't expect it to be quite as sensational as this.''

Rebecca did not believe she would be able to look at David. But she forced her eyes upward. He looked just exactly as his father had looked when they came into the room. As if he were carved of stone. Of white marble.

''I'm not a ghost,'' Julian said. ''But under the circumstances I don't suppose I can expect a tumultuous welcome, can I?''

David took a step forward. Julian dropped his arm from Rebecca's waist. And then the two men were in each other's arms, hugging each other tightly and wordlessly. David's eyes were tightly closed.

Rebecca looked across the library to the earl, who still had not moved, though he was watching the three of them. The stony look had gone from his face, to be replaced with a look of suffering so intense that it brought her back finally to full reality. He had had time to digest the fact of Julian's return and all its implications. She realized suddenly with a sick turning of the heart just how much there was to be digested, how many implications there were to be faced.

David was crying with noisy sobs. Julian was laughing. Rebecca touched his shoulder from behind, rubbed her palm along it, set her face against it. And felt an arm slide out from beneath her breasts and away—an arm that had been around Julian. Her husband's arm. David's arm. There was silence in the room again.

"I had no idea I had been reported dead," Julian said. "I thought you would have found me missing, Dave. I thought you would have come looking for me after the battle. But you were badly wounded, Father told me."

"Yes."

"And so everyone thought me dead," Julian said, "and some poor devil who is still thought to be missing is buried back there instead of me. Unless whoever was in charge of the burial detail just could not count. It's a queer feeling to find that you have suddenly been resurrected in people's eyes."

No one answered. Rebecca kept her face where it was. Her eyes were closed. There was a familiar smell about him, something quite unidentifiable, something she had never been aware of before. He was so unmistakably Julian.

"And so you and Becka married," Julian said.

"Yes."

"And have a son."

"Yes."

"It's one hell of a mess, isn't it?" Julian said. He chuckled, though the sound lacked his usual humor. "Whose wife is she, I wonder."

They all knew the answer to that one. Rebecca could hear someone crying and realized, startled, that it was her. She could not seem to stop.

"No, don't, David," she heard the earl say sharply and it was Julian who turned to take her into his arms and cradle her head against his shoulder.

"Becka," he crooned against her ear. "We'll sort it all out. I'm home, darling. I'm holding you in my arms again. Where you belong. They have been so empty without you. So very empty. You are glad to see me, aren't you? Tell me you're glad. Tell me you love me.''

An ache of the old tenderness washed over her and she cried harder against his shoulder. Her usual control had utterly deserted her.

"She is in shock," she could hear the earl's voice saying. "Take her upstairs, love, and get her something to calm her down and put her to sleep for a while. No, David, stay where you are. Louisa will know best what to do.''

She had not heard Louisa come into the room. The earl must have sent for her.

"Let her go, Julian," the cool voice of the earl continued. "Louisa will be the best medicine for her at the moment. We three have some talking to do.''

Julian was releasing his tight hold on her. She was still crying helplessly and observing her loss of control as if from a distance, as if she were two distinct persons, one observing, the other gone all to pieces.

"Come on, Rebecca," Louisa said. "We'll go upstairs and have a cup of tea and I'll have some medicine sent up and some hot bricks to get the bed nice and warm.''

The only way to do it was to stop thinking, that detached part of herself told Rebecca. She allowed Louisa to lead her away, past the silent, motionless figure of David, and out into the hall. David. Stop thinking. Her feet were climbing the stairs. She should go and check on Charles before doing anything else. *Stop thinking.*

"There's a nice cozy fire burning in your sitting room," Louisa said. "Shall we go there and sit down for a while, Rebecca? Tea should arrive almost as soon as we do. You will feel better with some hot tea inside you. One always does.''

Rebecca felt the insane urge to laugh. Julian had come back from the dead and was home. Her husband—her love—had come back to her after four years. She had two husbands. She was a bigamist. She had a child of a bigamous marriage. Charles was an illegitimate child. A bastard. And a cup of tea would make her feel better?

She did not laugh. If she did so, she realized, she

would lose the last vestiges of her control. If she started laughing, she might never be able to stop.

"A glass of brandy each would not come amiss," the Earl of Hartington said, crossing the library to a sideboard and setting out three glasses with great deliberation before filling them almost to the brim. "We will sit by the fire, the three of us, and talk this thing out." He handed a glass to his son and one to his godson as they obeyed his instructions silently, and went back for his own.

Talk this thing out. There was nothing to be talked out as far as David could see. But perhaps his father could see more clearly than he. His own mind was still numb with shock. He gazed in wonder at the foster brother he had shot more than three years before. Julian looked uncannily the same as he had when David last saw him except that he was not wearing uniform. He looked no older, no thinner, no less good-natured.

Julian was looking steadily back at him. "You really do look as if you have seen a ghost, Dave," he said. "Just the way I must have looked two days ago, I suppose, when Father told me where Becka was. You had better drink up."

David did so and concentrated for a few moments on the liquor burning its way down his throat and into his stomach. "You were dead," he said. "I turned your body over and felt your neck for a pulse."

"I seemed to hear nothing else for weeks or perhaps months except the opinion that I was dead and there was no point in wasting any more time on me," Julian said. "But I was alive for all that and fortunately there was at least one other person who saw it too. Those Russians never could shoot straight, could they?"

David's glass was empty already. He set it down and started to get to his feet. "I had better go and see how Rebecca is doing," he said before sinking back into his chair. God! His legs felt suddenly as if they were made of jelly.

There was a silence that no one rushed to fill.

"I had a long talk with the vicar yesterday, David," the earl said. "I requested an interview with the bishop.

He has kindly agreed to come here tomorrow. It will be better for him to come here, I suppose. He will probably wish to speak with all three of us. Perhaps with Rebecca too.''

David closed his eyes against a wave of dizziness.

''Some of the facts are quite clear, of course,'' the earl said. His voice was cool and matter-of-fact. Perhaps only David, who resembled his father to a remarkable degree, realized how much emotion it masked. ''Rebecca is Julian's wife. A few other matters are more tricky. The vicar was full of sympathy and understanding, but he was unable to give me an answer concerning the exact nature of her—er—marriage to David. The bishop will have to decide if that marriage constitutes bigamy.''

''She married me in good faith,'' David said, sucking in his breath. ''She believed Julian to be dead. She mourned him for almost two years.''

''You don't have to plead your case with me, David,'' his father said. ''The Church will have to make a decision.''

David looked at him in an agony. If only he could be a child again, he thought foolishly. If only he could look to his father and know that everything would be made better again. He felt all the overwhelming weight of adulthood and life on his shoulders.

Numbness was beginning to leave him. Rebecca was no longer his wife. She had never been his wife. She would no longer be at Stedwell with him. Their life together was at an end. She would no longer be any part of his life whatsoever. He closed his mind to panic.

''I'm sorry, Dave,'' Julian said. ''I truly am sorry. This is going to be hard on you, isn't it? But it's hard on me too, old chap. It's quite a shock to come home after such an ordeal, you know, to find that everyone thought you dead and that your wife has married your brother. To find that she has had a child by him.''

David leapt to his feet, reality hitting him finally like a fist low to his stomach. ''Charles,'' he said.

''It will be for the bishop to decide,'' the earl said, his voice as calm as before, his eyes troubled. ''Tomorrow, David. We must have patience.''

David sank back into his chair. His son illegitimate.

A bastard. Unable to inherit from him as his true heir. His son and Rebecca's. An innocent, happy little golden-haired child. The light of his life and of hers. The thoughts hammered at him.

"Perhaps I shouldn't have come back," Julian said. "Perhaps I should have stayed in Russia. It wasn't entirely unpleasant, you know. It was different. But I grew bored and homesick. There is nowhere like England when all is said and done. And I missed Becka."

David stared at him, unseeing and uncomprehending.

"You had to come home, Julian," the earl said quietly. "You are alive and this is where you belong, my boy. And this is where your wife is."

His wife. Julian's wife.

Rebecca!

David saw Julian suddenly. His brother. The man he had killed and suffered torment over for more than three years. Miraculously come to life again and restored to him again. The man he had hugged and shed tears over not so many minutes past before all the implications of Julian's return had begun to strike him.

Julian was alive. And home. He was sitting there, not six feet away, alive and warm and smiling and only a little pale. David forced himself to absorb the truth. He had not after all killed his brother. Julian was alive.

"Tell me what happened," he said. "Tell me all that has happened to you, Julian. It has been over three years since—since you disappeared."

The account was vague. Julian had been taken into someone's home and nursed back to health. That probably accounted for the fact that he had recovered at all. The Russians were not renowned for the care shown to their prisoners, especially the wounded ones. And women, Julian said with a grin, could get stubborn about refusing to let a fellow die when he wanted to slip away without any fuss.

It was a woman, then, who had nursed him.

After that he had been taken deeper into Russia—he was vague about what part—and kept in gentlemanly captivity. He had not even known until long after the fact that the war was over. It seemed that he had been forgotten about. When he had finally discovered the truth and broached the subject of his freedom, he had been told that he was free to go.

"A nice anticlimax after almost three years of captivity," Julian said. "One expects some sort of dramatic moment, some sort of fanfare, doesn't one? But I merely came home. And here I am."

"I thought all prisoners were released after the peace was signed," the earl said.

Julian shrugged. "I was one of the forgotten ones," he said. "I might have been there until I was ninety if I hadn't thought to ask if I could come home. 'Ask and thou shalt receive,' " he chuckled. "Do I have the quotation exact? I never was very good with chapter and verse of the Bible."

"I saw your grave," David said. "I went there and found it. It was a mass grave. I was furious that they had not done better for a captain of the Guards. Officers are not buried in mass graves."

Julian chuckled. "I missed hell from what I can gather," he said. "You went back to it, Dave, when you could have come home with your wounds? But then I would have expected no different from you. You were always the hero, always the dutiful officer. You would put duty before personal inclination any day of the year, wouldn't you? You were awarded a Victoria Cross?"

David nodded.

"And you defeated the bastards," Julian said. "I wish I could have been there for that. I missed almost all the fun, didn't I?"

They lapsed into silence.

"She took it hard," Julian asked at last, "when she thought I was dead?"

"She loved you dearly, Julian," the earl said. "I believe that for a long, long time she wished she could die too."

"Poor Becka," Julian said. "God, but I've missed her."

David stared into the fire.

"Well, I'm home to stay this time," Julian said. "I'm never going to be away from her again. I'm going to make up to her for all the lost years. I love her more than life, you know."

"Yes," the earl said, "you must cherish her, Julian. She has suffered greatly and this will not be easy for her. Especially if the bishop is a man who clings to the letter of church law more than to the spirit of Christian compassion."

"I'll make it up to her," Julian said. "I swear I will. I know you have looked after her, Dave. I know you have cared for her. But you needn't worry that I will neglect her or leave her again for the rest of her life. I'm going to make her the happiest woman who ever lived." He got to his feet, the old smiling, happy Julian. "I'm going to go up to see how she is."

It felt rather, David thought, as if someone had plunged a knife into his stomach and was twisting it. He had to stay sitting. He had to let Julian go—up to Rebecca's rooms, into her bedchamber. He had to sit quietly and let it happen.

Julian was her husband.

He sat very still, fighting panic again.

"Let her sleep," the earl said. "But she's your wife, Julian. You must do as you see fit."

"I'll not wake her," Julian promised.

David listened to the library door open and then close again. He set his elbows on his spread knees and rested his fists against his eyes.

"David," his father said after a lengthy silence. All the coolness had gone from his voice. It was raw pain. "My son, what can I say to you? There is nothing to say."

"No," David said, the weariness of ages in his voice, "there is nothing to say."

He was hit by the awful truth of the words. There was nothing to say. Nothing to do.

Nothing.

David was sitting on the edge of the bed when she woke up. She could feel him there. She felt as if she had been sleeping very deeply. She felt as if she wanted to cling to sleep, almost as if there was something she did not want to wake up to. And then she remembered all in a rush. She opened her eyes.

It was Julian sitting there.

Julian, smiling and good-looking and familiar and comfortable. Julian, her dearest love, come back from the dead. It was something she had dreamed of so many times during those first dreadful months—just this dream of waking to find him sitting on the bed. But she knew this was no dream. There was a heaviness in her as well as a surging of joy.

He set a finger along the top of her nose—a familiar, long-forgotten gesture. "Hello, sleepyhead," he said. "Feeling better?"

"Julian," she whispered to him. "Oh, Julian."

"Tears again?" he said. "Haven't you wept them all dry by now, Becka?"

"Julian," she said. "I thought I would die. I wanted to die. I did not know pain could be so intense."

"I'm home, darling." He set a hand on either side of her pillow and leaned over her, his eyes warm and tender. "I'm not going away again. I've dreamed of this moment for years."

His mouth felt familiar—closed, his lips pouted against hers. It had always felt warm and comfortable and wonderful to kiss with Julian. Now she set her hands against his shoulders and pushed. Now it felt—wrong? For a flashing moment she wondered what David would say if he knew that there was another man in her bedchamber, sitting on her bed, leaning over her, kissing her.

But David knew.

David was not her husband.

Julian was.

"What is it?" He withdrew his head only so far and gazed down into her face. "Aren't you happy to see me, Becka? Don't you love me any longer?"

She stared in bewilderment into his eyes and saw her beloved Julian. Always her love. All through her girlhood. All through their marriage. During her widowhood. And after her marriage to David. It had been understood from the start. David had understood it and accepted it. Julian was the love of her life.

He was alive. And here. And bending over her, waiting for her answer.

"I am so happy," she said, lifting her arms and locking them about his neck, "that I can feel only sadness,

Julian. Only the urge to cry and cry. And I have always loved you. Always. Even until today, when I still thought you dead. My love. Oh, my love, I can't find words.''

''You don't need to,'' he whispered. ''Becka, my darling.'' And he kissed her again, more firmly, more warmly. He slid his arms beneath her on the bed and tightened them about her. The weight of the upper part of his body came down on her.

She kissed him back with all the joy of the moment. He had been dead and he was alive. He had been taken from her and he had come back. He had been her love and he was in her arms again.

For a few moments she kissed him back.

And then she felt unease and fear and a terrible sense of wrongness. Where was David? What would David say? She should not be alone with another man. Kissing another man. It was wrong. Sinful.

She wanted David.

But he was Julian. She stared up at him blankly when he lifted his head from hers and smiled down into her eyes.

''Darling,'' he said. ''They should have taken me out and shot me when I first left you, shouldn't they? I should have risked a court-martial and stayed home with you. So many lost years, Becka. I'm going to make them up to you. Every one of them and every single day of them. Starting now. Just a moment, I'm going to lock the door.''

''No!'' she grabbed for his wrist as he sat up.

''No?'' He smiled at her.

''No.'' She gazed up into his beloved face. ''No, Julian. I can't. Not now. Not yet. I'm—. I can't. Oh, please understand. I—''

''I am being a bit of a dolt, aren't I?'' he said, smiling the boyishly charming smile that had always made her heart turn over. ''I have to give you time, Becka. Did he treat you well? Were you fond of him? You haven't gone and fallen in love with him, have you?''

Those wretched tears welled into her eyes again. ''I love *you*,'' she said, her voice high-pitched and unsteady.

''I'll give you time,'' he said, patting her hand. ''I understand, Becka. You feel some loyalty to him. Some affection. I don't' resent that. I love Dave dearly my-self.''

Even though David had shot him? But she did not want to explore that thought now. She closed her eyes.

''There's Charles,'' she said dully.

''Your son?'' he said. ''He must mean a great deal to you, Becka. I know how much you wanted a child. You can keep him. I won't mind. I'll love him as my own.''

Her eyes snapped open. ''Charles is David's,'' she said fiercely. ''He belongs to David, Julian.''

He lifted her hand and set it against his cheek. ''We'll talk about it all some other time,'' he said. ''God, I wish there had not been that wretched mix-up, Becka. It doesn't come easy to know that you have been with Dave for a year and a half, you know. It hurts like the very devil if you want to know the truth.''

Yes. It did. And worse than that.

''Well.'' His smile came back. ''We are together again, Becka. That's all that matters, isn't it? We'll work every-thing else out—tomorrow. Just tell me again that you love me.''

''I love you, Julian,'' she said.

He released her hand and got to his feet. ''And I you,'' he said. ''You're beautiful, Becka. More lovely even than I remembered. God, I've missed you. I'll leave you to get up and tidy yourself. My presence would probably embarrass you after all this time, wouldn't it?''

She did not reply.

''That will change,'' he promised. ''I am home, dar-ling. Home to stay.''

''Yes.'' She smiled at him.

22

Bishop Young was an imposing figure yet a kindly man. He arrived quite early the following day, having stopped in the village first to talk with the vicar. He was immediately closeted with the earl in the library for a lengthy interview, and then talked separately with both Julian and David. It would be unnecessary, he said at last, to disturb Lady Cardwell since she was understandably indisposed.

The four men ate luncheon together, Louisa having excused herself on the grounds that she was tending Rebecca.

Finally they were back in the library. David held his mind and his emotions dead, as he had since the day before. He had tried to tell himself during a sleepless night that he was glad to see Julian alive—and he *was* glad beyond words. He had even tried to tell himself that he was glad Rebecca was to be restored to the only man she had ever loved. But at that point his thoughts become too tormented to be borne and he had stopped thinking and feeling.

If only it was as easily done as it was to tell himself that he was doing it, he thought now, waiting for the bishop to speak.

Bishop Young chose not to accept the chair offered him. Perhaps he had learned from long experience that certain matters were best dealt with on his feet with utter formality and all the dignity of his office.

"I will have to take this matter higher, of course," he said, "before what I say is made official. But I feel confident that my decisions will be confirmed."

The earl made rumbling noises of assent.

"Lady Cardwell's first marriage must, of course, take

precedence over the second," the bishop said, "since her first husband is still living and the marital connection has been neither annulled nor severed in any other way."

None of the three men either moved or reacted visibly. This was not the important pronouncement. There had been no doubt in any of their minds that Rebecca was still married to Julian. Yet David grew a little colder inside and died a little further. What his head had told him since the day before, his heart now knew to be true. Lady Cardwell. Rebecca was Lady Cardwell.

"The second marriage, her marriage to you, Lord Tavistock," the bishop continued, his voice the official voice of the Church and yet sympathetic at the same time, "is of course invalid."

Yes. Rebecca was not his wife. Julian was alive.

"The question is," Bishop Young said, 'whether it has always been invalid. In a sense, of course, it has since Sir Julian Cardwell was alive when it was celebrated. And yet my investigations this morning have convinced me that the marriage was made in perfectly good faith by all concerned, that at the time of the ceremony there was no way anyone involved could have known that there was an impediment. Although the marriage became invalid the moment Sir Julian returned home, it was valid until then. It is my judgment that no sin was committed by either Lord or Lady Tavistock since sin involves a conscious decision to do what is evil."

David saw his father's hand clench and unclench on the arm of his chair. He closed his eyes.

"Therefore," the bishop said, "and I believe this is the point most at issue in this very sad matter, the child of that now invalid union was conceived within a real marriage and is legitimately your issue, Lord Tavistock. No stigma of bastardy will attach to his name."

David sat with closed eyes even after his father and Julian had risen to their feet to shake the bishop by the hand. If anyone—even the Church—had tried to suggest otherwise, he would have committed murder. And if anyone had suggested that Rebecca was . . . He opened his eyes, got to his feet, and extended his hand to the bishop, adding his thanks to those of his father.

The bishop would not stay longer. He had other business requiring his attention this day. He would send word as soon as his decisions were officially approved, he told them before the earl escorted him outside to his waiting carriage.

"I'll find Rebecca then and break the news to her," he said, looking back to his son and godson.

There was a great deal of agony to be faced in the coming days and weeks, David knew. But what he was finding hardest at the moment was curbing the instinct to go to her. Yesterday he had not been able to go up to see how she was feeling after she had nearly collapsed from shock. Instead he had had to watch Julian go to her. This morning he had not been able to go to her to find out how she had slept, how she was reacting to all that had happened. He had had to listen without comment to Louisa's claim that Rebecca was indisposed. Now he could not go up to tell her what had been decided about matters that concerned the two of them—and only the two of them and Charles. He had not even been to see Charles today, afraid that Rebecca would be with him.

"Well, Dave," Julian said. His voice sounded rather shaken. "I was not expecting all this, I must say."

David looked at him. It still seemed somehow impossible to believe that Julian really was there, alive and apparently healthy, and looking very much his old self.

"I really believed I had killed you," he said.

"That makes two of us, then," Julian said. "I was never more surprised in my life, Dave, as I was when you shot—and shot me, not Scherer. The bastard would have stabbed me in the back. It was sheer miracle that I turned and saw him just in time and managed to trip him. Though I'm not even sure I can claim credit for that. I think he might have caught his foot in a root. But he grabbed for his sword again and would have still killed me if I had not slashed down at his arm and kicked the sword away. How much of that did you see?"

"None of it," David said. "All I saw was you about to kill him."

"That explains it then, I suppose," Julian said. "It's just as I thought, in fact. I forgave you long ago, you know. You were just being Dave, of course—an officer first, my brother second. It must have looked damned sordid. And of course he caught me at a bad moment, when that lust to kill that always comes with battle had destroyed all my ability to reason. Maybe that's what made you shoot too, Dave. Did the bastard get himself killed some other way?''

"He survived," David said.

Julian winced. "Poor Cynthia," he said. "He was a brute to her, Dave. Nothing too physical beyond the odd beating. All mental. You wouldn't believe it. You should have let me kill him—and have him on my conscience for the rest of my life."

David said nothing.

Julian's smile was rather twisted. "Is that what I did to you, Dave?" he asked. "You really thought I was dead. Have I been on your conscience?"

"Yes," David said.

"They don't know, do they?" Julian asked. "You didn't tell them. Is that why you married Becka?"

David got to his feet and crossed the room to the window.

"You felt you had to look after her for me, Dave?" Julian asked. "Was that it?"

"I suppose so," David said.

"This is difficult for me, you know," Julian said. "Damned difficult. To think of you and Becka . . . And a child. She succeeded with yours while she didn't with mine. It hurts, Dave. I just wasn't expecting it, I suppose. I always thought of Becka as—mine. I thought she would wait forever."

"You were dead," David said. "She was twenty-four years old and living here with Papa and Louisa. She needed a home of her own and something to do with the rest of her life. She needed children."

"She had a home," Julian said. "Though you could have knocked me down with the proverbial feather when I found Louisa ensconced here as the mistress. She wasted no time in getting herself a title and fortune, did she?"

"I believe she is fond of Papa," David said. "They seem happy together."

"I'm glad anyway," Julian said, "that she is not guilty of bigamy or anything like that. Becka, I mean. It would have killed her Dave. Becka always has to do what is right and proper. And I'm glad the child isn't a bastard. That would have been hard on her.''

''Yes,'' David said tersely.

''I told her yesterday that she could keep the child,'' Julian said. ''I wouldn't mind if it would make her happy, Dave. I don't hold it against her or anything. I know you all thought I was dead.''

''What did she say?'' David wished suddenly that he had stayed sitting down. He rather thought he might black out.

''She said the child was yours,'' Julian said. ''I don't know how you feel, Dave. It's your heir and all that, isn't it? But I don't mind having it.''

It. To Julian Rebecca's child was an it. ''Charles is my son,'' David said quietly. ''I love him.''

''Yes, well,'' Julian sounded uneasy. ''This is damned awkward, isn't it, Dave? You'll have to find your son a new mother. That will be the best thing, won't it?''

He has a mother. By God, he has a mother. But if he said the words aloud, he would unleash with them passions that frightened him. He wanted to kill Julian, he thought in sudden horror. And yet all this was not Julian's fault.

''What have you been doing all this time?'' he asked.

''Captivity,'' Julian said. David turned in time to see him shrug.

''Chains and a barred cell and all that?'' David asked.

''By Jove, no,'' Julian said. ''The Russians are almost as civilized as we are, Dave. They treat their prisoners of officer rank as gentlemen.''

''It was a long time,'' David said. ''The war has been over for a long time. But they still would not release you?''

''Well.'' Julian shrugged again and for a moment his face relaxed into his characteristic charming smile. ''I suppose if I had asked.''

''Why didn't you?''

''I didn't know for a long time that it was over,'' Julian said.

''For a long time,'' David said. ''Did you ask for release the moment you did know?''

Julian laughed. "I shouldn't have had to ask," he said. "They should have sent me home, shouldn't they?"

David looked at him in silence for a few moments. "You couldn't bear to leave her?" he asked.

Julian laughed again. "A man has to counter boredom somehow," he said, "especially when he's a virtual prisoner and doesn't know when his captivity will come to an end. She meant nothing to me, Dave. It was always Becka. It got to the point where I couldn't think of anything else. And I started dreaming about her. I had to come home. That's when I asked."

David had often disapproved of Julian's actions in the past. After Julian's marriage he had been furious at the infidelities. But he could not remember hating him as he hated him now. He really did want to kill him, he realized anew.

"Don't look at me like that." Julian sobered and looked contrite. "It would never have happened if I hadn't been forcibly kept away from her, Dave. I love her. You know that. There has never been anyone but Becka. Now that I'm back things will be different once and for all. I'm not going to let her out of my sight."

"If I ever hear of another infidelity," David said, his hands clasped firmly at his back, his eyes holding Julian's, "even just one, Julian, I'll find you and kill you. And this time my aim will not be off by half an inch. Do you understand me?"

Julian's expression reminded David of the one that had been on his face when he fell on the Kitspur. He looked startled. "Damn it, Dave," he said. "You're in love with her, aren't you?"

"She's my wife," David said coldly. "Correction. She *was* my wife. She's the mother of my son. You talk about how difficult all this is for you, Julian. Imagine, if you can, what it is like for me, having to stand aside and watch her return to a miserable cur like you."

Julian's face had turned white. "She is my wife, Dave," he said. "I love her. I know I have treated her shabbily, but I mean to reform. I do love her. And she loves me."

"Yes," David said curtly. "You have that advantage over me too, don't you? I'll be returning to Stedwell tomorrow. But I meant what I said just now. One infidelity, Julian. Just one.''

"There'll be none," Julian said. "I promise, Dave. It's all different, isn't it? It's all changed. I thought you would be delighted to find that you had not done me any permanent damage after all—I didn't know that you thought you had killed me. I imagined how it would be coming home and seeing you and Father. And I pictured the look on Becka's face when she saw me. But nothing is the way I imagined it.''

"Julian," David said, his anger disappearing and leaving him feeling drained and utterly weary. "I am glad that you are alive. So is Father. And Rebecca.''

Julian nodded and ran the fingers of both hands through his hair.

"We are your family," David said. "You belong here. You are the brother I never had. Nothing essential has changed.''

Julian nodded again. "You've always loved her, haven't you?" he said. "I feel as if my eyes had suddenly been opened. That was why you were always so mad with me whenever—well, whenever I was weak. It was why you settled things with Flora.''

David said nothing.

'I'm sorry, Dave,'' Julian said. "But I mean to be the world's best husband from this moment on, if that is any consolation.''

It should have been. But it was not.

"I had better go and find her," Julian said. "She will be happy to know what the bishop decided. It will be a load off her mind. We have a lot of catching up to do, Becka and I, and a lot of planning. I'm going to see that she has fun. We are going to travel—all over Europe. Maybe for a year or more. She deserves some fun, don't you think, Dave?''

David did not answer. She would hate it. She would have no settled home, no realm of responsibilities, no sense of purpose or belonging. She would hate frivolity and the sort of transient friends they would make during constant travels. But how could he know for sure? She would be with Julian—with her beloved Julian. Perhaps he could be her whole world. Perhaps she would not need those things she needed with him.

"I'll see you later, Dave," Julian said and left the room.

David had always dreaded the waking part of his nightmares more than the sleeping part. Part of him had always known when he was dreaming that he would wake up. The real hell had begun after the dream because then he had known that he was awake and that there was no escaping his thoughts. He tried now to convince himself that he was asleep, that soon he would wake up to cope with a less terrifying reality. But he was wide awake. He knew it. And he was plunged deep into the darkest, most despairing corner of hell.

He wondered if seeing Charles would help him at all. She would be with his father and then with Julian. She would not be in the nursery. He left the library and climbed the stairs toward the nursery on legs that felt as if they were made of lead.

It was cold. Very cold with leaden skies and a brisk, cutting wind. The rosebushes looked brittle and dead. It was almost impossible to imagine that within a few months they would come back to life again and burst out into exquisite bloom.

She would never see the roses bloom in her own arbor.

It was not her arbor.

It was David's.

She sat inside the rose arbor at Craybourne, huddled inside a cloak that did not protect her from the bite of the wind. Her throat and chest were one harsh ache, but she could not cry. She had been unable to cry all night. And why would she want to cry? Julian was alive and home.

She deliberately felt the joy of the thought. And there *was* joy. Joy like a cup brimming over with sparkling wine. And at the same time a knifing agony. The mingling of two such opposing and extreme emotions was causing the tightness in her chest, the feeling that she must surely be going mad.

She looked up when someone came through the arch and sat quietly beside her. Her father-in-law's hand—no, he was no longer that—came to rest on her shoulder and squeezed. She wanted to tip her head sideways to rest against him, but she did not do so. There was no comfort. Why try to find some when there was none? She continued to sit very upright.

"The bishop has just left, Rebecca," the earl said. "The Church is to pronounce that your marriage to David was a real marriage from the day of your wedding until yesterday. It was a marriage made in good faith. No one concerned in it could have been expected to know that there was an impediment. You have not been guilty of bigamy."

The wind flattened her cloak against her for a few moments, but she did not feel the chill.

"And Charles is a legitimate child," he said. "He is the product of a marriage that was valid at the time of his conception and birth."

Would her arbor ever be as lovely as this one was in summer? she wondered. Would the fact that there had been trees where it had been built have spoiled the soil? It was not her arbor.

It was David's.

The earl's hand squeezed more tightly. "You will find both those facts reassuring," he said.

"Yes."

"Julian is so very happy to be home, Rebecca," he said. "It is a true miracle."

"Yes," she said. "It never seemed real to me. Because I never saw his body and never saw his grave, I could never quite accept that it was true. But all that pain. And emptiness."

"He is home now," he said gently. "Together you will be able to make up for all the lost years."

"Yes," she said.

"He loves you dearly, Rebecca," he said.

"Yes." She drew her cloak more tightly about herself, feeling the chill again. "And I love him, Father. It has always been Julian. For as far back as I can remember. I think of sunshine and laughter whenever I think of Julian. And now he is home. He has come back to me."

"You will be happy," he said, his voice curiously

heavy, "once you have recovered from the shock, Rebecca."

"I am happy," she said. "I am, Father." But why the leaden weight inside? "But David?" She swallowed. "And Charles?"

"David is returning to Stedwell tomorrow," he said. "It will be best if he leaves you alone with Julian. There will be too much awkwardness if he stays longer." He paused and patted her shoulder. "He will take Charles with him."

All the joy of Julian's return was gone again suddenly. *He will take Charles with him.* Charles! Her baby. Her sunshine.

Charles was David's son. He had been born of a marriage that no longer existed. His mother now belonged in another marriage.

Charles was David's. He was going home with David tomorrow.

Home!

Home was Julian. Home was wherever Julian was.

"Yes, that will be best," she said.

The earl got to his feet and reached out a hand to her. "Come inside, Rebecca," he said. "You will catch a chill out here."

"I want to sit here for a while," she said.

"It's winter," he said, "and a raw day. It is not the time to be sitting around outside."

"But summer will come," she said. "The roses will bloom again. Won't they?"

He leaned down, took her hands firmly in his, and drew her to her feet. "When they do," he said, "you may sit out here all day if you wish, Rebecca. Now you are coming indoors."

But they met Julian coming out as they neared the doors and the earl relinquished her arm.

"She is thoroughly chilled, Julian," he said. "I would advise you to take her indoors."

"Your nose is like a beacon," Julian said, drawing her arm through his and following the earl to the doors. "We'll go up to your sitting room, shall we, Becka? And talk? Did Father tell you what the bishop said?"

He was a familiar height. Walking with him, it seemed

impossible to believe that so many years had passed. That she had thought him dead. Part of her must have always known that he was alive, she thought. She smiled at him.

"Yes," she said. "It was good news. I'm glad it is all settled. Shall I have tea sent up, Julian? It will be good to talk, won't it? Just you and me? I was still drugged when you came to talk with me yesterday. And still in deep shock. You cannot imagine what it felt like to walk into the library and see you there. I am not sure I quite believe it yet."

"Oh, you can believe it, Beck." He released her arm as they climbed the stairs to set his own about her waist. It was something he had often done. It had used to embarrass her. She had used to scold him about it. What if his father saw? Or the servants? Hang the servants, he had used to say, grinning and shocking her, and perhaps Father could remember what it was like to have a young and lovely wife. It had seemed so very improper to her. And rather wonderful. "I am real flesh and blood." He set his mouth close to her ear. "And I'll prove it as soon as we have the door of your room closed behind us."

He wasted no time. He held to her wrist as he closed the door of her sitting room with a booted foot and leaned back against it. He drew her against him, set his arms about her, and kissed her.

She had always loved such closeness. If there had been only this, she used to think, and not all the embarrassing discomfort and unpleasantness of what he did to her in her bed, she would have considered the physical side of marriage true bliss.

She surrendered to the kiss, leaning into him, setting her arms about his neck, kissing him back, focusing all her thoughts, all her energies, all her being on Julian. Her husband. Her love.

"Steady, love, steady," he said, looking down at her with the lazy grin that stirred her with the ache of sudden memories. "If you are that eager, I had better get a mattress at your back."

"No," she said quickly. "No, let's just talk, Julian. Let's talk and talk and talk. I want to know all about the missing years." She took his hand—so familiar, broader and shorter-fingered than David's—and led him to sit beside her on a love seat.

"Where do you want me to begin?" He smiled into her eyes and lifted his free hand to caress her cheek lightly.

"At the beginning," she said, gazing eagerly into his much-loved face. "At the very start, Julian. Tell me everything. Every last little detail."

He laughed softly and lowered his head to kiss her once more before starting to talk. She listened avidly. She listened as if she were a girl again and back with her governess and knew that she had to write an examination on what was told her.

She pushed everything else ruthlessly from her mind— everything—and concentrated her full attention on him.

It was going to be wonderful, she told herself as he talked, her thoughts straying despite herself. He was back with her again. Everything was going to be wonderful. She had forgotten how soft and wavy his hair always looked, inviting fingers to feather through it. She had forgotten how large and expressive and smiling his gray eyes were. She had forgotten—oh, so much. But he was back home, back with her. She had a lifetime in which to relearn everything there was to know about him.

She wondered if Charles was having his afternoon nap. She had not seen him today. He would be wondering where she was.

She smiled and focused her attention on what Julian was saying.

She wondered what David was doing.

She leaned forward and kissed Julian's cheek, causing him to chuckle again and declare that he could not keep the thread of his story with her sitting so close to him and issuing such invitations.

She surrendered determinedly to his kiss again.

He was Julian and she loved him with her whole heart.

23

Rebecca had gone to the nursery during the evening, having dined alone in her sitting room. She had stood tentatively at the door looking in at her son, almost as if she expected him to look different, almost as if she expected him to reject her. But he had seen her almost immediately and had come crawling toward her, dragging along with him a toy of Katie's.

She had swept him up into her arms to find him red-cheeked and bright-eyed. He had not had his afternoon nap, his nanny had told her. He had refused to go to sleep. And so she had undressed him and changed his nappy and rocked him to sleep in her arms, though it had not been necessary for a couple of months, ever since he had been weaned. She had kissed the chubby hand he lifted to her face and watched his eyelids flutter until they finally closed and stayed closed.

And then she had set him down in his cot, her heart aching with love and grief.

That had been the evening before. Now today when she went to him late in the morning to say good-bye—though she could not use that word in her mind—all was different. He had slept through the night and on into the morning later than usual. He was full of energy and mischief and crawled determinedly after the toddling Katie, willing to fight her for every toy. Beyond a broad smile for Rebecca when she appeared in the nursery and helpless chuckling when she picked him up to twirl him about, he had no time for a mere mother.

And so when she finally picked him up to hold him close for the last time, her heart breaking, he merely objected loudly to having his game interrupted and squirmed to be free.

She set him free and her arms were empty and her heart worse than empty.

"Good-bye, sweetheart," she said softly, her eyes drinking in the sight of him. But her son was shrieking with laughter as Katie bashed him on the head with a rag doll.

They were to catch the early-afternoon train back to Stedwell. She knew that. She would stay in her rooms until they had left, she decided. She had even drawn the curtains across her windows so that she would not look down on the carriage as it left. Once they had gone, everything would be all right.

No. She was not naive enough to believe that. But it would be easier with them gone. Reality would be easier to accept. Once they were gone she would be able to concentrate on her love for Julian and spend her energies on building their marriage again.

She willed time to pass quickly.

Louisa followed the maid who brought her luncheon tray into her room. Her smile for Rebecca was rather strained. This must be very difficult on the whole family, Rebecca thought. Rejoicing over the return of Julian mingled with sadness over the mess of David's marriage.

David. She wished he were gone already.

"I'll eat here with you if you have no objection," Louisa said.

They ate in semidarkness, a fact that Louisa did not comment on. Indeed, they scarcely spoke for several minutes.

"William thinks you should come downstairs to say good-bye to him," Louisa said at last.

"No." Rebecca set down her fork.

"David said the same thing," Louisa said, "until William persuaded him that it would be best. Things left quite unfinished fester in the mind. Say good-bye to him, Rebecca. Alone. You need not feel the awkwardness of anyone else's presence."

"It would not be seemly," Rebecca said, "without my husband present."

"Rebecca." Louisa's voice was softly reproachful.

Did they not understand? Did they not realize what it must be like after a year and a half of marriage and parenthood, to find suddenly that the marriage no longer existed, that she was married and owed loyalty and obedience to another man? No, of course they did not realize. How could they? It was something beyond imagining.

"There is nothing to say," she said.

"Perhaps a word or two of kindness," Louisa said. "You would not want to remember that you have not exchanged a word with him since walking into the library two days ago."

She wanted him gone. She wanted to be with Julian. She wanted to resume their marriage and forget the years between. But how ridiculous her desire was. Forget Charles? Forget David?

"Very well," she said. "Where? Not the library. And not here."

"There is a fire in the drawing room," Louisa said. "Come down there with me now and then I'll go and find him and send him to you."

The drawing room was disconcertingly large and empty and chilly despite the fire. Rebecca stood gazing into it, warming her hands while she waited. She fought the urge to escape, to bolt from the room before it was too late. But Louisa was right. There must be a good-bye. And yet when the door opened and closed quietly behind her, it took every ounce of the discipline of years to turn calmly and look in his general direction. She could not look directly at him.

"The carriage is ordered to take you to the station?" she asked.

"Yes." He did not come far into the room, she noticed.

"I hope for your sake the train is not late," she said. "It is tedious waiting on platforms, especially during the winter. And Charles gets fidgety."

"I'll make sure the carriage stays until the train comes in," he said.

"Yes," she said. "That would be wise. He was in high spirits this morning. He is going to miss Katie."

"Yes," he said.

What else was there to say? There must be a world of other things to say. Her mind reached about for just one of those things. He was walking closer to her.

"Rebecca," he said, "I know this is hard on you. You were a good and dutiful wife to me. You have friends at Stedwell whom you will miss. And there is Charles . . ." He swallowed. "But I know that your heart must be bursting with joy over the miracle of Julian's return. He has always been your love. Once this difficult moment is past, let yourself be caught up in that miracle. Don't worry about me. I'll be happy to know that you are happy."

Her eyes shifted to his face at last. It was pale, set, harsh. Only his blue eyes suggested something different.

"I am happy to know that you did not kill him," she said. "For both your sakes."

"Yes," he said.

Yet again there was nothing to be said. Her eyes dropped to his mouth, his chin, his collar, and his neatly tied four-in-hand.

"Well," he said, "we had better have done with this, Rebecca. I'll have Charles's nanny send you reports every week. Good-bye." He did not hold out a hand to her.

"Good-bye." She watched him turn and stride across the room toward the door. And felt the most dreadful panic of her life. "David!"

He looked back over his shoulder, his hand on the doorknob.

She wanted to go with him—more than anything in life. For one quite unreasoned moment she wanted to wipe out the last few days and be back to normal again. She wanted to go with him and Charles. Back to Stedwell. Back home. But this was good-bye. Good-bye was forever.

"Nothing," she said lamely. And then she thought of something. She twisted his wedding ring, easing it over her knuckle and off her finger. She held it out mutely to him.

She thought he was not going to take it. He stood looking at it for endless moments before crossing the distance between them and taking the ring from her outstretched hand. Their fingers did not touch.

"Have a safe journey," she said. "I'll pray for you and for Charles."

"Yes," he whispered.

And he was gone.

Rebecca stood where she was, icy hands clasped before her while the fire roasted her back. She deliberately avoided either touching or looking down at her bare ring finger. She stood there for long minutes until Julian came to her.

It was a great deal easier with them gone. The earl kept much to himself, claiming the press of work. Rebecca had to deliberately seek him out in order to reclaim Julian's wedding ring. Louisa spent a great deal of time with Katie or out and about, fulfilling her many duties. Rebecca had a chance to be alone with Julian most of the time.

For a whole week she gave herself up to the joy of his return. They spent almost every waking minute together, talking, laughing, reminiscing. He told her stories about Russia, outrageously funny, lighthearted stories that would have had her almost believe that there had been no captivity at all. She told him nothing about her own life during the missing years, but she had always been a better listener than talker. Since Julian had always been the opposite, they suited well.

They walked outside, wrapped up warmly against the chill, though there were signs of early spring on some milder, sunnier days. They rode or took drives in the carriage. Sometimes they sat in her sitting room or in the conservatory. But it did not matter what they did or where they went. It mattered only that he was alive, that they were together again.

That she loved him.

She scarcely took her eyes off him during those days. His fair, wavy hair, his gray eyes with the laugh lines at their corners, his wide, good humored mouth and white teeth, his carefree laugh, his charm—she familiarized herself with everything again. They touched almost constantly when there was no one else in sight, and sometimes even then when she could not prevent him. They linked arms or held hands. They wrapped their arms about each other. They kissed.

There was only one thing wrong.

She was standing before the fire in her bedroom the

night David and Charles left, absently brushing through
her hair, gazing unseeing into the flames, trying not to
imagine what was happening now at this very moment at
Stedwell, trying not to think of anything else either, when
the door opened and Julian came inside, wearing a dressing gown over his nightshirt.

She had been half expecting him, she supposed, now
that David had left. He was her husband and had been
without her for four years. And he had always come to
her frequently, almost nightly. She was his wife. She
smiled at him and set down her brush.

She set her arms about him as he kissed her and let all
her love for him flow outward. It would not be as bad as
she remembered. She always loved it with D—. It would
not be bad. She loved him. And all else aside, it was her
duty.

"Mm, Becka," he murmured, lowering his head to
nuzzle her neck. "You're hot, love. Let's lie down."

She let him lead her to the bed and sat down on the
edge of it while he removed his dressing gown. She would
lie back against the pillow and he would lift her nightgown and . . . She could remember clearly how he did
it—always the same way.

But she was David's. Only David had the right to . . .
This was a stranger. Julian was a stranger.

She could not lie down.

"Julian," she whispered, "I can't."

He knelt on the floor before her, pushing her knees
apart so that he could move closer, drawing her head
down for a kiss. "Yes, you can," he said. "You love
me. Don't you Becka?"

Of course she loved him. "Yes," she said. "You know
I do, Julian."

"Lie down, then," he said, getting back onto his feet.
"I'll make it quick if you would prefer, Beck. I'll not
hurt you."

God. Oh, God, Oh, please dear God.

She lay down and closed her eyes. But when she felt
his hands at the hem of her nightgown, she panicked and
was up and fighting him like a wild thing before she knew
what she was about.

"No!" she was yelling at him. "No."

He looked white and shaken when she stopped fighting suddenly and looked at him in some horror.

"Julian," she said, "I'm so sorry. Please forgive me. It's just that three days ago I was married to D-David." Three nights ago David had made love to her in his usual passionate manner—and she had made love to him in the same way. Only three nights ago. "My mind can't adjust this fast. I need time. I'm so sorry."

It felt as if she were trying to commit adultery.

"I understand, Becka," he said, breathing rather hard. "It's just that it's been so damned long. And I didn't foresee any of this. All right. How much time?"

"A week," she said. "Give me a week, Julian. Let's spend our days together and get to know each other again and feel comfortable with each other. Let's fall in love again."

"Have we ever stopped being in love?" he asked her. "Did you stop loving me, Becka?"

"No," she said earnestly. "Not for a single moment. When I agreed to marry David, it was on the understanding that I would never be able to give him my love—or any other man either. It was agreed that I would always love you."

He touched her cheek with the backs of his fingers. "You're so beautiful, Becka," he said. "A week then. Not a moment longer, though. You can't know how difficult this is. It's not the same for women, but men have needs that can't easily be put off for a week."

"I know," she said unhappily—though she had always needed David every bit as much as he had needed her. "Thank you, Julian. I'm sorry." She grasped his wrist and turned her head to kiss his hand. "I love you. I love you so much it hurts."

"Good night, then, Becka," he said, turning to leave the room.

She sat on the edge of the bed for a long time, feeling utterly wretched. She knew that she had disappointed him. And she knew that for the first time in her life and in both of her marriages she had failed in the performance of her foremost marriage duty—she had refused herself to her husband. But she could not. She could not have allowed him inside her body.

Her body was David's.

She spread her hands over her face. Her body was Julian's. *She* was Julian's. She had a week in which to adjust her mind and her body to that fact. It would not be difficult, surely. She loved him.

And so for the week following the departure of David and Charles, she spent every waking moment loving her husband, adjusting herself to the new condition of her life, preparing for the night when he would become her husband again in true fact.

A letter came from home—from Stedwell—at the end of the week. A letter written in the neat hand of Charles's nurse. A letter that told of his beginning to cut another tooth and being a little cross and feverish with it but of his otherwise being his usual high-spirited self. He had been out each day for fresh air in his perambulator and had behaved very well at church on Sunday.

Rebecca read the letter with feverish haste. It was detailed but so very impersonal. There were none of the little touches that might help her feel as if she were there with him. Not a mention of his missing his mother. Surely he missed her. Oh, surely he did. He had always been closer to her than to anyone else, even David. Especially when he was tired or not feeling well. He was cutting a tooth without her being there.

Not a mention of David. She folded the letter carefully.

"Charles is cutting a tooth," she told Julian.

He set an arm about her shoulders and kissed her. "Children usually survive the ordeal," he said.

"Yes." She wondered sometimes how much interest he would have shown in his own children if she had not lost them. She wondered if he would have been as good a father as David. But it was unfair to wonder and compare. She could not expect him to show interest in a child she had had with another man.

"I can hardly wait for tonight," he murmured against her ear before kissing her again. "Has a week been long enough, Becka?"

"Yes," she said.

"I have never known a longer week in my life," he

said, looking down at her with the boyish grin that had always drawn an answering smile from her. "But tonight it will be at an end."

"What did Father want?" she asked him. The earl had taken Julian into the library after breakfast and kept him there for all of an hour.

"Just to know what my plans are," Julian said. "It's pretty difficult to plan anything right now, Becka. I have been officially dead for so long that it seems I have little more than my life and the clothes I stand in. And you, of course." He paused to kiss her lingeringly once more. "It's going to take a while before I get my property and fortune back. I haven't been in the mood to do much about it in the past week, but Father is bringing a solicitor down tomorrow to get things moving. He was mumbling about responsibility and my being a married man and all that. It was quite like old times." He chuckled.

"And when everything is settled we are going to go home at last?" she asked. "I have never even seen your home, Julian. It seems strange after six years of marriage, doesn't it?"

He wrinkled his nose. "I don't know if we will go there yet, Becka," he said. "I would prefer to have some fun while we are still young enough to enjoy it. I think we will travel for a year or two."

"But I'm twenty-six, Julian," she said. "I want a home. You don't have to think of traveling for my sake. I'll be happy just to be with you."

"I don't think I could settle if I tried, Becka," he said. "Not yet anyway. We'll travel. It will be fun, you'll see."

That was what he had said about joining the Guards six years before. She had told him then that she did not fancy the unsettled life, moving from place to place, never having a home that she could really call her own. But he had laughed and said it would be fun to move about and to mingle with other people.

Would he never want to settle? She gazed up at him, her head resting comfortably on his arm. But perhaps it would not matter. She would be with Julian. She would have all she could possibly want in life. But she remembered those two years of marriage with him and recalled something she had denied at the time or simply ignored.

She had been dissatisfied and frequently bored. Everything—her whole happiness—had depended upon Julian. When he was with her, everything had been wonderful. When he was gone, there had been nothing.

Perhaps that was why she had been so inconsolable in her grief when she had thought him dead. There had been nothing—nothing at all—apart from Julian. No meaning to life. No real sense of self. She had been nothing and nobody. Only his wife.

But that was enough. It was enough to be just his wife, wasn't it? She had been taught that that was all a woman needed for a sense of fulfillment.

"A penny for them," he said, rubbing his nose against hers.

"I was thinking it does not matter where we are provided we are together," she said.

That thought sustained her through the rest of the day and on until bedtime. She undressed, brushed her hair, dismissed her maid, and dabbed some perfume behind her ears—something she had never done before at bedtime. It was going to be a special night, one that would get her so deeply involved in her marriage again that all else would pale into insignificance. The marriage act was going to be as wonderful as it was with . . . It was going to be as wonderful as she knew it could be.

She was in bed when he came as she had always used to be. She was lying on her back, breathing deeply and evenly, her hands flat against the mattress at her sides. She smiled at him.

"We'll do it right this time, Becka," he said, dimming the lamp. "Perhaps it was the light that bothered you last time."

"No." she said. "It was just the newness of your return, Julian. Thank you for having patience with me."

"Well," he said, "I love you, you know."

She drew a deep and steadying breath as his hands lifted her nightgown to her waist and he came on top of her, pushing her legs wide with his own as he did so. She loved him, she told herself over and over. She was going to show her love in the ultimate way. She was going to give him what only a wife could give.

"I love you, Julian," she said as he positioned himself.

And then everything snapped again and she was fighting wildly, arms flailing, legs kicking, teeth gnashing, voice crying out.

"Shh! Hush! The devil!" he was saying when she had enough sanity to hear sounds from outside herself again. "What the devil? Hush up this minute, Becka. You'll have the whole household coming at a run. Hush or I'll be forced to slap you." His voice was harsh, quite unlike Julian's voice.

She went limp. She was lying across the bed, his weight heavy on her, his hands holding her arms clamped to her sides, his legs imprisoning her own between them.

"Julian." Her breath was coming in sobbing gasps. "Oh, what have I done? I'm sorry. I'm so sorry. I can't. Oh, please, I can't."

His weight was gone suddenly and she lay, gasping for air until the lamp flared again. She pushed hurriedly at her nightgown. He was looking flushed and furious. She could not remember seeing Julian angry before. He glared down at her.

"I've had enough of this," he said. "I can go elsewhere if you would prefer it, Becka. It's all the same to me. But if it's Dave you are hankering after, you can forget him. Do you hear me? He had you for over a year under false pretenses. But that time is over. I'm back whether you like it or not, and you're my wife. You will do well to understand that."

"Julian," she said, deeply distressed, "I love you."

His laugh was harsh. "A strange way you have of showing it, Beck," he said. "A damned strange way. If you love someone, you want to go to bed with him. You don't fight like a wild cat as soon as he's ready to make his mount."

She could feel the blood hot in her cheeks. She gazed up at him—this strange, angry, vulgar Julian—and was frightened by the nightmare into which she had propelled them. She loved him. She did love him.

But . . .

But there was David. Her body was David's.

"I need time," she said, her voice dull.

"How much time?" he snapped. "Another week? A month? A year? Ten damned years? What am I supposed to do in the meanwhile?"

"Give me another week," she said.

He leaned over her on the bed, an arm braced on either side of her head. "And do we have to go through this same performance at the end of the week?" he asked. She watched the anger ebb from his face as he gazed down at her. "I love you, Beck. You're my wife. Is everything spoiled? Is it Dave? Foolish question. It's Dave, isn't it?"

She shook her head. "It's not spoiled, Julian," she said. "I adored you for years before we married. I adored you after our marriage. I thought I would die of grief when you died. I married David because there seemed to be nothing else to do with my life and he needed help with Stedwell. But I didn't stop loving you for a moment. Give me time. Or give me a command. I don't think I could be disobedient to a command. I'm your wife." She raised a hand and touched her fingertips to his cheek.

He drew his head back. "You had better not touch me, Becka," he said, "or you may find yourself being forced even without the command. And if you think I am going to order you to spread your legs for me, you don't know me very well, do you?"

She flushed and bit her lip.

"We will have to work this thing out somehow," he said, running the fingers of one hand through his hair. "Just tell me one thing, Becka. You don't love him, do you?"

Her eyes widened. "David?" she said. "Of course I don't love him, Julian. I love you."

"We'll work it out, then," he said. "I daresay that letter upset you this morning. You care for the child pretty deeply, don't you?"

"Of course," she said. "He's my son, Julian. I carried him with great difficulty for nine months. I gave birth to him and suckled him."

He looked at her broodingly. "Does he look like Dave?" he asked.

"He has golden hair like mine," she said. But he had David's eyes and would have David's build.

"We'll have children of our own," he said. "Once you have got over your aversion to having the seed planted. You'll be happy again once we have a child."

"I'm happy now," she said.

His smile was just a ghost of his old grin. "Lord, Becka," he said, "I would hate to see you unhappy, then. We'll talk tomorrow, shall we? After that blasted solicitor has been here? We'll make plans. We'll decide where we are going to go on our travels."

"Yes," she said. "Tomorrow, Julian."

He left her room without another word.

Rebecca continued lying across the bed. She closed her eyes and let the thought come that had been hovering at the edge of her consciousness for many minutes. There would never be enough time. She would never be ready.

She had lied to him.

He had asked her if she loved David and she had lied to him. She had thought as she spoke the words that they were the truth. It was only after they were out that she knew she had lied.

Her answer had been a lie.

She lay on her bed, defenseless against the onslaught of horror.

And despair.

24

"When will they be leaving?" Louisa met her husband's eyes in the mirror of her dressing table. He was brushing her hair, something he liked to do occasionally at night after she had dismissed her maid. "They have been here almost a month."

The earl did not answer for a while. "This is their home," he said at last. "I have treated Julian as my son since he came here at the age of five. Rebecca has belonged here since she married him. You were always fond of her, my dear."

"And of course I still am," she said impatiently. "Don't deliberately misunderstand me, William. Rebecca could stay here forever and I would be happy."

"Julian is waiting for the solicitors to settle his affairs," he said. "He is waiting for what is his to be restored to him. Then they will be leaving. He is going to take Rebecca traveling."

"She will hate it," Louisa said. "But that is not the point. He has money, William. There is all the officer's pay that accumulated from the time he was presumed dead until the time when he came home and sold out. That must be fortune enough to keep them for a year or more abroad."

"You do not like Julian," he said, setting the brush down quietly on the dressing table.

"No," she admitted. "I'm sorry, William. I know you love him. After he employed me, I stayed only because I felt sorry for Rebecca. She deserved better. She deserved—well, David."

"And yet," he said, "she was deeply in love with Julian and had been for years before they wed."

"He was not worthy of her love," she said, rearranging pots and combs on her dressing table. "And is not. She is unhappy."

"Yes," he said quietly. "It is a sad situation especially with a child involved. And yet she loves Julian still. I cannot think there is real harm in him, my dear. He was rather wild and weak of character as a boy. Perhaps time has put that right."

"It has not," she said tersely.

"Louisa." He rubbed the knuckles of one hand over the back of her neck. "I have known you long enough to know when you wish to say something but do not quite know how or whether it should be said. You had better say it before we go to bed or I shall feel you like a coiled spring beside me all night."

"When Rebecca was expecting a child in London, before her miscarriage, before he left for Malta," she said, "he made—overtures to me. I made my indignation quite clear and he said no more. But I disliked him and despised him from that moment on."

"Poor Rebecca," he said. "Yes, I suspected that Julian would not be a constant husband. I really should have forced the truth from David—well, no matter. But again time may have healed his weakness. He was away from her long enough to have learned to value her, I believe."

"He made similar overtures this morning," Louisa said. "It seems that I cannot be quite satisfied with an aging husband and that I must be looking for a diversion."

The earl's hand stilled against her neck.

"It is rather comic in light of my condition," she said.

"No one yet knows of that except you and me—and the doctor," he said. "I shall have a word with him, my dear. It will not happen again. I do assure you it will not happen again. I beg your pardon that it happened in my own home while you are under my protection."

Louisa got suddenly to her feet and faced him, her face tight with emotion. "She should be with David," she said, "and Charles. It is with them that she belongs. She is pining away for them. One has only to look at her to see that."

He gazed mutely at her.

"Can't you do anything?" she asked.

"I wish I could be God for you," he said. "But perhaps it is as well I cannot be. I would have to choose which hearts were to be broken. She married him, my dear. She married for love. And marriage vows are for life."

Louisa sighed and the tension went from her face. "It seems unfair, that's all," she said. "Life is unfair. And I do believe you would do a vastly better job of ordering it than God does, William."

He chuckled and drew her into his arms. "Don't let the vicar hear you utter such blasphemies," he said. "I'll have a word—more than a word—with Julian tomorrow. I'll not have you being upset, especially at this particular time. Is it to be a boy or a girl this time?"

"Do you want a boy?" she asked, looking up into his face. "Does it matter to you?"

"Not one little bit," he said. "I love my son and my daughter equally. Gender is of no significance."

"But I would like a son," she said. "Don't drive them away, William, despite what I have said. At least here Rebecca has us."

"Sh," he said. "I am going to take you to bed and I want you to sleep, not worry. Do you understand me?"

"Yes, my lord," she said, her face relaxing into a smile.

Rebecca and Julian still spent a great deal of their time together, but not all of it as they had done during the first week. They still talked and touched and smiled and kissed. But the total openness between them was no longer there. Rebecca carried around with her always the guilt of knowing herself a poor wife. She was withholding what her husband had most right to, and what she knew he both needed and wanted. Sometimes she resolved to put duty before everything, as she had used to do, and invite him to her bed. But she could not do it.

She could not rid her mind of the thought that had been there from that first night. Her body was David's. She knew it was not so. And she knew that it never could be his again. But she could not offer it to any other man, even her husband. The time would come, she supposed, when she would have to. She could hardly withhold her favors from Julian for the rest of their lives. But she could not contemplate that time. She could do nothing to hasten it on.

Julian's sunny nature sometimes deserted him. She understood the reason and did not blame him. Her heart ached for him. She still loved him dearly—as dearly as ever. The knowledge was confusing. How could she love him and yet—not? She forgave him his lapses into anger and spite and frustration—they were not many or serious.

Sometimes when they were kissing, he would open her mouth with his and thrust his tongue inside, something he had never done before. It was the way David kissed her, but with Julian it seemed somehow insulting, as if he did it just to shock her. And once in the carriage he opened her jacket and her blouse and held her shoulders back with his hands, turning her to the light of the window so that he could look at her bared breasts above her stays. Again it was something he seemed to be doing for its shock value more than out of sexual desire. He released her after a while and watched her button herself back up with hands that began to shake.

Sometimes he would remind her of their childhood and some mischief or cruelty for which David had been punished. Almost as if he wanted to punish her with the memories.

And yet they were small matters compared to the cheerfulness of his normal manner and the affection and tenderness of his usual treatment of her. And she was more grateful than she could say for the patience that kept him from her room at night. She wanted more than anything to be able to give him her undivided love again. If only the correct report had come out of the Crimea! There would have been unimagined agony in knowing that he had been taken prisoner when so grievously wounded and in hearing nothing of or from him for so long. But at least her heart would have remained wholly his and now her joy would have been unalloyed. There would have been no David. No Charles.

She could not imagine a world without Charles.

She could not imagine her life without David. She could not put herself back in time to see him as she had seen him before their marriage.

She took to going out alone whenever she could. Sometimes she just walked for miles and miles without knowing afterward quite where she had been. Sometimes she went to see Flora Ellis.

Flora was happy. Mr. Chambers, the gentleman who had leased Horace's house and had been paying court to Flora for some time, had proposed to her at Christmastime. They were to wed in the summer. It was good to see her friend happy, Rebecca found. It was good to see that for some people there were happy endings. Mr. Chambers, it seemed, was fond of Richard and was quite prepared to adopt him as his own son.

Richard was a bright and cheerful little boy with sparkling gray eyes and a sweet, engaging smile.

"He is going to slay the girls one day with that smile and those eyes," she told Flora, laughing. "He is going to be a handsome young man."

It hurt her to see David's son. To know that he had two sons, not just Charles. But she could see none of Charles in Richard, though she looked closely for some resemblance. Richard had David's hair color and shape of face. Charles had David's eyes and build, and some indefinable facial expressions too.

"You have lost weight," Flora told her one day when they were sitting at the kitchen table drinking tea.

"Every woman's dream," Rebecca said. "I am sure there was weight to be lost."

"No," Flora said. "You were just right as you were. Are you going to be living at Craybourne permanently?"

"We are going traveling," Rebecca said, "as soon as Julian's affairs are settled. I can hardly wait. I am longing for us to be on our way."

"Are you?" Flora asked, looking at her penetratingly.

Flora was the only person in whom Rebecca sometimes confided. Even with Louisa she could not speak the heart's truth these days. With Louisa it seemed important to keep up appearances. She was, after all, married to David's father and Julian's godfather.

"Perhaps everything will be different once we are away from here," Rebecca said. "Perhaps I will be able to forget and focus all my love on Julian again. Perhaps we can be as happy as we used to be. I do love him, you know. It is just that—well, David is hard to forget. We have both had to live with that feeling, haven't we?''

Flora looked tight-lipped. ''No,'' she said bluntly.

''I suppose I'll never quite understand what was between you and David,'' Rebecca said. ''I cannot imagine having known him as you and I have known him and not—missing him. Did you not love him even a little?''

She was sorry she had asked the question as soon as it was out. She was not sure she wanted the answer to be yes.

''Oh, Rebecca.'' Flora sounded exasperated. ''I can't stand this. It was always hard. Now it is impossible. I never admitted that Lord Tavistock was Richard's father, you know. Never. To anyone.''

''But he is,'' Rebecca said, wide-eyed. ''Richard looks like him.''

''Richard looks like *me*,'' Flora said. ''The dark hair and narrow face come from me.''

There was a short silence. ''Are you saying that David was not the father?'' Rebecca asked.

Flora swirled the dregs of the tea in her cup. ''I am saying nothing,'' she said. ''And I am sorry for the outburst. I have told my betrothed the truth. I will tell no one else.''

''Forgive me,'' Rebecca said. ''It was none of my business.''

Flora drew breath as if to say more but shrugged instead and set her cup down. ''Do you want to hear about my trousseau?'' she asked. ''Bruce is insisting that I have one and that he pay for it. Aren't I the luckiest woman in the world?''

Rebecca smiled. ''Tell me about it,'' she said, ''down to the last flounce and bow.''

Richard Ellis was not David's, she thought as she admired patterns and sketches and small remnants of materials and laces. Flora had been telling her that as clearly as if she had put it into words. He was not David's.

The relief was enormous. She wanted to laugh for joy. He was not David's. David had not done that dreadful thing.

But there was puzzlement too. Why had Flora let her

believe for so long that it was David? Why had David himself not denied it? Why had he told her that he and his father were supporting Flora? And that was undoubtedly true. Why would they support her if her child was not David's?

Charles had her golden hair and David's blue eyes. Richard had Flora's dark hair and—gray eyes. Flora's were dark. Charles had some of David's facial expressions. Richard had that sunny smile and the beginnings of a charm that was going to set many a female heart to fluttering when he was older.

Rebecca concentrated on what Flora was saying. It was only as she was walking home later that the thoughts returned. If Richard was not David's son, whose was he? The earl's? The idea was preposterous. But it made sense that they would support Flora only if David or the earl were the father.

Or . . .

Her footsteps quickened. That idea was just as preposterous. It had happened only a few months before her wedding. She and Julian had been head over heels in love. Richard had been born about six months after her marriage and just after her first miscarriage.

No, the idea was preposterous. And yet it brought on a wave of dizziness and nausea that almost forced her to sit down on the damp grass for a few moments. Standing still instead with her head hung low while she took a few deep breaths enabled her to steady herself enough to go on.

Flora Ellis, had Rebecca but known it, stood at the door of her cottage gazing after her for many minutes after she had disappeared from sight. Flora had promised never to tell. She had broken that promise to tell Bruce, of course. She had volunteered the information before he had asked for it. But no one else. She had just come perilously close to telling the one person she had been most meant to withhold the information from.

But Rebecca should know.

Flora's jaw hardened in sudden anger. To think that he had come back. That very morning. Smiling and charming and handsome as ever and setting her stomach to churning just as if she did not know what he was and just as if she had never met and grown to love Bruce. But then Julian had always had that effect on her.

Without a word of apology for the past, without a word of inquiry about his son—Richard had been out riding with Bruce—he had held her and kissed her and made it very clear that he was ready to pick up their affair where it had ended—and started—just months before his marriage to Rebecca.

She was shamed—deeply shamed—to realize that for one brief moment she had been held thrall to the old love for him. But love could not thrive where there was contempt. And she had felt mostly contempt for Julian Cardwell since he had broken his promise to end his betrothal to Rebecca and marry her.

Poor Rebecca. Flora had almost hated her at the time. And she had mourned his loss for many long months while she carried and bore his son. But how fortunate she had been. She could see that now with blinding clarity. What a great escape she had had.

Poor Rebecca.

The weekly letter had come from Charles's nanny. Rebecca had always read them alone since that first one she had read with Julian sitting beside her. She went upstairs to her sitting room to read it, though she knew it would be short and unsatisfactory like all the others.

He had had the measles. He had recovered now but it had been a nasty bout. The doctor had called daily and ordered him kept quiet in a darkened room. He had been very ill when the last letter had been written, but she had not wanted to worry Lady Cardwell so had kept quiet about the illness until it was on the mend. There was nothing further to worry about.

Rebecca let the letter fall to her lap. How much else had been kept from her—so that she would not worry? Charles had been very sick in a darkened room at Stedwell, visited daily by the doctor. She looked back on what she had been doing a week before and during the days before and after. All that time Charles had been lying sick.

Perhaps he had been crying for his mama.

Or perhaps he had forgotten her already. Did young children forget so soon?

There was not a single mention of David. There never had been. Almost as if he was not even there. And perhaps he was not. Perhaps he had gone away, to London maybe. There was never a mention of him in connection with Charles. Did he spend time with him now as he had always used to do? Did he play with him? Take him outside? Had he worried during Charles's illness? Had he held him? Soothed him to sleep? Was he even there?

When a knock sounded at her door, she wanted to call out to tell whoever it was to go away. But there was too much soreness in her chest. The door opened and closed again.

"Bad news?" Julian's voice broke the silence. He was standing behind her.

She spread her hands over her face and did what she rarely did. She lost control. She cried and cried until she thought her heart would break. Until she wished it could and she would die.

"Becka." He was down on his haunches in front of her, massaging her shoulders with his hands. She leaned forward to rest her forehead on his shoulder and wept on.

"Ch-Charles had the measles," she wailed, "and they did not t-tell me. He m-might have died and I wouldn't even have been there. I d-don't even know if D-David was there."

"Sh." His arms were about her, warm and comforting. "He didn't die, did he, Becka? And he is better now? You have nothing more to worry about, you see. Wasn't it better not to know until it was all over?"

She fumbled for a handkerchief, drew back from him, and dried her eyes and blew her nose. "What did Father want this morning?" she asked. "He kept you a long time."

"Oh, nothing much," he said vaguely. "He reminded me that even before everything is settled I have the money from the army. And spring is the best time to begin travels, he said, with the whole of the summer ahead. I think he thought it would be better for you if I took you away from here soon. Fresh scenes and new people and all that."

"Can we go soon?" she asked. "Please, Julian? Can we? I can't bear to be here any longer. I want to be away—away from all the memories. I want to be alone with you. I want to love you again." She heard the echo of the last sentence but could not recall it.

He stood up and rested a hand on her head.

"I wish all this had not happened," she said wearily. "I wish you had not joined the Guards, Julian, just because David did. I wish there had not been that dreadful war and that mix-up in the Crimea. I can't understand how they could have thought they had buried you when you were still alive. I wish—I wish David had not come home. Oh, it's no good, is it? It did happen. But everything will be all right again. Once we are away from here it will be as it used to be. Won't it?"

He pressed his hand down a little harder on her head. "I'll start making the arrangements," he said.

David recognized the handwriting though he had not seen it for several years. He opened the letter with some reluctance. As long as there was no contact whatsoever he could somehow live on from day to day. He would not write even to his father. He had asked his father not to write to him.

He was keeping himself as busy as he could. Construction had just begun on three more laborers' cottages, and he spent some time each day at the site, often helping with the work. He had planned out the year's farming with his steward. He was considering the schoolmaster's plea for a new schoolhouse.

His neighbors had been understandably shocked at the news he had brought back from Craybourne. For several days they had even left him alone, too embarrassed perhaps to visit him, not knowing what they would say when they did so. But after church on Sunday he forced himself to stay and talk, Charles in his arms.

Although he had no desire to take up again with the social round, he did so. Nothing was going to change, he told himself. He was a bachelor again. Alone again. He would not become a hermit, much as he would like to do so. He had a child to consider. His son would need friends and neighbors.

The Sharps, he realized after a few more weeks, were visiting him and inviting him out more than any of his other neighbors. And Stephanie Sharp, who was still unattached despite a Season in London and despite considerable beauty, was usually paired with him. He felt sickened at first when he understood what was happening. But why not? he thought again. He was in need of a wife, wasn't he? Charles was in need of a mother.

Except that Charles had a mother and he had a wife.

He went through the motions of living much as before. It was a life he could perhaps continue to live provided there was no contact. But now a letter had come.

It was a short letter. "Becka is pining away for the child," Julian had written. "I think you had better send him for a visit, Dave. Better still, bring him yourself. I think there is some unsettled business among the three of us that needs taking care of before I take her away for a year or two. But she needs to see the child first."

She was pining for Charles. Not for him. For Charles. But the hurt he felt was ridiculous and self-pitying. Of course she was pining for their son. He remembered how badly she had wanted him, how patiently she had borne that month in bed, how frantic she had been when she had thought she was losing him, how ecstatically happy she had been when he was born. And how doting a mother she had been during the eight months before Julian came home.

Perhaps she would have another child soon. Unconsciously he crumpled the letter into a tight ball in his hand. He would have to advise Julian to keep her very quiet during the first and last months and to keep her in bed during the fourth. God! He closed his eyes very tightly.

He was on his way to the nursery a few minutes later—he had been on his way up there anyway to take Charles out for his morning dose of fresh air, riding up on his shoulders. Before they left, he gave instructions to his son's nanny to pack a bag for herself and Charles for a week or so at Craybourne. They would be leaving on the afternoon train tomorrow.

He would go too, he decided later. He would not have Charles going alone with only servants to take care of him on the journey.

Besides . . .

Besides, he was starved for news of her. For a sight of her. He had not even known until Julian's letter came that she was still at Craybourne.

25

There were wild daffodils growing around the lake. Rebecca strolled there with Julian during the afternoon of a beautiful day in early March. She was reminded of another walk she had once taken there, with the earl and Louisa and David. He had proposed marriage to her there for the second time. It seemed so long ago.

"I'm glad spring is here," she said. "I'm glad summer is coming. The dreariness of winter is behind us at last."

"You should live through a winter in Russia," Julian said with a chuckle.

She held more tightly to his arm and rested her head against his shoulder for a few moments. "I wish I could have lived through one with you there," she said. "I wish you could have got word to me, Julian. Would they not even allow you to write?"

"There was a war on, Becka," he said. "Or so I thought."

She tried to see and feel only the signs of spring all around her—the blue sky and water, the warmth of the sun, the fresh green of the grass, the gay yellow of the daffodils. She tried to let it all soothe her and heal her. More than anything she wanted to return to the bliss of those two good years she had had with Julian.

Except that there had not been real bliss. There had been the heartrending miscarriages, the unsettled nature of their lives, her boredom when Julian was not with her. There had been the intimacies, which she had never learned to enjoy.

But she would choose to look back on those years as blissful, she decided. She was too afraid to see them as they really had been—though she did so even while telling herself that she would not. She had been a girl in love with a boy. The realities of life had begun to trouble her and make her uneasy, but, young as she had been, she had ignored them and persuaded herself that all was bliss. It had not been the love of a woman for a man that she had experienced. Perhaps that would have come. Perhaps if there had not been the long separation, and if there had not been David, they would have grown up together and the bond of their love would have deepened.

But there had been the separation. And there had been David. She had grown up with David. She had learned with him what she should have been learning with Julian. And now perhaps it was too late to change things to what they might have been and should have been.

She wished it were possible. She hoped it still was.

"Julian?" she said, and she knew even as she spoke that perhaps she was starting something that she would not be able to stop, that perhaps she was about to destroy something that was already badly broken and in need of mending.

"Mm?" He smoothed his hand over hers as it lay on his arm.

"Flora Ellis's son, Richard," she said. "He is not David's."

His hand stilled for a moment and then continued stroking. "She told you that?" he said.

"More or less," she said. "She did not come right out and say it, but I understood her."

"Ah," he said. "Well, that's good news for you, isn't it, Becka? Did I hear that she is going to be marrying soon?"

"Mr. Chambers," she said. "He has leased Horace's house. David and Father have been supporting Flora since before Richard was born, Julian."

"Have they?" he said.

"Yes." She would say no more. Perhaps it was not too late to stay quiet. Perhaps after all she had not begun anything or destroyed anything. She tried to think of another topic of conversation that would put this one out of his mind.

"I suppose you know, Becka, don't you?" he asked quietly. "Or guess?"

"Yes," she said.

"It happened in a moment of thoughtless passion," he said. "I had to wait another endless few months for you and she was there. She said she loved me. Said she always had. It didn't mean anything, Becka. I swear it didn't mean anything."

"It didn't mean anything?" she said. "And yet Flora was ruined and cast off by her father. She had to bear her child alone and in shame. Richard was born a bastard. And if she meant what she said, she had a broken heart to contend with too. Yet it meant nothing? Flora was always a good girl. Did you promise her marriage, Julian?"

"Who knows what one promises at such times?" he said. "But I was engaged to you. The wedding was all planned. And I loved you. She knew all those things."

"She knew that you promised marriage only to get her to give herself to you," she said. "It meant nothing."

"I swear it didn't, Becka," he said. "She hasn't suffered, has she? She has been well looked after, and now this Chambers is going to marry her. He must be well set up if he can afford your brother's home."

There was nothing to say. There was no point now at this late date in anger and outrage. There was no point in expressing horror at the callousness of his present attitude. Now after all he was trying to defend himself to her as best he could. Perhaps at the time he had suffered. Perhaps he had known dreadful pangs of conscience. Good heavens, his son had been born after his wife had miscarried.

"It was a long time ago, Becka," he said. "And it was before our marriage. You aren't going to get all upset about it now, are you?"

"David must have agreed to take the blame," she said. "He did nothing to stop the rumors. Even when I accused him of it after he came home from the Crimea, he did not deny it. Why did he agree to such a thing?"

"Habit, I suppose," he said. "Dave was always a good sort that way."

"A good sort?" she said. "In what way?"

He shrugged. "He might have hated me," he said, "and been jealous of me. He had had all of Father's attention after all until he was seven or so. He could have seen me as an intruder especially when Father made it clear that he was going to treat me as a son. But he didn't. He treated me as a brother and always tried to make sure that I didn't get any harsher treatment than he just because I was not really Father's son. I think he was afraid sometimes that I was going to get kicked out.''

"How did he make sure?'' She was almost holding her breath, she realized.

"I was a mischievous lad,'' he said. "If David thought I had done something worse than usual, he would sometimes tell Father that he had done it. Poor Dave. Father had a heavy hand and the cane in later years was no lighter. He didn't spare either the hand or the cane when he thought we had deserved it.''

"You let David take the blame for things you had done?'' she asked with widened eyes. "You let him be beaten for you?''

He grinned. "He wanted to do it,'' he said. "Dave was always stronger than I was. I used to quail at the very thought of the cane. Dave never let out a sound.''

"And yet,'' she said, "you never stopped doing the things that would earn punishment—for David.''

"Oh, Beck,'' he said, chuckling and patting her hand again, "we were just children. Children get into trouble. It's what childhood is all about.''

"Father was always a stern man,'' she said. "But he was never cruel. He would have used a cane only for misdeeds that he thought particularly serious. That incident with the gardeners' daughters being locked in a hot shed for hours on end . . .''

"I forgot all about them.'' He laughed. "They were almost roasted alive, weren't they?''

"And the kittens taken from their mother . . .''

"I meant to take them back,'' he said. "I forgot. I had a lamentable memory in those days. None of them died as it happened, though one came close, didn't it? Ned had to feed it by hand for days until it could go back to the mother cat. I was a wretched child, wasn't I?''

"I was a very prim and prudish girl,'' she said. "I grew to dislike David heartily on the strength of such incidents.''

"Poor Dave," he said. "I think he quite fancied you at one time, but you would have nothing to do with him."

And she had fancied David too except that her conscience and her moral upbringing had forced her to repudiate the attraction she had felt. He had not been worthy of her regard, she had told herself. And so she had turned her love to Julian and away from the man both her parents and his had chosen for her.

She had married Julian when she might have married David.

"And so," she said, "he did it once more when Flora was got with child. He took the blame. Was he still afraid that Father would turn you off?"

"No," he said. "I must admit that I begged and groveled on that occasion, Becka. I was afraid that you would be upset if you knew. I loved you too much to see you upset. And there would have been a dreadful scandal if you had felt it necessary to call off the wedding. You would have suffered too much."

"Didn't you think I had a right to know?" she asked. "A right to decide if I still wanted to marry you?"

"Your love wouldn't have been a very strong thing, Becka," he said, "if you had sent me packing for one transgression."

"Didn't David think I had a right to know?" she asked. "And Father."

"Oh, Lord," he said, "Father doesn't know. There would have been all hell to pay if he had found out."

"So even David's father thought him guilty of that villainy," she said. 'Poor David. It must have been difficult to quell the urge to justify himself just so that I would not be upset. Did you promise him that no such thing would ever happen again?"

"It was an easy promise to make, Becka," he said. "Believe me it was easy."

"And have you kept it?" she asked.

"Of course I've kept it," he said, squeezing her hand. "Of course I have, Becka. How could there be anyone else but you? I love you."

They had come to the end of the lake where the reeds grew out of the water. They were worse this year. It seemed more like bog than lake. But it still had the wild beauty that Louisa had admired.

It was a difficult thing, Rebecca thought, to adjust one's mind to someone falling off a pedestal. She had always thought Julian near perfect. The sunny-natured, charming boy of her youth had been her idol. He had seemed worthy of her love, and so, like the sensible girl she had been, she had fallen in love with him. Deeply. She had not been able to do anything by half measures as a girl—perhaps she still could not. She had been totally wrapped up in her love for Julian.

Yet all the time he was the one who had committed those occasional cruelties. And he was the one who eventually had committed that dastardly wrong against Flora. Richard was Julian's son. All those times she had wept because it had seemed that she could not present him with a child, he had had a son living in a cottage on the grounds of Craybourne. A son conceived a mere few months before their wedding. Even while that wedding ceremony was being performed, Flora was pregnant.

He had got Flora to lie with him by promising to marry her. Doubtless by telling her too that he loved her. She did not believe that Flora would have done that with him if she had not been convinced that he returned her love.

Julian was a very flawed mortal, after all. He was no glittering hero. Rebecca's heart was heavy.

And yet, believing David guilty of all those things, she had nevertheless grown to love him. She had come to love him despite far worse villainies. David had had an affair with a married lady in the Crimea and then had shot Julian who had tried to intervene in the inevitable confrontation with the wronged husband. She had grown to love him despite all that and the fact that she had believed he had actually killed Julian.

Well, then. There was no reason for her love for Julian to die. He had been a mischievous, thoughtless, and sometimes cruel boy. He had ruined and abandoned Flora, something for which he had doubtless suffered in conscience in the years since. Who was she to judge? And Flora probably had not been entirely blameless. It was very unlikely that what had happened to her had been rape.

There was no reason to come to hate and despise Julian. She had loved him totally. She had loved as a girl loves. And she had married him. She still loved him. There was a deep tenderness in her feelings for him. If she worked very hard, as she must, perhaps her love would deepen and broaden again. Perhaps she would come to love him as a woman loves. As she loved David. No, never that, she realized as soon as the thought came.

David had once assured her that affection was enough, that they could make a workable marriage if they could but feel affection for each other. Well, then, she felt an abundance of affection for Julian. Even if there was never anything else, there was that. She would make it enough. She would have to make it enough.

"Are you disgusted with me, Becka?" Julian asked after the silence had stretched. "Do you hate me?"

"No, of course not," she said. "Oh, of course not, Julian. We all make mistakes. We all do things for which we are desperately sorry afterward. And sometimes it seems that those things just cannot be put right. But we have to go on. I can't judge you. There is too much of which I could accuse myself."

"You, Becka?" he said. "You are an angel." He bent his head to kiss her briefly on the lips.

And yet, she thought, she was even then committing one of the greatest sins of all. She loved a man who was not her husband. But she would fight against it. For the rest of her life she would fight. She was going to love Julian again with her whole heart and soon she was going to be a proper wife to him again. She would force herself, letting duty be her armor. She had forced herself for those two years.

Perhaps in some strange way it would be easier knowing what she now knew about him. He was just an ordinary, erring human.

She smiled at him. "You would not be biased by any chance, would you?" she asked.

"Guilty as charged," he said, drawing her around into his arms to that he could kiss her properly. "My sweet angel. My darling."

She wondered as she relaxed into his kiss if he had ever seen his son. Or if he cared. But she would not ask the questions. Or think about them any longer. There was the whole of spring to be enjoyed. And Julian's love.

Both the earl and Louisa were in the hall when David arrived with his son. No one else. He breathed a sigh of relief as Louisa hugged him and kissed his cheek and his father shook his hand, squeezing it tightly and looking him up and down as he did so.

But Charles, in his nanny's arms and tired and cross as he usually was when something happened to destroy the routine of his afternoon nap, would have none of Louisa's kisses and then objected loudly when his nanny would have carried him up to the nursery. Charles wanted his father and he was going to let everyone within earshot know it.

David took him and nodded to the nurse to let her know that he would bring the child up in a little while. Louisa tried to wheedle a smile from him while David and his father exchanged news.

"Julian told me he was sending for the baby," the earl said. "I approved. She needs him badly, David."

"But Rebecca does not know," Louisa added. "Julian was too afraid that you would not be willing for Charles to come and she would be disappointed."

"Not be willing for his own mother to see him?" David said. "Don't pull Papa's hair, sweetheart."

"They are out walking," Louisa said. "I think they were going to the lake."

"Good," David said. "Charles can have his nap before she returns. He is in a wicked mood. Aren't you, imp? Hair hurts when it is pulled, you know." He wanted to make his escape upstairs. It had been a mistake to come, he realized now that he was here. He really did not want to see her. It could serve no purpose whatsover to see her and would only rub raw again wounds that had scarcely started to heal. "I'll take him up."

But he had hardly turned toward the stairs before the front doors opened behind him. He looked back.

"Hello, Dave," Julian said cheerfully. "You came, then, and brought the child. It was good of you. I had Dave bring your son, darling, as a surprise." He laughed.

Only his heart recognized her. Even with the full skirt

of her dress and the jacket bodice she looked thin. Her face was thin and colorless. Haggard even. Her eyes had dark smudges beneath. Her hair had lost its shine. She was standing absolutely still, her eyes passing over him and focusing on Charles, who was gripping his neck and looking the other way.

"Oh," she said.

It was only a breath of sound, but Charles turned his head sharply. And then he reached out his arms toward her, almost causing David to drop him, and set up a pitiful wailing. David hurried toward her.

She stood where she was, but her eyes were huge and bright with tears by the time David got close, and her arms reached out. He held out their son and her arms closed about him and Charles's about her neck even as her eyes closed and her mouth opened in a silent cry of agony.

David stood back as his son wailed and clung to the mother he had not seen in over a month and as she held him in an ecstasy of pain. And then she turned sharply and hurried across the hall to her left.

"Open the door," the earl said to a servant who was standing there.

She disappeared into a salon and the servant closed the door behind her.

"I told you she needed him, Dave," Julian said from behind him. "You can see that for yourself, can't you? Women are like that with their children, aren't they? It comes from carrying them around inside for nine months, I suppose. She'll be better after a day or two with him."

He should turn around and greet Julian. Say something pleasant to him. After all, Julian was guilty only of having survived a bullet that should have killed him. It was unreasonable and unfair to resent him, to hate him.

"When was the last time she had a decent meal or a decent night's sleep?" he asked. His voice sounded cold, accusing. "Can't you look after her better than this, Julian?"

"She has been missing the child," Julian said. "I have been doing my best, Dave. I sent for him."

David turned and held out his hand. "I'm sorry," he said. "Yes, you did, Julian. Thank you. Charles has been needing her too. This is proving to be a difficult home-coming for you, isn't it?''

Julian clasped his hand and said something whose sense David did not even grasp. All he could think of was that the hand now shaking his touched Rebecca at night. Touched his wife. Hatred constricted his breathing.

And yet she looked haggard enough to be almost unrecognizable. Haggard only because she missed Charles? That sadness should have been countered with ecstasy over the return of her love. Why was it not?

What was wrong?

''I had better go up and tell the nurse that Rebecca has Charles and will bring him up later,'' he said, turning abruptly and striding toward the stairs.

''Come to the drawing room for tea as soon as you have done that,'' Louisa said behind him.

He was soft and warm and smelled of powder and soap. He was surely bigger and heavier, though perhaps that was just her imagination. He could not have grown a great deal in a month. He had a death grip on her neck and showed no signs of stopping crying.

She did not believe she had ever felt happier in her life. There was misery too, she knew, just beyond the bounds of the happiness, but she would not let it in. Life had so few moments of happiness. Experience was teaching her that each one was to be grasped and accepted with gratitude. She held on tightly to her moment of happiness.

''Sh, sweetheart,'' she crooned to her son. ''Mama has you safe. No one is going to take you away. Just you and Mama, sweetheart. Sh.'' She rocked him, talked softly to him, rubbed her cheek over his soft hair, and listened as the wailing gave place to drowsy sobs with silences between. He settled his cheek more comfortably on her shoulder. Soon the extended silence and the greater warmth of his body told her that he slept. She continued to rock him.

There was a forgotten shawl of Louisa's tossed over the back of a chair. Rebecca picked it up, lowered herself slowly onto a comfortable chair and sat back, her child cradled against her. She covered him with the shawl and gave herself up to the sheer joy of holding her sleeping child. She had always set him down soon after he had fallen asleep. There was some theory that it would spoil a child to be held too much. But she did not care a fig for theories at this moment. She would sit here for as long as he cared to sleep. She would hold on to her little piece of happiness for as long as she could.

His mouth must have fallen open. She could hear him breathing deeply and evenly.

Louisa tiptoed in about half an hour later and set down a cup of tea and a piece of cake at Rebecca's elbow. She smiled though she said nothing, and she leaned forward impulsively to kiss Rebecca on the forehead.

Rebecca leaned her head back when she was alone again and closed her eyes. He had lost weight. His face looked thin and harsh, his eyes bleak. He looked much as he had looked when he came home from the Crimea. He was suffering. Perhaps it had been only a marriage of affection, but it had been important to him. He was suffering.

She had not even realized that she had looked at him that closely until she saw him now behind her eyelids, holding Charles, coming toward her, putting their child into her arms.

He was suffering.

Poor David. Ah, poor David. Perhaps he had been the cause of it all—her own misery, Julian's, his own—but he was suffering dearly for his sins. Too dearly.

26

He would not stay, David decided overnight. He would come back for Charles after a week or possibly two. His father had told him that he had been encouraging Julian to take Rebecca away as soon as possible. Surely they would be leaving within a week or two. She must have Charles until then, hard as it would be to be without him himself.

She had spent all the rest of the day with their son. She had sat in the salon with him while he slept, keeping him in her arms, according to Louisa, and had then taken him to the nursery, where she had played with him, fed him, and eventually rocked him to sleep for the night. David had not gone there himself.

He went there in the morning. Early enough to see Charles before she came, he hoped. But there she was in the middle of the nursery floor, lying flat on her back with Katie sitting on her stomach and Charles crawling about her head and throwing himself across her face. She was looking unusually disheveled. She was laughing.

David stood in the doorway, watching, during the minute or two before his son noticed him and came crawling toward him. She lifted Katie to her feet and got to her own, brushing at the full skirt of her dress and trying to check her hair at the same time. Her face had considerably more color than it had had the day before. She did not look at him.

David picked up his son, who played briefly with his watch chain, patted his cheeks and pulled his hair, and then wriggled to get down. He went crawling off after Katie to visit their two nannies, who were gossiping in a corner.

"He seems well," Rebecca said, fixing her eyes somewhere on a level with David's tie. "I was worried when I knew he had had the measles."

"He had them quite badly," he said.

"You should have let me know, David," she said. "I should have known."

"I instructed Nurse to wait," he said. "I did not want you to have the frustration of being here knowing that he was there and ill."

"I would have come," she said.

Now that the flush of playing with the children had left her face, she looked as pale and haggard as she had the day before. Her eyes were large with unhappiness.

"I'll be catching this afternoon's train home," he said. Her eyes flew to his. "No, no, Charles will be staying here for a week or two. You will be able to enjoy his company better with me gone. There are a few matters we should discuss, though." He had become aware of the fact that the two older women had stopped talking, though Katie's jabbering must have made it difficult for them to eavesdrop. "Shall we go somewhere else?"

She hesitated for a moment and then came toward him. He opened the door for her and set a hand at the small of her back, a gesture so habitual that he did not realize he had done it until her back arched away from him and she hurried along the corridor ahead of him and led the way to her sitting room.

He closed the door behind them. "Charles needs both of us," he said. "And we both need him. We are going to have to come to some sort of arrangement, Rebecca, so that he spends part of his time with each of us. It is not a thoroughly satisfying plan for him, but I think it is the best we can manage under the circumstances."

"You are willing to let me have him some of the time?" she asked. She was looking at his tie again.

"Of course," he said. "You are his mother. You saw yesterday how much he has missed you, and it is painfully obvious how much you have missed him. There is no need to give you both such pain. Neither of you has done any wrong that deserves punishment, after all."

She closed her eyes briefly. "It will mean so much to me to see him occasionally," she said. "You can't imagine how much it will mean, David."

"Perhaps I can," he said. "Julian has said that he will not mind. He is being very decent about it. You and he will be going away soon, I believe?"

"He is going to take me traveling," she said. "I can hardly wait to go. He says we will be away for a year or two, but if I can have Charles, I will persuade him to return to England for a week or so every few months. Will that be too often, David?"

"No," he said.

"Thank you." Her eyes lowered still further. He suspected that they were filled with tears. Rebecca did not like to be seen showing emotion. "Thank you, David."

He took a few steps toward her though he knew he should take a brief farewell and leave. "Is he treating you well, Rebecca?" he asked.

"Yes." Her eyes shot to his face and down again. "He is my husband and loves me. And I him."

"Yes." He smiled wryly at the stupid surging of pain. "It is only because of Charles, then, that you have been unable to eat or sleep properly?"

"What makes you think . . ."

"I have only to look at you," he said. "It is just because of Charles?"

He watched her draw a deep breath and release it slowly through her mouth. "It's not easy," she said, "to give up a way of life so abruptly. How is everyone—the Applebys, the Sharps, the Mantrells, everyone? Are the children still going to school? Are my ladies still knitting? Are my girls still learning the seamstress's art? Have you built any more cottages? Is Stephanie going back to London for a second Season? Do you still play with Charles? Does he cry for me?" She drew a deep breath again. "I am not expecting answers. But it is not easy not to know."

And it was not being replaced by Julian. She looked deeply unhappy.

"I wish," he said, "I had taken longer to kneel beside his body to discover that after all there was a pulse."

"But you did not," she said.

"But I did not."

She spread her hands before her and looked down into

the palms, then curled her fingers into them, and lowered them to her sides.

"I'll come back for Charles, then, in a week or ten days' time," he said.

"Yes. Thank you, David," she said.

"Good-bye, then."

"Good-bye."

But instead of turning to leave the room, as he should have done, he reached out a hand toward her. It stopped halfway. No, that would not do. But he did not immediately lower it to his side. She looked at it for what seemed endless moments and then lifted her own hand until their fingertips touched. She swallowed and closed her eyes.

Could it be? Could it possibly be that he too was part of her misery? But she loved Julian. She always had. She had been quite clear on that point even when she had agreed to marry him. And there was no point in the surging of hope he felt. She was Julian's wife and the soul of honor.

"David," she whispered without opening her eyes, "I have not slept with him."

But the foolish, pointless hope surged higher.

"I can't stop feeling married to you." She was still whispering. "It is a terrible sin as is telling you like this. It is why I want to go away. I love him. I want to be his wife. I want to be a good wife."

But she could not stop feeling married to him.

"You know I did not marry you only because I felt responsible for you or because I needed help with Stedwell, don't you?" he said.

She shook her head from side to side and lowered her hand. "Don't, David," she said. "Please don't. It is a terrible sin to indulge ourselves like this. I belong to Julian. I love him."

. . . to indulge ourselves like this. I can't stop feeling married to you. I have not slept with him. David let his own arm fall to his side. Yes, it was a foolish and pointless indulgence. And yet he wanted to say the words to her. He wanted to hear her say them.

"And none of this would have happened," she said, "if you had not . . . That woman . . . And if Julian had not tried to prevent a duel. Oh, what is the use?'' She spread her hands over her face.

He turned to leave.

"David." Her voice stopped him for a moment. "I know about Flora and Richard. And all those childhood incidents. Julian told me yesterday.''

But not about Cynthia Scherer? He turned the door-knob slowly.

"He could not have had deeper love or devotion from a real brother,'' she said. "I just wish I had known as I was growing up.''

Why? Would it have made a difference? Would she have loved him if she had known that he was not capable of all the petty cruelties? More than she had loved Julian? But Julian had had all that sunny charm.

"I wish I had known,'' she said softly. "I was a fool-ish girl. I thought love had to be earned. I grew up close to the church and yet I understood my religion little enough to believe that.''

He opened the door, stepped out into the hall, and closed the door quietly behind him.

The train was late. A brisk March wind whistled along the platform, causing David to hunch his shoulders against it. He could have got back inside his father's carriage, which still waited outside the station. He had told Vinney that he might leave, but the groom, obe-dient to orders from his master, waited until the train had left.

It felt strange to be alone, to be without Charles. It was going to feel even stranger at home without him. The house, which had seemed large and silent and shabby during the last month without Rebecca, was going to seem like a tomb without Charles either. David began to understand something of the emptiness that Rebecca must have felt when Charles was taken from her. Except that she had thought she would not see him again.

The train was coming at last, a good twenty minutes late. Its departure must have been delayed in London. He could see the steam billowing up into the sky and hear the rhythmic chugging of the steam engine. He watched the engine pass him and the carriages slow beside him.

He dug his hands into his pockets and hunched his shoulders again. It would be good to get in out of the wind. It was spoiling an otherwise lovely spring day.

He waited while five passengers got out onto the platform. He nodded to the first one, the village smith, and exchanged pleasantries with him. And then he found himself being hailed and had a strange feeling of déjà vu.

"Ah, Major," Sir George Scherer said, his voice hearty, his right hand extended, "well met. Returning to Stedwell, are you? You are leaving your son with Lady Cardwell for a while? Very generous of you, sir. Very generous, indeed. Don't you agree, Cynthia?"

Lady Scherer, as always, was just behind her husband, like a silent shadow. She neither replied nor looked at David.

"What are you doing here, Scherer?" he asked, not even trying to remain polite. It was perfectly obvious why Scherer was there—as well informed as he always seemed to be. David wondered which servants at Stedwell and Craybourne were getting rich with bribes from him.

"We heard, purely by chance, didn't we, my love, that Captain Cardwell survived the Crimean War after all," Sir George said. "We were never more glad of anything in our lives. Especially Cynthia. She was once fond of him, you know. Nothing would do but we had to come to pay our respects."

"You would do better to write if you feel you must," David said. "Why not join me on the train and visit Lady Scherer's relatives in Gloucester?"

Sir George laughed. "Captain Sir Julian Cardwell and I have some unfinished business," he said.

Yes. David had wondered how long it would be before the man discovered that Julian was still alive. Something would have to be settled there, he supposed, since the wronged husband had had no satisfaction in the Crimea. And Scherer was obviously not the man to let the past die. But Rebecca was at Craybourne. And so was Charles. And Scherer had already demonstrated that his almost insane hatred extended beyond Julian himself to anyone who was connected with him—even to the man who had apparently killed him.

David nodded to the guard of the train, who was looking at him with some impatience, and waved him on.

"There is a carriage outside the station," he said. "I'll convey you and your wife to the inn, Scherer, so that you may take a room for the night. I'll wait for you there and take you on to Craybourne. Perhaps Julian will consent to speak with you."

"How extraordinarily kind of you," Sir George said, his words half drowned in the loud hiss of steam that preceded the train's departure from the station. "Is he not kindness itself, Cynthia, my love? The village inn, you say? The Earl of Hartington is not as generous a host as you, Major?" He chuckled.

David turned to lead the way out of the station. He should have let Julian kill the man, he thought. But he had given in to that eternal urge to interfere in Julian's affairs. He had seen what had looked to be the imminence of cold-blooded murder and he had interfered on behalf of the man who would have stabbed Julian in the back just moments before he came on the scene. And the man who had tormented his wife for years for her transgression and had stalked Julian's wife and the foster brother who had robbed him of the pleasure of killing Julian for himself.

David wished the mist had been thicker or that he had come through it just one second later than he had.

One second. Less.

He turned to hand Lady Scherer into the carriage, but she ignored his hand and took her husband's instead.

Rebecca and Louisa took their children for a walk in the afternoon, though the coldness of the wind threatened to spoil the outing somewhat. Julian had decided not to come. She was to run along and enjoy herself with the child, he had said.

Charles was almost always just "the child" to Julian. But she would always be grateful to him for sending to Stedwell for him. It must be difficult for him to accept the fact that she had a child by David and that she was finding it an agony to live without that child. He seemed not at all annoyed to know that Charles would be staying with her for a week or two.

"I am happy for you, darling," he had said, drawing her into his arms and kissing her when they were alone together for a few minutes after luncheon. "You look brighter already. You must enjoy the week. Spend as much time with the child as you want. I'll understand."

She had hugged him tightly and asked him to come out walking with them later. She had been consumed with guilt at the memory of those minutes she had spent alone with David and of what she had said to him. She felt almost as if she had been unfaithful to Julian. And in a sense she had. When she had touched David's fingertips, she had felt as deep a stabbing in her womb as if he had put himself inside her. And she had wallowed in the feeling, hugging it to herself, keeping the contact with him even after she had realized its erotic nature.

She had hugged Julian and kissed him and resolved silently that she would never allow herself to err again.

"You run along," he had said, "and have fun with the child and have a good gossip with Louisa. I'll go out for a ride."

It was bitingly cold—so unlike the day before when she had walked beside the lake with Julian—but bracing. And it felt good to draw fresh air into her lungs. And even better to watch Charles crawling across the grass after Katie, heedless of either wind or cold or grass stains.

"One thing I will always bless Julian for," Louisa said, "is sending for Charles. I hate to imagine how I would feel if Katie were taken away from me."

Rebecca smiled. She thought of David on the train, on his way back to the empty house at Stedwell. For the rest of Charles's childhood and boyhood one or other of them was going to feel empty and deprived. She thought of his saying that he had not married her for any of the reasons he had given her when he had proposed marriage to her. She wished for a moment that she had allowed him to complete the thought. The words he had been about to say would have warmed her for a lifetime. And chilled her for as long.

And she should not even be reliving that meeting with David.

"You don't like Julian, do you?" she asked Louisa.

"Oh." Louisa looked uncomfortable. "It is not my place either to like or dislike him, Rebecca. I suppose it is just that William and I watched in wonder as your marriage of convenience to David developed into a love match. It did, didn't it?"

"I love Julian," Rebecca said. "I always have."

"Yes, of course," Louisa said. "Forgive me. How dreadful of me to remind you. Do forget I said anything, Rebecca. Put it down to my condition." She laughed in an obvious attempt to cover up her faux pas. "Yes, I am in a *condition*. What is sometimes called an interesting one. Say you're happy for me. Somehow it seems far more of a surprise the second time. Goodness, can I do this again? was my first reaction. I want a son this time. I think it would be enormously clever to have a son. William says it does not matter. But then he already has a son. I don't. Oh, Rebecca, forgive me for saying what I just did."

But Rebecca was laughing too and she turned to hug her former companion. "I am happy for you," she said, "and for Father. It must be a strange and wonderful feeling for him to be having a second family. Perhaps it is possible to have a second family, do you think? Perhaps Julian and I . . . But it's too soon to think of that. When is it to happen?"

But their conversation was interrupted by the necessity of settling a loud and physical quarrel over a daisy head between the two children.

When they finally returned to the house, it was to be greeted by the news from the butler that there were visitors in the drawing room.

"Oh, dear," Louisa said, looking down at her grass-dotted skirt. "Do I look as bad as you do, Rebecca? We had better hurry and change and comb our hair. William and Julian will not appreciate having to entertain alone."

They left the children to their nurses' care and hurried to their rooms. Ten minutes later Rebecca came back downstairs and let herself into the drawing room. The

earl was there and Julian. And David. There were two
visitors. Sir George Scherer was getting to his feet, a
broad smile on his face, his right hand outstretched. Lady
Scherer was sitting silent and white-faced.

The earl and Louisa made polite, if labored, conversation through tea. They must surely have felt a strangely
tense atmosphere, but basic good manners dictated that
they treat with courtesy the former comrade David had
met at the station and accompanied back to Craybourne.
The explanation, offered with hearty good humor by Sir
George Scherer, that he had just discovered the good fortune of his former friend and fellow officer, Captain
Cardwell, and had come to pay his respects, seemed a
reasonable one. They had, of course, met the Scherers
briefly at the station at Stedwell.

It was a three-way conversation. The earl, Louisa, and
Sir George talked. Lady Scherer watched her hands in
her lap. David and Rebecca exchanged occasional
glances. Julian looked uncomfortable. He got to his feet
finally, when it seemed that good manners should have
set the Scherers to taking their leave.

"A word with you, Scherer, if you please," he said.
"Perhaps you would care to step outside. There are many
things to reminisce about and we would not wish to bore
the ladies with military talk."

"My sentiments exactly," Sir George said, getting up
and rubbing his hands together as he inclined his head to
the ladies and smiled about at them. "You will stay and
converse with Lady Hartington and Lady Cardwell, my
love?"

Cynthia Scherer looked up briefly at Julian but said
nothing. Louisa smiled and looked determinedly cheerful. It was not going to be easy to converse with a silent
guest.

"Well," Julian said when the two men were outside
on the terrace. "I have lived on to be stabbed in the back
again, Scherer. Do you have a hidden knife about your
person, by any chance? Or a gun? I assume this was not
a purely social call."

"I was delighted to hear that you lived," Sir George
said.

"I'm quite sure you were," Julian said. "You must have felt cheated when you thought me dead. You may name the time and the place and weapons, Scherer. But not here if it is all the same to you. I would not bring disgrace or scandal on the man who has been a father to me since childhood."

"A duel," Sir George said. "That is an honorable settlement of differences, Cardwell. But I am not convinced you deserve to be treated with honor."

Julian clucked his tongue with impatience. "I have a strange aversion to being stabbed in the back," he said. "It is not an honorable way to dispatch an enemy, Scherer. I think we are about even on that score, don't you?"

"I wonder," Sir George said, "what you will tell your wife, Cardwell."

"Leave my wife out of this," Julian said curtly.

"I wish you had left my wife out of it," Sir George said. "You are fond of Lady Cardwell, so I have been told. You have allowed her to have her bastard son for a few weeks. Of course, her preoccupation with him gives you more time to spend with your inamorata, I suppose. Nancy Perkins, I believe? You have lowered your sights, though, Cardwell. It used to be ladies, not common laboring wenches."

"You are well informed, I see," Julian said curtly. "And any more slurs on my wife's name and I will be the one issuing a challenge. What exactly do you want?"

Sir George shrugged. "Oh, this is merely a social call after all," he said. "Cynthia had a hankering to see you again, Cardwell. I understand she fell rather hard for you. One has to pander to one's wife's wishes occasionally, doesn't one?"

"I see," Julian said. "It is to be a cat and mouse game, is it? You always were a worm, Scherer. I am to be left guessing, then, am I? And watching my back?"

"I should have had an eye over my shoulder in Malta and the Crimea," Sir George said. "Shouldn't I?"

Julian shrugged. "If you have nothing more to say," he said, "perhaps you should rescue Lady Hartington and my wife from the necessity of entertaining a woman who would clearly rather be any place else on earth.''

''In other words, 'Get out'?'' Sir George said.

''Exactly,'' Julian said. ''If you wish satisfaction from me, Scherer, you know where to find me.''

''Oh, always,'' Sir George said. ''Of that you can rest assured, Cardwell.''

27

Rebecca had not had a restful night. Sir George Scherer was like a constant millstone about all their necks. She had thought that perhaps they had heard the last of him once Julian came home. She had thought that he would be satisfied with the disaster that had overtaken David. Surely he did not need more revenge. Except for the fact that he had nothing to do with bringing this particular one about, of course. Perhaps there was no real personal satisfaction for him in it. Besides, Lady Scherer had said that he was almost deranged.

It was unfair, Rebecca thought, for him to have come to Craybourne to drag the earl, Louisa, and Julian into his net. Especially Julian. Julian had saved Sir George Scherer's life. Did the man feel no gratitude? But perhaps it was part of his plan to make David utterly miserable.

Rebecca did not approve of dueling, and yet sometimes she wished that Sir George had just challenged David when they were both in the Crimea and been done with it. One of them would probably have been dead, but at least innocent people would not have been involved.

She spent an hour of the following morning in the nursery, bathing and dressing Charles, giving him his breakfast, and playing with him. Then she sought out Julian. He was still in his dressing room in his shirtsleeves. He dismissed his valet before kissing her.

"Are you putting me to shame?" he asked. "You look as if you have been up for hours."

"I have been with Charles," she said. "Children usually wake early."

"That is why they have nannies," he said.

"I have him for only a week or so," she said. "Though

David says I must have him regularly. Will you mind, Julian?''

"Why should I mind?" he asked, satisfied with the knot in his four-in-hand and shrugging into his coat. "Have you had breakfast?"

"No," she said.

"Neither have I." He set an arm about her waist and turned her against him to kiss her more thoroughly. "But I could be persuaded to miss it." He grinned. "Or to take nourishment of another kind."

She sagged against him and rested her forehead on his shoulder. It would be so easy to say yes. But it was so impossible to do so. He had almost died trying to stop David from killing the man he had wronged. And yet she could not give herself to Julian because of her love for David. Love could destroy all rationality, she was discovering, and all devotion to duty.

"We need to talk, Julian," she said.

He sighed and then chuckled. "At least you did not say you have a headache," he said. "Let's go and get something to eat."

Louisa was in the breakfast room. She had been late getting up, she explained apologetically, because Katie had been awake half the night with aching gums and had insisted on her mother's presence.

Rebecca and Julian went outside to stroll after breakfast. He linked her arm through his and clasped her hand.

"You were wondering when we are going to be on our way?" he asked. "Next week, I think, Becka. We'll make Paris our first stop, shall we? It is the place to be these days. The Emperor Napoleon and the Empress Eugenie have a glittering court, and all is gaiety and busy activity. We can stay there for as long as we want and then move on somewhere else. Where do you most want to go?"

She shrugged. "It doesn't matter. As long as I am with you I'll be happy."

"Will you, Beck?" He looked down into her face, his own serious.

"Julian," she said, "that man invited himself to Stedwell a few times before you returned. Sir George Scherer,

I mean. David and I met him in London. He called at Hartington House to thank David for saving his life.''

"Ah," he said quietly. "Then you know the whole story, do you, Becka? I was hoping to keep it from you."

"Yes, I know what happened," she said. "It was a foolishly brave thing you did, Julian."

He looked at her.

"The only thing I don't know," she said, "and I suppose it makes a world of difference—it has worried me. What I don't know, Julian, is whether Sir George had a gun too or not. Was it a type of duel they were engaged in, or was David going to shoot him down in cold blood? That possibility has haunted me."

Julian did not answer for a while. "What is the story you have been told, Becka?" he asked.

"Oh, I know all the sordid truth," she said. "I know David was having an affair with Lady Scherer. And I know that Sir George found out. I know that they had a confrontation in the middle of the Battle of Inkerman and that you stopped David from shooting Sir George by taking the bullet yourself. But did Sir George have a gun too? Tell me the truth, Julian. I need to know."

"Dave told you all this?" he asked.

"I pieced it all together," she said. "He did not deny it. And Lady Scherer told me that she loved him. That makes it hard to bear too. I don't think he loved her. He was just using her and forcing her into committing adultery. But I must not judge. I really must not."

"She said she loved Dave?" Julian asked. "Those were her exact words, Becka?"

"Yes," she said. "I did not imagine them. She told me that she had loved my husband. I wonder if she still does, poor lady. She is dreadfully withdrawn and unhappy. Was she always so, Julian? Did you know her in the Crimea? But I am straying from the point, perhaps because I am afraid of the answer. Did he have a gun?"

"No," he said. He passed a hand over his face.

"No." Her voice was bleak. "Ah, this is what I feared. I have tried to believe that he could not have been capable of such villainy. I am well out of that marriage, aren't I?"

And yet she wanted to howl with grief.

"I always used to let him do it," Julian said. "I always used to convince myself that I had more to lose than he did. And he never seemed to mind. He had broad shoulders. He has less to lose this time too."

She was not really listening. She was grappling with one more count against David.

"You love him, don't you?" Julian said.

"Who? David?" she said. "No, of course not. I love you. It's just that—"

"It's just that you love him," he said. "He did it one more time for me, Becka. For your sake, I suppose. So that you would be able to keep your belief in me intact. So that you would be able to remember me as a hero."

She did not have to ask him what he meant. The truth came rushing at her with such force that it seemed impossible to believe that she had not seen it before. Especially after she had discovered the truth about Flora and about all those childhood escapades.

And of course it was just the sort of thing David would have done, even though she had been married to him at the time and they had both thought Julian dead. He had risked the future of their marriage so that she could cling to a youthful attachment that she had convinced herself was the love of her life.

Lady Scherer had loved her husband. Yes. Oh, yes.

David had shot Julian because—because Julian was about to kill Sir George?

Julian had been the one having an affair with Lady Scherer. They had both been committing adultery. While she had been at Craybourne, miserable with missing him, living with daily and nightly anxiety for his safety, loving him, he had been having an affair with Lady Scherer. Flora just before their marriage, Lady Scherer two years after. How many more had there been?

"I'm sorry, Becka," he said. "It would have been better if you had never known. But I couldn't let you go on thinking that David was the villain of that piece. Not when he is your child's father. Not when you love him. I'm sorry. She didn't mean anything to me, you know. I was just lonely. I was missing you."

"She loved you," she said, "and so did I. You betrayed us both, Julian."

"Yes," he said. "I'm sorry, Becka."

Adultery. It had always seemed one of the worst possible sins to her. That physical act was such a momentous thing. So very, very intimate. The joining of bodies. That one could betray one's spouse to do it with someone else seemed inconceivable to her. Especially when the other person meant nothing. She could have understood better if he had said that he had loved Cynthia Scherer. But she had meant nothing to him. Flora had meant nothing to him.

"Has there been anyone since?" she asked.

"No, of course not," he said. "I was wounded and in captivity. And now I am back with you. I love you, Becka. You must believe that. I can't tell you how my world would shatter if you did not believe that." There seemed to be genuine panic in his voice.

"And yet," she said, "I have refused to be a proper wife to you, Julian. I could hardly blame you if you turned elsewhere, could I? I am sorry to have put such temptation in your way. Is there someone else now?"

"No," he said. "No, of course there is not, Becka. You are my wife. I am prepared to wait for you as long as it takes."

"It won't be much longer," she said. "When we leave here next week, Julian, I'll be your wife again. The very first night we are away from Craybourne. I'll be yours whenever you need me. But there must be no one else. I'll not share you. I'll not let you come to me after being with someone else. There have been others apart from Flora and Lady Scherer, haven't there? Tell me the truth. Please? There is need of truth between us."

"A few," he admitted uneasily. "Not many, Becka, I swear. I don't want there to be any others. I want to be a good husband to you. I love you."

"I know." She rested her head on his shoulder for a brief moment. "I know you do, Julian."

She marveled that almost all her life she had known him and liked and admired and loved him and not seen until now his essential weakness. He was a sunny-natured, charming boy—even now he was more a boy than a man. There was no viciousness in him, but only a lack of control, a lack of responsibility. He was well-

meaning but self-indulgent. There would be other
women. She knew it as surely as she knew that she would
never leave him. He loved her. In his own way he really
did. More important, he needed her. He needed her
strength just as he had needed David's all through his
boyhood.

"Will you forgive me, then, Becka?" he asked, his
voice miserable. "I'm pretty far from being the hero you
have always thought me, aren't I?"

"I forgive you, Julian," she said. "You suffered for that particular sin, Julian. You nearly died. Paris I think will be
lovely. Perhaps I will even be utterly frivolous and have
the famous Mr. Worth make some dresses for me."

"I will so load you down with finery," he said, turning her against him and kissing her fiercely, "that you
will need ten extra trunks by the time we come home,
Becka. And I'll make you forget him, I promise. You are
going to fall in love with me all over again. Deeply. Head
over ears. Consider yourself warned."

"All right," she said when she could. "We will be a
couple of lovestruck children all over again, Julian, and
the envy of everyone we meet."

But she could think of only one thing as he kissed her.
Sir George Scherer had come to see Julian, not David. It
was against Julian his real quarrel was. Perhaps believing
Julian dead he had been prepared to vent his bitterness
against Julian's widow and against the man who had put
Julian beyond his grasp. But now Julian was back and
Sir George had a grievance against him that had had sev-
eral years in which to fester.

Sir George would not leave Julian alone. She did not
know if the man and his wife were still at the village inn,
or if they had left today. But they would be back. Sir
George Scherer would not be satisfied until he had killed
Julian. But perhaps it would take him a long time to come
to the point. He would delight in stalking Julian for a
while. They could expect him and his wife to follow them
to Paris and wherever in Europe they chose to go.

She wondered if Julian realized that too.

David had just returned from a ride. He had gone with
his father about some estate business, but had not ridden

back to the house with him, claiming the need for more fresh air. He was not sure if he was going to resume the journey that had been interrupted the day before. He certainly had no wish to spend time at Craybourne before Julian and Rebecca left there. But there was something that had to be checked out before he left.

He did not even need to stop at the inn to make discreet inquiries. He passed Sir George and Lady Scherer on the village street. He nodded curtly to them, touched his hat to Lady Scherer, and rode on, despite the fact that Sir George beamed at him and looked as if he was ready for a conversation. They had not left, then, although the morning trains in both directions had already gone.

And David knew that he would not leave either. If he could have taken Rebecca and Charles with him, then perhaps he would have gone. Julian, after all, would have to face the music sooner or later. Scherer would want some sort of satisfaction, and Julian would doubtless give it to him. Cowardice in such circumstances was not one of Julian's shortcomings.

But Rebecca was now Julian's wife. And Charles had been promised to her for a week or more. Neither one of them could be taken away. And so David would stay with them. Protecting Rebecca was Julian's responsibility, of course. But David would protect her too. She could not stop feeling married to him, she had said the day before. Well, he could not stop feeling married to her either. She was his wife, whether it was true in reality or not. He would not leave her at Craybourne as long as the Scherers were in the vicinity.

He went upstairs as soon as he got back home to change for luncheon. He came out of his dressing room half an hour later to find when he turned toward the stairs that Rebecca was just rounding the top of them. She stopped when she saw him and his hand remained on the handle of the door. If he could, he would have retreated inside again. But it would have looked childish. He prepared some commonplace to say as he took a few steps toward her.

And then she hurried toward him, quickening her pace as she came close. His arms opened almost by reflex and she walked right into them and circled his waist with her arms. He hugged her tightly, robbed of breath for a moment by the aching familiarity of her slim, well-corseted figure against him. She smelled of clean soap as she always did.

"David." She looked earnestly up into his face and her eyes brightened with sudden tears. "You are the kindest man who ever existed. I am sure you must be. I am deeply shamed that I ever allowed myself to believe all the evil I heard of you. I chose to believe even though all the evidence of my mind and senses told me otherwise. And I chose to believe my own interpretation of what happened in the Crimea even though it all seemed so alien to your character. I am so sorry. Please, please forgive me."

She knew, then. Julian must have told her. "There is nothing to forgive," he said. "I never denied any of it."

"Because you loved Julian," she said, "and cared for me. You did, didn't you? That was why you did not contradict me when I thought what I did about Lady Scherer and about the shooting. You did not want to spoil my memories of Julian. Because you cared for me."

"I cared," he said quietly, watching one tear spill over and trickle down her cheek. "I care, Rebecca."

She stared mutely up at him. He doubted if she fully realized yet what she had just done. He did realize, but he was finding the temptation to hold her for a few moments longer too strong to resist. He lowered his head, but when his mouth was a whisper away from hers he caught movement in the corner of his vision. Julian had followed her upstairs.

David straightened, drew her arms away from about his waist, and lifted one of her hands briefly to his lips before turning back to his dressing room. She looked bewildered, and the beginnings of a painful awareness of what she had just done were clouding her face even though she did not yet know that Julian was standing a short distance behind her.

David closed his door from the inside and leaned back against it, his eyes closed. *I care for you. I love you.* He wondered if she understood that that was what his words had meant. What had the expression in her eyes been

telling him? It had been naked enough. And yet he dared
not believe it. And even if he did, what then?

She was Julian's wife.

Nancy Perkins lived with her mother in a small house
at the edge of the village. Her mother earned something
of a living by taking in laundry. Nancy helped her. But
quite a number of times during the past month she had
been absent for hours at a time—usually in the afternoons, two or three times at night.

Julian escorted her back to the usual copse of trees,
which was as close as he dared go to the village with her.
He bent his head to kiss her, although he had already
told her that he would not be seeing her again. But she
was crying, and he could not bear to see her cry, especially since he had grown rather fond of her. For almost
a month, since he had first tumbled her behind a hedge-
row when she was on her way back to the village after
delivering some clean laundry, she had been flatteringly
adoring.

"Don't cry, my sweet," he said against her lips. "I'll
see you again when I return from my travels. I'll bring
you some pretty trinkets from Paris."

"I d-don't want trinkets," she said.

He had paid her well after each lay, but he knew that
Nancy would not have demanded even a single penny.
She was in love with him. He felt rather wretched.

"You are the loveliest, sweetest girl in the whole
world," he said. "If I weren't married, Nance . . ." But
he felt even more wretched at the lie.

Finally he had to let her go, knowing that he had
doomed her to weeks and perhaps months of misery,
knowing that she had given the treasure of her virginity
to a man who did not really care for her. He hoped he
had not left her with child.

He started on the long walk back home. He had
not brought a horse today. He felt doubly wretched—
partly because he had hurt Nancy and partly because
he had lain with her today before breaking the news to
her. He had sworn to himself that he would not so
much as touch her ever again. He had sworn that he was

going to remain faithful to Becka for the rest of his life.

He felt unclean. He felt a sympathy for those people who were addicted to such substances as alcohol or opium. One's head and one's heart—the whole of one's being, in fact—could steel one with determination to resist the great temptation and yet when it presented itself there were really no defenses against it at all. He must be addicted to his need for women.

Perhaps it would change once they had left Craybourne, he thought. Becka had promised that she would start sleeping with him again once they were away. She had promised that he might have her as often as he wished. It was a cheering thought. Except that sex had never been good with Becka. Sometimes he felt as if he worshiped her more than he loved her. She embodied for him all that was perfect womanhood, all that he wished he could attain and deserve. He could never deserve Becka. Never. She was as far beyond him as the stars.

He had always been afraid when in bed with her— afraid of shocking her, disgusting her. Becka was a lady. Sex to her must seem the basest of human activities. He had never really enjoyed bedding her even though he had done so with determined regularity during those first years of their marriage. There had seemed something almost obscene about forcing her to do that with him.

Julian hurried along the country lane that would take him to the gate of Craybourne, his head down. And now she had even stopped loving him. She loved Dave. It had always amazed him that she had chosen him rather than Dave, who had all the looks and all the other qualities of character that Julian had craved all his life. But she had chosen to love him, and he had squandered the gift.

She loved Dave now. And Dave, of course, had always loved her. They had been man and wife for a year and a half. They had had a son together. And Becka, the soul of honor and propriety, had been in Dave's arms this morning when he had arrived at the top of the stairs. They had been about to kiss.

Yet instead of wanting to kill them both, he had wanted to cry. There had been a strange rightness to their being together. Their son had been one floor above them, in the nursery. That child who had Becka's hair and Dave's eyes.

He should have stayed in Russia, Julian thought. But he knew he could not have done that. He had been in an alien culture and he and Katya had been growing tired of each other. And he had had a craving for home and for Becka.

"Well, talk of the devil," a pleasant voice said, and Julian's head snapped up.

"Straight from hell, pitchfork in hand," he said. "What are you doing still here, Scherer? I thought you would have gone back to London this morning. Hello, Cynthia."

"Julian." She looked at him briefly, much as Nancy had looked at him a few minutes ago.

"And miss the chance for some country air in the springtime?" Sir George said. "We decided to prolong our stay, didn't we, my love?"

"You decided that we must stay," she said.

"Enjoying the company of your little whore, were you?" Sir George asked. "She makes a soft and shapely mattress against the hard ground, I would guess."

"There is a lady present," Julian said, tight-lipped.

"Cynthia?" Sir George said. 'Oh, no, no, Cardwell, Cynthia is no lady. She too enjoys lifting her skirts for any handsome figure of a man who happens along, don't you, my love?"

"If you want to meet me, name the time and place," Julian said as Lady Scherer turned her face sharply away. "Otherwise let's have it out here with fists. Any man who talks so of his own wife deserves punishment. Lady Scherer was blameless, if you want the truth of it. I forced her."

"Julian," she said.

"I raped her," Julian said. "Do you want to punish me for that, Scherer? Do so, but stop punishing her. She looks as if she has had more than enough."

"Well, my love," Sir George said, laughing. "You have done a great deal of crying for a man who raped

you, haven't you? We will leave it until another day,
Cardwell. We would not wish to show violence in front
of a lady, would we? Or even in front of a whore.'' He
drew her arm through his. ''Come, my love, we will
return to the village. ''I am wondering, Cardwell, since
you seem so concerned for the feelings of ladies, how
your wife would enjoy hearing of this afternoon's, ah,
frolic, and of certain events that happened overseas prior
to your near-demise. Now there is a real lady. Cynthia
says it constantly, don't you, my love? 'Lady Cardwell is
a real lady,' she says.''

Julian nodded and stepped aside to let the other two
pass. ''It takes two to play that sort of game, Scherer,''
he said. ''I am not playing. It is as simple as that. I shall
call on you at your inn tomorrow afternoon. There we
will arrange to settle matters between us. If you will not
slap a glove in my face, then I shall in yours. Good day.
Good afternoon to you, Cynthia.''

She darted him a look of mingled yearning and fright
and warning. Sir George chose only to smile cheerfully
at him and walk on.

And there it was again, Julian thought, staring after
them. The destruction he had wrought in other people's
lives. Cynthia had come to him willingly enough and had
been an eager and lusty bed partner. They had been well
into their affair before he had discovered to his surprise
that he was the first man with whom she had committed
adultery. And that she fancied herself in love with him.
He had continued the affair anyway—even knowing that
she would ultimately be hurt.

As he had known that Flora would be hurt.

It had never seemed to matter as long as he had a good
time.

And now Becka was being dragged into it all. She
already knew the truth about him. She knew what a sorry
apology for a man she had married. And Scherer was
trying to drag her into his cat and mouse game. In fact,
perhaps he had already done so. He had visited Dave and
her a few times at Stedwell, she had said, after calling
on them in London. She had not said why he had called,
and Julian had not thought to ask.

He resumed his walk and turned in at the gates of

Craybourne, his eyes trained on the ground ahead of him. For perhaps the first time in his life he was realizing what suffering his own pursuit of pleasure had caused other people. And now Becka was suffering. Becka, who meant more to him than life itself. She really did, despite his more than shabby treatment of her.

28

David had been expecting it. Rebecca was in the nursery putting Charles to bed. Louisa had just returned from there and was sitting in the drawing room with the three men. Julian suggested a game of billiards with David.

Of course they did not play. They went into the billiard room and closed the door behind them, but neither of them made a move to set a game in progress.

"It was not quite what it seemed," David said, "though I am aware that that is a familiar line. She was upset because she had misjudged me most of my life. She was apologizing."

"With her arms about you," Julian said. "You were about to kiss her."

"Yes." There was a short silence. "It is difficult to break a habit of mind. She would have been horrified afterward—in fact, she probably is anyway—and so would I. You need not fear having an unfaithful wife, Julian."

"A habit of mind," Julian said. "And of body? Were you very close, Dave?"

"We were married," David said curtly, though he recognized Julian's right to ask such questions.

"I was so shocked to learn that," Julian said, "that I closed my mind to the implications. I tried to pretend, I suppose, that you must never have had sex together. I don't know where I thought the child had come from. I just couldn't bear the thought of Becka . . ."

"Her heart was always yours," David said. "She married me only on the understanding that that would always be so."

"I just want to know something," Julian said. "Would you have her back? I mean, if I were to drop dead suddenly or something, would you marry her again? Or are you thinking yourself well out of it?''

"She is your wife, Julian," David said rather harshly. He had imagined Julian's death too often during the past month or so. He was not proud of himself. All that was decent and rational in him recoiled at the thought of Julian's dying. "What you saw upstairs this morning has not happened since your return and will never happen again. I can assure you of that. I know Rebecca will say the same."

"That was not my question," Julian said. "I need to know, Dave. Do you love her? Would you marry her if you could?"

David hesitated. "I married her once," he said. "I made vows that bound me to her for life. Since you came home it has struck me that I am free and that I could and perhaps should take another wife. But I don't believe I ever will. I will always think of Rebecca as my wife. There. Are you satisfied now?" His tone had become annoyed. "But I'll not be trespassing on your preserves, Julian. She is yours. Just make sure you value her properly and treat her well."

Julian had been staring intently at him, his normally good-humored face drawn and rather pale. He nodded. "That's what I needed to know," he said. "But just one more thing before we return to Father and Louisa. Thank you, Dave. For shouldering the blame over Cynthia, I mean. I know you did it for Becka, not for me, but I'm grateful anyway. You have been the best of friends to me. The best of brothers." He held out his right hand.

David took it, frowning. "This sounds like good-bye," he said. "And what is this talk of death? You aren't planning anything foolish, are you, Julian? If you are, think of Rebecca and Papa. And of me. You will not solve anything for any of us by taking your life."

Julian grinned. "I'm not the type, Dave," he said. "I love life too much. Besides, I'm too much the coward. No, I'm not planning anything so drastic."

David continued to frown. "Scherer?" he said. "He is still here, isn't he? Has he been in touch with you today? Has he issued a challenge?"

"No." Julian laughed. "He prefers to play cat and

mouse. I am going to have to take the initiative, it seems. Tomorrow afternoon. I'll go to the inn and call him out if he won't call me. It will serve him right if I kill the bastard. I would certainly be doing Cynthia a favor, don't you think, Dave?''

David looked steadily back at him. "Do you want me to come with you?" he asked.

"So that I can hide behind your coattails?" Julian chuckled. "No, those days are over, Dave. I'll go alone. I may call upon you as a second, but tomorrow is just for the challenge.''

"There must be another way," David said.

"Not with someone like Scherer." Julian shrugged. "Cynthia always used to say he was crazy. I didn't realize at the time that she meant it literally. I'll deal with it, Dave. I'm not going to have him breathing down my neck all my life. I wronged the man, I'll admit that, but there's an honorable way to deal with a man who has wronged you. Scherer is not an honorable man.''

"No," David said. "He is not. I should have let you kill him when you had the chance, shouldn't I?"

Julian clapped a hand on his shoulder and led him to the door. "But then you would not have been true to yourself," he said. "You would not have been Dave. Besides, I think I was meant to learn something about myself. Perhaps I would never have learned had I killed Scherer that day. Undoubtedly I would not, in fact. Let's get back to the drawing room. Unless you really want a game of billiards, that is.''

"No," David said. "You always beat me anyway. Why invite unnecessary punishment?"

Julian laughed.

Julian had mentioned next week as the time of their departure for Paris. The days were slipping by and soon she would be parted from Charles again for an indefinite length of time. She wanted to spend every moment of every day with him. If she had only herself to consider, she would have had him to sleep in her bed at night. But it was better for him to sleep in his own cot in the nursery.

Everything that took her from him for any length of

time was an annoyance. And yet Julian was very insistent that they take a morning walk again. He smiled and shook his head when she suggested taking Charles too.

"I think not, Becka," he said. "I want to talk."

She stifled her disappointment and hurt. Perhaps he would keep her out no longer than an hour. There would be plenty of the day left. She and Louisa were gong to take the children to the lake for a picnic in the afternoon. And the weather was cooperating. It was a glorious day, more like a fresh summer's day than spring. The sun beamed down from a clear blue sky.

"Summer is coming," she said, lifting her face to the warmth of the sun as they left the house. "Is summer in Paris pleasant, Julian?"

"I don't know," he said.

She glanced at him. He was not his usual ebullient self.

"If it is not," she said, "we will move on somewhere better. But probably not too far south. Italy is said to be dreadfully hot in summer. I don't like too much heat. Do you, Julian? I must be a true Briton."

"It's better than the rain, I suppose," he said.

"I can hardly wait to leave," she said, smiling at him. "There will be so many new places and things to see. So much to do. And just you and me together, Julian. I love Father and Louisa dearly, but it will be good to be alone together, won't it? Like a second honeymoon."

"Becka," he said quietly, "you don't have to do this."

"Do what?" She looked at him, bewildered.

"You don't have to pretend to an enthusiasm you don't feel," he said.

She merely stared at him. She could think of no answer. He seemed very unlike his usual self.

"I can remember," he said, "when we were first betrothed, that you were excited at the thought of going home with me. You wanted your own home and your own place in society. You must have been very upset when I bought my commission."

She had been. Dreadfully. "It was what you wanted, Julian," she said. "I always wanted what you wanted."

"You never complained," he said. "You never really enjoyed the life of an officer's wife, though, did you? And if we had not been doing so much gadding about, maybe you wouldn't have lost those two babies.''

"Oh, Julian," she said, "don't blame yourself. I married you because I loved you and because I wanted to be with you. The only time I was really unhappy was when you went to Malta and I had to stay home.''

"You were always so dutiful and so obedient," he said, "that I was given altogether too much of my own way. You should have ranted and raved, Becka.''

"But it was your duty—'' she said.

"I mean even before I bought the damned commission," he said. "I did it only because I wanted to be as good as Dave, you know. Because I wanted Father to love me as much as he loved Dave.''

"Oh, he always did, Julian," she said, distressed.

"Not really," he said. "Oh, he tried. He was a good father to me and still is. But it is understandable that Dave means more to him. I'm not blaming him. I owe him a great debt of gratitude. But anyway, Beck, I was the world's worst husband to you.''

"You were not." She hugged his arm, tears in her eyes. "Julian, I loved you. I was happy with you. Oh, I was. And we will be happy again. Once we get away from here and there are just the two of us, we will be the happiest couple alive.''

"I think you found with Dave what you had always been dreaming of," he said. "Dave gave you everything you most wanted, Becka—a home of your own, meaningful work to keep you busy there, friends, a child, his undivided devotion. I should have tried to give you those things but didn't. I wanted my own life and you too. I don't suppose I would ever have been able to give what Dave did, though. I don't think I am capable of it, Becka.''

"We are all different," she said. "You like a more varied and exciting life. I will enjoy that too.''

"No." He cut her off. "No, you won't. You won't be happy anywhere but at Stedwell with Dave and the child. It's the type of life you need." He drew a ragged breath. "And he's the man you need. Dave is the one, Becka.''

"No," she said, blinking to rid her eyes of the annoying tears. "I was fond of him, Julian. But I love you.''

"He always was the one," he said. "You would have seen it if you hadn't demanded so much in the man you were to spend your life with. And if we had told the truth, he and I. Actually he did live up to your expectations if you had but known it. Dave always was your man, Becka—firm and steady and loyal."

"No." She did not know where this was leading, but her voice was shaking. There could not be this much truth between them. Not now. How were they to go on if they admitted all this to each other? How were they to cope with the rest of a lifetime together?

"I want you to divorce me, Becka," Julian said.

She stopped walking abruptly. The world began to darken at the edges of her vision.

"What?" The word was whispered.

"Divorce is allowed now," he said. "Even I know about the new law, even though I've been away. I want you to divorce me. For adultery. I can give you grounds. You know of the one infidelity, and I admitted to others yesterday. I'll give you all the grounds you need, Becka."

"No!" She was still whispering. But she found her voice. "No, Julian. I don't care what the new law says. Divorce is wrong. There should be no such thing. To me there cannot be. We married in church. We made vows before God. For better or for worse we have to remain together."

"I could live until I'm ninety, Becka," he said. "In all that time you would never be able to admit to loving Dave, even to yourself. You would never be able to touch him again or confide in him or laugh with him or make love with him."

"You are my husband," she said.

"And you'd see the child only for a week or two here and there," he said. "He would grow up almost a stranger to you, Becka. And he would have no brothers or sisters unless Dave gets them with another woman."

She did not intend to moan, but she heard herself do it.

"I don't think he will," he said. "You are his wife, Becka, and unlike me, Dave will never be unfaithful even if it means being celibate for the next forty or fifty years."

"Julian, don't." She was angry suddenly and turned to walk briskly onward. "There can be no question of divorce. The very idea is unthinkable."

"It is something I need too, Beck," he said, catching up to her. But she stopped walking again. "Put yourself in my shoes. I come back expecting everyone to have been waiting for me for years, expecting to find you pining away for me. And what do I find? I find that I was reported dead and that life has continued without me and really turned out rather well for everyone. I find you and Dave married and in love and parents of a child. I know I deserve it all, but the only way I can be punished is to punish everyone else. It would be punishment to me to remain married to you, Becka, because I would know I was punishing two of the three people who mean most to me in the world—you and Dave. And the third one would suffer too—Father's heart is aching for Dave. Somehow I have to start again. Perhaps I can do better than I have thus far. But first you have to divorce me."

"No." But it was an anguished protest rather than a firm denial. How could she divorce him? She would be breaking every rule, every moral principle, every religious scruple she had ever held dear if she divorced him. If she did so, she would never be able to marry David or anyone else. For in her own mind she would never believe that her marriage was ended and her marriage vows void.

"Think about it, Becka." He took both her hands in his and squeezed them tightly. "I know you love me, darling, and you know I love you. But it's not the sort of love that should ever have led us into marriage. The best way we can show our love is to set each other free."

She shook her head slowly. "I can't, Julian," she said. "Don't talk me into it. Don't force me into it. This is not something on which I must be obedient. You are asking me to do something that is wrong. I would not be able to live with myself."

"So four lives are to be blighted," he said. "Yours, mine, Dave's, and the child's."

"Justifying something does not make it right," she said. "There is such a thing as right and wrong, Julian. It is not just what feels good or what causes least suffering. Certain things are wrong regardless of the good that might come out of them.''

His smile was twisted as he drew her into his arms. ''You precious little fool, Becka,'' he said. ''I am trying to do something for you for a change. I am trying to do something decent in my life. Think about it. Will you promise me that? Talk to other people about it if you wish. Let's talk again tomorrow. Agreed?''

She set her hands on his shoulders and looked into his pale face.''Julian,'' she said. ''Oh, Julian, my love. My happy, charming, handsome boy. What happened?''

''I think it is called growing up, Beck,'' he said, grinning at her and looked suddenly once more like the Julian she remembered. ''Once this is all over we will be able to look back without pain and remember all those good times.''

''Or we can go on and recapture them,'' she said.

He kissed her firmly on the lips and hugged her to him. ''Promise me you will give it some thought and not decide finally until at least tomorrow,'' he said.

How could she keep an open mind when there was nothing to decide? ''I promise,'' she said.

''Good girl.'' He patted the sides of her waist and put her from him. ''Now back to the house. And back up to the nursery with you. Don't you get tired of frolicking with an infant all the time?''

''No,'' she said.

''He is a pretty little thing, I must confess,'' he said. ''Those blue eyes alone are going to be ladykillers when he grows up. Now, tell me all about your plans for this afternoon so that we have something to talk about between here and the house.''

''We are going on a picnic,'' she said.

''The details, please,'' he said cheerfully.

David was worried about Julian. He would have felt far happier if he could have gone to the inn with him. What if a duel was arranged for somewhere in the vicinity of Craybourne? It was unthinkable. The thought of a duel at all was dreadful so long after the provocation. One of them was going to end up dead. And then there was always the possibility that Julian would simply shoot

Scherer right at the inn and end up hanging for murder. The very thought made David break out in a sweat.

But he recognized Julian's need to go alone. And his own need to stay away. Protecting Julian, keeping him from harm, not trusting him to do the right thing when left alone were so deeply ingrained in him from childhood that it was difficult now to break the habit. And yet it was ludicrous not to. Julian was twenty-eight now and he was thirty. Neither of them, by any stretch of the imagination, could be called a boy.

And so he schooled himself to await the outcome of the confrontation and watched glumly as Julian rode off down the driveway in the direction of the village. In the meantime he had other worries. He felt uneasy about Scherer's hanging about in the neighborhood and worried about Rebecca. She was, after all, Julian's wife. And if he could not protect Julian, then he could do something about keeping an eye on Rebecca.

The trouble was that she and Louisa had gone on a picnic to the lake, taking the children with them. They had walked there and were having the food taken by wagon.

It was ridiculous to worry. They would be on Craybourne land all afternoon. Besides, it was Julian that Scherer was really after, and he knew that Julian was coming to the inn to give him any satisfaction that he might demand. But David could not help worrying. He had had too many encounters with Sir George Scherer to take anything for granted.

He could not simply invite himself on the picnic. But he would persuade his father to take a walk with him in the direction of the lake when he returned from a call he had had to make on a tenant. He had not expected to be long. They could walk around the lake, David decided, without disturbing the women and children. He would be happier having her in his sight until he knew exactly what had come of Julian's call at the inn.

David instructed a servant to call him as soon as his father returned and then got ready for the walk. He hesitated for a long time in front of a certain chest of drawers in his dressing room before pulling one of the drawers open and withdrawing a pistol—the same one that had shot Julian. It was carefully wrapped and perfectly clean, but he checked it with slow deliberation and loaded it before tucking it into the waistband of his trousers.

His legs were shaking, he found as he walked away. And he was being ridiculous. But he did not put the gun back.

There was a knock on his door a few minutes later and his valet came into his dressing room. There was a message from the earl, the man explained. A boy had been sent with it. Viscount Tavistock was to join the earl with all haste at the cottage of Paul Wiggins.

"Wiggins?" David said with a frown. "He lives miles away. What on earth is my father doing there? I thought he was on his way somewhere close."

His valet was unable to give any satisfactory answer.

"And what on earth can he want with me?" David's frown deepened. "Where is the boy?"

"He left, my lord," his man said. "It was a verbal message with no answer required. But he did stress that his lordship said the matter was urgent."

"Then I had better go," David said, striding from the room. The picnic would doubtless be long over by the time they could get back home again and walk to the lake. But it was probably just as well. Rebecca would be able to relax and enjoy the afternoon far more without him in sight.

As he readied his horse in the stables and swung into the saddle, he turned his mind to his father and the strange summons. He also felt suddenly the weight of his pistol, which he had forgotten to put back in the drawer in his haste to be on his way. He thought of handing it to a groom, but he shrugged and rode out of the stable-yard. After all, for many years, when he had been an officer of the Guards, his pistol had been almost like an extra limb.

Sir George and Lady Scherer had taken the second room on the right at the head of the stairs, the innkeeper's wife told Julian when he made inquiries downstairs. He climbed the stairs grimly and knocked on the door. He did not know quite what to expect, but of one thing he was certain. He was not going to let Scherer play games with him any longer. He had slept with the man's wife four years ago and the two men had had it out then though Dave had interrupted the final act. It was time the whole thing was put to rest.

There was no answer to his knock. Julian was furious. Another move in the game. Scherer had known he was coming and had deliberately absented himself. Well, he would wait, Julian decided, until the man and his wife returned. They had obviously not gone back to London or the innkeeper's wife would have told him. Damn it all, he would wait.

But as he turned from the door, he heard a sound. A muffled sound, but nevertheless quite distinct. It was coming from inside the room. He knocked again.

"Hello," he called. "Scherer? Are you in there?"

Again the sound. Damn it, the man had left his wife behind and trussed her up. Julian thought. That was the sound—the sound of someone who could not call out because she was gagged or come to the door because she was tied up somewhere. The door was locked. But he was down the stairs and back again with an extra key all within a minute. The innkeeper's wife had not argued when she saw his face.

It was as Julian had thought. A chair had been tied to the leg of the bed and Cynthia Scherer to the chair. She had been gagged with one of her own stockings.

"Where is he?" he asked, removing the gag before tackling the knots that bound her. "Are you hurt?"

"No," she said, licking the dryness from her lips. "Just stiff. I think he meant for you to hear me as soon as you knocked. He just wanted the timing to be to his liking. He did not want me running to warn anyone too soon."

"Warn them of what?" he asked, chafing one of her hands and wrists as she winced.

"She is going on a picnic this afternoon, isn't she?" she said. "To the lake on the estate with her son."

"Becka?" He jumped to his feet and paled. "He is not going after Becka, is he?"

"Yes," she said, her voice dull. "And he made sure I knew it. He intends for you to go there too, Julian."

"I'm on my way," he said, dashing toward the door.

"Julian." Her voice stayed him for a moment. "He is mad. He is quite mad. Be careful. He means to kill."

"And I am furious," he said. "I suppose that makes us even, Cynth. Perhaps I will kill him for you and set you free."

She laughed without humor, but he did not hear her. He was rushing along the upper corridor and descending the stairs two at a time. The innkeeper's wife looked up with interest as he dashed past her.

If Scherer laid one finger on Becka, Julian thought—one single finger—he was a dead man. He thought with regret of the fact that he had no weapon, but there was no time to return to the house. His hands would have to do. He would tear the man limb from limb with his bare hands if he had to.

He swung himself up into the saddle of his horse and spurred it into a gallop even before he had left the village behind him.

29

Rebecca and Louisa walked to the lake, taking a considerable amount of time to get there since Katie could not walk a straight line and had to explore the hidden side of every tree within twenty feet of their route. And Charles was not willing to stay in Rebecca's arms but had to go down and walk part of the distance, both of his hands stretched above his head and held firmly by his mother. And he too insisted on seeing what was behind a few of the trees.

"Ah," Louisa said when they finally reached her favorite part of the lake—the wild, overgrown end, "peace and quiet and relaxation." She helped Rebecca spread the blankets they had brought with them and sank down onto one of them.

But both women were laughing rather ruefully no less than two minutes later when they had to step in to break up a fierce quarrel between the two children.

"We were so careful to bring two almost identical rag dolls," Rebecca said, laughing, "and yet they have to fight over the same one. Will I ever teach Charles to be a gentleman, do you suppose?"

But the thought sobered her. She would not have a chance to teach Charles much of anything. Unless . . . But Julian's suggestion was unthinkable. And she would not think of it, though she had promised him that she would do just that. Not this afternoon. This afternoon was purely for pleasure. She had decided that before they had left the house.

"Perhaps as soon as I teach Katie to be a lady," Louisa said with a sigh. "And to think I am about to inflict another little monster on the world. Are we women mad, Rebecca?"

But finally there seemed to be a moment of peace. Katie who had won the argument over the doll, had promptly lost interest in it and was now playing with the other. Charles had convinced himself that there was something of great interest beneath the blankets and was trying to worm his way beneath the one on which Louisa sat.

"Ah, bliss," Louisa said, closing her eyes and lifting her face to the sun. "I wonder for how many minutes or seconds it will last? Should I count?" She laughed.

It was unlikely that they would be able to do much relaxing with the children present, Rebecca thought, but it was bliss anyway. Next week she would no longer have Charles, and perhaps it would be months before she saw him again. But she ruthlessly blocked the thought and set herself to enjoy the afternoon to the full. But something caught her eye at the edge of the trees through which they had walked just ten minutes or so before.

"Oh, no," she said. "Who told him we were going to be here, I wonder."

Louisa glanced over her shoulder to where Rebecca was looking and pulled a face when she turned back again. "What a strange man he is," she said. "I know he came down to Craybourne because he had found out Julian was alive and wanted to pay his respects. And he was all amiability when he called. But I could not like him. You too, Rebecca?"

But there was no time for further speech. Sir George Scherer was upon them and greeting them effusively and commenting on the perfection of the day and the beauty of the lake. Louisa smiled politely at him. Rebecca looked up at him, tight-lipped.

"My pardon for trespassing, ma'am," he said, bowing to Louisa. "But fresh air and the beauty of the countryside called to me."

"I can understand that, sir," Louisa said. "This is a beautiful part of the world. But you did not bring Lady Scherer out with you?"

"Cynthia is tied up with other concerns, ma'am," he said, rubbing his hands and looking about him.

Rebecca felt uneasy. Sir George Scherer, she suspected, did nothing out of a love of beauty or fresh air.

He had known that they were at the lake having a picnic, just as he seemed to know so much about their
movements—hers and David's and Julian's. He had
known and so he had come to spoil the afternoon for
her. It seemed strange to see him without his wife.
When he answered Louisa's question, Rebecca formed
a literal image of his words. It sounded almost as if he
meant them literally.

She wondered if he meant to kill Julian or if he merely
meant to torment Julian's family.

"Won't you sit down on the blanket, sir?" Louisa suggested politely. "Our picnic tea should be arriving
soon."

"That is very civil of you, ma'am," he said, "but I
would not wish to intrude on a scene of such domestic
bliss. I shall continue my walk and leave you ladies to
enjoy a little peace and quiet."

But he did not move on immediately. Instead, he went
down on his haunches to laugh at Charles, who was hauling himself to his feet, using Louisa's arm as a prop, and
then sitting down in a rush again when he lost his bal-
ance.

"You have a handsome little man here, ma'am," he
said, patting Charles on the cheek with one finger. "He
will be walking and leading you a merry dance before
you know it."

Rebecca felt a shiver claw down her back as he touched
her son and told herself not to be silly. But she wished
people would not announce that they were leaving unless
they meant what they said. She was angry with the man.
How dare he intrude, especially when he was trespassing.

"Oh, Charles is Rebecca's," Louisa said. "Katie is
my child." She indicated her daughter, who was playing
quietly with the rag doll a short distance away.

"But of course," Sir George said. "I should have remembered that Major Tavistock's child was a son. And
this little lad has Lady Cardwell's golden hair. How proud
you must be of him, ma'am." He turned his head to
smile at Rebecca.

"Yes," she said stiffly.

"It is my one regret in an otherwise perfect mar-

riage,'' he said, ''that Cynthia has never been able to
present me with little ones. I dote on them, ma'am.'' He
addressed himself to Louisa.

Go away, Rebecca told him silently and wished she
had the courage that David must have had to ask him to
leave Stedwell on two occasions. And then her heart leapt
right into her throat and she reached out with both arms.
Sir George Scherer had taken Charles's hands and drawn
him to his feet and was moving backward on his knees
while Charles toddled toward him. Sir George was
chuckling. ''That's my little man,'' he said.

Rebecca lowered her arms. Hatred was a dreadful
thing. It made one mindless and unreasonable. She had
almost expected for a moment that Sir George was about
to whip her son up and make off with him. She deliberately looked about her and reminded herself that she was
on Craybourne land during a lovely spring day in the
middle of the nineteenth century. But she wished Louisa
had not mentioned tea. Surely he would not invite himself to stay after all, would he?

Her stomach lurched suddenly as Sir George did
just what she had been expecting him to do a few moments before—or part of it anyway. He straightened up
to a standing position, taking Charles with him. His
smile broadened as he looked off in the direction of the
trees.

''Oh, do set him down,'' Rebecca said. ''He does not
like to be held. I'm afraid he has too much energy.'' She
glanced over her shoulder. Julian was walking toward
them rather slowly, his eyes fixed on Sir George. Oh,
now they were in for trouble, she thought. ''Do set him
down.'' Charles was already beginning to wriggle.

''Ah, Cardwell,'' Sir George said, raising his voice,
''I was fortunate enough to run into the ladies and their
children during my afternoon walk. Come for tea, have
you?''

''Please set him down.'' Rebecca had got to her feet
and reached out her arms to take Charles, but Sir George
took a step back, not taking his eyes off Julian.

''Well met, Scherer,'' Julian said pleasantly. ''I called
on you at the inn but there was no one there. Now I can
see why. It is a lovely day, isn't it? Let's take a walk

around the lake, shall we? Set the boy down.'' He chuckled. ''He is not averse to biting if held against his will,
and the last time I held him I ended up with a wet arm
and chest. I was not amused at the time, was I, Becka?''

Julian had never held Charles. Rebecca was frightened suddenly. No longer just annoyed or uneasy, but
definitely frightened. Sir George was walking slowly
backward, a smile fixed on his face. He still held
Charles in his arms, though the child was wailing a
protest now.

''Do have a care,'' Rebecca said, one hand creeping
to her throat. ''The lake is behind you, sir.'' He was
getting perilously close to it. ''Please put Charles
down.''

''I say,'' Louisa said, sounding both puzzled and annoyed. ''This is not courteous, sir. Please give the baby
back to Rebecca.''

''Let's walk,'' Julian said, his tone a little tauter than
it had been before. ''We have matters to discuss.''

''No, Cardwell,'' Sir George said. ''We have nothing
to discuss. An eye for an eye is, I believe, what the Bible
permits. You sullied my wife and destroyed my marriage.
I must do something similar to you. It is only fair, I think
you would agree. The fairest thing might be for me to
take your wife before your very eyes. Don't think I have
not been tempted. She is a luscious morsel. But unlike
you, Cardwell, I don't believe in adultery. A man must
have his scruples, you know. Besides, I don't particularly
fancy a woman who whored with another man while you
were away.''

''Oh, my dear God.'' Louisa's voice was shaking. She
had snatched up Katie in her arms.

He was not going to let Charles go. Rebecca held off
the panic that threatened to engulf her by a sheer effort
of will.

''This is between you and me,'' Julian said coldly.
''Let's go somewhere where we can settle it man to man.
Put the child down. You are very close to the bank.''

One step, two steps more . . . There was no air to
breathe suddenly. Charles was protesting loudly. Sir
George lifted one hand and swatted him hard across the

bottom. The protests come to an indignant halt and then renewed themselves at a louder volume.

"I had to ask myself," Sir George said, having to raise his voice to be heard above Charles's complaints, "what was more important to your wife than anything else, Cardwell. What could most effectively destroy your marriage and bring hatred into it as you brought hatred into mine? I did not have to look very far to find my answer."

"Dear God," Louisa said.

Rebecca could not react at all.

Julian took two determined steps forward and then came to an abrupt halt. Sir George Scherer, still smiling, held Charles with one arm, and whipped a pistol from his pocket with his free hand. It was pointed directly at Julian's heart.

"I wouldn't if I were you," he said.

The thought struck Rebecca that she must be in the middle of a particularly bizarre and nasty nightmare. But she knew she was not. She hardly dared breathe. Charles's attention was caught by a new toy and he stopped his bawling to reach for the gun. He was jerked back and bawled anew.

"What do you want?" Julian's voice was clipped but curiously calm.

"I thought I had already made that clear," Sir George said. "I want you to suffer as I have suffered, Cardwell. I want your wife to hate you as no one has ever hated."

He was going to kill Charles. Rebecca gasped for air.

"Shoot me, then," Julian said, contempt in his voice. "Kill me and get it over with. But let the child go. He is not even mine. Why should I care what happens to him? You can't get to me by harming him."

Sir George laughed. "That was not even a decent try, was it, Cardwell?" he said. "You will all stand exactly where you are or there will be more than one death this afternoon."

"You are insane," Louisa shrieked. "Put the gun down this instant. Put Charles down. Get away from here. Get off my husband's land."

There was a shout—more than one—from the direction

of the trees, but they did not register in Rebecca's mind. She heard only the next words and saw only what happened next before screaming and screaming and screaming.

"Put the brat down?" Sir George said, laughing. "Certainly, ma'am." He swung his arm back and flung Charles out into the water and among the reeds.

Julian saw the gun and knew very well that it was going to be used to hold off anyone who might try to save the child's life. He knew that the child was intended to drown before their eyes. He did not hesitate. He dived low, beneath the gun and into the water. He felt heat in his right shoulder and knew he had been hit, though curiously he had not heard the shot. But he ignored the pain and the welling of blood into the water.

The child had not been flung far. He was spluttering and gasping and trying to cry as Julian grasped him and lifted his head free of the water. At any moment he expected to feel another shot or to see the baby jerk as it was hit. He turned to set his body between the child's and the bank, well aware that when he was killed he would drag the child under with him.

And then Becka's screams penetrated his mind—she had been screaming since her son had been tossed into the water—and a voice shouting. Dave's. He turned his head to look over his shoulder and winced. Dave was kneeling on the bank, arms outstretched to him. Becka was standing just behind him, no longer screaming, with Father holding her tightly. Louisa was a few feet away, holding her daughter. He could not see Scherer.

"Hand him to me, Julian," David said, "and then you can get yourself disentangled. Scherer's dead."

He was lying facedown a little to David's right. And trust Dave to be sounding perfectly calm and every inch Major Lord Tavistock. Julian almost grinned except that his shoulder was paining him like a thousand devils and both boots had become entangled in the reeds and the child was squawking in his ear.

"I can't move, Dave," he called. "Here. You'll have to catch."

It was not easy to throw a child when one's arms were

already at chest level and one shoulder had been shattered by a pistol bullet and the child was squirming. But the distance was not great and Dave was leaning far out. The baby landed in the water, but Dave was able to fish him out in a trice and was on his feet and setting him in Becka's waiting arms.

The devil, Julian thought, these reeds were a death trap. They held his legs like the tentacles of a giant octopus. He drew a deep breath and went under to disentangle himself. And yet he had only one leg free before having to surface to suck in air again.

He glanced toward the bank, but nobody was yet taking any notice of him. They knew he was a strong swimmer and in no real danger. All attention was focused on the child, who was crying in Becka's arms while Dave held them both tightly and Louisa was wrapping one of the blankets about the baby. Father was holding his daughter and watching. Only a few seconds had passed since Julian had tossed the baby out of the lake. Soon they would turn to him, he knew. He knew that they loved him—Becka and Dave and Father. He knew that Dave and Father had always loved him and treated him as brother and son from the moment of his arrival at Craybourne, bewildered at the strange disappearance from his life of his own mama and papa.

They loved him and yet they were a perfect family group there on the bank without him. Father with his new wife and family. Dave and Becka and the child—the three of them clasped firmly together, heedless of the fact that they no longer belonged together—because there was Julian. And Becka would not divorce him, he knew. It was never Becka's way to take the easy way out if the easy way involved what she conceived to be sin.

The image of family and the thought of his own intrusion into it despite his conviction of being loved all imprinted themselves on Julian's mind within a second and several seconds before those on the bank thought to turn back to him in concern.

He could feel reeds wrapping themselves annoyingly about his free boot again. And his right arm was becoming numb beneath the wounded shoulder. He could still free himself easily. He had always been quite at home in water. And he could always call on Dave for help if his arm really was incapacitated. But . . .

His eyes picked out Rebecca again. She was holding the awkward blanketbound bundle of the son who meant more to her than life and her head was tipped sideways and resting on Dave's broad shoulder.

He wanted to do something for her, he had told her just that morning. He wanted to do something decent in his life for a change. Well . . .

He went under the water to disentangle his legs without first gulping in lungfuls of air. He felt fear as he pulled at the reeds, his decision not quite made. It was still not too late. If he wrenched with his legs as well as tearing with his workable hand, he would be free in no time at all.

And then, before he could make the mistake of thinking too much and before he could allow cowardice, the bane of his life, to control him, he breathed in deeply through his mouth.

David had met his father by the sheerest chance just three miles from home. It was at a crossroads with thick trees on all sides. Another minute either way and they would surely have missed each other. As it was the earl had hailed David, who was so intent on getting quickly to his distant destination that he was not looking about him.

The earl had looked blank and puzzled when asked what was the matter and why he was riding home when there was supposed to be a matter of great urgency at the Wiggins' cottage. The earl had not been near Wiggins in almost three weeks.

And then the truth had struck David with utter certainty. He had felt no doubt at all that Scherer was behind the strange message and that his purpose had been to draw David out of the way. But why? Out of the way of what? David had been planning to go to the lake because the women and children were there. Did Scherer also know that? But of course he knew. He always seemed to know everything concerning Julian or Rebecca or himself.

And if it seemed necessary to Scherer to make sure

that David and his father did not go to the lake, and if Scherer knew that Julian was on his way to the inn . . .

"Is that horse of yours fresh?" he had asked his father. "Can it gallop? We have to get to the lake as fast as we possibly can."

His father had frowned, but such was the urgency with which David spoke that they were both galloping back toward Craybourne before he began to ask questions. David had answered them as briefly as possible. He could not quite imagine what danger Rebecca was in, but he had no doubt that she was in danger. Scherer was deranged. Rather than challenge Julian to a duel and attempt to kill him for an admitted wrong, he would harm Rebecca.

They had left their horses when they were among the trees surrounding the lake. Trying to ride through the trees would only slow them down. They had run the rest of the way, the earl falling only a little way behind David.

The sight that met David's eyes when he came in sight of the lake almost paralyzed him for one moment. Scherer was standing with his back to the lake, very close to it, Charles clutched in one arm, a pistol in the other hand. Julian was a few feet away, poised to leap. Rebecca was standing on one of the blankets, both hands in tight fists pressed to her mouth. Louisa was holding Katie.

David shouted and heard his father do the same. At almost the same moment Scherer drew back his arm and flung Charles into the lake. Rebecca screamed, Julian dived for the water, and Scherer fired at him.

David heard the shot and then another, almost simultaneous one. There was an uncanny feeling of déjà vu for a brief moment. Sir George Scherer turned to look at him, surprise on his face, and then pitched forward. David looked down at the smoking pistol in his hand.

But the moment lasted perhaps less than a second. In the next instant he was racing for the lake, past an hysterically screaming Rebecca, and seeing blood in the lake and Julian with Charles's head blessedly above the water. The baby was coughing and spluttering. He was alive, then.

David checked the instinct to dive in after them and forced himself to think like an officer again. Panic had never saved any lives. He glanced quickly to his right, but there was no doubt about the fact that Scherer was dead. His head was turned to the side. His eyes were staring. Blood was oozing from his mouth. David set down his pistol on the grass, called to Julian, and reached out his arms.

Julian, he could see, once calm had been ruthlessly imposed on his mind, was wounded. It looked like a shoulder wound and probably hurt like the devil, but it had not incapacitated him and was doubtless not very serious. Charles was squawking and squirming, a welcome sight under the circumstances. Rebecca had stopped screaming.

"Hand him to me, Julian," he called, keeping his voice deliberately calm. He knew from military experience that panic around him tended to recede if he kept himself calm. But Julian, of course, was tangled up in the reeds and had to toss Charles, who landed with a plop, short of the bank. David had him out of the water almost before he had hit it.

It was only when he felt the wet body of his son and got to his feet that reality began to hit. Charles might have drowned. Their son might be dead by now. He turned and set the child in Rebecca's arms and reached for them both, folding them against him as if by the sheer strength of his arms he could keep them safe from all harm forever after.

"Sh," he said over and over again as Charles whimpered and Rebecca gasped and moaned. "He's safe now, love. No one is going to hurt him ever again. Or you. You are both safe."

Louisa had pushed her way between them to wrap one of the large blankets about Charles, but David folded them to himself again when she moved back. Rebecca set her head on his shoulder. Their son was crying with cold and discomfort and with self-pitying indignation.

David did not know how much time passed—seconds or minutes—before he remembered guiltily that he had no right to be holding Rebecca and that Julian would be needing a hand to help him up onto the bank.

Julian had saved Charles's life and was being thoroughly ignored as a reward.

But there was no sign of Julian when David looked out onto the lake. "He must be having a time of it disentangling himself," David said to his father. "I had better go out there and help him." He shrugged hastily out of his coat and dragged off his boots.

And then, just when Julian's head should have bobbed up to take another breath of air, Julian appeared all right—on his front, with his arms stretched loosely out to his sides. His face and his head were still underwater.

"God!" David said and dived.

It took him only a few strokes to swim up to the limp form of his foster brother. He trod water, careful to move his legs up and down instead of swishing them about and giving the reeds a chance to wrap themselves about him. He hauled Julian's head up by the hair. He was unconscious.

And then his father was there too, diving down to free Julian's legs, swearing as one of his own was caught, kicking free, and helping David to swim toward the bank with Julian's inert form between them.

The two women were busy undressing Charles, toweling him dry with the blanket in which he had been wrapped, and then wrapping him warmly in the other blanket. Two servants were approaching, having abandoned the food wagon when they saw that there was trouble. Lady Scherer was standing in the shadow of the trees.

But David saw none of it. He got Julian onto the bank with his father, turned him onto his side and thumped his back to try to dislodge the water he must have swallowed, and rolled him over onto his back.

"Come on, Julian," he said harshly. "Time to wake up, old fellow."

"He's dead," his father said, a hand against Julian's neck.

But David remembered saying the same thing in the Crimea after finding no pulse at Julian's neck. "No," he said. "He's not dead, just unconscious. Come on, Julian."

He shook him, slapped his cheeks, pressed on his chest to try to get his heart beating again. He even tried breathing into his mouth.

"Bring the blanket," he ordered his father, ruthlessly suppressing the panic that was threatening to take his control. "He's cold."

"He is dead, David." His father's voice was very quiet but appallingly distinct.

"No." David kneeled to one side of Julian, set his hands one over the other on Julian's heart, and tried to pump for it. "Come on, breathe, damn you. Where the devil is that blanket? Bring the damned blanket. Breathe!"

Someone was kneeling beside him, beside Julian's head. David did not waste energy looking to see who it was.

"Breathe, damn you. Wake up, Julian."

"He is dead, David." His father, standing behind him, rested one hand on his shoulder.

And finally he knew it to be the truth. Julian was dead. Julian had died while he, David, had been wallowing in the feeling of relief and rapture as he had held Rebecca and their son in his arms. Julian had died saving Charles's life. He had been left to drown.

Julian was dead. Cold and wet and still on the ground. And quite, quite lifeless.

David leaned forward, buried his face against Julian's stomach, and wept with deep, painful sobs.

Beside him Rebecca knelt still and quiet looking down at the dead face of her husband.

"Julian," she whispered, and she reached out a hand and smoothed the wet hair out of his face. "Julian." She took a handkerchief from the pocket of her dress and dried his face with gentle thoroughness. "Julian." She gazed down at him, at the face of her sunny-natured, charming boy, now surprisingly peaceful in death.

He was dead. She had thought him dead for so long and had mourned him bitterly. And then he had been miraculously restored to her. For a short time. For such a pitifully short time. Now he was dead again. Dead forever this time.

"Julian." She smoothed a hand over his cheek and

across his lips. There was no warmth of breath. No breath at all. He was dead. "Oh, Julian, my love. My love." She slid an arm beneath his neck and bowed over him, resting her warm cheek against his cold one.

She wept.

30

Rebecca sat down on the grass, arranging her black skirts around her so that they would not crease too badly. She removed her black bonnet with its heavy veil and set it down beside her. The weather was still gloriously sunny and warm for the time of year. It was good to feel air and warmth against her head and face.

She had chosen almost the exact spot on which she and Louisa had spread their blankets a week before. It was peaceful again as it had been then at first. Sunlight sparkled off the water among the reeds.

Perhaps it was morbid to come back to this very place so soon afterward. Louisa had looked horrified when Rebecca had mentioned where she was going. She had probably been relieved too, Rebecca thought, to know that there was no question of her being asked to go as well. The earl had insisted that Louisa spend a few days in bed before the funeral yesterday, and he was still keeping her very quiet. Poor Louisa—she had gone all to pieces.

It was just there he had died, Rebecca thought, looking at the sparkling, lovely waters of the lake. Not very far from the bank and among reeds that should not have been so very dangerous to a man who could swim. But Julian had died.

Of course, both the earl and David had explained very emphatically to the magistrate who had come to the house, Julian had been badly injured and had lost a lot of blood in the water. And the water had still had its early spring chill. And Julian's heavy clothes and boots would have made it extra difficult for him to keep his head above water. And the reeds were quite treacherous.

Both men had stressed every single point that might have accounted for the fact that Julian had died.

His death had been an accident, aggravated by a deadly assault. That had been the magistrate's final decision. Father and David had shown almost open relief. So had she. It would have been dreadful if this death had been ruled . . .

Rebecca drew in a deep, steadying breath.

The killing of Sir George Scherer had been ruled quite justified under the circumstances. David had shot him through the heart. Through the center of the heart, not an inch higher this time. Lady Scherer had had the body taken away and had disappeared from Craybourne. She had refused the help the earl had offered.

Rebecca had a strange memory of Lady Scherer that afternoon—though perhaps it was not so strange after all. Rebecca had been too distraught with her own grief to notice much at the time, but later she had remembered Lady Scherer standing silently a little removed from the family, gazing stony-faced, not at her husband's body, but at Julian's.

Rebecca could remember Lady Scherer saying that she had loved Rebecca's husband. Julian. It had seemed clear that afternoon that her love had never died. Poor lady. But at least now she was free of that villain, who had made her suffer for years for loving Julian.

Rebecca was aware suddenly that someone was coming up behind her. She even knew who it was. She did not turn. Julian's death had driven something of a wedge between them. They had both grieved deeply during the past week, but separately, not together. It was almost as if they both felt guilty, as if they both felt they had been partly responsible for Julian's death.

He came down on his haunches beside her. She gazed out across the lake.

"Papa was concerned about your being here alone," he said. "You needed to come back, Rebecca?"

She nodded.

"Would you rather be alone?"

"No." She shook her head, and he sat down on the grass beside her. "He was always a very strong swimmer, David."

"Yes."

"And the wound was not so very bad, was it?"

"He had survived worse," he said.

"And he could easily have called for help even though we were all selfishly gathered around Charles."

"Yes."

"He wanted me to divorce him," she said. "There were grounds. I suppose you knew that there were other women even after our marriage, didn't you?"

"Yes," he said.

"I was to think about it and give him my answer the next day," she said. "But I think he knew it was something I just could not do."

David said nothing.

"Did I drive him to it?" she asked. "Because I could not have that on my conscience, did I force him into this?" She gestured with one hand toward the lake.

"No," he said. "I have blamed myself too, Rebecca. I let myself hold you and almost kiss you at the house and he saw us. I held you and Charles after Julian had rescued him. He must have seen us. I did not turn immediately, as I should have done, to help him out of the water. I assumed that he was in no danger. But it was not my fault or yours."

"Whose, then?" she asked.

"I think it was a gift," he said quietly. He drew breath as if to explain his meaning, but it did not need to be explained. He said no more.

"Did he think we wanted him dead, then?" she asked. "And did we? Did he know how many times I had thought that it might have been better if he had not come back?"

"And how many times I had thought it?" he said.

"David," she said, "I loved him. He was my dearest boy. He was my love."

"I loved him too," he said. "He was my friend and my brother."

"And we owe Charles's life to him," she said.

"Yes."

"I used to be annoyed because he showed no interest in Charles," she said. "Because he only ever referred to him as 'the child.' But he gave his life for Charles."

"Yes," he said. "And for us."

It was unsettling to feel so many conflicting emotions. It was disturbing to feel that she no longer knew whom she loved or even what love was. Perhaps that was because she had never suspected that love could be so many dimensional. She had loved Julian and David. Both of them as lovers and husbands. Both simultaneously. Did one of those loves have to be real and the other imaginary? Could they not both have been real?

The terrible gloom that had engulfed her with the black crape since the week before seemed suddenly eased. She had not forced Julian into what he had done. She had not betrayed him. She had not failed in her love for him.

Of his own free will he had given her a precious, precious gift. Two gifts. First, her son, and then her freedom. Perhaps three gifts—he had given her precious memories of him. She only hoped . . . Oh, she only hoped . . .

"Do you think he knew that I loved him?" she asked.

"Yes," David said. "He knew. And he knew that Papa and I loved him too."

"So it was not done out of bitterness or despair?" she asked.

"No," he said. "It was done out of love. He spoke the truth when he said that none of those other women meant anything to him, Rebecca. He had a weakness that he could not seem to conquer. But he did love you. You were the only woman who meant anything to him. He worshiped you."

"Yes," she said. *He died for me.* But she did not say the words out loud. "And so he died a hero after all."

"Yes."

They sat side by side in silence for a long while. But it was neither a bitter nor a grief-stricken silence. It was a peaceful one. Rebecca found that she could look at the spot where Julian had drowned and at the place on the bank where she had wept over his body and feel only deep love, not the wrenching pain she had been feeling for a week. She lifted her face to the healing warmth of the sun.

"I am going back to Stedwell tomorrow, Rebecca," David said at last.

She had not thought of the future. She had deliberately kept her mind on the present and the past. She did not know what to expect of the future.

"I'll leave Charles here," he said. "I'll stay away for two months. May I come back then—to you?"

She nodded. "Yes."

"I don't think we need to wait a full year," he said. "It will not be disrespectful to wait less. Ours are exceptional circumstances. And there is Charles to think of."

"Yes," she said. "He needs both of us."

"We should wait at least the two months, though," he said. "I'll go home tomorrow."

"Yes," she said. "I think that is a good idea, David."

They would remarry, then. Without any fuss or romance. Without any declarations of love or passion. Because it was what Julian had died to make possible. Because Charles needed both of them. And for another reason too. She knew there was another reason, but it was not the time either to think or to talk about that.

It felt right to come to a quiet agreement this way.

"I want another child." She did not know where the words or the idea came from, but she knew as she heard what she had said that it was what she passionately wanted. Life reaffirmed. Love growing and spreading to more and more people. For that was what love was. That was what she had discovered during the past week.

"We'll have another, God willing," he said. "Together."

Yes, they had had Charles together. Although it had been in her womb that he had been carried, keeping him there had been a joint effort. A combined labor of love.

They sat in silence again, both gazing out across the lake. After a while he set his hand palm up on the grass between them, not touching her. She was aware of it though she had not looked down, and she set her own hand palm down on top of it. He laced their fingers together and held her hand in a firm clasp.

The July wedding in the village church at Stedwell was a rather subdued affair since the family of the bride and groom and even the couple themselves all wore mourning. And yet it was neither a gloomy nor an unhappy event.

The church was crammed full, partly with guests from other places, most notably the Earl and Countess of Hartington and the bride's brother and sister-in-law. But it was filled too with the viscount's friends and neighbors of all social stations. All had been overjoyed to learn that they were to have their viscountess back again after a lengthy absence.

Some of those neighbors had decked the church with flowers. The schoolchildren, standing outside with their schoolmaster during the ceremony, waited with excited impatience to pelt the bride with blooms as soon as she emerged from the church.

There was a more than ordinary sense of tension in the church when the rector asked if anyone knew of any impediment to the marriage about to be solemnized. There was a collective sigh of contentment later when bride and groom said "I do," and again when the rector pronounced them man and wife. Charles, standing on his grandfather's lap, stabbed one finger in the direction of the couple, turned triumphantly to Katie, and announced for all the church to hear, "Mama!"

The groom kissed his bride and again there was that whisper of a sigh. Charles turned, having lost interest in the proceedings, and hunted for his grandpapa's watch chain. Louisa narrowly averted disaster by drawing a favorite toy out of her handbag when Katie seemed about to take exception to the fact that another child was monopolizing her papa's lap.

And then everyone was outside the church and wanting to greet the newly married couple. For a few moments it rained flowers. The bride laughed and turned her face up to them. The groom caught one and threaded it into her hair beneath the brim of her bonnet, the pink of the bloom a startling contrast to the unrelieved black in which she was clothed.

Everyone had been invited to Stedwell for breakfast. Everyone. The bride had been quite adamant about that. And all would eat together and mingle together. Tables were spread out along the terrace and guests milled around them, filling plates and lifting glasses from large

trays, and strolled about on the lawns and down beside
the river and onto the bridge.

The gardens were looking a great deal better cared for
than they had looked for years, several people agreed—
those who had known Stedwell before the viscount returned to it two years before.

They were fortunate to have a pleasant day for the
wedding, since the weather through most of the summer
so far had been indifferent at best. It was so much more
festive to be able to remain outdoors than to have to crowd
into the ballroom, which had been the alternate site for
the breakfast.

Everyone wanted to kiss the bride again and shake the
groom by the hand before leaving. Although it had been
nominally breakfast that they were eating, it was well
into the afternoon before everyone except the house
guests had driven away. The house guests themselves
were quite content to drift back into the house and seek
out their rooms for an hour or so of relaxation. The children, who had excited themselves to exhaustion during
the celebrations, which they had been allowed to attend,
gave in reluctantly to the insistence of their nannies that
it was nap time with no arguments allowed.

The wedding was over.

"Are you tired?" David asked. They were standing in
the hall, having just watched the earl escort a quite largely
pregnant Louisa upstairs.

"No." Rebecca shook her head. "I am too excited to
be tired."

"Come, then," he said, taking her hand and lacing
his fingers with hers. "I have something to show you."

He led her outside again and along the terrace to the
side of the house, where they had set up the rose arbor the
year before. The hedges had grown high enough now to
shield it from both wind and prying eyes. Rebecca had not
seen it. She had returned to Stedwell only the afternoon
before with the earl and Louisa and the children.

"Oh," she said, coming to a halt under the trellised
archway—which was covered with budding and blooming
roses. "Oh, David." It quite took her breath away. It
was a private little heaven, rich with blooms and their

scent. The fountain was shooting sprays of water into the air.

"I was working on it anyway," he said. "But I have given our gardeners no peace over it in the last three months, since I knew you were coming back."

"You said the roses would bloom this year," she said.

"And they have." He looked gravely down at her.

She stepped inside the arbor and turned all about, reveling in the sights and the smells. She had not realized until this moment how much her vision had been bounded by black since Julian's death.

"I love it," she said. "Is it my wedding gift, David? It is the most beautiful gift in the world. Living beauty and the promise of endless springs, endless summers. Oh, thank you."

He came toward her and framed her face with his hands. She gazed up into his eyes, all barriers gone, all defenses down, all self-deception in the past, all misunderstandings over and done with. She wanted the moment to last forever.

"Are you happy?" he asked her.

For answer she felt tears welling to her eyes. But she smiled and nodded. "Yes. Oh, yes, I am, David."

"It is not just because of Charles, then," he said, "and of what you feel you owe Julian? Not just because you want another child?"

"It is because of those things, yes," she said. "For all three. They are such important reasons, David. But not just for those. Perhaps not even mainly because of them."

"What, then?" he asked.

She gazed into his eyes. So very blue. She had not realized quite how much she had missed them. "Because you are my life," she said.

He kissed her softly with closed lips and smiled down at her. His eyes were so lovely when they smiled. He had smiled so little during their first marriage. There had been so much to mar their joy then. But they were being given a second chance. And she knew that neither of them would squander that chance. She smiled back.

She had smiled so little during their first marriage. He had not even realized it fully until now, when she was smiling at him with quiet joy. *You are my life.* The words warmed him to the innermost recesses of his heart.

"And you are mine," he said. "Did you know that I have always loved you?"

"Always?" Her eyes widened.

"Always," he said. "As a boy I adored you. I have adored you ever since. Every moment of every day. I adore you today. I'll always love you."

"David," she said. "Oh, David, I'm glad all the clouds have gone away. They have, haven't they? There were so many clouds. But I grew to love you despite them. I didn't expect to or even want to. I almost did not realize I did until it was time to force myself to stop loving you."

There was a brightness in her face that confirmed her words despite the tears. All the clouds had rolled away. Only sunshine was left. And he held his sunshine in his arms. She was his bride, his wife.

"Put your arms about my neck," he said. They were spread against his chest.

"Why?" She did as she was told, smiling at him. She was expecting to be kissed.

"For this reason," he said. And he lifted her firmly by the waist and twirled her around and around until they were both dizzy and laughing.

"How foolish," she said when he set her feet back on the ground. She was flushed and still laughing. He drank in the wonder of her happiness. "I thought you were going to kiss me."

"I was," he said. "I am. I was just warming up to it."

She laughed and tightened her arms about his neck. "Let's see how warm you are, then," she said.

He tipped his head back and grinned down at her. Rebecca being risqué? He could not have imagined it until this moment.

"Are you sure you want to find out?" he asked.

Her laugh gave place to wistfulness. "Yes, I do, please, David," she said. He watched her eyes grow luminous. "I want you so much. I did not know that love could be so very beautiful in its physical form until you taught me."

She had never learned it with Julian? That was why she had been afraid of his lovemaking at first?

He lowered his head and kissed her. It was a sweet and a tender kiss for a long time, mouths molding to each other, caressing, tasting, tongues touching, twining, pushing, exploring, arms holding, tightening. There was all the wonder of their wedding day in their kiss and of the fact that they were together again after being so disturbingly torn apart.

It was a kiss that satisfied for a time. It was a kiss that told of affection and love and promise. But his mouth and his tongue were gone after a while and she opened her eyes to find him smiling at her from a few inches away. David. Her husband. Her friend. Her love.

"I am glad we came here," he said, "to discover alone together that we have married for all the right reasons." His smile deepened. "And for love too. We needed to discover those things here, Rebecca, where summer and roses are blooming. I knew you loved me and you knew I loved you. But it needed to be said."

"Yes," she said.

"But having said it," he said, "there is really nothing more to be added, is there?"

She shook her head.

"I love you," he said. "And I want to be your lover. Now."

"And I want to be yours," she said. "Now."

"In our bed," he said, "where we started Charles, the little imp. Did you hear him in church this morning?"

She chuckled. "Who didn't?" she said. "I want another, David."

"Despite all the trouble and anxiety?" he asked.

She nodded.

"In our bed now, then," he said, taking her hand and lacing his fingers with hers again. "Just because you want my seed, Rebecca?"

"For that reason, yes," she said. "But not just for that."

"What, then?"

She wondered how many years would pass before he had permanent laugh lines in the corners of his eyes.

They were going to make him look impossibly attractive. Though he was already that.

"Because I want you," she said. "All of you, David. Everything you have to give."

He stopped briefly under the trellised arch to kiss her lips. "Can you offer a similar gift?" he asked.

She nodded. "Everything I have and am is yours from this day on," she said. "I love you, David."

"What more could a man ask for?" he said. But he grinned suddenly. "Perhaps that his bedroom was a great deal closer than it is?"

They both laughed as their hands parted and their arms slid around each other's waist.

To hell with what the servants might think, David thought. It was his wedding day.

She hoped there were no servants in sight, Rebecca thought. But surely they would make allowances for the fact that it was her wedding day.

Their wedding day. Hers and David's.